The Truelove

The sails of a square-rigged ship, hung out to dry in a calm.

1 Flying jib
2 Jib
3 Fore topmast staysail
4 Fore staysail
5 Foresail, or course
6 Fore topsail
7 Fore topgallant
8 Mainstaysail
9 Maintopmast staysail
10 Middle staysail
11 Main topgallant staysail

12 Mainsail, or course
13 Maintopsail
14 Main topgallant
15 Mizzen staysail
16 Mizzen topmast staysail
17 Mizzen topgallant staysail
18 Mizzen sail
19 Spanker
20 Mizzen topsail
21 Mizzen topgallant

Illustration source: Serres, Liber Nauticus.
Courtesy of The Science and Technology Research Center,
The New York Public Library, Astor, Lenox, and Tilden Foundations

By Patrick O'Brian

THE AUBREY/MATURIN NOVELS
Master and Commander
Post Captain
H.M.S. Surprise
The Mauritius Command
Desolation Island
The Fortune of War
The Surgeon's Mate
The Ionian Mission
Treason's Harbor
The Far Side of the World
The Reverse of the Medal
The Letter of Marque
The Thirteen Gun Salute
The Nutmeg of Consolation
The Truelove
The Wine-Dark Sea

NOVELS
Testimonies
The Catalans
The Golden Ocean
The Unknown Shore
Richard Temple

TALES
The Last Pool
The Walker
Lying in the Sun
The Chian Wine

BIOGRAPHIES
Picasso
Joseph Banks

ANTHOLOGIES
A Book of Voyages
The Rendezvous and Other Stories

The Truelove

Patrick O'Brian

W·W·Norton & Company
New York   London

For information about permission to reproduce selections from this book,
write to Permissions, W. W. Norton & Company, Inc
500 Fifth Avenue, New York, NY 10110

Library of Congress Cataloging-in-Publication Data

O'Brian, Patrick, 1914–2000
[Clarissa Oakes]
The truelove / Patrick O'Brian.—1st American ed.
p.   cm.
Originally published under title: Clarissa Oakes.
I. Title.
PR6029.B55C57   1992
823'.914—dc20   91-44345

ISBN 978-0-393-03109-6

W. W. Norton & Company, Inc.
500 Fifth Avenue, New York, N.Y. 10110
www.wwnorton.com

W. W. Norton & Company Ltd.
Castle House, 75/76 Wells Street, London W1T 3QT

6 7 8 9 0

for Mary, with love and
most particular gratitude

The Truelove

Chapter One

Standing at the frigate's taffrail, and indeed leaning upon it, Jack Aubrey considered her wake, stretching away neither very far nor emphatically over the smooth pure green-blue sea: a creditable furrow, however, in these light airs. She had just come about, with her larboard tacks aboard, and as he expected her wake showed that curious nick where, when the sheets were hauled aft, tallied and belayed, she made a little wanton gripe whatever the helmsman might do.

He knew the *Surprise* better than any other ship he had served in: he had been laid across a gun in the cabin just below him and beaten for misconduct when he was a midshipman, and as her captain he too had used brute force to teach reefers the difference between naval right and naval wrong. He had served in her for many years, and he loved her even more than his first command: it was not so much as a man-of-war, a fighting-machine, that he loved her, for even when he first set foot aboard so long ago neither her size nor her force had been in any way remarkable, and now that the war had been going on for twenty years and more, now that the usual frigate carried thirty-eight or thirty-six eighteen-pounders and gauged a thousand tons the *Surprise*, with her twenty-eight nine-pounders and her less than six hundred tons, had been left far behind; in fact she and the rest of her class had been sold out of the service or broken up and not one remained in commission, although both French and American yards were building fast, shockingly fast: no, it was primarily as a ship that he loved her, a fast, eminently responsive ship that, well handled, could outsail any square-rigged vessel he had ever seen, above all on a bowline. She had also repaired his shattered fortunes when they were both out of the Navy – himself struck off the list and she sold at the block – and he sailed her as a letter of marque; but although that may have added a certain immediate fervour to his love, its true basis was a disinterested delight in her sailing and all those innumerable traits that make up the character of a ship. Furthermore, he was now her owner as well as her captain, for Stephen Maturin, the frigate's surgeon, who bought her when she was put up for sale, had recently agreed to let him have her. And what was of even greater importance, both man and ship were back in the Navy, Jack Aubrey reinstated after an exceptionally brilliant cutting-out expedition (and after his election to Parliament), and the frigate as His Majesty's hired vessel *Surprise* – not quite a full reinstatement for her, but near enough for present happiness.

Her first task in this particular voyage had been to carry Aubrey and Maturin, who was an intelligence-agent as well as a medical man, to the west coast of South America, there to frustrate French attempts at forming an alliance with the Peruvians and Chileans who led the movement for independence from Spain and to transfer their affections to England. Yet since Spain was then at least nominally allied to Great Britain the enterprise had to be carried out under the cover of privateering, of attacking United States South-Sea whalers and merchantmen and any French vessels she might chance to meet in the east Pacific. This plan had been betrayed by a highly-placed, a very highly-placed but as yet unidentified traitor in Whitehall and it had had to be postponed, Aubrey and Maturin going off on quite a different mission in the South China Sea, eventually keeping a discreet rendezvous with the *Surprise* on the other side of the world, in about 4° N and 127° E, at the mouth of the Salibabu Passage, the frigate in the meantime having been commanded by Tom Pullings, Jack's first lieutenant, and manned, of course, by her old privateering crew. Here they sent her more recent prizes away for Canton under the escort of the *Nutmeg of Consolation*, a charming little post-ship lent to Captain Aubrey by the Lieutenant-Governor of Java, and so proceeded to New South Wales, to Sydney Cove itself, where Jack hoped to have his stores renewed and several important repairs carried out against their eastward voyage to South America and beyond, and where Stephen Maturin hoped to see the natural wonders of the Antipodes, particularly Ornithorhynchus paradoxus, the duck-billed platypus.

Unfortunately the Governor was away and Jack's hopes were disappointed because of the ill-will of the colonial officials; and the fulfilment of Stephen's very nearly killed him, for the outraged platypus, seized in the midst of his courting-display, plunged both poison-spurs deep into the incautious arm. It was an unhappy visit to an unhappy, desolate land.

But now the odious penal shores had sunk in the west; now the horizon ran clean round the sky and Jack was in his old world again, aboard his own beloved ship. Stephen had recovered from his distressing state (immensely swollen, dumb, blind and rigid) with extraordinary speed; the bluish leaden colour of his face had returned to its usual pale yellow; and he could now be heard playing his 'cello in the cabin, a remarkably happy piece he had composed for the birth of his daughter. Jack smiled – he was very deeply attached to his friend – but after a couple of bars he said 'Why Stephen should be so pleased with a baby I cannot tell. He was born to be a bachelor – no notion of domestic comforts, family life – quite unsuited for marriage, above all for marriage with Diana, a dashing brilliant creature to be sure, a fine horsewoman and a capital hand at billiards and whist, but given to high play and something of a rake – quite often shows her wine – in any case quite improper for Stephen – has nothing to say to books – much more concerned with breeding horses. Yet between them they have produced this baby; and a girl at that.' The wake stretched away, as true as a taut line now, and after a while he said 'He longed for a daughter, I know, and it is very well that he should have one; but I wish she may not prove a platypus to him,' and he might have added some considerations on marriage and the relations, so often unsatisfactory, between men and women, parents and children, had not Davidge's voice called out 'Every rope an-end' cutting the thread of his thought.

9

'Every rope an-end.' The cry was automatic, perfunctory, and superfluous: for having put the ship about (with rather more conversation than was usual in a regular man-of-war but even more neatly than in most) the Surprises, in the nature of things, were rapidly coiling down the running rigging, braces and bowlines, just as they had done thousands of times before. Yet without the cry something would have been missing, some minute part of that naval ritual which did so uphold sea-going life.

'Sea-going life: none better,' reflected Jack; and certainly at this point in time he had something like the cream of it, with a good, tolerably well-found ship (for the returning Governor had done all he could in the few days left), an excellent crew of former Royal Navy hands, privateersmen and smugglers, professional from clew to earing, with his course set for Easter Island, and many thousand miles of blue-water sailing before him. Above all there was his restoration to the list, and though the *Surprise* was no longer in the full sense a King's ship both her future as a yacht and his as a sea-officer were as nearly assured as anything could be on such a fickle element. In all likelihood he would be offered a command as soon as he came home: not a frigate alas, since he was now so senior, but probably a ship of the line. Possibly a small detached squadron, as commodore. In any event a flag, being a matter of seniority and survival rather than merit, was not so very far distant; and the fact that he was member of parliament for Milport (a rotten borough, in the gift of his cousin Edward) meant that independently of his deserts this flag would almost certainly be hoisted at sea, for rotten borough or not, a vote was a vote.

This certain knowledge had been with him ever since the Gazette printed the words *Captain John Aubrey, Royal Navy, is restored to the List with his former rank and seniority and is appointed to the Diane of thirty-two guns*, filling his massive frame with a deep abiding happiness; and now he had another, more immediate reason for joy, his friend having made this astonishing recovery. 'Then why am I so cursed snappish?' he asked.

Five bells. Little Reade, the midshipman of the watch, skipped aft to the rail, followed by the quartermaster with the log-ship and reel. The log splashed down, the stray-line ran gently astern; 'Turn' said the quartermaster in a hoarse tobacco-chewing whisper, and Reade held the twenty-eight second glass to his eye. 'Stop,' he cried at last, clear and shrill, and the quartermaster wheezed 'Three one and a half, mate.'

Reade gave his captain an arch look, but seeing his grim, closed expression he walked forward and said to Davidge 'Three knots one and a half fathoms, sir, if you please,' directing his voice aft and speaking rather loud.

The wake span out, rather faster now than Jack had foretold – hence the arch look. 'Cross in the morning and bloody-minded with it, like an old and ill-conditioned man. It is discreditable in the last degree,' he said, and his thoughts ran on.

Profound attachment to Stephen Maturin did not preclude profound dissatisfaction at times: even lasting dissatisfaction. For a quick and efficient refitting of the ship, good relations with the colonial administration had been of the first importance; but in that very strongly anti-Irish and anti-Catholic atmosphere (Botany Bay had been filled with United Irishmen after the '97 rising) the presence of Stephen, irascible, more or less Irish and entirely Catholic, rendered them impossible. Or to put it more fairly not just his presence but the fact that he had resented an insult after a Government House dinner on his very first day in the penal colony – blood all over the bath-stoned steps. Jack had had to endure weeks of official obstruction and harassment – the vexatious searching the ship for convicts trying to escape, the stopping of her boats, the arrest of mildly drunken liberty-men ashore – and it was only when the Governor returned that Jack had been able to put a stop to all this by promising him that the *Surprise* should carry no absconder from Port Jackson.

Stephen, poor fellow, could not really be blamed for the misfortunes of his birth, nor for having resented so very gross an insult; but he could be blamed, and Jack did blame him, for having, without the least consultation, planned the escape of his former servant Padeen Colman, equally Popish and even more Irish (virtually monoglot), whose sentence of death for robbing an apothecary of the laudanum to which, as Stephen's loblolly-boy, he had become addicted, had been commuted to transportation to New South Wales. The matter had been presented to Jack when he was exhausted with work and last-minute preparations, frustrated beyond description by a light froward conscienceless woman, liverish from official dinners in the extreme heat; and their difference of opinion was so strong that it endangered their friendship. The escape did in fact take place in the confusion that followed Maturin's encounter with the platypus and Padeen was now on board: it took place with the consent of Padeen's master and of the entire crew; and it could be said that Captain Aubrey's word was unbroken, since the absconder came not from Port Jackson but from Woolloo-Woolloo, a day's journey to the north. Yet for his own part Jack dismissed this as a mere quibble; and in any event he felt that he had been manipulated, which he disliked extremely.

That was not the only time he had been manipulated, either. Throughout the voyage from Batavia to Sydney Jack Aubrey had been chaste: necessarily so, given the absence of anyone to be unchaste with. And throughout his anxious, frustrating negotiations in Sydney he had been chaste, because of total exhaustion by the end of the day. But after Governor Macquarie's return all this changed. At several official and unofficial gatherings he met Selina Wesley, a fine plump young woman with a prominent bosom, an indifferent reputation and a roving eye. Twice they were neighbours at dinner, twice at supper-parties; she had naval connexions, an extensive knowledge of the world, and a very free way of speaking; they got along famously. She had no patience with Romish monks or nuns, she said; celibacy was great nonsense – quite unnatural; and when during the interval in an evening concert given in some gardens outside Sydney she asked him to walk with her down to the tree-fern dell he found himself in such a boyish state of desire that his voice was scarcely at his command. She took his arm and they moved discreetly out of the lantern-light, walked behind a summer-house and down the path. 'We have escaped Mrs Macarthur's eye,' she said with a gurgle of laughter, and her grasp tightened for a moment.

Down through the tree-ferns, down; and at the bottom a man stepped out of the shadows. 'There you are, Kendrick,' cried Mrs Wesley. 'I was not sure I should find you. Thank you so much, Captain Aubrey. You will find your way back easily enough, I am sure, steering by the stars. Kendrick, Captain Aubrey was so kind as to give me his arm down the path in the dark.'

He had other causes for discontent, such as the faint and even dead contrary airs that had kept Bird Island in sight for so long and then the curious falsity of the trade wind that obliged the ship to beat up close-hauled day after day, wearing every four hours. Other causes, some of them trivial: he had taken only two midshipmen from the *Nutmeg* into the *Surprise*, two for whom he felt a particular responsibility; and both of them were extremely irritating. Reade, a pretty boy who had lost an arm in their battle against sea Dyaks, was over-indulged by the Surprises and was now much above himself; while Oakes, his companion, a hairy youth of seventeen or eighteen, went about singing in a most unofficer-like manner – a kind of bull-calf joy. Jack skipped over the matter of Nathaniel Martin, the Reverend Nathaniel Martin, an unbeneficed clergyman, a well-read man and an eager natural philosopher who had joined the *Surprise* as assistant surgeon to see the world in Maturin's company. It was impossible to dislike Martin, a deeply respectable man, though his playing of the viola would never have recommended him anywhere; yet Jack could not love him either. Martin was of course a more suitable companion for Stephen in certain respects, but it seemed to Jack that he took up altogether too much of his time, prating away about primates in the mizen-top or endlessly turning over his collections of beetles and mummified toads in the gunroom. Jack passed quickly on – he did not choose to dwell on the subject – and came to the strange, unaccountable behaviour of the frigate's people. Obviously they were not like a Royal Navy crew, being much more talkative, independent, undeferential, partners rather than subordinates; but Jack did not dislike that at all; he was used to it, and he had thought he knew them intimately well from his cruises with them as a privateer and from this long run from Salibabu to New South Wales. Yet something seemed to have happened to them in Sydney. Now they were fuller of mirth than before; now they had private expressions that caused gales of laughter in the forecastle; and now he often saw them look at him with a knowing smile. In any other ship this might have meant mischief, but here even the officers had something of the same oddness. At times even Tom Pullings, whom he had known since his first command, seemed to be watching him with a considering eye, hesitant, quizzical.

Causes for discontent, vexations, of course he had them; and none rankled like that caper in the tree-ferns nor came more insistently into his humiliated mind, so full of unsatisfied desire. Yet all these put together, he thought, could not account for this growing crossness, this waking up ready to be displeased, this incipient ill-humour – anything likely to set it off. He had never felt like this when he was young – had never been made game of by a young woman either.

'Perhaps I shall ask Stephen for a blue pill,' he said. 'For a couple of blue pills. I have not been to the head this age.'

He walked forward, the windward side of the quarterdeck emptying at his approach; and as he passed the wheel both the quartermaster at the con and the helmsman turned their heads to look at him. The *Surprise* instantly came up half a point, the windward leaches of the topsails gave a warning flutter and Jack roared 'Mind your helm, you infernal lubbers. What in Hell's name do you mean by leering at me like a couple of moonsick cowherds? Mind your helm, d'ye hear me there? Mr Davidge, no grog for Krantz or Webber today.'

The quarterdeck looked suitably shocked and grave, but as Jack went down the companion-ladder towards the cabin he heard a gale of laughter from the forecastle. Stephen was still playing and Jack walked in on tiptoe, with a finger to his lips, making those gestures that people use to show that they are immaterial beings, silent, invisible. Stephen nodded to him in

14

an absent way, brought his phrase to a full close and said 'You have come below, I find.'

'Yes,' said Jack. 'Not to put too fine a point on it, I have. I know this is not your time for such things, but I should like to consult you if I may.'

'By all means. I was only working out a few foolish variations on a worthless theme. If what you have to say is of an intimate nature at all let us close the skylight and sit upon the locker at the back.' Most consultations shortly after a ship had left port were for venereal diseases: some seamen were ashamed of their malady, some were not: in general the officers preferred their state not to be known.

'It is not really of an intimate nature,' said Jack, closing the companion nevertheless and sitting on the stern-window locker. 'But I am most damnably hipped . . . cross even in the morning and much ill-used. Is there a medicine for good temper and general benevolence? A delight in one's blessings? I had thought of a blue pill, with perhaps a touch of rhubarb.'

'Show me your tongue,' said Stephen; and then, shaking his head, 'Lie flat on your back.' After a while he said 'As I thought, it is your liver that is the peccant part; or at least the most peccant of your parts. It is turgid, readily palpable. I have disliked your liver for some time now. Dr Redfern disliked your liver. You have the bilious facies to a marked degree: the whites of the eyes a dirty yellow, greyish-purple half-moons below them, a look of settled discontent. Of course, as I have told you these many years, you eat too much, you drink too much, and you do not take enough exercise. And this bout I have noticed that although the water has been charmingly smooth ever since we left New South Wales, although the boat has rarely exceeded a walking pace, and although we have been attended by no sharks, no sharks at all, in spite of Martin's sedulous watch and mine, you have abandoned your sea-bathing.'

'Mr Harris said it was bad in my particular case: he said it closed the pores, and would throw the yellow bile upon the black.'

'Who is Mr Harris?'

15

'He is a man with singular powers, recommended to me by Colonel Graham when you were away on your tour of the bush. He gives you nothing but what grows in his own garden or in the countryside, and he rubs your spine with a certain oil; he has performed some wonderful cures, and he is very much cried up in Sydney.'

Stephen made no comment. He had seen too many quite well educated people run after men with singular powers to cry out, to argue or even to feel anything but a faint despair. 'I shall bleed you,' he said, 'and mix a gentle cholagogue. And since we are now quite clear of New South Wales and of your thaumaturge's territory, I advise you to resume both your sea-bathing and your practice of climbing briskly to the top-most pinnacle.'

'Very well. But you do not mean me to take medicine today, Stephen? Tomorrow is divisions, you remember.'

Stephen knew that for Jack Aubrey, as for so many other captains and admirals of his acquaintance, taking medicine meant swallowing improbable quantities of calomel, sulphur, Turkey rhubarb (often added to their own surgeon's prescription) and spending the whole of the next day on the seat of ease, gasping, straining, sweating, ruining their lower alimentary tract. 'I do not,' he said. 'It is only a mixture, to be followed by a series of comfortable enemata.'

Jack watched the steady flow of his blood into the bowl: he cleared his throat and said 'I suppose you have patients with, well, desires?'

'It would be strange if I had not.'

'I mean, if you will forgive a gross expression, with importunate pricks?'

'Sure, I understand you. There is little in the pharmaco-poeia to help them. Sometimes' – waving his lancet – 'I propose a simple little operation – a moment's pang, perhaps a sigh, then freedom for life, a mild sailing on an even keel, tossed by no storms of passion, untempted, untroubled, sin-less – but when they decline, which they invariably do, though they may have protested that they would give anything to be free of their torments, why then unless there is some evident physical anomaly, all I can suggest is that they should learn to control their emotions. Few succeed; and some, I am afraid, are driven to strange wild extremes. But were the case to apply to you, brother, where there *is* a distinct physical anomaly, I should point out that Plato and the ancients in general made the liver the seat of love: Cogit amare jecur, said the Romans. And so I should reiterate my plea for more sea-bathing, more going aloft, more pumping of an early morning, to say nothing of a fitting sobriety at table, to preserve the organ from ill-considered freaks.' He closed the vein, and having washed his bowl in the quarter-gallery he went on, 'As for the blue devils of which you complain, my dear, do not expect too much from my remedies: youth and unthinking happiness are not to be had in a bottle, alas. You are to consider that a certain melancholy and often a certain irascibility accompany advancing age: indeed, it might be said that advancing age equals ill-temper. On reaching the middle years a man perceives that he is no longer able to do certain things, that what looks he may have had are deserting him, that he has a ponderous great belly, and that however he may yet burn he is no longer attractive to women; and he rebels. Fortitude, resignation and philosophy are of more value than any pills, red, white or blue.'

'Stephen, surely you would never consider me middle-aged, would you?'

'Navigators are notoriously short-lived, and for them middle-age comes sooner than for quiet abstemious country gentlemen. Jack, you have led as unhealthy a life as can well be imagined, perpetually exposed to the falling damps, often wet to the skin, called up at all hours of the night by that infernal bell. You have been wounded the Dear knows how many times, and you have been cruelly overworked. No wonder your hair is grey.'

'My hair is not grey. It is a very becoming buttercup-yellow.'

Jack wore his hair long, clubbed and tied with a broad black bow. Stephen plucked the bow loose and brought the far end of plait round before his eyes.

'Well I'm damned,' said Jack, looking at it in the sunlight.

17

'Well I'm damned; you are quite right. There are several grey hairs . . . scores of grey hairs. It is positively grizzled, like a badger-pie. I had never noticed.'

Six bells.

'Will I tell you something more cheerful?' asked Stephen.

'Please do,' said Jack, looking up from his queue with that singularly sweet smile Stephen had known from their earliest acquaintance.

'Two of our patients have been to the two islands you mean to pass. That is to say Philips has been to Norfolk Island and Owen has been to Easter Island. Philips knew the place before it was abandoned as a penal station, and he knew it extremely well, having spent – I believe Martin said a year, for it was to him that Philips spoke about the place – in any event a great while after the ship to which he belonged was wrecked. I forget her name: a frigate.'

'That must have been the *Sirius*, Captain Hunt, heaved on to a coral reef by the swell in the year ninety, much as we were so very nearly heaved on to the rocks of Inaccessible on the way out. Lord, I have never been so terrified in my life. Was you not terrified, Stephen?'

'I was not. I do not suppose there is my equal for courage in the service: but then, you recall, I was downstairs, playing chess with poor Fox, and knew nothing of it until we were delivered. But as I was saying, Martin was delighted to hear that the mutton-birds would be there by now. He loves a petrel even more than I do; and the mutton-bird, my dear, belongs to that interesting group. He very much hopes that we may go ashore.'

'Certainly. I should be happy to oblige him, if landing is possible: sometimes the surf runs very high, by all accounts. I shall have a word with Philips; and I shall ask Owen to tell me all he knows about Easter Island. If this breeze holds, we should raise Mount Pitt on Norfolk tomorrow morning.'

'I hope we shall be able to go ashore. Apart from anything else there is the famous Norfolk Island pine.'

'Alas, I am afraid it was exploded years ago. The enormous great spars would not stand even a moderate strain.'

'To be sure: I remember Mr Seppings reading us an excellent paper at Somerset House. But what I really meant was that so prodigious and curious a vegetable as the Norfolk pine may well harbour equally prodigious and curious beetles, as little known to the world in general as their host.'

'Speaking of Martin,' said Jack, who did not give a pinch of snuff for beetles, however singular, 'I thought of him twice yesterday. Once because while I was going through the mass of estate-papers with Adams, trying to get them in some kind of order – they came from seven different lawyers after I had paid off my father's mortgages, and the children had tumbled them about to get at the stamps – he pointed out that I had three advowsons and part of a fourth, with the right of presenting every third turn. I wondered whether they would interest Martin.'

'Are they of any value?'

'I have no idea. When I was a boy, Parson Russell of Woolcombe kept his carriage; but then he had private means and he had married a wife with a handsome dowry. I have no notion of the others, except that the vicarage at Compton was a sad shabby little place. I went to sea when I was no bigger than Reade, you know, and hardly ever went back. I had hoped that Withers' general statement of the position would reach me in Sydney: that would give all the details, I am sure.'

'What was the second circumstance that brought Martin to your mind?'

'I was restringing my fiddle when it occurred to me that love of music and the ability to play well had nothing to do with character: neither here nor there, if you follow me. Martin's two Oxford friends, Standish and Paulton, were perfect examples. Standish played better than any amateur I had ever heard, but he was not really quite the thing, you know. I do not say that because he was perpetually seasick or because he ratted on us; nor do I mean he was wicked; but he was not quite the thing. Whereas John Paulton, who played even better, was the kind of man you could sail round the world with and never a harsh word or a wry look all the way. What astonished me is that Martin should have played with two such very capital hands and that neither should ever have persuaded him to tune somewhere near true pitch.' Jack regretted this fling against Stephen's friend as soon as it was out – it sounded malignant – and he quickly went on, 'And it is odd that they should both have become Papists.'

'You find it odd that they should revert to the religion of their ancestors?'

'Not at all,' cried Jack, feeling low. 'I only meant it as though there were an affinity between music and Rome.'

'So we are to have divisions tomorrow,' said Stephen.

'Yes. I was sorry to miss them last week. They have a good effect in pulling the crew together after a long run ashore, and they allow one to take the ship's pulse, as it were. The people have surely been behaving rather strangely, simpering, making antic gestures . . .'

Jack's tone was that of enquiry, but Stephen, who knew perfectly well why the people were simpering and making antic gestures, only said 'I must remember to shave.'

The *Surprise*, in her present state, carried no Marines and a much smaller crew than a regular man-of-war of her rate – no landsmen, no boys, and very little in the way of gold lace and glory: but she did possess a drum, and at five bells in the forenoon watch, the ship being under a great spread of sail with the gentle, steady breeze one point free, the sky perfectly clear and Mount Pitt in Norfolk Island sharp on the horizon at twelve or thirteen leagues, West, the officer of the watch, said to Oakes, the mate of the watch, 'Beat to divisions.' Oakes turned to Pratt, a musically gifted seaman, and said, 'Beat to divisions,' whereupon Pratt brought his poised drumsticks down with a fine determination and the generale boomed and roared throughout the ship.

This surprised no one: shirts and duck trousers had been washed on Friday, dried and prettied on Saturday; during the long breakfast of Sunday morning the word 'Clean to muster' had been passed, and in case anyone had not seized the message Mr Bulkeley the bosun had bawled down the hatches 'Do you hear there, fore and aft? Clean for muster at five bells.' While his mates, even louder, called 'D'ye hear there?

Clean shirt and shave for muster at five bells.' Long before this the forenoon watch had brought up their clothes-bags and had stowed them in a hollow square on the quarter deck abaft the wheel, leaving a space over the companion to let daylight into the cabin; and at four bells the watch nominally below brought up theirs and made a pyramid of them on the booms before the boats, not without a good deal of jocular shoving and calling out, laughter and jokes about Mr O in the middle watch. It would never have done for the Royal Navy, and some of the old man-of-war's men tried to quieten their privateer shipmates: but by the time their officers had lined them up, and by the time each had reported his division 'present, properly dressed and clean, sir' to Pullings they really looked quite presentable, and Pullings was able, with a clear conscience, to turn to Captain Aubrey, take off his hat, and say 'All the officers have reported, sir.'

'Then we will go round the ship, if you please,' replied Jack, and all fell mute.

The first division was the afterguard, under Davidge, who saluted and fell in behind his captain. All hats flew off, the seamen stood as straight and as motionless as could be in the heavy swell, and Jack walked slowly along the line, looking attentively into the familiar faces. Most retained their ceremonial expression – Killick, standing there with his mouth set in disapproval, might never have seen him before – but in a few he thought he detected a look of something he could hardly name. Amusement? Knowingness? Cynicism? In any case a lack of the usual frank amiable vacuity.

On to West – poor noseless West, a victim of the biting frost far south of the Horn – and his division, the waisters; and as Jack inspected them, so down in the sick-berth one of their number, an elderly seaman named Owen, absent from divisions because of illness, said 'And there I was on Easter Island, gentlemen, with the *Proby* clawing off the lee shore and me roaring and bawling to my shipmates not to desert me. But they were a hard-hearted set of buggers, and once they had scraped past the headland they put before the wind – never started a sheet until they crossed the Line, I swear.

And did it profit them at all, gentlemen? No, sirs, it did not; for they was all murdered and scalped by Peechokee's people north of Nootka Sound, and their ship was burnt for the iron.'

'How did the Easter Islanders use you?' asked Stephen.

'Oh, pretty well, sir, on the whole; they are not an ill-natured crew, though much given to thieving: and I must admit they ate one another more than was quite right. I am not over-particular, but it makes you uneasy to be passed a man's hand. A slice of what might be anything, I don't say no, when sharp-set; but a hand fair turns your stomach. Howmsoever, we got along well enough. I spoke their language, after a fashion . . .'

'How did that come about?' asked Martin.

'Why, sir, it is like the language they speak in Otaheite and other islands, only not so genteel; like the Scotch.'

'You are familiar with the Polynesian, I collect?' asked Stephen.

'Anan, sir?'

'The South Sea language.'

'Bless you, sir, I have been in the Society Islands this many a time; and sailing on the fur-trade run so long, to north-west America, when we used to stretch across to the Sandwiches in the winter when trading was over, I grew quite used to their way of it too. Much the same in New Zealand.'

'Anyone can speak South Seas,' said Philips, the next patient on the starboard side. 'I can speak South Seas. So can Brenton and Scroby and Old Chucks – anyone that has been in a South Seas whaler.'

'And then I had a girl, and she helped me to a lot of their words. We lived in a house, built by the old uns a great while ago, and ruined, though our end was sound enough: it was a stone house shaped like a canoe, about a hundred foot long and twenty wide, with walls five foot thick.'

'On Norfolk Island me and my mates cut down a pine two hundred and ten foot high and thirty round,' said Philips.

Captain Aubrey, accompanied by Mr Smith the gunner and Mr Reade, reached the end of the next division, made up of the captains of gun-crews, quarter-gunners, and the armourer; and as he looked attentively at the bearded Nehemiah Slade, the captain of the gun called *Sudden Death*, the ship, impelled by a freakish double crest, gave a great lee-lurch. Although Jack had been at sea from his boyhood, even his childhood, he could still be caught off balance, and now, while the gunners were all heaved back to leeward against the hammock-netting, he plunged into Slade's bosom.

The general roar of honest mirth that followed this might account for the amusement in the next division, the fore-topmen, the youngest, brightest, most highly decorated members of the ship's company, who were led by Mr Oakes. Although he was a plain, thick-faced youth he was unusually popular; he was often drunk, always jolly, with a great flow of animal spirits; he never tyrannized nor did he report any sinner; and although he was no great seaman in the navigational or scientific way he would run up to the iron crosstrees with the best of them and there hang upside down.

'And then another wonderful thing about Easter Island,' said Owen, 'is what they call moles.'

'There is nothing wonderful about moles,' said Philips.

'Pipe off, Philips,' said Stephen. 'Go on, Owen.'

'Is what they call moles,' said Owen, rather more distinctly than before. 'And these here moles is platforms built on the slopes of hills, with the walls on the seaward side maybe three hundred foot long and thirty foot high, all made of squared stone sometimes six foot long. And on the platforms there are huge great images carved out of grey rock and brought there to be set up, images of coves as much as twenty-seven foot high and eight across the shoulders. Most of them were thrown down, but some of them were still standing, with great red round stone hats on the top of their heads: and these here hats, because I sat on one with my girl, one that had been thrown down, is four foot six across and four foot four high, measured with my thumb.'

With a certain sense of relief Jack came to the forecastle,

where he was received by Mr Bulkeley the bosun and Mr Bentley the carpenter, in their good West-of-England broad-cloth coats, grave men, but scarcely graver than the forecastle hands, prime middle-aged seamen who, having taken off their hats to the Captain, smoothed their hair over pates that were sometimes bald on top and whose waist-length pigtails were often eked out with tow. Behind these, in the days when the *Surprise* was in regular commission, there would have stood the ship's boys, under government of the master-at-arms; but a privateer had no room for boys, and their place, ludicrously enough, was now taken by two little girls of even less value in fighting the ship, Sarah and Emily Sweeting, Melanesians from the remote Sweeting's Island, the only survivors of a community wiped out by the smallpox brought by a South Seas whaler. They had been carried aboard by Dr Maturin, and the task of looking after them naturally fell to Jemmy Ducks, the ship's poulterer, who now whispered to them 'Toe the line, and make your bob.'

The little girls fixed their bare black toes exactly on a seam in the deck, plucked the sides of their white duck frocks and curtseyed.

'Sarah and Emily,' said the Captain, 'I hope I see you well?'

'Very well, sir, we thank you,' they replied, gazing anxiously into his face.

On to the galley, with its coppers shining like the sun, the cheerful cook and his sullen assistant Jack Nastyface, whose name, like Chips for the carpenter or Jemmy Ducks, went with the office. On to the lower deck, where the hammocks swung by night, but empty now, with a candle in each berth and a variety of ornaments and pictures laid out pretty on the seamen's chests; not a hint of dust, not even a gritting of fine sand underfoot, and the light sloping down through the gratings, such elegant shafts of parallel rays. Jack's heart lifted somewhat, and they came to the midshipmen's berth, cabins built up on either side and reaching as far aft as the gunroom, too small in the days when the frigate carried so many master's mates, midshipmen and youngsters, too big now that she had only Oakes and Reade, particularly as Martin, the surgeon's mate, and Adams, the Captain's clerk, lived and messed in the gunroom, where the purser's, master's and Marine officer's cabins all stood vacant.

They did not look into the gunroom, though it would have borne the severest, most hostile inspection, even the stretchers of the officers' table having been polished above and below, but went down towards the sick-berth, which Stephen preferred to the traditional bay, airier but far more noisy, a place where affectionate messmates found it easier to make his patients drunk.

'And another thing that would please you gentlemen,' said Owen, 'is the noddies, or terns as some say. They arrive when the stars and the moon are just so, and the people know it to a day; they arrive in thousands and thousands, all screaming, and make their nests on an island just off shore, rising like the Bass Rock, only much more so.'

'On Norfolk Island there are millions and millions of mutton-birds,' cried Philips. 'They come in at dusk, dropping out of the sky and going to their burrows; for they live in burrows. And if you go to the mouth of the burrow and call ke ke ke he answers ke ke ke and pokes his head out. We used to kill twelve or fourteen hundred a night.'

'You and your mutton-birds,' began Owen: then he stopped, his ear cocked.

Jack opened the door: Stephen, Martin and Padeen stood up: the invalids assumed a rigid posture.

'Well, Doctor,' said the Captain, 'I hope you find our pumping has answered?' Ever since Stephen had spoken of the *Surprise*'s stench below as compared with the *Nutmeg*'s purity, sea-water had been let into her hold every night and pumped out in the morning, to purify her bilges.

'Tolerably sweet, sir,' said Dr Maturin. 'But it must be confessed that this is not the *Nutmeg*; and sometimes, when I recall that the ship was originally French, and that the French bury their dead in the ballast, I wonder whether there may not still be something of a charnel-house down there.'

'Quite impossible. The ballast has been changed again and again: scores of times.'

'So much the better. Yet even so I should be grateful for another ventilating pump. In this heavy breathless air the patients have a tendency to grow fractious, even to quarrel.'

'Make it so, Captain Pullings,' said Jack. 'And if any hand should presume to quarrel, let his name be entered in the defaulters' list.'

'Here, sir,' said Stephen, 'are the men I was speaking about: Philips, who knows Norfolk Island well, and Owen, who spent several months among the Easter Islanders.'

'Ah yes. Well, Philips, how are you coming along?'

'Wery indifferent, sir, I am sorry to say,' said Philips in a weak, gasping voice.

'And Owen, how are you?'

'I do not complain, sir; but the burning pain is something cruel.'

'Then why the Devil don't you keep out of brothels, you damned fool? A man of your age! Low knocking-shops in Sydney Cove of all places, where the pox is the worst in the world. Of course you burn. And you are always at it: every goddam port . . . if your pay were docked for venereals as it is in the regular service you would not have a penny coming to you when we pay off, not a brass farthing.' Captain Aubrey, still breathing hard, asked the other patients how they did – they were all much better, thank you, sir – and returning he said to Philips, 'So you were in *Sirius* when she was heaved ashore: was there no good holding-ground near the island?'

'No, sir,' said Philips, speaking like a Christian now. 'It was terrible: coral rock everywhere inshore.'

'It was far worse off of Easter Island, sir: coral rock far offshore too, then no bottom with the deep-sea line; and an almighty surf,' said Owen, but in an undertone.

'We could not land on the south side of the island, sir, so we went round to the north-east: and there we were lying to with a light breeze off the shore and all hands fishing for gropers when the *Supply* brig, who was laying outside of us, hailed Captain Hunt that we was being heaved inshore.

26

Which was true. It was all hands make sail, and make sail we did; but then the flood set in – it sets from the north on that side of the island, sir – and what with that and the swell we could not make head against it, not even with the breeze on our quarter. We let go both bowers, but the coral cut their cables directly; we let go the sheet-anchor and the spare and they parted too; and at one bell in the afternoon watch we struck, drove farther over the reef, and cut away our masts. Our captain gave orders to open the after hatchway and stave all the liquor . . .' All this Philips had delivered with barely a pause; now he drew breath, and in the interval Owen said, 'On Easter Island, sir . . .'

'Doctor,' said Jack, 'I shall ask Mr Adams to see these men separately and take notes of what they have to say. Now I am going forward to see what your pumping has done about our rats as well as our smell. Colman, the lantern, there.'

In his hurry Padeen dropped the lantern, lit it again, dropped it once more, and was cursed for an unhandy grass-combing lubber in a tone of much greater severity and exasperation than was usual in Captain Aubrey, who left a disapproving silence behind him, and a certain consternation.

Stephen did not discuss the ship's captain with anyone, nor obviously did he discuss his friend Jack in the gunroom; but he could perfectly well speak of the patient Aubrey with Martin, a man of strong good sense and exceptionally wide reading. Reverting to Latin he said 'I have rarely, perhaps never, seen such a high degree of irascibility, so continuous and as it were cumulative irritation in this particular subject. It is clear that there has been no good effect from either my enemata or my cholagogue; and this steady and increasing exacerbation makes me fear that this is not an ordinary congestion of the hepatic ducts but some disease acquired in New South Wales.'

In his medical capacity Martin had nothing to do with moral values and he replied 'When you say disease, do you refer to that which is so usual among seafaring men, high or low?'

'Not in this case. I put the question directly: had there been any commerce with Venus? No, said he with surprising vehemence, there had most certainly not, adding a remark that

I did not catch. There is something strange here; and it is with real concern that I recall dear Dr Redfern's account of the various forms of hepatitis he has seen in the colony, sometimes associated with hydatic cysts . . . he showed me one from a person who had lived entirely on kangaroo and rum, and there was an unparalleled degree of cirrhosis. But worse than that for our purposes was his case-book showing long-drawn-out histories of general bilious indisposition, melancholy, taedium vitae sometimes reaching mere despair, extreme irascibility: all this with no known agent, though autopsy showed an enlarged quadrate lobe studded with yellow nodules the size of a pea. He calls it Botany Bay liver, and it is this or some one of the other New Holland diseases that I fear our patient may have caught. The vexation and more than vexation of spirit is certainly present.'

'It is deeply saddening to see what disease can do to a whole cast of mind, to a settled character,' said Martin. 'And sometimes our remedies are just as bad. How it appears to draw in the boundaries of free-will.'

'The Doctor may say what he likes, Tom,' said Captain Aubrey, 'but I think the *Surprise* smells as sweet as the *Nutmeg*, or sweeter.' They were approaching the cable-tier now – for the *Surprise* had a cat-walk that allowed uninterrupted progress from the after-platform right forward – the cable-tier where the great ropes lay coiled, together with the hawsers and cablets. These always came aboard sodden, often stinking and covered with slime, there to lie dripping through spaces between the planks down into the hold, but now, since the *Surprise* had lain at moorings in Sydney Cove or had tied up to bollards, they were warm and dry: Jack remembered luxuriating in their folds when he was young, sleepy from the morning watch and willing to escape from the din of the reefers' berth.

'Sweet to be sure, sir,' said Pullings, 'but there are still vermin about for all our pumping. I have seen a score since the sick-berth.' He made a nimble kick at one far-travelled and particularly audacious Norway rat that had come aboard at

28

Sydney and sent it flying over the nearest coil to the lattice bulwark behind. With a shrill screech a figure darted from behind the cables, brushing the rat away.

'What the Devil are you doing here, boy?' cried Jack. 'Did you not hear the drum beat for divisions? Who the Devil are you?' Then relaxing his iron grip and standing back a little, 'What is this, Mr Pullings?'

Pullings held up the lantern and said in a neutral voice 'It is a young woman, I believe, sir.'

'He is wearing a reefer's uniform.' Jack took the lantern, and looking even bigger than usual in its light he studied her for a moment: Pullings was obviously right. 'Who brought you here?' he asked with cold displeasure.

'I came of myself, sir,' said the girl in a trembling voice.

This was utter nonsense. It could be demolished in a minute, but he did not wish to make her lie and lie until she was driven into a corner and forced to bring out the name – obvious enough, in all conscience.

'Let us carry on, Mr Pullings,' he said.

'What, and leave her here?'

'You heard me, sir. Take the lantern.'

They silently inspected the sail-rooms, the bosun's, gunner's, carpenter's store-rooms, the pitch-room and so returned to the open air, where all hats came off once more and where all faces changed at the sight of Captain Aubrey's pale severity.

'We shall not rig church, Captain Pullings,' he said. 'The Articles will do very well for this occasion.'

The parade, such as it was, dissolved and the hands moved aft, lining the quarterdeck as far as the companion hatchway and sitting on benches or stools or capstan-bars poised between two match-tubs, or on the belaying-bitts round the mainmast: chairs were placed for the Captain and the officers on the windward side, for the midshipmen and the warrant-officers to the lee.

A sword-rack covered with an ensign and holding the Articles of War stood in front of Captain Aubrey; and all this time the sun shone from a clear sky, the warm air breathed across the deck, slanting from forward with just enough strength to fill her great array of canvas: there was very little sound from the breeze, the rigging or the blocks, and the water only whispered down the side. Norfolk Island, rising and falling on the long even swell beyond the larboard bow, was perceptibly nearer. Nobody spoke.

'Silence fore and aft,' called Pullings; and after a moment Jack stood up, opened the thin boards that held the Articles and began: there were thirty-six of them, and nineteen of the offences named carried the death sentence, sometimes qualified by the words 'or such other punishment as the nature and degree of the offence shall deserve, and the court-martial shall impose'. He read them deliberately, with a powerful voice; and the Articles, already inimical, took on a darker, more threatening tone. When he had finished the silence was still quite as profound, and now there was a greater uneasiness in it.

He closed the boards, looked coldly fore and aft, and said 'Captain Pullings, we will take in the royals and haul down the flying jib. When they are stowed, hands may be piped to dinner.'

It was a quiet meal, with little or none of the shouting and banging of mess-kids that usually greeted the Sunday plum-duff and the grog; and while it was being eaten Jack walked his quarterdeck as he had so very often walked it before: seventeen paces forward, seventeen paces aft, turning on a ring-bolt long since polished silver by his shoe.

Now of course the half-heard jokes, the covert allusions to Mr Oakes's weariness, his need for a sustaining diet and so on, were perfectly clear. He turned the situation over and over in his mind; flushes of pure exasperation interrupted his judgment from time to time, but he felt in perfect command of his temper when he went below and sent for the midshipman.

'Well, Mr Oakes,' he said, 'what have you to say?'

'I have nothing to say, sir,' replied Oakes, turning his oddly mottled face aside. 'Nothing at all, and I throw myself on your mercy. Only we hoped – I hoped – you would carry us away from that horrible place. She was so very unhappy.'

'I am to take it she was a convict?'

'Yes, sir; but unjustly condemned, I am sure.'

'You know perfectly well that I have turned away dozens, scores of others.'

'Yet you let Padeen come aboard, sir,' said Oakes, and then clasped his hands in a hopeless, stupid attempt at unsaying the words, doing utterly away with them.

'Get away forward,' said Jack. 'I shall take no action, make no decision today, this being Sunday: but you had better pack your chest.'

When he had gone Jack rang for his steward and asked whether the gunroom had finished their dinner. 'No, sir,' said Killick. 'I doubt they are even at their pudding yet.'

'Then when they *have* finished – when they have quite finished, mind – I should like to see Captain Pullings. My compliments, and I should like to see Captain Pullings.'

He looked doggedly through the sheets of physical observations he had made for Humboldt, temperature and salinity of the sea at various depths, barometric pressure, temperature of the air by wet and dry bulb thermometer, a chain of observations more than half way round the world, and he derived a certain satisfaction from them. Eventually he heard Pullings' steps.

'Sit down, Tom,' he said, waving to a chair. 'I have seen Oakes, and the only explanation he could bring out was that she was very unhappy: then the damn fool threw Padeen in my teeth.'

'You did not know, sir?'

'Of course I did not. Did you?'

'I believe it was common knowledge in the ship, but I had no certainty. Nor did I enquire. My impression was that the situation being so delicate you did not choose to have it brought to your attention or for there to be any question of returning to Botany Bay.'

'Was it not your duty as first lieutenant to let me know?'

'Perhaps it was, sir; and if I have done wrong I am very sorry for it. In a regular King's ship with a pennant, a party of Marines, a master-at-arms and ship's corporals I could not have avoided knowing it officially, and then in duty bound I should have been obliged to inform you. But here, with no Marines, no master-at-arms and no ship's corporals I should have had to listen at doors to be certain. No, sir: nobody wanted to tell either me or you, so that you, officially in the dark until it was too late, could not be blamed – could sail on for Easter Island with an easy conscience.'

'You think it is too late now, do you?'

'Wittles is up, sir, if you please,' said Killick at the door of the dining-cabin.

'Tom,' said Jack, 'we left that odious wench in the starboard cable-tier. I dare say Oakes has fed her, but she cannot stay there watch after watch: she had better be stowed forward with the little girls until I have made up my mind what to do with her.'

This was one of the few Sundays when no guests had been invited to the cabin, the Captain feeling so out of sorts, one of the few Sundays when Dr Maturin dined in the gunroom, and Aubrey sat in the solitary splendour usual in some captains but rare in him – he liked seeing his officers and midshipmen at his table and particularly his surgeon. Not that Stephen could in any way be called a guest, since they had shared the cabin these many years, and until recently he had actually owned the ship.

He might have been expected for coffee, but in fact Jack saw nothing of him until the evening, when he walked in with a dose and a clyster: he and Martin had spent the intervening hours describing the more perishable specimens from their tour in the bush, and writing to their wives.

'Here's a pretty kettle of fish,' cried Jack. 'An elegant God-damned kettle, upon my word.' Solitude and a heavy afternoon sleep had increased his ill-humour, and Stephen did not at all like the colour of his face. 'What's afoot?' he asked.

'What's afoot? Why, the ship is turned into a bawdy-house – Oakes has had a girl in the cable-tier ever since we left Sydney Cove – everybody knew, and I have been made a fool of in my own command.'

'Oh, that? It is of no great consequence, brother. And as for being made a fool of, it is no such matter but rather a mark

32

of the people's affection, since they wished to avoid your being placed in a disagreeable posture.'

'You knew, and you did not tell me?'

'Of course I did not. I could not tell my friend Jack without at the same time telling Captain Aubrey, authority incarnate; and you are to observe that I am not and never have been an informer.'

'Everyone knows how I hate a woman aboard. They are worse than cats or parsons for bad luck. But quite apart from that, quite rationally, no good ever came of women aboard – perpetual trouble, as you saw yourself at Juan Fernandez. She is an odious wench, and he is an ungrateful scrub.'

'Have you seen her, at all?'

'I caught a glimpse of her in the cable-tier just after leaving you this morning. Have you?'

'I have, too. I went along to ask the little girls how they did and to hear them their piece of catechism and there I found a midshipman with them, a young midshipman I did not know, a handsome youth: then I perceived that he was a young woman and I begged her to sit down. We exchanged a few words – her name is Clarissa Harvill – and she spoke with a becoming modesty. She is clearly a woman of some family and education: what is ordinarily called a gentlewoman.'

'Gentlewomen do not get sent to Botany Bay.'

'Nonsense. Think of Louisa Wogan.'

Jack gave the unanswerable Louisa a passing glance and returned to his fury. 'Bawdy-house,' he cried. 'It will be the lower deck full of Portsmouth brutes next, and a Miss in every other cabin – discipline all to pieces – Sodom and Gomorrah.'

'Dear Jack,' said Stephen, 'if I did not know that your liver was speaking rather than your head or God preserve us your heart this righteous indignation and solemnity would grieve me, to say nothing of your broadside of first stones, for shame. As you told me yourself long ago the service is a sounding-box in which tales echo for ever, and it is perfectly well known throughout the ship that when you were about Oakes' age you were disrated and turned before the mast for hiding a girl in that very part of the ship. Surely you must see that this pope-holy sanctimonious attitude has a ludicrous as well as a most unamiable side?'

'You may say what you please, but I shall turn them both ashore on Norfolk Island.'

'Pray take off your breeches and bend over that locker,' said Stephen, sending a jet from his enema through the open stern window. A little later, and from this position of great moral advantage, he went on 'What surprises me extremely in this whole matter is that you should so mistake the people's frame of mind; but then in many ways, as their surgeon, I am closer to them than you are. It appears to me that you do not sufficiently distinguish between the ethos of the man-of-war and that of the privateer. The prevalent feeling or tone of this community is far, far more democratic; consensus is required; and whatever the law may say, you command the *Surprise*, the *Surprise* as a privateer, only because of the respect the people have for you. Your commission is neither here nor there: your authority depends wholly upon their respect and esteem. If you were to order them to put a callow youth and a slip of a girl down on a virtually abandoned island and sail on with me and Padeen you would lose both. You have many old followers on board who might say *My Captain, right or wrong*; but you have no Marines, and I do not think the followers would prevail, with the community as it now stands and with its overriding sense of what is fair and right. You may put your breeches on again.'

'Damn you, Stephen Maturin.'

'And damn you, Jack Aubrey. Swallow this draught half an hour before retiring: the pills you may take if you do not sleep, which I doubt.'

Chapter Two

Like most medical men Stephen Maturin had seen the effects of addiction, full-blown serious addiction, to alcohol and opium; and like many medical men he knew from inner experience just how immensely powerful that craving was, and how supernaturally cunning and casuistical the deprived victim might become. It was therefore only with the greatest reluctance that he had included one small square case-bottle of laudanum (the alcoholic tincture of opium, alas) in his medicine chest. Once laudanum had come aboard by the carboy, and indulgence in it under stress had very nearly wrecked his own life and Padeen's; now, although he was reasonably sure of himself he had not the same confidence in Padeen, and this single bottle, often disguised and sometimes filled with an emetic, was kept in an iron box, far from the ordinary drugs.

A ship had to be provided with a certain amount, since there were cases in which the tincture alone would give relief; and the square bottle was the very smallest that could still be called reasonable – that could be reconciled with Stephen's medical conscience. 'It is a curious thing,' he said to Martin, turning the key in the iron box, 'that a man who knows perfectly well that in decency he must not practise on his friends has not the slightest hesitation in doing so when it comes to medicine. We give strongly-coloured, strongly-flavoured, physically inoperative draughts, pills, boluses in order to profit by the patient's belief that having been dosed he now feels much better – a belief whose invaluable physical effects you have often seen. In this case I exhibited the tincture in the unusually powerful dose of five and thirty drops, disguising it with asafetida and a little musk and suppressing its name, since the patient has a horror of opium, while at the same time, to deal with the

initial stimulation that often accompanies the ingestion of nar-
cotics by those unaccustomed to them, I provided four pills
of our usual pink-tinted chalk, to be taken in the event of
wakefulness. The patient, comforted by the thought of this
resource, will pass the first ten minutes or so in placid contemplation, ignoring the slight excitement, and then he will plunge
into an oblivion as deep as that of the Seven Sleepers, or
deeper. I flatter myself that this deep peace, this absence of
vexation and irascibility, will allow the organs to carry on with
their usual task unhindered, responding to my cholagogues,
eliminating the vicious humours and restoring the former
equilibrium.'

The Seven Sleepers however had not been brought up from
boyhood with a ship's bell. At the second stroke in the morning
watch Jack Aubrey flung himself from his cot on the leeward
roll and staggered, dazed and half blind, to the starboard
chain-pump, where the hands were gathering. He took his
place, tall there in the twilight with the warm air wafting his
nightshirt. He said 'Good morning' to his dimly-apprehended
neighbours, spat on his hands and cried 'Way oh!'

This horrid practice had begun long ago, well north of
Capricorn, so long ago that the people no longer looked upon
it as a grievance but rather as part of the nature of things, as
inevitable and perhaps as necessary as dried peas – so long ago
that Jack's hands were now as horny as his shipmates'.
Stephen's would have been equally harsh and rough, for since
he had unwittingly set the whole process in motion he felt
morally obliged to rise and toil; and he did rise and toil; nearly
destroying himself, until the Captain very kindly told him that
it was his duty to keep his hands as smooth as a fine lady's, in
order to be able to take a leg off like an artist rather than a
butcher's boy.

'Way oh!' he cried, and the water gushed along the pump-
dales, shooting clear of the side. On and on, an exuberant
flood; in half an hour he was dripping sweat on to the deck
and his wits were gathering themselves together through the
clouds of Stephen's five and thirty drops. He recalled the
events of yesterday, but without much emotion; on the edge

36

of his field of vision he noticed that the tide of wet, followed by sand, followed by holystones and then by swabs was coming steadily aft; at length he said 'Some zealous fool must have kept the sweetening-cock open half the watch', and he began to count his strokes. He had nearly reached four hundred when at last there came the welcome cry, 'She sucks'.

They stood away from the pump-brakes and nodded to one another, breathing hard. 'The water came out as clear and sweet as Hobson's conduit,' said one of his neighbours.

'So it did,' said Jack, and he looked about him. The *Surprise*, still on the same tack, but under topsails alone, had drawn in with Norfolk Island, so that the nearer shore could be seen on the rise, and along the heights the outlines of monstrous trees stood sharp against the sky – a sky that was as pure as ever, apart from a low cloud-bank right astern: the lightest night-blue overhead changing imperceptibly to aquamarine in the east, with a very few high clouds moving south-east on the anti-trade, much stronger up there than its counterpart below. Down here the breeze was much the same as before: the swell if anything heavier.

'Good morning, Mr West,' he said when he had examined the log-board. 'Are there any sharks about?' He handed the log-board back – it had told him exactly what he expected – and tossed his sodden nightshirt on to the rail.

'Good morning, sir. None that I have seen. Forecastle, there: are there any sharks about?'

'Never a one, sir: only our old dolphins.' And as the cry came aft so the sun sent up a fine brilliant orange sliver above the horizon; for a moment it could be looked at before eyes could no longer bear it, and a simile struggled for life in Jack's mind, only to be lost as he dived from the gangway, utterly forgotten in the long bubbling plunge with his hair streaming out behind in the pure water, just cool enough to be refreshing. He dived and dived again, revelling in the sea; and once he came face to face with two of the dolphins, cheerful creatures, inquisitive but discreet.

By the time he came aboard again the sun was well clear of the sea, and it was full day, glorious indeed, though lacking

37

that sense of another world entirely. There was Killick, too, standing by the stanchion with a large white towel and a disapproving look on his face. 'Mr Harris said it would close the pores, and throw the yellow bile upon the black,' he said, wrapping the towel about Jack's shoulders.

'Is high water the same time at London Bridge and at the Dodman?' asked Jack, and having stunned Killick with this he asked him whether the Doctor were about. 'Which I seen him in the sick-bay,' said Killick sulkily.

'Then go and ask him whether he would like to have a first breakfast with me.'

Jack Aubrey had a powerful frame to maintain, and this he did by giving it two breakfasts, a trifle of toast and coffee when the sun was first up and then a much more substantial affair shortly after eight bells – any fresh fish that happened to be at hand, eggs, bacon, sometimes mutton chops – to which he often invited the officer and midshipman of the morning watch, Dr Maturin being there as a matter of course.

Stephen came even before Killick's return. 'The smell of coffee would bring me back from the dead. How kind to let me know: and a very good morning to you, my dear sir. How did you sleep?'

'Sleep? Lord, I went out like a light, and remember nothing at all. I did not really wake up until the ship was pumped almost dry. Then I swam. What joy! I hope you will join me tomorrow. I feel a new man.'

'I might, too,' said Stephen without conviction. 'Where is that mumping villain Killick?'

'Which I am coming as quick as I can, ain't I?' cried Killick: and then, putting down the tray, 'Jezebel has been rather near with her milk.'

'I am afraid I shall have to leave you very soon,' said Stephen after his second cup. 'As soon as the bell strikes we must prepare two patients for surgery.'

'Oh dear,' said Jack. 'I hope it is not very serious?'

'Cystotomy: if there is no infection – and infection at sea is much rarer than in hospital – most men support it perfectly

38

well. Fortitude is called for, of course; any shrinking from the knife may prove fatal.'

The bell struck. Stephen quickly ate three more slices of toasted soda-bread, drank another cup of coffee, looked at Jack's tongue with evident satisfaction and hurried away.

He did not emerge until quite well on in the forenoon watch, and as he came up he met a usual morning procession that had just reached the quarterdeck from the leeward gangway: Jemmy Ducks bearing three hencoops, one empty; Sarah carrying the speckled hen in her arms; and Emily leading the goat Jezebel, all bound for the animals' daytime quarters abaft the wheel.

Greetings, smiles and bobs; but then Emily said in her clear child's voice 'Miss is weeping and wringing her hands, way up forward.'

Stephen was thinking 'How well animals behave to children: that goat is a froward goat and the speckled hen a cross ill-natured bird, yet they allow themselves to be led and carried without so much as an oath', and it was a moment before he grasped the force of her remark. 'Ay,' he replied, shaking his head. They moved on with their livestock, greeted by a great quacking of ducks, already installed in a coop with legs.

He was considering Miss Harvill, the island (much closer now), its cliffs, its tall and strangely ugly trees, when he heard Jack cry 'Jolly-boat's crew away,' and he became aware of the tension on the quarterdeck. All the officers were there, looking unusually grave, and from the forecastle and along the gangways the people gazed steadily aft. All this must have been in train for some time, since getting even a jolly-boat over the side was a laborious business. The hands ran down to their places: the bowman hooked on and they all sat there looking up as boat and ship rose and fell.

'There is a Norfolk Island petrel,' said Martin at Stephen's elbow; but Stephen only gave the bird a passing glance.

'Pass the word for my coxswain,' called Jack.

'Sir?' said Bonden, appearing in a moment.

'Bonden, take the jolly-boat into the bay between the cape

39

and the small island with the trees on it and see whether it is possible to land through the surf.'

'Aye aye, sir.'

'You had better pull in, but you may sail back.'

'Aye aye, sir: pull in and sail back it is.'

Jack and Bonden had served many years together; they understood one another perfectly well, and it appeared to Stephen that in spite of their matter-of-fact words and every-day expression some message passed between them; yet though he knew both men intimately he could not tell what that message was.

They pulled away and away, and once it had set a rise of the swell between itself and the ship the jolly-boat disappeared, reappeared, disappeared, reappeared, smaller each time, heading straight for the land, two miles away. White water on the small island with trees close inshore to the east; white water between that island and the iron-bound coast; white water on the headland to the west; and the bay between had a fringe of white. Yet whereas all the rest of the coast in sight had cliffs dropping almost sheer, this bay possessed a beach, probably a sandy beach, running well back to a moderate slope; and there seemed to be a fairly clear passage in.

They watched intently, saying little; but at five bells Jack, turning abruptly from the weather-rail, said 'Captain Pullings, we will stand off and on until the boat returns.' And pausing on the companion-ladder he added 'On the inshore leg we might try for soundings' before hurrying below.

'Philips tells me that there are also parrots, parakeets, gannets and pigeons on the island,' said Martin. 'How I hope we may go ashore! If we cannot land on this side, do you think we may be able to do so on the other?'

For once Stephen found Martin a tedious companion. Was it possible that the man did not know what landing on Norfolk Island might entail? Yes: on reflexion it was quite possible. Just as Captain Aubrey had been the last person to know that there was a woman aboard his ship, so Nathaniel Martin might be the last to know that this woman and her lover were in danger of being marooned there. The threat was after all very

40

recent: the officers were unlikely to have discussed it in the gunroom and it could scarcely have reached Martin from the lower deck – Martin had no servant of his own and Padeen was hardly capable of telling him even if he had wished to. On the other hand it was possible that Martin, having heard of the threat, did not take it seriously. For his own part Stephen did not know what to say. There were times when Jack Aubrey was as easy to read as a well-printed book; others when he could not be made out at all, and this formal, public dispatch of the boat seemed to Stephen incomprehensible, in total contradiction with the cheerful, familiar, sea-wet Jack of early breakfast.

The *Surprise* edged nearer to the wind and Pullings gave orders for the deep-sea line. Stephen walked along the gangway to the bows: as he reached the forecastle the hands gathered round the bitts fell silent and slowly dispersed. From the rail he had a perfect view of the bay, and his pocket-glass showed him the jolly-boat's crew pulling steadily in; they were more than half way now, and as he watched Bonden took the boat round a sunken rock with an ugly swirl of water over it. The ship barely had steerage-way and although the shrouds gave a creaking sigh each time the long swell raised her up or let her down there was very little noise in the bows. He heard the cry of 'Watch, there, watch,' as each man in succession along the side let go his last turn of the deep-sea line, and then Reade's shrill report 'Sixty-eight fathom, sir: coral sand and shells.'

Six bells. The boat had reached the edge of the breakers over by the small island and was working its way westwards along the shore. The triangular sail in front of him, the foretopmast staysail in all likelihood, filled, and the *Surprise* began her turn, sailing gently away from the land. Martin, who could take a hint as well as any man, had retired to the mizen-top, which now commanded an excellent view of Norfolk Island, and Stephen thought of joining him there. But a disinclination for talk combined with the exaggerated movement of the mast now that the ship was heading directly into the swell kept him to the quarterdeck, where he stood at the taffrail and watched

41

the jolly-boat making its way towards the cape that limited the bay, keeping to the edge of the surf – from this level the little boat seemed to be almost in the breaking rollers, and in great danger of being swamped.

He was still there, pondering, when the jolly-boat reached the far end, hoisted a sail and stood out to sea; and he was so lost in his reflexions that he was quite startled when Jack tapped him on the shoulder, saying with a smile, 'You are in a fine study, Doctor. I hailed you twice. How did your patients do? I see' – nodding at the dried blood on Stephen's hand – 'that you have been opening them.'

'Quite well, I thank you: they are as comfortable as can be expected, and with the blessing they will soon be more so.'

'Capital, capital. I shall pay them a visit.' Then in a much lower tone he added 'I have been to the head myself. I thought you might like to know.'

'I am heartily glad of it,' said Stephen, and asked him exact and particular questions; but Jack Aubrey was more prudish than might have been supposed about such matters and he only answered 'Like a horse,' walking forward out of range.

He brought the ship round again to meet the boat, but Stephen stayed where he was. With the turn the island slid out of view, to be replaced by a vast expanse of ocean; and today the ocean had a horizon as taut and sharp as could be desired, except in the west-south-west, where the early morning's cloudbank had grown, working up against the wind as thunder-clouds and squalls so often did, contrary to all sense of what was right and natural by land.

'I beg your pardon, sir,' said Reade at his side, 'but the Captain thought you might like me to pour this water over your hand.'

'God love you, Mr Reade, my dear,' said Stephen. 'Pray pour away, and I will rub. I did wash at one time, I recall; but I dare say I adjusted a dressing afterwards. Fortunately, however, I turned back the cuffs of my coat, or I should be in sad trouble with . . .' He stopped abruptly, for here was Bonden coming up the side.

'Well, Bonden?' asked Captain Aubrey on the silent, listening quarterdeck.

'No landing, sir,' said Bonden. 'A wicked surf and a worse undertow, though the tide was on the ebb.'

'No landing at all?'

'None at all, sir.'

'Very good. Captain Pullings, since there is no possibility whatsoever of landing we will hoist in the jolly-boat and make all possible sail on our former course.'

'On deck there,' hailed the lookout at the masthead. 'A sail right astern. Fore-and-aft, I reckon.'

Jack took the watch telescope and ran aloft. 'Where away, Trilling?' he called from the crosstrees.

'Right astern, sir, on the edge of that ill-looking bank,' replied Trilling, who had moved out along the yard.

'I can't see her.'

'Why, to tell you the truth nor can I now, sir,' said Trilling in that amused, conversational tone more usual in a letter of marque than a man-of-war. 'She comes and goes, like. But you could see her from the deck, was it to clear a little: she ain't a great way off.'

Jack returned to the deck by way of a backstay, as he had done when he was a boy. 'As I was saying, Captain Pullings,' he went on, 'we will make all possible sail on our former course. There is not a moment to be lost.'

The jolly-boat was hoisted in and made fast, the topgallants were sheeted home and hoisted to the strange musical cries of the Orkneymen aboard, the bowlines hauled to the one chant the Royal Navy countenanced 'One! Two! Three! Belay oh!', and Martin said to Stephen 'I was much astonished to hear that the surf made landing impossible. From my vantage-point I could have sworn I saw a relatively smooth stretch just this side of the cape. I hope you are not too deeply disappointed, Maturin?'

'Faith, if I were to repine at every promising island I have been swept past in my naval career, I should have run melancholy mad long since. We have at least seen the mutton-bird and the monstrous pines, bad luck to them. I think them as ugly as they are tall; the ugliest vegetables known to man except for that vile *Araucaria imbricata* of Chile, which in some ways it resembles.'

They talked about the conifers they had seen in New South Wales; they watched the upper-yard men race aloft to set the royals; and Martin, looking round to see that no one was at hand, said in a low voice 'Tell me, Maturin, why are they said to be set flying? *Flying*? I have been at sea so long I do not like to ask anyone else.'

'Martin, you lean on a broken reed: we are in the same boat, as reeds so often are. Let us comfort ourselves with the reflexion that not all of our shipmates could tell how an ablative comes to be so very absolute, on occasion.'

'Sir,' called West, who was standing on the leeward hammock-nettings with a telescope. 'I believe I make her out on the rise. I think she may be wearing a pennant; and if so she is the cutter we heard about.'

Pullings relayed this to the Captain, adding 'When we were in Sydney they spoke of a fast fourteen-gun cutter called the *Eclair* that was coming up from Van Diemen's Land.'

'I heard about her,' said Jack, training his telescope aft. 'But I see nothing.'

Noon. The officers took their altitudes: Pullings reported that the sun was on the meridian: Jack allowed that it was twelve o'clock and that the new naval day might now begin. Eight bells struck; the hands hurried to their dinner; and a curious noise they made, not the muffled anxiety of the day before, but still restrained and as it were conspiratorial.

When the din was over and when the hands were perhaps half way through their dinner (oatmeal, ship's bread and cheese, Monday being a banyan day) West repeated that he was sure of the cutter now, and almost certain of her pennant.

'You may be right, sir, though I see nothing of it,' said Jack. 'But even if you are, there is nothing extraordinary about a cutter being sent to Norfolk Island. There are still quantities of Government stores ashore, and several people, I understand.'

'Surely they are throwing out a signal, sir?' cried West a moment later.

'I do not see it, sir,' said Jack coldly. 'Besides, I have no time for idle gossip with a cutter.' And Davidge, who was quicker than his shipmate, murmured 'Tace is the Latin for a candlestick, old fellow.'

When the hands and therefore the midshipmen had finished their dinner Jack went below and sent for Oakes. 'Sit down, Mr Oakes,' he said. 'I have been considering what to do with you, and although it is clear that we must part – apart from anything else no women are allowed in the *Surprise* – I do not mean to discharge you until we reach some reasonably Christian port in Chile or Peru, where you can easily take the passage home. You will have enough money to do so: there is not only your pay but also the probability of some prize-money. If we should take nothing then I will advance what is necessary.'

'Thank you very much, sir.'

'I shall also give you a recommendation to any naval officer you may choose to show it to, mentioning your good and seamanlike conduct under my command. But then there is your . . . your companion. She is under your protection, as I take it?'

'Yes, sir.'

'Have you considered what is to become of her?'

'Yes, sir. If you would be so extremely kind as to marry us, she would be free; and if that cutter were to come aboard we could bid them kiss our – we could laugh in their faces.'

'Have you made her an offer?'

'No, sir. I supposed . . .'

'Then go and do so, sir. If she agrees, bring her back here and let me hear her confirm it: be damned to Hell if I allow any forced marriage in my ship. If she don't, we shall have to find some place for her to sling her hammock. Cut along now. You may be as quick as you like. I have many things to do. By the way, what is her name?'

'Clarissa Harvill, sir.'

'Clarissa Harvill: very well. Carry on, Mr Oakes.'

They came panting aft, and Oakes urged her through the

45

cabin door. She had heard of her lover's summons; she had had time to do what could be done to clothes, hair, face, against all eventualities, and looked quite well as she stood there, slim and boyish in her uniform, her fair head bowed.

'Miss Harvill,' said Jack, rising, 'pray be seated. Oakes, place a chair and sit down yourself.' She sat, her eyes cast down, her ankles crossed, her hands in her lap, her back quite straight, looking as nearly like one wearing a skirt as possible, and Jack addressed her: 'Mr Oakes tells me that you might consent to marry him. May I take it that this is so, or is the fish wather to – that is to say, or does he flatter himself?'

'No, sir: I am quite ready to marry Mr Oakes.'

'Of your own free will?'

'Yes, sir: and we shall be infinitely obliged for your kindness.'

'Never thank me. We have a parson aboard, and it would be most improper for a layman to take his place. Have you any other clothes?'

'No, sir.'

Jack considered. 'Jemmy Ducks and Bonden could run you up a smock of number eight sailcloth, the kind we use for royals and skysails. Though perhaps,' he went on after some thought, 'canvas might be looked upon as improper – not sufficiently formal.'

'Not at all, sir,' murmured Miss Harvill.

'I have some old shirts, sir, that could perhaps be pieced out,' said Oakes.

Jack frowned, and raising his voice to its usual pitch called 'Killick. Killick, there.'

'Sir?'

'Rouse out the bolt of scarlet silk I bought in Batavia.'

'I doubt but we should have to rummage the whole after-hold, my mate and me, with a couple of hands to heave and then put it all back again, all back again,' said Killick. 'Hours of heavy toil.'

'Nonsense,' said Jack. 'It is next to the lacquer cabinets in my store-room, packed in matting and then blue cotton. It will not take you two minutes: even less.' Killick opened his

46

mouth; but weighing up Captain Aubrey's present mood he closed it again and retired with an inarticulate grunt of extreme displeasure. Jack went on, still addressing Miss Harvill, 'But I am sure you can sew perfectly well yourself?'

'Alas, sir, only the plainest of seams, with large stitches, and very slow – scarcely a yard in an afternoon.'

'That will never do. The gown must be ready by eight bells. Mr Oakes, there are two young men in your division who embroider their shirts uncommon pretty –'

'Willis and Hardy, sir.'

'Just so. They can each take a sleeve. Jemmy Ducks can run up a skirt in half a glass, and Bonden can look after the – the upper part.' There was a pause, and to fill it Jack, who was always rather nervous with women, said 'I trust you do not find the weather too hot, Miss Harvill? With squalls brewing astern, it often grows oppressive.'

'Oh no, sir,' said Miss Harvill with more animation than her modesty had allowed hitherto. 'In such a very beautiful ship it is never too hot.' The words were idiotic, but the inclination to please and to be pleased was evident; and the compliment to the ship could not go wrong.

Killick came in, so pinched with disapproval that he could not bring himself to say anything but 'Which I took off the matting.' Jack said 'Thankee, Killick,' turning the bolt in his hands. He opened the blue cotton wrapping and the silk appeared, a heavy, discreetly gleaming silk, deeper than scarlet, extraordinarily rich in texture and above all in colour, with the sun coming diagonally across from the stern windows. 'Mr Oakes,' he said, 'carry this bolt to Jemmy Ducks: it is a fathom wide, and a suitable length cut from the end square with the leech will cover the young lady from top to toe. Tell Jemmy what is to be done and ask him whether there are any better tailors in the ship, and if so to carry on with their help: there is not a moment to lose. Miss Harvill, I hope to have the pleasure of seeing you at eight bells.' He opened the door; she made as though to curtsey, realized the absurdity and gave him a most apologetic look, saying 'I do not know how to thank you, sir. Lord, it is the most beautiful, beautiful silk I have ever seen in my life.'

The interview, though short, had been curiously wearing, and Jack sat at his ease for some time on the stern-window locker with a glass of madeira at his side. Through the open companion he could hear the usual sounds of the ship: Davidge, the officer of the watch, calling out for an even tauter foretopsail bowline; Dirty Edwards, the quartermaster at the con, telling the helmsman 'to ease her a trifle, Billy, then luff and touch her'; then Davidge again, 'I cannot tell you where to put it, Mr Bulkeley. You will have to wait until the Captain comes on deck.'

Jack finished his wine, stretched, and came on deck. As soon as he appeared, blinking in the sunlight, Davidge said 'Sir, Mr Bulkeley wants to know where the hands can hoist the wedding garland.'

'Wedding garland?' said Jack; and glancing into the waist of the ship he saw several men from Oakes's division gazing up. As he looked they mutely raised the traditional set of hoops, all decked out with ribbons and streamers. Where indeed was it to go? If Oakes had been a seaman it would have gone to the mast he belonged to; if he had commanded the ship, then to the maintopgallant stay; but in this case? 'Hoist it to the foretopgallant masthead,' he called down, and walked slowly aft. That garland had not been made during this last half hour. The streamers were not even very fresh. The infernal buggers had known what he would do — had foretold his decision — had made game of him. 'God damn them all to Hell: I must be as transparent as a piece of glass,' he said, but without particular anger. In any case his mind was diverted by the sight of Dr Maturin showing Reade a series of extraordinarily exact and rapid steps from an Irish dance. 'There,' he said, 'that is a way we have of tripping it at a marriage; but you must never wave your arms or show any emotion, far less hoot aloud, as some unhappy nations do: a most illiberal practice. Here is the Captain himself, who will tell you that hallooing as you dance is not at all genteel.'

'It is an odd thing,' said Jack, when Reade had withdrawn,

'but I seem to bring no news in this ship. The hands have had the garland ready pretty well since we weighed, and here you are showing young Reade how to dance at a wedding, though it was arranged only ten minutes ago. I doubt whether I shall even be able to astonish Mr Martin, when I ask him to officiate. He dines with us today, as I am sure you recall.'

'How I wish he may not be late: my belly fairly groans for its food. Though that may be the effect of terror. You have noticed the ship pursuing us, I make little doubt? A ship flying a man-of-war's pennant?'

'I pass over your calling a cutter a ship, but allow me to object to your *pursuing*. To be sure, she is sailing approximately the same course; and to be sure, she would probably like to speak to us. But she may very well be putting into a bay on the north-western side, the leeward side, of Norfolk Island on some official business; and although she is alleged to be wearing a pennant I believe I may safely ignore her. I have no time for gossiping, and we are sufficiently far apart for it not to be offensively obvious, not court-martial obvious; and we shall certainly stay far enough ahead until nightfall.'

'Can we not outsail her? Run clean away?'

'Of course not, Stephen. How can you be so strange? Both vessels are moving through the water at much the same pace, but whereas we, as a ship, a square-rigged ship, can only come up to within six points of the wind, she can come up to five; so all things being equal she must overhaul us in the long run – unless of course we put before the wind, which would put us far out of her reach but which would also be a clear proof of criminal evasion. If she is still there in the morning – if she has not run into the lee of Norfolk Island – and if there is no extraordinary change in the weather, I shall have to heave to. To stop,' he added, for a person who could call a cutter a ship after so many years at sea might need even simpler terms explained. 'But by that time Oakes's companion will be a free woman, Martin having done her business with book, bell and candle.'

'You would never be forgetting Padeen, I am sure?' said Stephen in a low voice.

'No,' said Jack, smiling. 'I am not. We have no Judases aboard, I believe; and even if we had it would be a bold cutter-commander who would find him in my ship.' For some minutes he studied the *Eclair*, the cutter in question, through his glass. She was well handled, and she might in fact be moving a little faster than the *Surprise* as well as lying closer to the wind; and her pennant was now quite certain when she came about: but she could not reach him by nightfall and the likelihood of her running beyond Norfolk Island into the main ocean was very small indeed even if she was in pursuit of him. He closed the telescope and said 'It is a very surprising thing, you know, the power of a young woman that sits quiet, self-contained and modest, looking down, answering civil – not like a booby, mark you, Stephen – civil, but not very much. A man could not speak chuff to such a girl, without he was a very mere Goth. Old Jarvey could not speak chuff to such a girl.'

'It is my belief, brother, that your misogyny is largely theoretical.'

'Ay,' said Jack, shaking his head. 'I love a wench, it is true; but a wench in her right place. Come, Stephen, we must shift our clothes. Tom and Martin will be with us in five minutes.'

In five minutes Captain Pullings in all his glory and Mr Martin in a good black coat walked into the great cabin: they were at once offered drinks to whet their appetite (a wholly unnecessary form at this time of the day) and as the bell struck they took their places at table. For the first part of dinner both sailors tried to make both medical men understand, really understand, why a craft that came up to within five points of the wind must eventually overtake another, moving at the same speed but coming up only six points, it being understood that they were both sailing close-hauled. After the roast mutton had gone away, a very mere skeleton, Jack in desperation sent for Reade and told him to ask Mr Adams for some bristol card and to cut out two isosceles triangles, the one with an apex of $135°$, the other of $112°30'$.

By the time triangles came the cloth had been drawn and Jack would have traced lines showing the direction of the wind

50

and the turning points in port on the gleaming mahogany had Killick not cried out 'Oh sir, no sir, if you please: let me stretch lengths of white marline.'

The marline stretched, Jack said 'Now, gentlemen, the wind is blowing right down the middle, from the Doctor's waistcoat to mine; the parallel lines on either side show approximately where the vessels go about, beating up into it, towards him. Now I lay the six-pointer's triangle on the left-hand line with its base at right angles to the wind: I trace the ship's course, close-hauled, as far as the right-hand line, where she goes about; and I mark the place with a piece of bread. I do the same for each leg until I reach the turning-point of the sixth leg, marked with this dead weevil. Now I take the cutter's five-point triangle; I do the same; and as you see the cutter's fourth leg coincides almost exactly with the frigate's sixth. The distance made good to windward is pretty well four to three in favour of the fore-and-aft rig.'

'It cannot be denied,' said Stephen, looking closely at the weevil. 'But my head is more fully convinced than my heart – such a fine tall ship, that has run down so many enemies of superior force.'

'Would a trigonometrical proof please you more?' asked Tom Pullings.

Stephen shook his head and privately drew the weevil towards his plate. 'I looked into a book on trigonometry once,' said Martin. 'It was called *A Simple Way of Resolving All Triangles, invaluable for Gentlemen, Surveyors, and Mariners, carefully adapted for the Meanest Understanding*: but I had to give it up. Some understandings are even meaner than the author imagined, it appears.'

'At least we all understand this capital port,' said Stephen. 'A glass of wine with you, sir.'

'By all means,' said Martin, bowing over his plate. 'It is indeed capital port; but this must be my very last. I have a ceremony to perform within the hour, as you know, and I should not wish to mumble and stumble my way through it.'

After dinner Stephen, who attended no services but funerals, retired to the sick-berth where Owen told him about

51

his voyages to the mainland and islands of north-western America for furs and thence across by the Sandwich Islands, particularly Hawaii, to Canton, or sometimes home by way of the Horn or the Straits, with perhaps a stop at Más Afuera for seal skins. And about other parts of the South Seas he had been to, especially Easter Island, which Stephen found more interesting than the rest, above all because of the prodigious figures on their exactly-dressed stone platforms, set up by an unknown people who had also left records on wooden tablets, inscribed in an unknown script and an unknown tongue. Owen was an intelligent, clear-headed man, who took pleasure in measuring things and pacing out distances and who, though nearly sixty, still had quite a good memory. He was still talking, though rather hoarse by now, and Stephen was still questioning him, when Martin came down for the evening doses and dressings.

'How I long to see Easter Island,' said Stephen to him. 'Owen here has been telling me more about the place. Do you remember how far off it is?'

'I believe the Captain said five thousand miles; but really, the bottle passed with such insistence after the ceremony that I am scarcely to be relied upon, ha, ha, ha.'

Padeen of course was present, as loblolly-boy: he had been in a pitiful state of anxiety ever since the cutter was sighted, and now as they all walked into the dispensary he bent to whisper in Stephen's ear, 'For the Mother of God, your honour will never forget me, I beg and beseech.' 'I will not, Padeen, upon my soul: I have the Captain's word itself,' said Stephen, and partly by way of reassuring him he went on in an ordinary tone to Martin, 'How did the service go? Well, I hope?'

'Oh yes, I thank you. Apart from the pitching, which nearly had us over twice, it might have been a private wedding in a drawing-room. The Captain gave away the bride very properly; the armourer had made a ring out of a guinea piece; all the officers were present and everything was entered in the log and signed. The bride startled me by appearing in a scarlet dress, but she thanked me very prettily when I offered my congratulations afterwards.'

'Had you not seen her before?'

'Certainly I had. I went forward earlier in the day to speak to her about the nature of the ceremony and to make sure she understood it – I had supposed she was quite a different kind of woman, barely literate . . . She was still wearing the clothes she had come aboard in, and I must say that although she looked very well as a bride, she looked far better as a boy. Her slight but not unattractive form gave me if not an understanding of paederasty then something not unlike it.'

Stephen was surprised. He had never heard Martin make such an unreserved and almost licentious observation: perhaps he was now more a medical man than a parson. And perhaps, Stephen reflected as they rolled their pills and Padeen wound the bandages, this was one of the effects of bringing a woman into a celibate community. He was no chemist, but some of his friends were and he had seen a Swedish savant let a single catalysing drop fall into a clear untroubled liquid that instantly grew turbid, separated, and threw down fire-red crystals.

'Come,' said Martin. 'We must not be too late. There are to be great doings on the forecastle. *Jack's Alive* and horn-pipes, of course, and some of the old dances, like *Cuckolds All Awry* and *An Old Man's a Bed Full of Bones*. We used to dance them when I was at school.'

'What could be more suitable?' said Stephen.

The *Surprise* had always been a tuneful ship and much given to dancing, but never to such a degree as this evening, when the crowded forecastle saw the ranks of country-dancers advance, retreat and caper in perfect time despite the swell, while fiddles, horns, jew's harps and fifes played with barely a pause on the bitts and even perched on the windward cathead. Hornpipes, with several dancing at once, each encouraged by his own division; jigs; the strange evolutions of the Orkney-men, and their rhythmic howls.

'They are enjoying themselves, sir,' said Pullings.

53

'Let them gather their peasecods while they may,' said Jack. 'Old Monday he's a-dying. They will have a ducking before we muster the watch.' They both glanced up through the cloud of sails at the thickening sky – barely a star showing through. 'But I am just as glad of it. That damned cutter will throw up another blue light in a minute, but we shall not be able to see this one either.'

Indeed, as the current hornpipe was ending in feats of extraordinary agility, two faint blue glows appeared far astern, but the third, completing the conventional signal, could not be made out at all.

'Even so,' said Jack, 'let us keep all standing at eight bells. That fellow is sure to shorten sail for the night: he is not cracking on hot-foot after some thumping great prize. Two escaped convicts without a penny on their heads are not a thumping great prize.'

'He might be after promotion, sir.'

'Very true. But taking two very small absconders would not win him a ha'porth of promotion, whereas cracking on, being brought by the lee and limping home under a jury-rig would certainly earn him some very bitter words indeed, naval stores being what they are in Sydney. No. With topgallants and royals we shall draw so far away from him in the night that I do not believe even promotion would bring him on, supposing there were any. But in any event I am morally certain that in an hour's time he will put down his helm and steer for the north side of the island.' Jack paused, sniffing the air, taking in the whole vast series of strains and stresses acting on the ship. 'Yet with such a top-hamper and the possibility of thick weather . . .' A double flash of lightning startled the dancers and a first swathe of warm rain untuned the fiddle-strings. '. . . I should like you to take the middle watch.'

It was rare that Captain Aubrey misjudged a naval situation, but at first dawn the next day the thump of a distant gun drew him from his sleep and a moment later Reade appeared in the twilight by his cot. 'Captain Pullings' duty, sir, and the cutter is half a mile on our starboard beam. She has thrown out a signal and fired a leeward gun; and she is lowering down a boat.'

'What does the signal say, Mr Reade?'

'We have not been able to make out the hoist yet, sir, the light being so indifferent, but we think *governor* and *dispatch* is part of it.'

On deck a somewhat drawn Pullings said 'I am sorry to pull you out of your bed so soon after you turned in, sir, but there you are. She never reduced sail any more than we did: she cracked on to make all sneer again, and she must have crossed our wake about four bells.'

'There is nothing to be done about it. Prepare to receive boarders as civilly as we can. Flog the gangway and preddy the deck as far as possible. I shall put on a uniform. Mr Reade, you will have to change those filthy trousers. They seem to be whipping an extraordinary number of objects over the side,' he added, from the head of the companion-ladder. Below he roused Stephen Maturin and said 'You may call me Jack Pudding if you choose, but that cutter is alongside and I must receive her captain. I shall invite him to breakfast. If you join us, pray do not forget to shave and put on a shirt, a good coat and your wig. Killick will bring hot water.' He then roared for his steward: 'Uniform: tell my cook to prepare a breakfast fit for visitors and to stand by in case they stay dinner. Pass the word for Bonden.' And to Bonden, privately, 'Stow Padeen.' Both Jack and Bonden had had a great deal of experience in pressing hands out of merchantmen, hands hidden, often enough, with wonderful ingenuity; and they were confident that no one, unless he were allowed to fumigate the ship with sulphur, could discover their hiding-place.

The boat came slowly across, taking care to row dry with so many packages aboard, and presently a lieutenant, followed by a midshipman, came aboard to the wail of bosun's calls. He saluted the quarterdeck, which returned the salute, and advanced with his hat tucked under his arm and a waxed-sailcloth packet held in his left hand. 'Captain Aubrey, sir?' he said. 'I am M'Mullen, commanding the *Eclair*, and I have been honoured with orders from His Excellency to deliver this to you personally.'

'Thank you, Mr M'Mullen,' said Jack, taking the official packet with due gravity and shaking M'Mullen's hand.

'And then, sir, I have a quantity of mail for *Surprise* that came in two ships, one after another, just after you sailed.'

'That will be very welcome to all hands, I am sure,' said Jack. 'Mr West, pray have it brought aboard. I hope, sir, that you will breakfast with me?'

'I should be delighted, sir,' said M'Mullen, whose red round young face, hitherto solemn and official, now beamed out like the sun.

'And Mr West,' said Jack, looking at the *Eclair*'s long-legged midshipman on the gangway, 'I am sure the gunroom will look after the young gentleman and see that the boat's crew have all they want.'

In the cabin M'Mullen looked about him with the keenest attention, and on being introduced to Stephen shook his hand long and hard, and in the course of breakfast he said 'I had always longed to be aboard the *Surprise*, and to meet her surgeon, for my father, John M'Mullen, held the appointment in ninety-nine.'

'The year of the *Hermione*?'

'Yes, sir; and he told me about it in such detail that it seemed almost like Troy, with all the people and the places on the heroic scale.'

'Mr M'Mullen will correct me if I am mistaken,' said Stephen, 'but I can think of no more concentrated heroism in the Iliad. After all, the Greeks had ten years in which to accomplish their feats: the Surprises in 1799 had not as many hours.'

'I should be the last to contradict Dr Maturin,' said M'Mullen. 'For not only do I abound in his sense, but my father has always mentioned him with the greatest respect. He told me, sir, that he looked upon your *Diseases of Seamen* as the most luminous, perspicuous book on the subject he had ever read.'

'He flatters me far beyond my deserts,' said Stephen. 'May I help you to a slice of bacon, sir, and a double-yolked, delicately browned egg?'

'You are very good, sir,' said M'Mullen, holding out his plate: and when he had emptied it he said to Jack, 'Captain Aubrey, sir, may I beg you to indulge me? I have undertaken to sail for the mainland in half an hour; and if I might spend those minutes in running about the ship with a midshipman – tops, fighting-quarters and so on – and in looking at the sick-berth for my father's sake, it would make me extremely happy.'

'But ain't you going to stay dinner?' cried Jack.

'Sir, I regret it exceedingly; nothing would have given me greater pleasure,' said M'Mullen. 'But alas my hands are tied.'

'Well,' said Jack, and called 'Killick. Killick there.'

'Which I'm just behind your chair,' said Killick.

'Then pass the word for Mr Oakes,' said Jack, with a look that meant 'Tell him not to look too squalid, for the honour of the ship.'

The moment Mr M'Mullen had left the cabin with Oakes, Tom Pullings came in and said 'Sir, the officers and men are very urgent with me to beg you will open the mail.'

'No more urgent than I am, Tom,' said Jack, hurrying out on to the half deck, where there stood a surprising heap of boxes, chests and bags. With no pleasure Jack recognized the bulk of it as legal papers in corded legal trunks: he heaved them to one side and seized the undoubted mail-sacks. He broke the seals, emptied the contents on to the broad, wide stern-window locker, and hurrying through them for Sophie's well-known hand he called for his clerk. 'Mr Adams,' he said, 'pray sort these for me, will you. Those for the lower deck may go forward at once.'

He carried his own little heap and the official packet away to his sleeping-cabin: there he opened the waxed sailcloth first from a sense of duty; as he had expected it contained three large Admiralty enclosures for Stephen together with a cover from the Governor – compliments, no doubt – and then he laid them all aside for his letters from home. Dear Sophie had at last learnt to number her envelopes, so he was able to read them in order; and this he did with a happy smile set on his face and his soul ten thousand miles away, watching his son's progress in Latin under the Reverend Mr Beales and in horsemanship under his cousin Diana (a female centaur), and his daughters' in history, geography and French under Miss O'Mara, in dancing, drawing and deportment at Mrs Hawker's establishment in Portsmouth, progress all more or less supported by notes in their own hands, proving that they were now at least partially literate. But the smile abruptly left his face when he came to a later reference to Diana, to their cousin Diana, Stephen's wife. Sophie had always been most unwilling to say anything disagreeable about anyone, and when it came to her cousin the adverse criticism was so hedged about, qualified and softened that its meaning was not at all easy to catch. Something was amiss, but a second reading did not make it clear and he had no time for a third before Oakes knocked at the door and said 'If you please, sir, Mr M'Mullen wishes to take his leave.'

'Thank you, Mr Oakes: pray let the bosun know.' Jack came on deck and found M'Mullen poised to go, the *Eclair* lying to within pistol-shot.

'I thank you very heartily indeed, sir,' he said, 'and give you joy of the finest sixth-rate I have ever seen, finer even than my father told me.'

They parted on the kindest terms: the cutter put before the wind and spread her wings. When last seen she was setting topgallant studdingsails, tearing away to a young woman in the suburbs of Sydney. But long before this Jack had returned to the great cabin, followed by all the officers, and when he had handed round their post he said 'Gentlemen: although Mr Oakes may leave us at the next convenient port in South America, since the *Surprise* carries no wives, in the meantime he remains a midshipman and must be treated by all hands with the respect due to anyone who walks the quarterdeck. The same of course applies to Mrs Oakes. I intend inviting them to dinner and I look forward to the pleasure of your company.'

They all bowed, said they would be charmed, delighted, very happy, and hurried off to read their letters. Jack, having passed the massive enclosures to Stephen, went back to his sleeping cabin; and he was about to return to Ashgrove Cottage and this question of Diana when the Governor's envelope, addressed to Captain Aubrey, Royal Navy, MP, FRS, etc. etc., struck him as larger than usual for even very flowery compliments.

Yes, indeed. These were orders, wholly official and direct; and like most orders they left the door ajar, so that the man who carried them out could be blamed for either closing or opening it. There had been trouble in Moahu, an island to the south of the Sandwich group: British ships had been detained and British mariners misused. It appeared that there was a war in progress between the queen of the southern part and a rival from the north: Captain Aubrey would proceed to Moahu without a moment's loss of time and take appropriate measures to secure the release of the ships and their crews. It appeared that the forces were evenly balanced. The presence of His Majesty's ship would no doubt decide the issue. On mature consideration Captain Aubrey would decide which side was the more likely to acknowledge British sovereignty and receive a resident counsellor with an adequate guard, and he would bring his influence to bear in favour of that side: it was desirable that there should be only one ruler for Government to deal with. Although any unnecessary bloodshed was to be deprecated, if moral force proved insufficient to induce compliance, Captain Aubrey would consider other arguments. Moahu was of course British, Captain Cook having taken possession of the archipelago in 1779; and Captain Aubrey would bear in mind the importance of the island as a base for the fur-trade between north-west America and Canton on the one hand and for a potentially far more important commerce with Korea and Japan on the other. He would also reflect upon the benefits likely to accrue to the inhabitants from British protection, a settled administration . . . superstition, barbarous customs, undesirable practices . . . medical instruction . . . enlightenment . . . missionary stations . . . commercial development. Jack's eye skimmed over the usual set piece at the end, but he did notice that it had been written in haste and that although the variation about *the end justifying the means* had been thought better of, there had been no time to write the whole afresh and the words had been attempted to be scratched out, which gave them a ghostly emphasis.

Moahu. Jack walked into the great cabin, to the chart table, and having pored over it he returned to the quarterdeck and said 'Mr Davidge, we will alter course, if you please: north-north-east. Spritsail and spritsail topsail; the staysails I need not name.'

The guests – there were only seven of them – gathered in the coach, normally Stephen's sleeping-cabin when he did not prefer to go down to his little booth opening off the gunroom and at all times his study, but now tweaked and scrubbed into the likeness of an ante-room; and when Stephen himself appeared Martin said to him 'I am so sorry about Easter Island.'

'So am I,' said Stephen. 'I was vexed to the heart when first the Captain told me, but now I count it as just one more disappointment in a radically miserable life; and I console myself that the ornithology of these new islands has barely been touched upon. I understand that Moahu is no great way from Hawaii, which is known to possess a wide variety of honeysuckers and even a gallinule with a scarlet forehead.'

'Yes. And presently you will also have the consolation of seeing Mrs Oakes in the remarkable scarlet gown I told you about.'

The door opened, but no scarlet gown appeared. The blue cotton that protected Jack's bolt of silk had been transformed by Heaven knows what ingenuity and pains into a dress that looked very well with a seaman's black shore-going Barcelona handkerchief worn over it as a fichu. Jack stepped forward to welcome Mrs Oakes and her husband, and in due course he led her, followed by all the rest, into the great cabin: it was more than usually splendid, for although the long table, ablaze with silver, was laid for eight, and they spread well apart, there was still a great deal of space on every hand, a space filled with the sun reflected from the wake and the dancing sea, vivid and full of life, flooding in through the stern sash-lights, a range of windows running across the whole width, a fourth and inwardly slanting wall of bright glass panes that made the cabin the most beautiful room in the world. Clarissa Oakes looked about her with evident pleasure, but she said nothing as he sat her on his right hand and the other chairs began to fill: Davidge was opposite her and Reade was on her right with Martin over against him. Tom Pullings was of course at the foot of the table with Oakes on his right hand and Stephen on his left. There were few seamen servants and no red-coated Marines, only Killick behind Jack's chair and his mates to carry dishes and bottles, Padeen behind Stephen's, and a young foretopman each for Pullings and Davidge, but the scene had a seamanlike grandeur in which a twelve-pounder on either side did not look at all out of place.

'We had an agreeable visitor this morning, ma'am,' said Jack, helping her to soup. 'The captain of the *Eclair*. He was most uncommon eager to see the ship, because his father had served in her in ninety-nine, the year of her famous action at Puerto Cabello. Well, I say famous – a trifle of sherry, ma'am? It is a very innocent little wine – because it made a great deal of noise in the service; but I do not suppose you ever heard of Puerto Cabello or the *Hermione* by land?'

'I do not believe I ever did, sir, though naval actions have fascinated me ever since I was a child. Please would you tell me about Puerto Cabello? A first-hand account of a battle at sea would be of the very first interest.'

'Alas, I was not there. How I regret it! I was indeed a midshipman in the *Surprise* at one time, but that was some years before. However, I will give you a bald statement of the facts. Mr Martin, the bottle stands by you, sir. Well, the *Hermione* was in the hands of the Spaniards, who at that time were our enemies, allied to the French: I will not go into how they came to have her because it is not to the point, but there she was, lying in Puerto Cabello on the Spanish Main, moored head and stern between two very powerful batteries at the mouth of the harbour, yards crossed, sails bent and all ready for sea.

'Captain Hamilton – Edward Hamilton, not his brother Charles – who then had the *Surprise*, took her in to have a look at the *Hermione*. She was a thirty-two gun frigate and 365 men aboard: the *Surprise* had twenty-eight guns and 197 men and boys: but he decided to cut her out, and his people agreed. He had room for only 103 in his six boats, so he made a very careful plan of attack and explained it as clearly as ever he could. An hour or so after sunset, and all wearing blue – not a scrap of white anywhere – they set off in two divisions, the captain in the pinnace with the gunner, a mid and 16 hands; the launch with the first lieutenant – who was the first of the *Surprise* at Puerto Cabello, Captain Pullings?'

'Frederick Wilson, sir: and the midshipman was Robin Clerk, now master of the *Arethusa*.'

'Aye. And then there was the jolly-boat with another mid, the carpenter and eight men. The next division was made up of the gig, commanded by the surgeon, our friend M'Mullen's father, and 16 men . . . but I must not be too particular. Six boats in all, counting the two cutters. So they pulled along, each division in tow, and each boat with a distinct task. The jolly-boat for example was to board on the starboard quarter, cut the stern cable and send two men aloft to loose the mizen topsail. It was a dark night with a smooth sea and a breeze off the land and all went swimmingly until they were within a mile of the *Hermione*, when they were seen by two Spanish gunboats rowing guard. "Be damned to them," said Hamilton. He cut the tow, gave three cheers and dashed straight for the frigate, confident that all the rest would follow him. But some of them, eager to be knocking Spaniards on the head, set about these wretched gunboats and Captain Hamilton and his boat's crew found themselves almost alone when they boarded on the starboard bow and cleared the forecastle. There was a tremendous din going on and they found to their astonishment that the Spaniards were at quarters below them blazing away with the great guns at some imaginary foe that had not yet arrived. So the Surprises made their way aft along the gangway for the quarterdeck, where they met with violent resistance. By now the Doctor and the gig's crew had boarded on the larboard bow, but forgetting that they were to rendezvous on the quarterdeck they went for the Spaniards on the gangway and cut them up most dreadfully; but this left Hamilton alone on the quarterdeck and four Spaniards knocked him down. Happily some Surprises darted aft and rescued him and a moment later the Marines boarded on the larboard gangway, formed, fired a volley down the after hatchway and then charged with fixed bayonets. But there were a very great many Spaniards aboard and it was still nip and tuck until the Surprises managed to cut the bower cable, whereupon they loosed the foretopsail and with the boats towing the *Hermione* stood out to sea. The batteries fired at her of course as long as she was in gunshot, but they only knocked away the gaff and some rigging; and by two in the morning she was out of range with all prisoners secured. In that bout the *Surprise* had no one killed and only twelve wounded, though the poor gunner – I knew him well – who steered the *Hermione* as she made her offing, was shockingly knocked about. The Spaniards, out of 365, had 119 killed and 97 wounded. Captain Hamilton was knighted, and after that the *Surprise* was nearly always allowed a third lieutenant, an unofficial but a customary indulgence.'

'Heavens, sir, that was a famous victory,' cried Mrs Oakes, clasping her hands.

'So it was, ma'am,' said Jack. 'Allow me to carve you a little of this soused hog's face. Mr Martin, the bottle stands by you, sir. But in a way your running fight, tearing down the Channel for example in a heavy sea with all possible sail aboard, a lee-shore within pistol-shot, both sides evenly matched and both blazing away like Guy Fawkes' night is even finer. Mr Davidge, could you tell about the *Amethyst* and the *Thétis* in the year eight, do you think? Lord, that was such an action!'

'Pray do, Mr Davidge,' said Mrs Oakes. 'Nothing could please me more.'

'A glass of wine with you, Mr Davidge, while you collect your mind,' said Jack, at the same time filling Mrs Oakes's.

'Well, ma'am,' said Davidge, wiping his mouth, 'in the autumn of that year we were close in with the coast of Brittany, the wind at east-north-east, a topgallant breeze, when late in the evening we saw a ship – a heavy frigate she proved to be – slip out of Lorient, steering west by south. We instantly wore in chase . . .'

The tales followed one another, each amplified with details, names, accounts of various officers by the rest of the table, a fine general hum of talk accompanying but never breaking the central theme; and all this time Jack, true to the naval tradition, filled and refilled his guest's wineglass. While he was calling down the table, asking Pullings who it was that had taken the *Eclair* in the first place, she said privately, 'Mr Reade, I am sadly ignorant, but I have never dined with the Royal Navy before, and I do not know whether ladies usually retire.'

'I believe they do, ma'am,' whispered Reade, smiling at her, 'but not until we have drunk the King; and, you know, we drink him sitting down.'

'I hope I shall hold out till then,' she said; and in fact she was still upright, steady, hardly flushed at all and by no means too talkative (which could not be said for her husband) when the port came round and Jack, with a formal cough, said 'Mr Pullings, the King.'

'Madam and gentlemen,' said Pullings, 'the King.'

'Well, sir,' said Clarissa Oakes, turning to Jack when she had done her loyal duty, 'that was a delightful dinner, and now I shall leave you to your wine; but before I go may I too give a toast? To the dear *Surprise*, and may she long continue to *astonish* the King's enemies.'

Chapter Three

After this quite brilliant occasion Clarissa Harvill or rather
Oakes faded from Stephen Maturin's immediate attention. He
saw her of course every fine day – and the *Surprise* sailed
north-north-east through a series of very fine, indeed heart-
lifting days until she reached the calms of the equator – sitting
well aft on the leeward side of the quarterdeck, taking the air,
or sometimes on the forecastle, where the little girls taught
her games with string, cradles far beyond the reach of any
European cat; but although he saw her and nodded and spoke,
this was a time when he was very much taken up with his
intelligence work, and even more so with trying to decipher
Diana's letters and make out what underlay their sparsity,
brevity and sometimes incoherence. He loved his wife very
dearly, and he was perfectly prepared to love his unseen
daughter with an equal warmth of affection; but he could not
really get at either through the veil of words. Diana had never
been much of a correspondent, usually limiting herself to times
of arrival or departure or names of guests invited, with brief
statements of her health – 'quite well' or 'cracked a rib when
Tomboy came down at Drayton's oxer'. But her notes or letters had always been perfectly straightforward: there had
never been this lack of real communication – these lists of
horses and their pedigrees and qualities that filled paper and
told him nothing: very little about Brigid after a short account
of her birth – 'most unpleasant; an agonizing bore; I am glad
it is over' – apart from the names of unsatisfactory nurses and
the words 'She seems rather stupid. Do not expect too much.'
Unlike Sophie Diana did not number her letters, nor did she
always date them with anything more than the day of the week,
so although there were not a great many of them he found it

impossible to arrange the series in any convincing order; and often when he should have been decoding the long reports from Sir Joseph Blaine, who looked after naval intelligence, he found himself rearranging the sequence, so that Diana's ambiguous phrases took on a different meaning. Two or three things were clear, however: that she was not very happy; that she and Sophie had disagreed about entertainments, Sophie and her mother maintaining that two women whose naval husbands were away at sea should go out very little, certainly not to assemblies where there was dancing, and should receive even less – only immediate family and very old friends. And that Diana was spending a good deal of time at Barham Down, the big remote house with extensive grazing and high downland she had bought for her Arabians, rather than at Ashgrove Cottage, driving herself to and fro in her new green coach.

He had hoped that having a baby would make a fundamental change in Diana. The hope had not been held with much conviction, but on the other hand he had never thought that she would be quite so indifferent a mother as she appeared in these letters, these curiously disturbing letters.

They were worrying in what they said and perhaps more so in their silences; and Jack's behaviour made him uneasy too. Ordinarily when letters came from home they read pieces out to one another: Jack did so still, telling him about the children, the garden and the plantations; but there was a constraint – almost nothing about Barham Down or indeed Diana herself – and it was not at all the same frank and open interchange.

As Jack worked his way systematically through Sophie's letters he found that her very strong reluctance to say anything unpleasant gradually diminished, and by the time he read the last he knew that the baby 'was perhaps a little strange' and that Diana was drinking heavily. But he had also been told with great force that he must not say anything; that Sophie might be quite mistaken about Brigid – babies often looked strange at first and turned out charming later – and that Diana might be entirely different once she had Stephen at home again. In any case it would be pointless and wicked to put poor dear Stephen on a rack for the rest of the voyage and Sophie knew that Jack would not say anything at all.

This was bad. But there had been an area of silence between Jack and his friend years ago, and about Diana too, before Stephen and she were married. On the other hand, from their very first days at sea together, there had never been anything that Jack had had to keep from him in the line of naval warfare: intelligence and action complemented one another and Captain Aubrey had often been officially told in so many words to consult with Dr Maturin and seek his advice. This time however his orders made no mention of Stephen at all: was the omission deliberate or did it arise merely from the fact that they originated in Sydney rather than Whitehall? The second was the probable answer, since the occasion for the orders, the trouble in Moahu, had only just arisen; but there was a faint possibility that Sydney, informed by Whitehall, might know as much about Dr Maturin's views on colonialization, muscular 'protection', and the government of one nation by another as did Jack, who had so often heard him speaking of 'that busy meddling fool Columbus and that infernal Borgia Pope', of 'the infamous Alexander', 'that scoundrel Julius Caesar' and now worst of all 'the scelerate Buonaparte'. It seemed to him that he was now bound to offend Stephen either by asking him to collaborate in what might look very like annexation or to wound him by an evident neglect. Some infinitely welcome compromise might present itself in time, but for the moment it was a worrying position; and this was not Jack Aubrey's only source of worry either. Not long since, he had succeeded to two inheritances, the first on his father's death, which brought him the much-encumbered Wool-hampton estate, and the second on that of his very aged cousin Edward Norton, whose much more considerable possessions included the borough of Milport, which Jack represented in Parliament (there were only seventeen electors, all of whom had been Cousin Edward's tenants). And inheritance, above all the inheritance of land, brought with it a mass of legal procedures to be followed, duties to be paid, oaths to be sworn: Jack had always been aware of the fact and he had always said 'Fortunately there is Mr Withers to deal with the whole thing'. Mr Withers being the Dorchester attorney, the family's man of business, who had looked after both estates ever since Jack was a midshipman.

But while Jack was on the high seas – in the Straits of Macassar, to be exact – Mr Withers died, and his successor could think of nothing wiser to do than to send a great mass of papers, asking for instructions on scores or even hundreds of such matters as enclosures, mineral rights, and the disputed successions to Parsley Meadows, which had been in Chancery these twelve years, matters of which Jack knew nothing but which he was now trying to reduce to order with the help of his clerk Adams in spite of the contradictions at every turn, missing documents, vouchers, receipts.

'At least,' he said, coming into Stephen's cabin with a sheet of papers, 'I have the particulars of the advowsons I told you about some time ago. But tell me, is Martin an idoneous person?'

'Idoneous for what?'

'Oh, just idoneous. Two of the livings, if you can call them livings, are vacant; and this letter says I am required to present an idoneous person.'

'As far as benefices are concerned no one could be more idoneous, fitting or suitable than Martin, since he is an Anglican clergyman.'

'That makes him idoneous, does it? I was not aware. Well, here are the particulars of those in my gift: Fenny Horkell and Up Hellions are the vacant ones, and they should have been filled before this; but since I am on active service the Bishop has to wait until I can send home. They are in the same diocese, in spite of being so far apart. I am afraid neither could be called anything remotely like a plum, but Fenny Horkell has a decent house, built by a wealthy parson forty years ago for the sake of the fishing, which I know Martin would enjoy: it has sixty acres of glebe, poor plashy stuff, but it has the Test flowing through from one end to the other; yet the tithe only amounts to £47.15.0, although there are 356 parishioners. The next, Up Hellions, is rather better, with £160 a year and 36 acres of glebe – excellent wheat land – extraordinary number of hares – and there are only 137 souls to look after. If they interested Martin he could have a curate in Hellions, a dreary place, as the other man did.' As Stephen said nothing Jack went on 'I suppose you would not care to put it to him? I feel a little awkward about offering what might be looked upon as a favour, though a precious meagre one, above all with this monstrous income-tax. Perhaps he might prefer to wait for Yarell, with more than three times the income. It is held by the Reverend Mr Cicero Rabbetts, a very ancient gentleman, well over seventy, who lives in Bath.'

'Take heart of grace, brother, and put it to him directly: show him the papers and desire him to turn the question over in his mind.'

'Very well,' said Jack reluctantly, leaving the cabin; and as soon as the door closed Stephen returned to his letter, one of those rambling sea-letters so often written by sailors five thousand miles and more from the nearest post-office. He had by now calmed his mind somewhat by the reflexion that Sophie's quiet, staid, middle-class, provincial world had always disapproved of Diana's; that Sophie herself disliked horses as dangerous, smelly, unpredictable animals, and had no taste for wine, drinking elder-flower in summer and elder-berry in winter. Clearly when she had visitors this would not do, but as far as claret was concerned she felt that one glass was enough for any woman: a view that Diana despised. Indeed it was surprising to see how much of Mrs Williams' early influence was still to be seen in her daughter, who could not take much pleasure in Diana's active social life, her fox-hunting, or her driving the new green four-in-hand with only one servant up behind. Stephen mused for a while on the curious interpenetration of English classes by which it came about that two quite close cousins might belong to two widely different cultures, a state of affairs guaranteed to cause disagreement, even if Diana had been a devoted mother, which she quite obviously was not – disagreement, and as a natural consequence even in so sweet-natured a woman as Sophie, an unbalanced account with never a lie from beginning to end but essentially untrue.

He dipped his pen and wrote on: 'In the brief note that was all I had time to scribble before the *Eclair* left us I believe I told you how I discovered that the platypus (a warm shy inoffensive soft furry animal, devoid of teeth) had unexpected means of defence, spurs extraordinarily like the serpent's fang and equally capable of injecting venom, and how I survived the discovery; I also spoke, perhaps too facetiously, of dear Jack's first conscious encounter with middle age; but I do not think I described the new member of our ship's company, a young person brought aboard, dressed as a boy, by one of the midshipmen and kept *under hatches* as we say until it was too late for Jack to turn back and deliver her up to the authorities of that infamous penal colony as he would in duty have been bound to do had New South Wales not been so far away. Poor Jack was in a terrible passion to begin with, quite pale with fury, and he repeatedly called out that they should be marooned. To keep up the necessary façade he made as though to carry out this dreadful sentence the next day, and the people very gravely went through the motions of inspecting the strand on that side of the island most exposed to the swell and reporting that the surf made landing impossible. He was very much incensed against the wench – hates women aboard, troublesome, unlucky creatures, capable of using fresh water to wash their clothes – but she is quite pretty, modest and well-bred, not at all the trollop that might have been expected, and now he is reconciled to her presence. The two were married in the cabin by Nathaniel Martin, and Miss Clarissa Harvill became Mrs Oakes; Mr Oakes (though eventually to be discharged) was restored to his office or station, and his wife, legally recovering her civil freedom by this ceremony, also acquired the freedom of the quarter-deck. I write their names in this indiscreet, improper way, my dear, because this is little more than the ghost of a real letter: it will almost certainly never be finished, never be sent; but I do love communing with you, if only in thought and upon paper. So on the quarterdeck she sits, under an awning when the weather is

70

fine, as it nearly always is, and sometimes I am told in the warm night when her husband is on duty. I do not know her well, since my own work has taken up much of my time, but I have already perceived that there are two women in her. No uncommon state of affairs, you will say; but I have never known it in this high degree. Ordinarily she is anxious for approval, willing to agree; there is a general complaisance in her air and the civil inclination of her head; she is a good listener and she never interrupts. The officers all treat her with a proper respect, but like me they are eager to know what brought a young gentlewoman out to Botany Bay. All they can learn from her husband is what he knows: to wit, that at a house he visited outside Sydney she was teaching the children French, music, and the use of the globes. The information does not satisfy them of course and sometimes they angle for more. When this happens, the complaisance (the perfectly genuine complaisance, I am sure) vanishes and the second woman appears. Once to my surprise Jack was a little insistent about the voyage out – had she seen any islands of ice south of the Cape? – and there was Medea rather than Clarissa Oakes. She only said "I am under great obligations to you, sir, and I am extremely grateful; but that was a very painful time and you will forgive me if I do not dwell on it," yet her look was more eloquent by far, and he withdrew at once. Davidge, on the other hand, when he made enquiries of the same nature was told that her usual answer to an impertinent question was – I forget exactly what but "vulgar curiosity" came into it; and I think she has not been troubled since.'

East-north-east the frigate sailed, rarely exceeding a hundred miles a day between noon and noon in spite of perpetual close attention to her great array of canvas; but on a Sunday, immediately after church, the south-east trades returned to their duty, and although the royals and flying kites had been taken in, the *Surprise* awoke to a life she had not known since leaving Sydney Cove. Her deck sloped, she leant her larboard bow well down, overtaking the swell and splitting it with a

71

fine broad slash of white. All the tones of the rigging – quite different for the various sets of stays, shrouds and backstays and of course for all the cordage – rose and rose, and by the first dog-watch the resultant voice of all these sounds combined and sent forth by the hull reached the triumphant pitch that Stephen associated with ten knots. The wind, blowing under a sky beautifully mottled with white and an even purer blue, brought with it flying spray, and an uncommon freshness. At two bells the log was heaved and to his intense satisfaction Stephen heard Oakes report 'Ten knots and one fathom, sir, if you please.'

The satisfaction was general. All hands loved to feel their ship running fast, with this urgent heave and thrust and the water bubbling loud along her side, the bow-wave hollowing out amidships to show her copper. It was not quite the weather for dancing on the forecastle, but they stood all along the weather rail, smiling and looking pleased.

Clarissa Oakes shared in the *Surprise*'s cheerfulness. The awning had been struck long since, but she sat there, her seat made fast to the taffrail, her hair, apart from some flying wisps, done up in a handkerchief and her rather pale face showing much more colour than usual. She was alone for once and Stephen walked over to ask her how she did. 'Very well, sir, I thank you,' she said, and then 'I am glad you are come: I had almost made up my mind to send you a note asking if I might consult you. But perhaps female disorders lie far outside the purview of a naval surgeon?'

'In the nature of things he has little to do with them. But I am also a physician and therefore omniscient. I should be happy to be of service whenever you are at leisure – now, if you choose, whilst we have light and there is time before my evening rounds. Perhaps your husband would like to be present?'

'Oh no,' she said, getting up. 'Shall we go?' And as they passed the binnacle she called 'Billy, the Doctor is so good as to take me now.'

'How very kind of him,' replied Oakes, smiling gratefully at Stephen.

'As for place,' said Stephen on the companion-ladder, 'the sick-bay is clearly out of the question; and female disorders being what they so often are, your own cabin would hardly provide light enough, while in this heat lanterns are most disagreeable. My cabin has much to be said for it, but it wants privacy: every word uttered there may be heard on deck – I do not suggest any deliberate eavesdropping on the part of my shipmates, but the fact is there: within a yard of the skylight stands the helmsman – sometimes two helmsmen – and the quartermaster, to name only the foremast hands.'

'Perhaps we might speak French?' suggested Clarissa. 'I am reasonably fluent.'

'Very well,' said Stephen, opening the door for her and bolting it against intrusion.

'By the way,' she said, pausing with her hand on the fastening of her dress, 'it is true even at sea, is it not, that medical men never talk about their patients?'

'It is true for officers and their wives; but where the hands are concerned there are some diseases that have to be recorded. Where I am consulted personally I speak to no one, not even my assistant or a specialist, without the patient's consent. The same applies to Mr Martin.'

'Oh what a relief,' said Mrs Oakes, and as she slipped off her dress Stephen observed that she now possessed a pair of drawers, made of number ten sailcloth, so windworn and sunbleached as to be almost as soft as cambric, a gift no doubt from the sailmaker, whose perquisite it was – she was very popular among the foremast hands, whose gaze followed her with a fond longing.

At the end of his examination he said 'I think I may assert without much fear of error that your notion of pregnancy is quite mistaken. And I am obliged to add, that the likelihood of any such state is exceedingly remote.'

'Oh what a relief!' cried Mrs Oakes again, but with much greater emphasis. 'Mr Redfern told me that; but he was only a surgeon, and I am so glad to have his words confirmed by higher authority. I cannot tell you what a curse it is to have hanging over one's head. Anyhow, I loathe children.'

'All children?'

'Oh of course there are some dear little creatures, so pretty and affectionate; but I had rather have a pack of baboons in the house than the usual little boy or girl.'

'Sure, there are few amiable baboons. Now I shall send you some physic to be taken every night before retiring, and next month you will come to see me again.'

This conversation was carried on in French, perfectly current on either side, with a slight English accent on Clarissa's and a southern intonation on Stephen's; and no sooner was it finished and the patient gone than Martin walked in. If he had chosen his moment with care he could hardly have given a better proof of the rarity of places for private talk in a man-of-war, for having a confidential matter that he wished to discuss with his friend before their evening duties he said, in Latin, that he would have suggested their climbing to the mizen-top, tertii in tabulatum mali, if there had not been such a wind blowing – nodi decem – that he was afraid to make the ascent; besides, there were papers that might blow away.

He spoke lightly but it was clear to Stephen that he was much agitated. 'Captain Aubrey has just made me the very generous offer of two livings that are in his gift. I know he spoke to you of the matter, but as you may have forgotten the details I have brought them' – passing the sheets – 'As he observed himself, from the worldly point of view neither is at all desirable, but he suggested that the two combined, with a curate looking after the smaller, might answer tolerably well. On the other hand, he added, I might prefer to wait for Yarell, whose present incumbent, a valetudinarian of over seventy, lives in Bath. This page deals with Yarell. And finally, in the kindest way, he told me to turn the matter over in my mind for as long as I pleased. This I have been doing ever since, but I am still undecided. At first I was delighted with the idea of Yarell, which would eventually enable me to do my duty by my family handsomely and which for the immediate future would allow me to devote a few more years to this delightful rambling. It must be admitted that Fenny Horkell, with half a mile of both banks of the Test, was wonderfully tempting;

74

but since I am totally opposed to non-residence I could not possibly hold the remote Up Hellions at the same time; and without Up Hellions, Fenny could barely maintain its parson. The big parsonage was built by a man with ample private means some forty years ago.'

'*Il faut que le prêtre vive de l'autel*, say the French,' observed Stephen, thinking of the Martin he had first known, who would have been radiant with joy at the prospect of a benefice of any kind, of a living more modest by far than Up Hellions or even Fenny: but of course he was a bachelor then.

'Very true,' said Martin. 'So there I was, quite happy in my mind about Yarell, when all at once it occurred to me that although Captain Aubrey's prime motive was no doubt to do me a kindness and I honour him for it, there may also have been the wish to set me firmly ashore, to dispose of me by land. For some time, as you know, I have been aware that the Captain does not very cordially like my presence, and alas in the gunroom I have begun to see what it means to be shut up with a man you cannot stand, for months and months, seeing him every day for an indefinite period. It therefore appears to me that I should accept Up Hellions and take myself off as quickly as I can, as soon as this voyage is over. Do you not agree? I should have said earlier that it seemed to me Yarell was mentioned only in passing, as an afterthought.'

'Do I agree? I do not. Your premises are mistaken and so necessarily is your conclusion. The acceptance of Yarell would *not* allow you a few more years of this kind of sailing, the naturalist's delight, because when with the blessing we reach home the *Surprise* will be laid up and Captain Aubrey will be condemned to regular naval warfare in a ship of the line on blockade or to the command of a squadron: no more carefree rambling, no more far foreign strands or unknown shores. Secondly, Captain Aubrey does *not* dislike you: the fact of your being in orders imposes a certain restraint on him, sure; but he does not dislike you. Thirdly, you are mistaken in thinking that Yarell was brought in as an afterthought: he spoke of it to me in the first place: it was in the forefront of his mind, and unless there is some rule against it in your

75

church, I cannot for a moment see that with his general good-will towards you and Mrs Martin he would not offer you the living when it falls vacant. There. Let you not refine upon these aspects, but revolve the matter again on a sound basis; and let me beg you not to suppose, as many good men do, that whatever is desirable is wrong.' 'Clarissa Harvill is desirable' he thought in a quick parenthesis, but aloud he said 'I see you have your particulars folded into Astruc's *De Lue Venerea*,' in a purely conversational tone.

'Yes,' said Martin, who also had his private consultations, some men (the bosun on this occasion) being ashamed to go to Stephen. 'I have a case that puzzles me: Hunter asserts that the diseases are essentially the same, that both are caused by the same virus. Astruc denies it. Here I have symptoms that fit neither.' For some little while they spoke of the difficulty of early diagnosis, and as they prepared for their evening rounds Stephen said 'Sometimes it is still harder with long-established residual infections, particularly with women: eminent physicians have been deceived by the fluor albus, for example. We swim in ignorance. Where these diseases are not wholly characteristic, sharply marked and obvious, they are difficult to detect; and when we have detected them there is still little we can really do. Apart from general care our only real resource is mercury in its various forms, and sometimes the remedy is worse than the disease. Do but consider the effects of the corrosive sublimate in bold, unskilled hands.'

Thursday was the anniversary of the frigate's launching, and her captain took the afternoon watch. This enabled all the gunroom officers to sit down together, and Stephen, who had not dined with them these many days, took his familiar seat with Padeen stationed behind him. The seat was familiar enough; so were the faces, but the atmosphere was one he had not known before and almost at once he saw what Martin had meant by the disagreeableness of being confined to a ship with a man one could not stand. West and Davidge were obviously on bad terms. Tom Pullings at the head of the table, Adams, the oldest man present in both years and service, in the purser's place at the foot, and Martin, opposite Stephen, were doing their best to ease things along, while both lieutenants were sufficiently well-bred to be generally civil. But as a feast, a celebration, it was a failure and at one point Stephen found himself saying 'As I understand it our path across the ocean runs by Fiji. I have great hopes of Fiji,' to an apathetic table.

'Oh certainly,' cried Martin, recovering himself after only a moment's pause. 'Owen, who spent some time there, tells me they have a great god called Denghy, in the shape of a serpent with a belly the girth of a tun; but as he pays little attention to human beings they usually pray to much smaller local gods – many human sacrifices, it appears.'

'They are a cruel lot,' said Adams. 'They are the worst man-eaters in the South Seas and they knock their sick and their old people on the head. And when they launch one of their heavy canoes they use men tied hand and foot as rollers. Though it must be admitted they are fine shipwrights in their line of craft, and tolerable seamen.'

'A man can be a tolerable seaman and a damned fool,' said Davidge.

'Man-eaters: so they are too,' said Stephen. 'And I have read that on the main island there grows the solanum anthropophagorum, which they cook with their favourite meat, to make it eat more tender. I long to see the Fiji isles.'

Stephen dined that day in the gunroom but he supped in the cabin, the two of them eating lobscouse with hearty appetite. 'I left my messmates arguing about what they should give to the Oakeses when they invite them to dinner,' he said. 'Martin was sure there would be hogs in Fiji, and he knew Mrs Oakes was fond of roast pork; but the sailors all said the wind might not carry us so far. Can this be true, brother?'

'I am afraid so. The trades often fall away before twenty south: even now that fine steadiness has gone. It was very remiss of them not to have sent their invitation long before this: if they had done so before all their sheep died there would have been no talk about these foolish Fiji hogs.'

'It was a strange sudden pestilence, upon my word. But tell

77

me, Jack, is it possible that I shall not see Fiji at all? It lies in the direct road.'

'Stephen,' said Jack, 'I cannot command the wind, you know, but I promise I shall do my best for you. Keep your heart up with another cup.'

They were by this time drinking their coffee, and when they had followed it with a glass of brandy apiece they took out their scores and music-stands, carefully arranged the lights, tuned their instruments and dashed away with Boccherini in C major, followed by a Corelli they knew so well that there was no need for a score.

Bell after bell they played, taking the liveliest pleasure in their music; and then, just after the changing of the watch, Jack laid down his bow and said 'That was delightful. Did you notice my double-stopping at the very end?'

'Certainly I noticed it. Tartini could not have done better. But now I believe I shall *turn in*. Sleep is creeping upon me.'

Stephen Maturin valued sleep and wooed it, generally in vain now that he had abandoned laudanum; Jack Aubrey valued it no more than the air he breathed and it came to him at once. His cot had not swung three times before he was lost to the sensible world. Stephen's first swings were promising, promising; the verses he recited inwardly had begun to repeat themselves, growing confused; consciousness flickered; and then in the next cabin began that oh so familiar deep powerful shameless snoring, interrupted only by bestial climaxes. Stephen thrust the wax balls deeper into his ears, but it was no good; a barrier three times that depth would not have kept out the din and in any case fury and a pleasant torpor could not inhabit the same bosom. When this happened (and it happened frequently) Stephen usually went down to his official surgeon's cabin, but tonight he felt a distaste for the gunroom and as sleep was now improbable before the grave-yard watch he put on shirt and breeches and went on deck.

It was a dark night: the moon had set, and although there was a fair sprinkling of stars among the high clouds, including a prodigious Jupiter, by far the brightest light came from the binnacles. The warm breeze still flowed in over the frigate's quarter, and though it had certainly lessened it was still fair for the Fiji islands and the ship was sailing towards them with an easy roll and pitch at perhaps five knots. Before his eyes had grown used to the dimness he began walking aft and almost at once he tripped on a coil of rope. 'Let me give you a hand, sir,' said the voice of the unseen Oakes who steadied him, begging him 'to watch out for that goddam sister-block', and led him to his usual station by the taffrail calling out 'Clarissa, here's company for you.'

'I am so glad,' said Clarissa. 'Billy, pray bring the Doctor a chair.'

Stephen usually went to the taffrail to lean over it and either contemplate the birds that followed, particularly in the high southern latitudes, or to lose himself in the hypnotic wake; he had rarely sat looking forward and now the sight of the tall pale topsails reaching up and up into the night sky absorbed him for several minutes. The ship heaved and sighed upon the swell, the voices of seamen talking quietly under the break of the quarterdeck came aft, and an attentive ear could easily catch the sound of Captain Aubrey's sleep.

'I hope, Dr Maturin,' said Clarissa, 'that when I spoke in that intemperate way about children on Monday you did not feel I was making the slightest reflexion on Sarah and Emily? They are very, very good little girls, and I love them dearly.'

'Lord no,' said Stephen. 'It never occurred to me that you would put a slight on them. I am no great advocate for children in general, but if my own daughter – for I have a daughter, ma'am – grows up as kind, affectionate, clever and spirited as those two I shall bless my fate.'

'I am sure she will,' said Clarissa. 'No. I was talking about children that have not been properly house-trained. Left to their own impulses and indulged by doting or careless parents almost all children are yahoos. Loud, selfish, cruel, unaffectionate, jealous, perpetually striving for attention, empty-headed, for ever prating or if words fail them simply bawling, their voices grown huge from daily practice: the very worst company in the world. But what I dislike even more than the natural child is the affected child, the hulking oaf of seven or

79

eight that skips heavily about with her hands dangling in front of her – a little squirrel or a little bunny-rabbit – and prattling away in a baby's voice. All the children I saw in New South Wales were yahoos.'

In their slow progress, with declining winds, towards Fiji there were several of these night-conversations, for more and more Stephen avoided the gunroom, where the ill-feeling seemed to have spread; but few were as decided as the first, Mrs Oakes being usually as complaisant and anxious to please as could be, agreeing with the views expressed and amplifying them. Occasionally this led to awkwardness, as when she found herself wholly committed to both sides in a disagreement between Stephen and Davidge – for other officers often appeared, sometimes forestalling him – on the relative merits of classical and romantic music, poetry, architecture, painting.

Yet there were times when Stephen happened to be alone with her and she spoke in her earlier manner. From some context that he could not recall Stephen had mentioned his dislike of being questioned: 'Question and answer is not a civilized form of conversation.'

'Oh how I agree,' she cried. 'A convict is no doubt more sensitive on the point but quite apart from that I always used to find that perpetual inquisition quite odious: even casual acquaintances expect you to account for yourself.'

'It is extremely ill-bred, extremely usual, and extremely difficult to turn aside gracefully or indeed without offence.' Stephen spoke with more than common feeling, for since he was an intelligence-agent even quite idle questions, either answered or evaded, might start a mortal train of suspicion.

'I have always disliked it,' said Clarissa after a pause in which six bells sounded and clean round the ship look-outs called 'All's well'. 'When I was young I formed the opinion that impertinent questions, arising from a desire to be talking or from vulgar curiosity, did not deserve true answers, so I used to say whatever came into my head. But I can't tell you how difficult it is to maintain a lie for any length of time with any countenance, if it has assumed any importance and if you are bound to it. You skip from emergency to emergency, trying to remember what you said before, running along the roof-top at full speed: sadly wearing. So now I just say it is a subject I prefer not to discuss. What is that steadily repeated noise? Surely they cannot be pumping the ship at this time of night?'

'It may be mutiny to reply, but in your private ear I will tell you that it is Captain Aubrey, alas.'

'Oh dear. Cannot he be turned over? He must be lying on his back.'

'He always lies on his back. His cot is so constructed that he cannot lie on anything else. Many a time have I begged him to have it made longer, wider, deeper; but as regularly as a clock he replies that man and boy he has slept in that cot, and he likes what he is used to. In vain do I point out that with the years he has grown taller, broader, even more portly – that in the course of nature he has changed to larger boots, larger small-clothes . . .' He sighed and fell silent: a long, companionable silence.

From well forward came Davidge's voice – he had the watch. 'Mr Oakes, there. Jump up to the foretop with a couple of hands and look to the windward laniards.' After they had gone aloft Davidge turned, paused a while to write on the log-board and then came right aft. 'Are you still here, Doctor?' he cried. 'Don't you ever go to bed?'

This was said in a tone that Stephen had never heard from Davidge, drunk or sober: he made no reply, but Mrs Oakes said 'For shame, Davidge. Doctor, pray give me your arm down those stairs. I am going to my cabin.'

On the companion-ladder they met Captain Aubrey hurrying on deck to see what was amiss in the foretop, the heaving on the first purchase having pierced through his sleep, whereas the thunderous holystoning of the decks some hours later left him quite unmoved, wheezing gently now and smiling as though some particularly agreeable dream were going on behind his closed eyelids.

Morning after morning, now that the sweetening-cocks were left in peace, did their remote commander too sleep at his ease, making up for countless hours on deck at night – for though of course he kept no particular watch, a commander of Jack Aubrey's kind might be said to keep the whole round of them, above all in dirty weather – and laying in stores of resistance for the hurricanes, lee-shores and uncharted reefs that must surely lie ahead, if past experience were anything to go by.

He slept, quite undisturbed by all the ordinary routine noises that accompanied the ship's warm, calm, slow, unadventurous progress towards Tonga, not rising up for his morning swim until the sun was well above the horizon and sometimes even missing his first breakfast. He slept a great deal these days, often stretching on the stern-window locker after dinner as well as keeping to his cot most of the night; and he dreamt a great deal. Many of his dreams were erotic, some most specifically so, for New South Wales had proved cruelly frustrating; and he found that Clarissa entered not only his dreams, which he could not prevent, but also his waking mind to an unsuitable degree, which he could, and should. He was no more a rigid moralist than most full-blooded sanguine men of his age and service, but this was not a question of morals: it concerned discipline and the proper running of a man-of-war. No captain could make a cuckold of a subordinate and retain his full authority.

Jack knew this very well: he had seen the effects of the contrary behaviour on a whole ship's company, that delicately-balanced, complex society. In any event, on principle he regarded naval wives as sacred, except in the rare event of one giving unmistakable signs that she did not wish so to be regarded: and Mrs Oakes had certainly never done anything of the kind. She was therefore doubly sacrosanct, never to be thought of in a carnal light; yet again and again licentious images, words and gestures would come into his mind, to say nothing of the far more licentious dreams.

He tended therefore to avoid the quarterdeck when she was there, sitting by the taffrail, sometimes tatting in an inexpert fashion but much more often talking to the officers who came aft to ask her how she did. He consequently missed several developments such as the beginning of Pullings' and West's intimacy with Mrs Oakes. They were both of them much disfigured, Pullings by a great sword-slash right across his face, and West by the loss of his nose, frost-bitten south of the Horn; they were diffident where women were concerned and for hundreds of miles they said nothing more than 'Good day, ma'am' or 'Ain't it warm?' when they could not avoid it; but her open, candid friendliness and her simplicity had encouraged them, and in time they took to joining Dr Maturin, who quite often combined sitting with her and watching for Latham's albatross (reported from these latitudes) now that his laborious deciphering was done and now that the sick-berth had returned to its usual fine-weather blue-water somnolence, all ordinary sources of infection left far astern.

In the nature of things Jack also missed Stephen's words to Davidge the day after Davidge had sent Oakes into the foretop. That morning Stephen did not take his breakfast in the cabin, and when Killick heard that his place was to be laid in the gunroom he gave a satisfied nod. The two men at the wheel and the quartermaster had heard the words and they had been reported throughout the ship.

West, who had had the middle watch, was still asleep, but all the other officers were there when Stephen walked in and said 'Good morning, gentlemen.'

'Good morning, Doctor,' they all replied.

Stephen poured himself a cup of what passed for coffee in the gunroom and went on 'Mr Davidge, how came you to speak so petulantly to me last night as to say "Don't you ever go to bed?" '

'Why, sir,' said Davidge flushing, 'I am sorry you should take it amiss. It was only meant in a rallying way – in the facetious line. But I see that it missed its mark. I am sorry. If you wish I will give you any satisfaction you choose to name when we are next ashore.'

'Not at all, at all. I only wish to be assured that when you

83

see me conversing with Mrs Oakes at the back of the poop you will allow me to finish my sentence. I might be on the very edge of an epigram.'

Well before the ship took her position by measuring the noonday height of the sun, almost all her company knew that the Doctor had checked Mr Davidge something cruel for speaking chuff in the first watch last night; had dragged him up and down the gunroom deck, flogging him with his gold-headed cane; had made him weep tears of blood. At this point Jack knew perfectly well that the dear *Surprise* was about to cross the tropic of Capricorn; but he had no notion of how her surgeon had savaged her second lieutenant.

Nor did he know until several days later that Martin was teaching Mrs Oakes to play the viola. A more than usually discordant shriek came aft when he and Stephen were getting ready to work their way through a Clementi duet, one of the many scores that had followed them half round the world with such perseverance. 'Lord,' said Jack, 'I have heard poor Martin make many a dismal groan, but never on all four strings at once.'

'I believe that was Mrs Oakes,' said Stephen. 'He has been trying to teach her to play the instrument for some time now.'

'I never knew. Why did you not tell me?'

'You never asked.'

'Has she any talent?'

'None whatsoever,' said Stephen. 'Pray do not, I repeat do *not*, endeavour to conceal my rosin in your breeches pocket.'

During this somewhat withdrawn period Captain Aubrey, with the help of Adams, nominally his clerk but in fact the frigate's purser as well, and a highly efficient secretary, caught up with his paperwork and advanced well into the dreadful maze of legal papers. He also spent more time than usual writing to Sophie, and he began his Tuesday's sheet (the fourth) with a detailed plan for increasing the Ashgrove

Cottage plantations from the southern edge of Fonthill Lane right down to the stream, with timber, then chestnut coppice, so useful for staves, and alders at the bottom, always leaving room, however, to cast a fly. He had had this scheme in mind, maturing for a great while, but it was only now that he had the leisure and tranquillity of mind to deal with it: he did the subject justice, going on at some length about the virtues of the ash, beech and durmast oak that would delight their great-grandchildren and even drawing a creditable view of the wood in its prime. Then came a pause while he sat reflecting and gently chewing his pen; this was a habit of his boyhood, and he found the taste of ink favourable to composition; but as it had very often happened in the past, his chewed pen was too much weakened to do its duty and he had to mend it, very carefully paring off the sides with a razor he kept for the purpose and squaring its end with a clipper. The pen now traced an elegant treble clef and he went on 'Our unlikely marriage seems to be answering quite well. Oakes is more serious and attentive to his duty than he was, and I have rated him master's mate, which will be an advantage to him in his next berth. And Mrs Oakes is well-liked by the people and the officers. Little Reade is quite devoted to her – it is pretty to see how kind she is to him and the little girls – while Stephen and the other officers so often sit with her on the quarterdeck that it is a positive saloon. For a variety of reasons such as Humboldt's measurements and the estate papers I am rarely there except where the management of the ship is concerned, and I hardly know what they talk about; but Tom at any rate rattles away famously, laughing in a way that would astonish you, he being so shy in company. No: at present I am rather out of things, as captains so often are, yet I do see that she is very popular with them – so much so that I wonder the gunroom has not yet given her the feast that is her due as a bride. Though I believe it was their intention to sway away on all top ropes, to do the thing handsomely, with a hecatomb among their livestock; only their sheep died, their fowls had the pip, and as we could not put into Fiji for hogs, contrary winds obliging us to bear away for Tonga, she may be a mother before ever she sits down to the banquet, unless they will be content with a plain sea-pie accompanied by dog's-body and followed by boiled baby. She does not take it ill, however, but sits there tatting away, listening to their stories; and her presence adds to the gaiety of the ship. Not only the quarterdeck's, either: when the hands are turned up to dance on the forecastle in the evening they know very well she is there and they skip higher and sing sweeter. She certainly adds to the gaiety of the ship. I only wish she may not add too much. In your ear alone I will say that I am a little afraid for Stephen, who is so very often there. It is not that she is a raving beauty in any way – would never set Troy on fire. She is quite well-looking, however, with fair hair and grey eyes, in spite of a rather pale face and a slight figure; nothing really remarkable, though she does hold her head very well. On the other hand she is cheerful, has unaffected good manners – neither missish nor eager to put herself forward – agreeable company and a great change from the ordinary well-worn gunroom round. And of course a woman, if you understand me, is a woman; and in this case the only one for hundreds of miles. "Oh Stephen is in no danger," I hear you cry. "Stephen is so high-minded and philosophical that he is in no danger." Very true: I know no one more sober or temperate or less likely to play the fool; yet these feelings may come upon a man before he is aware, and even the wisest can go astray – he told me himself that St Augustine was not always quite the thing where young women were concerned – and I should be very sorry if it were to happen to him.'

Some inner clock told Jack that in a few minutes he would hear two bells in the first dog-watch; and in fact before he had closed his writing-desk there was Mr Bentley the carpenter and his mates breathing at the door, waiting to hurry in with mallets and unship all bulkheads, all doors, to destroy all privacy and make the great cabin indistinguishable from the rest of the upper deck – the famous clean sweep fore and aft in full readiness for battle that had been carried out aboard the *Surprise* almost every day at sea ever since he first had the delight of commanding her. On the necks of the carpenters there breathed Killick, Killick's mate and the far more powerful Padeen, ready to seize all portable property and strike it down below, and at what could only just be called a decent distance behind them the crews of the four twelve-pounders stood on one another's toes, fidgeting to get at their guns.

Jack put on his coat, walked quickly through them and ran up the companion-ladder. There on the windward or at least the starboard side of the barricade stood Pullings, the officer of the watch, with the drummer close at hand. The quartermaster at the con uttered the Royal Navy's ritual cry of 'Turn the glass and strike the bell' to a wholly imaginary Marine: having done so he turned it himself and hurried forward to the belfry.

At the second stroke Jack said 'Captain Pullings, beat to quarters.'

There were the usual repetitions, followed by the usual thundering of the drum, the usual muffled rushing sound of bare feet running fast to their action-stations, the usual report of 'All present and sober, if you please, sir' relayed to the captain, and Jack stood contemplating the silent, attentive deck, the crews grouped in their invariable pattern round their guns, the match-tubs sending up their smoke, the whole fighting-machine ready for instant action.

Nothing could have been more improbable. The whole towering array of canvas, from courses to skyscrapers, hung limp, sagging in the bunt; the smoke rose straight from the tubs; and both to larboard and to starboard there were unruffled mirror-pools of sea, miles in length and breadth, oddly purple in the declining sun. And nowhere, in the cloudless sky or on the smooth disk of enormous ocean, was there anything that moved, living or dead.

In the silence Dr Maturin's harsh voice could just be heard telling a very deaf dyspeptic seaman that his disorder was 'the remorse of a guilty stomach', that he must chew every mouthful forty times, and 'abjure that nasty grog'.

'Well, Captain Pullings,' said Jack at last, 'since tomorrow is a saluting-day we will just rattle them in and out half a dozen times. Then let us take in the flying kites and topgallants and give the rest of the day to the King.'

The King, poor gentleman, had been very fond of the infant Mozart, sitting by him at the pianoforte and turning the pages of his score, and perhaps he would have liked the pieces they played that evening, all as purely Mozartian as love of the great man could make them; for although there were no canonical violin and 'cello duets to be played, a bold mind could transcribe those for violin and viola as well as a variety of songs, the fiddle taking the voice and the 'cello something resembling the accompaniment, while boldness on quite another scale could wander among the operas, stating various passages in unison and then improvising alternately upon the theme. It might not have pleased everybody – it certainly angered Killick – but it gave them the greatest pleasure; and when they laid down their bows after their version of *Sotto i pini* Jack said 'I can think of nothing in its particular way so beautiful or moving. I heard La Salterello and her younger sister sing it when I was a master's mate, just before I passed for lieutenant: Sam Rogers – a drunken whoremaster if ever there was one, God rest his soul – was sitting next to me in the silent house and you could absolutely hear the tears pittering on his knee. Lord, Stephen, joy makes me sleepy. Don't you find joy makes you sleepy?'
    'I do not. You are much given to sleep these days, I find; and sure your tedious anxious careworn endless weeks or even God forbid months in that vile penal colony required a deal of reparation; but you are to consider that sleep and fatness go hand in hand, like fas and nefas – think of the autumn dormouse, the hibernating hedgepig – and I should be sorry if you were to grow even heavier. Perhaps you should confine yourself to one single dish of toasted cheese before turning in. I smell it coming.'
    'Some other time certainly,' said Jack. 'But tonight is Guy Fawkes' Eve, and must in common decency be celebrated to the full. Anything else would be close to treason, tasting of rank Popery – oh Lord, Stephen, I am laid by the lee again. I am so sorry.'

*

88

The extraordinary smoothness of the sea and the consequent immobility of his cot gave the sleeping Captain Aubrey a very strong impression of being at home, an impression so strong and a sleep so profound, his whole body limp and relaxed, that even the double swabbing of the deck and flogging it dry (this being a saluting-day) did not pierce through to his ordinary consciousness. Nor was it easy for Reade to wake him when he came bounding down at six bells to tell him that the ship had been pierced.

'Captain Pullings' duty, sir, and the ship's side has been pierced below the waterline just abaft of *Wilful Murder*. He thought you might like to know.'

'Are we making water?'

'Not exactly, sir. It was a swordfish, and his sword is still plugging the hole.'

'When you have finished playing off your humours on me, Mr Reade, you may go and tell the Doctor. I suppose the fish was not taken up?'

'Oh but he was, sir. Awkward Davies flung a harping-iron into him so hard it went right through his head. They are trying to get a bowline round his tail.'

Awkward Davies was rated able because he had followed Captain Aubrey into ship after ship whatever Jack might do and because the *Surprise* carried no landsman or ordinary seamen, but he possessed no seamanlike ability whatsoever apart from being able to throw the harping-iron with frightful strength, a skill that he had never been able to exercise in any commission for the last ten or twelve years. By the time Jack came on deck the swordfish, slow to acknowledge death, had at last ceased lashing; the bowline had been passed; and a gang from the afterguard, entirely directed by Davies, who would allow nobody, officer or not, to have any part in it, was gently raising the fish from the sea, brilliant in the early sun, its grey dorsal fin hanging down.

'He is one of the histiophori,' said Stephen, standing there in his nightshirt. 'Probably pulchellus.'

'Can he be ate?' asked Pullings.

89

'Of course he can be ate. He eats better by far than your common tunny.'

'Then we shall be able to have our feast at last,' said Pullings. 'I have been growing so shamefaced this last fortnight and more I could hardly meet her eye, a bride and all. Good morning, sir,' he cried, seeing Jack standing at the hances. 'We have caught a fish, as you see.'

'I caught him, sir,' cried Davies, a big, powerful, swarthy man, usually withdrawn, dark and brooding but now transfigured with joy. 'I caught him. Handsomely there, you goddam swabs. I flung the iron right through his goddam head, ha, ha, ha!'

'Well done, Davies. Well done upon my word. He must weigh five hundred pounds.'

'You shall have his tail and belly, sir: you shall blow out your kite with his tail and belly.'

Chapter Four

'At least the ship has steerage-way,' said Jack, taking off his
shirt and trousers and placing them in the hammock-netting
well clear of the trail of shining scales. 'I do so loathe plunging
into the accumulated filth of two, no, *three* days and nights.
Ain't you coming?'

'With your leave I shall attend to the anatomy of this noble
fish – Mr Martin, how do you do? – before the slightest change
sets in.'

'You can't have the deck above half an hour, Doctor,' said
Pullings. 'This is a saluting-day, you know, and everything
has to be tolerable neat.'

'Mr Reade, my dear,' said Stephen, 'may I beg you to run
– to jump – downstairs and bid Padeen bring me the large
dissecting-case, and then go forward and tell the little girls to
bear a hand, to lend a hand; but in their old, dirty pinafores.'

Their old, dirty pinafores had already been put to soak; new
pinafores were out of the question: they came aft naked, as
naked as worms, their small black figures exciting no comment, since they were in and out of the water much of the day
in this calm weather. They were valuable assistants, with their
little neat strong hands, their total lack of squeamishness –
they would seize a ligament with their teeth if need be – their
ability to hold almost as well with their toes as their fingers,
and their eagerness to please. Padeen was useful too in heaving
on the very heavy parts, and even more in warding off Davies,
the ship's cook, the gunroom cook, the captain's cook, the
ship's butcher, and all their respective mates, who were urgent
to have their pieces out of the sun and into the relatively cool
part of the ship or the salting-tubs; for swordfish was like

mackerel in these latitudes, mate, prime before sunset, poor-john the second day, and rank poison the third.

But with all their dispatch – and the seamen hurried off with their prizes the moment they were released by the anatomists – they were not hasty enough for Pullings. He had already sent the gunroom's compliments to Mr and Mrs Oakes and would be honoured by their presence at dinner, while Jack had accepted even before diving: the first lieutenant therefore had to set everything in train for a feast that would make up for the long delay, and at the same time he had to prepare the ship, dressed all over, for the grave ritual of saluting the Fifth of November. He and the bosun had of course laid aside great quantities of bunting and streamers, but they knew very well that nothing could be sent aloft until everything below was so clean that a maiden could eat her dinner off of it – until all guns and their carriages were spotless, until what little unpainted brass the ship possessed outshone the sun, until a whole catalogue of tasks had been carried out, all of them calling for great activity.

Early in these strenuous preparations Stephen handed the fishy little girls over the side, and having seen them thoroughly dipped, and having learnt from Jemmy Ducks that their divisional pinafores were ready for the ceremony, he hurried aft, drawn by the scent of coffee, to have breakfast with Jack, who had also invited West and Reade: it was a pleasant meal, yet with so much to be done none of the sailors lingered.

Stephen followed them on deck, but at the sight of the turmoil he retired to his cabin, and there, having smoked a small paper cigar out of the scuttle, he sat to his desk, reflected for a while and then wrote 'My dearest love, when I was a child and had to have my paper ruled for me I used to begin my letters "I hope you are quite well. I am quite well." There the Muse would often leave me; yet even so, as a beginning it has its merits. I hope you are very well indeed, and as happy as ever can be. Come in,' he cried. Killick opened the door, laid Stephen's best uniform, cocked hat and sword on the table with a significant look, nodded, and walked off. 'When last I sat at this desk,' continued Stephen, 'I was telling you, if I do not mistake, about Mrs Oakes: but I think I never described her. She is a slim, fair-haired young woman, a little less than the average size, with a slight figure, grey-blue eyes, and an indifferent complexion that I hope will be improved by steel and bark. Her chief claim to beauty is an excellent, unstudied carriage, not unlike yours. As for her face – but where faces are concerned, what can description do? All I will say is that hers reminds me of an amiable young cat: no whiskers, no furry ears, to be sure, but something of the same triangularity, poise, and sloping eyes. Its expression, though modest, is open and friendly, indeed markedly friendly, as though she were eager if not for downright affection then at least for general liking. This, or even both, she has certainly acquired; and a curious proof of the fact is that whereas some time ago all hands were intensely eager to know what crimes or misdemeanours had brought her to Botany Bay, she is now no longer troubled with any of the ill-bred hints that she at one time dismissed with a firmness that I admired – I believe that the very curiosity itself has died away, she being accepted as a person belonging to the ship. The question of guilt or reprobation is quite left aside.

'She is, there is no doubt at all, good company, willing to be pleased, taking an unfeigned interest in naval actions – I was there when West gave her a detailed account of Camperdown and I am sure she followed every stroke – and she never interrupts. She never interrupts! Yet I must insist that there is nothing in the least forward or provocative or inviting about her manner, nothing whatsoever of the flirt, she does not put out for admiration and although some of the officers feel called upon to say gallant things she does not respond in kind – no protestation, no simpering – a civil smile is all. Indeed I should say that she is in general much less aware of her sex than those she is with; and this I say with the more confidence since I have sat with her for hours, right through the afternoon watch for example, when her husband was on duty and I was looking out for Latham's albatross, or on occasion through much of the night, when it is close below and fresh on deck. We have few things in common: she knows little about birds, beasts or flowers, little about music; and although she has read a certain amount no one could call her a *bas bleu*; yet we talk away in a most companionable manner. And through all our conversations by day or by night, I might have been talking to a modest, agreeable, quite intelligent young man; though few young men I know are more conciliating, more willing to be liked – and none more capable of resisting intrusion on his privacy. Without being in the slightest degree what is called mannish, she is as comfortable a companion as a man. You may say that this is because I am no Adonis, which is very true. But unless I mistake it is the same with Jack, on those rare occasions when he comes to exchange the time of day; the same with Davidge, a more constant attendant; and both are reckoned tolerably good-looking men. Tom Pullings and West, whose nose mortified on the outward voyage, are even less lovely than I am: they are treated with the same friendliness. So is one-eyed Martin, though he, poor fellow, is not always discreet, and has sometimes seen the cold side of the moon, the Medea I spoke of long ago.

'Whether this unguarded friendliness is very wise or in the event very kind I do not know. Men are sadly apt to misinterpret such conduct and even when no masculine vanity or self-love steps in, a tenderness may arise in some bosoms, I fear. A tenderness or perhaps something with a grosser name in certain cases, or a mixture of the two in yet others: for after all, the lady came aboard in circumstances that could never be called ambiguous, and even the faintest remains of a bad reputation are wonderfully stimulating.

'Dear Jack, who is not insensible to her charms, keeps very much aloof; but to my astonishment I find that he is anxious for my peace of mind. For *my* peace of mind. Some of his more obscure general remarks upon human happiness became clear to me on Tuesday, when he surprised me extremely by repeating the sonnet that begins *Th' expense of spirit*, saying it in his deep voice better than I thought he could possibly have done, and ending

All this the world well knows, but none knows well
To shun the heaven that leads men to this hell

with the fine sullen growl it calls for, generally in vain. I was transfixed. And the words *savage, extreme, rude, cruel, not to trust* echoed strangely in my mind.

'The bell tells me that I shall see the lady in five minutes, unless she sends to cry off, which is not unlikely, she being to dine with the gunroom today; and although she may have some manly virtues I am sure she is woman enough to spend some hours dressing for a feast, so I shall leave this sheet unfinished.'

Stephen was not infallible. He was by no means infallible. The tap at his door five minutes later was his patient, true to her hour. The coming feast had brought some colour into her cheeks and she looked very well, but in point of fact he found neither improvement nor deterioration in her physical state; and when the examination was over he said, 'We must persevere with the steel and bark; I believe I shall increase the dose a trifle, and I shall also send a little wine forward, to be drank medicinally, a glass at noon and two glasses in the evening.'

'How very kind,' said Clarissa, her voice muffled in the folds of her dress; and again he reflected that she took no more notice of her nakedness than if they had both been men. Perhaps this was because he was a physician and did not count; yet most of his few women patients had made some gestures in the direction of modesty. Clarissa made none, any more than a professional painter's model would have done. But when her head emerged and she had buttoned herself and smoothed her hair she said, with a certain awkwardness, 'Dear Doctor, may I beg you to do me another kindness, nothing to do with medicine?' Stephen smiled and bowed and she went on, 'Something disagreeable happened yesterday. Mr Martin was showing me how to tune the viola when his little cat – you know his little cat?'

The little cat's mother had joined the ship in Sydney Cove, and had been tolerated so long by Jack-in-the-Dust – she was

95

a good mouser – that it was thought inhuman to turn her ashore when she proved to be in kit: and Martin had adopted this survivor from the litter, a stupid, persecuting animal.

Stephen bowed again. 'Well, it suddenly jumped on my lap, as it so often does. I dislike cats and I pushed it off, perhaps a little harder than usual. "Oh," cries he, "do not be unkind to my little cat, I beg. Were you not brought up with cats? Were there no cats at home when you were a child?" And a whole string of enquiries. As you know, I dislike questions as much as I dislike cats, and I may have answered him a little sharply.'

'Perhaps you did, my dear.'

'And I am afraid he may think I am still cross. But what is worse, the wretched creature disappeared last night and he may possibly imagine that I threw it overboard. Please would you seat him next to me at dinner? I should be so sorry if we were not friends.'

Stephen, feeling that his eyes might betray his reflexions, looked down and said in a neutral voice 'I have no say in these things: Pullings is the president of our mess. But I will mention it to him if you choose.'

Another tap at the door, and this time it was Reade, bringing the Captain's compliments: if Dr Maturin should wish to attend the ceremony he had between four and five minutes in which to change. The message was delivered in an embarrassed mumble, and when Mrs Oakes asked Reade whether her husband was already on deck he flushed and said 'yes, ma'am,' neither smiling at her nor looking at her, which was in so great a contrast to his usual attitude of open admiration that each gave him a quick, penetrating glance.

Stephen however had little time for quick penetrating glances. Killick was fuming there at the door and even before Mrs Oakes was quite out of the room he had whipped Stephen's greasy old coat off – a steady stream of nagging reproach.

Dr Maturin, properly uniformed, was propelled up the companion-ladder to the quarterdeck as the noon observation was in progress. He was somewhat astonished first by the flood of midday light after the shaded cabin and then by the colours all about him, high, low and on every hand, a variety of reds and yellows and blues, square, oblong, triangular, swallow-tailed, chequered, strangely brilliant after the eternal blue or grey, for the ship was now dressed over all, a splendid sight under a most luminous and perfect sky. There was just enough breeze to waft out all the flags and streamers that clothed the masts, yards and rigging – a startling multitude of them, blaz-ing away there in the sun: the whole ship too was very fine, her hammock-cloths stretched to a gleaming white unwrinkled smoothness, everything exactly as a sailor could wish it, decks, guns, falls, a quarterdeck alive with gold lace, the gangways and forecastle filled with hands in high Sunday rig, duck trousers, bright blue brass-buttoned jackets, embroidered shirts, ribboned hats.

'Make it twelve, Mr West,' said Jack, noon being reported to him, and his words were still floating in the air when eight bells struck.

But whereas they were ordinarily followed by the bosun's pipe to dinner and a wholehearted Bedlam of cries and tram-pling feet and thumping mess-kids, now there was a total silence, all hands looking attentively aft. 'Carry on, Mr West,' said Jack. 'Away aloft,' cried West, and the mass of the frigate's people raced up the shrouds on either side in a swift and even flow. 'Lay out, lay out,' called West, and they ran out on the yards. When the last light young fellow was right at the end of the starboard foretopgallant yardarm, holding on by the lift, Jack stepped forward and in a voice to be heard in Heaven he uttered the words 'Three cheers for the King.'

'You must pull off your hat and call out Huzzay,' whispered Pullings into Stephen's ear: the Doctor was staring about him in a very vacant manner.

Huzzay, huzzay, huzzay: the cheers pealed out like so many rolling broadsides, and after the last nothing could be heard but Sarah and Emily, beside themselves with glee, who huzzayed on and on, 'Huzzay, huzzay for Guy Fawkes', very shrill, until Jemmy Ducks suppressed them.

'Mr Smith,' said Jack, 'carry on.' And the gunner in his

97

good black Presbyterian-elder's coat stepped forward with a red-hot poker in his hand: the salute, beginning with Jack's own brass bow-chaser, came solemnly aft on either side at exact five-second intervals, the gunner pacing from one to the other with the ritual words 'If I wasn't a gunner I wouldn't be here: fire seven.' When he had reached 'fire seventeen' he turned aft and took off his hat. Jack returned his salute and said 'Mr West, the hands may be piped to dinner.'

A last wild long-drawn cheer, and before the white clouds of smoke had rolled a cable's length to leeward the usual midday hullaballoo rose to a splendid pitch.

'By land, in the northern parts of Ireland, I have seen the fifth of November celebrated with fireworks,' observed Stephen.

'Nothing can exceed the cannon's noble roar,' said the gunner. 'Squibs and burning tar-barrels, even sky-rockets at half a crown apiece, is mere frippery in comparison of a well-loaded gun.' Since he was to take the afternoon watch, thus releasing the whole gunroom for their feast, he was now on the quarter-deck, and turning to Jack he said 'Well, sir, me and my mate will take our bite now, with your leave, and be on deck in half a glass. Are there any special instructions?'

'No, Mr Smith: only that I am to be told of any considerable change in the breeze and of course of any sail or land.'

Half a glass went by and then apart from the gunner and his mate and the men at the wheel, the quarterdeck was empty. Stephen and Padeen had carried up two dozen of a pale sherry that had survived the voyage to Botany Bay, entrusting them to the gunroom steward: Stephen had spoken of Mrs Oakes's wish to poor anxious Pullings, had shown the gunroom steward's mate an unusually elegant way of folding napkins, had proposed decorating the table with seaweed, producing examples, and had been desired by all his messmates, their differences temporarily overlooked, to go and watch for his Latham's albatross until four bells. There really was not room for so many people to mill about in so confined a space; besides, it consumed what little fresh air there was – Martin had already gone into the mizen-top, carrying his silk stockings in his pocket.

Stephen wandered aft to where the Captain was taking his ease in the great cabin, stretched out on the stern-window locker with one foot in a basin of water.

'Do you suffer, brother?' he asked, 'or is this part of the Navy's superstitious horror of the unclean?'

'I suffer, Stephen,' said Jack, 'but moderately. Do you remember how I stood on the dumb-chalder when Dick Richards and I cleared the *Nutmeg*'s rudder?'

'The dumb-chalder. Sure I think of it constantly: it is rarely from my mind.'

'Well, it gave me a shrewd knock, and I limped for weeks. And just now I caught my ankle against the linch-pin there, hitting it in just the same place. How I roared!'

'I am sure you did. Will I look at it, now?'

Stephen took the foot in his hands, considered it, pressed it, heard the catch of breath, and said 'It is a little small piece of the external malleolus, trying to come out.'

'What is the external malleolus?'

'Nay, if you can oppress me with your dumb-chalders, I can do the same with my malleoli. Hold still. Should you like me to take it out now? I have a lancet over there, among the seaweed.'

'Perhaps we might wait until after the feast,' said Jack, who very much disliked being cut in cold blood. 'It feels much better now. I put a great deal of salt into the water.'

Stephen was used to this; he nodded, mused for a while, and said 'So the gunner has the watch. Tell me, Jack, is it not very amazingly strange that a gunner should have a watch?'

'Oh Lord, no. In a frigate it is unusual, of course, but in many a sloop with only one lieutenant, many an unrated ship, it is quite common for a steady, experienced bosun or gunner to stand his watch. And in our case there is an *embarras de choix*. I said there is an *embarras de choix*.'

'I am sure of it,' said Stephen absently.

'So many of our Shelmerstonians understand navigation and

have even commanded vessels of their own that if the whole quarterdeck were wiped out –'

'God forbid.'

'God forbid – they could still carry the barky home.'

'That is a great comfort to me. Thank you, Jack. Now I believe I shall go and read for a while.'

In the coach Stephen spread out his authorities, Wiseman, Clare, Petit, van Swieten, John Hunter. They were prolix about men, but although they had little to say about women they all agreed that there was no diagnosis more difficult than in those cases where the physician was confronted with a deep-seated, atypical, chronic infection. He was still reading Hunter with the closest attention when the bell told him he must join his messmates to welcome the gunroom's guests.

The gunroom was almost silent, in a state of high anxiety, with West and Adams both frowning at their watches. 'There you are, Doctor,' cried Tom Pullings. 'I was afraid we might have lost you – that you might have taken a tumble down the ladder like poor Davidge here, or fallen out of the top, like Mr Martin – do you think the table looks genteel?'

'Uncommon genteel,' said Stephen, glancing up and down its geometrical perfections. He noticed Davidge standing by the far end, his hand to his head: Davidge caught his eye, stretched his mouth in a smile and said 'I took a toss down the companion-ladder.'

'The bride sits on my right hand, in course,' said Pullings, 'and then Martin, then you, and then Reade. Mr Adams at the foot. The Captain on my left, then Davidge – you are all right, Davidge, ain't you?'

'Oh yes. It was nothing.'

'Then West, and then Oakes on Mr Adams' right. What do you think of that, Doctor?'

'A capital arrangement, my dear,' said Stephen, reflecting that Davidge's nothing was a damned heavy, turgid, uncomfortable one, a dark swelling from his left temple to his cheekbone.

'I do wish they would come,' said Pullings, 'the soup is sure to spoil,' and West looked at his watch again. The door opened; Killick walked in, said to Pullings 'Two minutes, sir, if you please,' and took up his place against the side, behind Jack's chair.

Martin edged his way round and with a decently restrained triumph he said 'Do not beat me, Maturin, but I have seen your bird.'

'Oh,' cried Stephen, 'have you indeed? And I wearing out the day watching. Are you sure?'

'There can be no doubt, I am afraid. Yellow, blue-tipped bill, a strong dark eyebrow, a confiding expression, and black feet. He was within ten yards of me.'

'Well, who ever said the world was fair? But I am sorry to hear that you fell out of the top.'

'That was a base slander. In my hurry to come down and tell you my foot made a trifling slip and I hung for a moment or two by my hands, perfectly safe, perfectly in control, and if the well-meaning John Brampton had not heaved me up by main force I should have regained the platform with ease. In any event I came down entirely unaided.'

Stephen sniffed and said 'Please to describe the bird.'

'Well,' said Martin and then stopped to turn and bow to Captain Aubrey: the gunroom welcomed their guest, pressed him to take a whet; Davidge once again explained that he had taken a toss on the companion-ladder and Pullings told Jack that he was uneasy about the soup.

Those near the door listened attentively for the Oakeses coming, but in this case there would be no steps on the ladder down to warn them as it had warned them of Jack's approach, since the midshipmen's berths, one of which the Oakeses inhabited, were only a short way along the passage that led from the gunroom door forward to the great screened-off expanse of the lower deck, deserted now, where the foremast-hands slung their hammocks. Even so, Adams' quick ear caught the swish of silk and he opened the door to the splendid scarlet glow that Stephen had never yet beheld.

'Upon my honour, ma'am,' he said when it was his turn to greet her, 'I have never seen you look so well. You fairly light up our dim and shabby dining-room.'

'Dim and shabby dining-room,' said the gunroom steward to Killick in a sea-going whisper, 'Did you ever hear such wickedness?'

'That is what we call a genteel compliment,' said Killick. 'Which it ain't meant to be believed.'

'It is all due to Captain Aubrey's kindness,' she said, smiling and bowing to Jack as she sat down. 'Never was such glorious silk.'

The sound of chairs being drawn in, the arrival of the swordfish soup and the ladling of it out filled the gunroom with the pleasant confusion of sounds usual at the beginning of a feast; but presently they began to die away. The ill-feeling between Davidge and West was so great that even now, with their Captain present, they barely exchanged a word: Oakes, always more at home in a pot-house, was even more than usually mute, a dogged look on his pale face. Reade, on Stephen's right, answered with no more than 'Yes, sir', 'No, sir', looking quite pitifully sad: whilst on his left, Martin maintained his reserved, though perfectly correct, attitude towards Clarissa throughout the soup. Stephen, Adams, and to some extent West made a reasonable amount of noise at the far end of the table about swordfishes they had known, the different kinds of swordfish, the inveterate enmity between the swordfish and the whale, instances not only of ships but even ships' boats being pierced, and the anguish of those sitting on the bottom, between the thwarts. Jack and Pullings found a good deal to say about tunny in the Mediterranean, with asides to Clarissa about the Sicilian and Moorish way of catching them.

The subject however had its limits, and although both Jack and Pullings would have been happy to engage Mrs Oakes, they were a little shy of doing so. There was the relief of taking soup plates away with a fine mess-deck clatter and bringing on the swordfish fritters, and during the interval both Stephen and Jack reflected upon the amount of ordinary dinner-table conversation taken up by 'do you remember?' or 'were you ever at?' or 'you probably know Mr Blank' or 'as I dare say you are aware', questions or implied questions that might offend the lady; or by personal recollections, in which she never indulged.

Stephen, Jack and even more Pullings felt the awful approach of silence, and Jack for one turned to his infallible standby: 'A glass of wine with you, ma'am.' Infallible, but not long-lasting; and he was grateful when West made some sudden, prepared observations about the saw-fish. Stephen took up this creature (such was the table's indigence), and compelled both Oakes and Reade to acknowledge that they had seen its mummified head in an apothecary's shop in Sydney and had speculated on the use of the saw.

Half-way through the fritters he found to his relief that Clarissa, who was not only beautifully dressed but who was also in looks, with colour in her cheeks and sparkling eyes – Clarissa, who had laid herself out to be amiable throughout the soup, had by now won her point: Martin's reserve had been overcome and they were talking away at a great rate.

'Oh, Mr West,' she called across the table, 'I was going to tell Mr Martin about your particular share in the Glorious First of June, but I am sure I would make some foolish landlubber's blunder. May I beg you to do it for me?'

'Well, ma'am,' said West, smiling at her, 'since you desire it, I will, though it don't redound much to my credit.' He considered, emptied his glass, and went on, 'Everyone knows about the Glorious First of June.'

'I am sure I do not,' said Stephen. 'And Mr Reade may not either; he was not born at the time.' Roused from his unhappiness for a moment, Reade looked at him reproachfully but said nothing.

'And I only know that you were wounded,' said Clarissa.

'Well, ma'am,' said West, 'just the most general lines, for those who may not have been born or who may never have seen a fleet action –' This was aimed at Davidge, who, until Jack took him aboard the *Surprise*, had seen very little action of any kind: his only acknowledgment of the hit was to drain his glass. 'In May of the year ninety-four, then, the Channel fleet put to sea from Spithead, with Earl Howe in command, the union at the main: the wind had come round into the north-east at last and we all got under way directly, forty-nine men-of-war and the ninety-nine merchants that had gathered at St Helen's, the East and West Indies convoys and those for Newfoundland – an uncommon sight, ma'am, a hundred and forty-eight sail of ships.'

'Glorious, glorious,' cried Clarissa, clasping her hands with unfeigned enthusiasm, and all the sailors looked at her with pleasure and approval.

'So we tore down the Channel, and off the Lizard we sent the convoys away with eight line-of-battle ships and half a dozen frigates to look after them: six of those ships of the line were to cruise in the Bay for a very important French convoy from America. That left Lord Howe with twenty-six of the line and seven frigates. We lay off Ushant – I was a youngster in his flagship, the *Queen Charlotte*, at the time – while a frigate looked into Brest. She saw the Frenchmen, twenty-five of the line, lying in the roads. So we cruised awhile in thick weather, looked in again, and they were gone. Some recaptured prizes told us where they were heading, and since the six ships cruising in the Bay were strong enough to deal with the French convoy, Lord Howe pursued the French fleet with a great press of sail. But it was light, variable airs nearly all the time and thick weather, and we did not catch sight of them until the morning of May 28th, twenty-six of the line now, directly to windward. Well, they bore down to about nine miles from us and formed their line ahead, directly to windward; but they had the weather gage, and seeing they did not seem very anxious to use it and attack, all we could do was to work to windward and harass them as much as possible. The Admiral sent four of the most weatherly ships forward and there was something of an action; there was another the next day, when we did manage to get to windward of them, though in no very good order and too late in the afternoon to force any decisive battle – we had quite a sea running, and the *Charlotte*, with her lower-deck ports little more than four foot from the surface, shipped so much water she had to pump all night. And her mizen-yard was so wounded that for a while she could not tack. The day after that the weather grew thicker and thicker – the French disappeared – and although the Admiral threw out the signal for our van ships to keep close order there were times when you could not see your second ahead or astern. But however it cleared a little by nine the next morning – this was the thirty-first, ma'am – and we saw how scattered we were. It was a very horrid sight, and we were very much afraid we had lost the Frenchmen. They came in sight about noon: some fresh ships had joined them, and as some of the ships had not behaved very sensibly in the last engagement, Black Dick – we called the Admiral Black Dick, ma'am, but though it sounds disrespectful, it was not so in fact, was it, sir?'

'Oh dear me no,' said Jack. 'It was affectionate: but I should never have dared use it to his face.'

'No. Well, Black Dick decided against an action that might last until darkness, and he hauled to the wind, steering the course he judged the French would follow. He was quite right. At dawn there they were on our starboard bow, about two leagues to leeward, in line of battle on the larboard tack. Moderate sea; breeze steady in the south by west. We bore down and then hauled to the wind again at seven, four miles from them. The Admiral signalled that he should attack the enemy's centre – that he should pass through the enemy's line and engage to leeward. Then we had breakfast. Lord, how I enjoyed my burgoo! When that was ate, we filled and bore down under single-reefed topsails in line abreast: they were in a close head and stern formation.'

'Sir,' whispered the gunroom steward in Pullings' ear, 'cook says if we don't eat our swordfish steaks this selfsame minute he will hang himself. I have been signalling your honour this last half glass.'

The steaks arrived in style, the dishes covering the middle of the table, while in the intervals and at the corners there were small bowls of such things as dried peas beaten into a paste with a marline-spike and flavoured with turmeric, and white sauce beautified with cochineal. Davies' dreadful whiskered face could be seen in the doorway, leering in: he had arranged all the dishes by hand. Martin was an accomplished anatomist, and Stephen noticed that he helped Mrs Oakes to some particularly tender pieces with great complaisance. He also noticed that Reade was filling his glass every time the wine came within reach.

'I had no idea that swordfish could be so very good,' said Clarissa, above the sound of knives and forks.

'I am so happy you like it, ma'am,' said Pullings. 'May I pour you a glass of wine?'

'Just half a glass, Captain, if you please. I long to hear the rest of Earl Howe's battle.'

After a decent reluctance, and encouragement by most of the table, West said 'I am afraid I have been far too long-winded; but now rather than try to describe the whole battle, I shall only say that when their line was perfectly clear, the Admiral rearranged our heavy ships to match theirs, and so we bore down, each to steer for her opposite number, break their line and engage her independently from to leeward. Well, some did, and some did not; but everyone knows we took six of them, sunk one, crippled many more, and lost none of our own, though it was nip and tuck at times, they fighting with such spirit. So having said that, may I just speak of a few things I saw? For I was on the quarterdeck, acting as our first lieutenant's runner, and some of the time I stood quite close to the Admiral's chair – you must understand, ma'am, that Lord Howe was a very ancient gentleman, seventy, if I do not mistake, and he sat there in a wooden elbow-chair. Now our opposite number was of course the French admiral's flagship, the *Montagne* of a hundred and twenty guns, and her next astern was the *Jacobin*, of eighty. They started firing at half past nine, but as the wind was blowing from us to them, their smoke rolled away to leeward; so we could see them perfectly well, and the Admiral, setting topgallants and fore-course, aimed for the gap between them, meaning to pass through, luff up on the *Montagne*'s starboard side and fight her yardarm to yardarm; but when we were within pistol-shot, the *Jacobin*, disliking the idea of being raked by our starboard guns as we broke through the line ahead of her, began to move up into the *Montagne*'s lee. "Starboard," calls the Admiral, in spite of the *Jacobin*'s being in the road. "My lord, you will be foul of the French ship if you don't take care," says Mr Bowen, the master – the master, ma'am, handles the ship in battle. "What's that to you, sir?" cries the Admiral. "Starboard." "Damned if I care, if you don't," says old Bowen but not very loud. "I'll take you near enough to singe your black whiskers." He clapped the helm hard astarboard and the ship just scraped through, the *Montagne*'s ensign brushing the *Charlotte*'s shrouds and the *Charlotte*'s bowsprit grazing the *Jacobin*'s as she flinched away; and then lying on the *Montagne*'s quarter we raked her again and again, at the same time battering the *Jacobin* with our starboard broadside. We mauled them terribly – blood gushing from the scuppers – but presently we lost our foretopmast – chaos forward – and they were able to make sail from us into the great bank of smoke to leeward. The rest of their line was breaking too, and the Admiral threw out the signal for a general chase. After that everything grew more confused of course, but I remember very well that late in the afternoon I received my only wound. The first lieutenant had just jumped down into the waist, and the Admiral said to me "Go and tell Mr Cochet to make the forecastle guns stop firing at that ship: she is the *Invincible*." I went down, and we ran forward. "Stop firing at *Invincible*," says Mr Cochet. "But she's not *Invincible*. She's a French ship that has been firing at us all along," said Mr Codrington, and Mr Hale agrees. "I know that," says Mr Cochet. "Let's have a shot." The gun was run in, sponged, loaded, run out: he pointed it just so, waited for the roll, waited again, and fired. The shot went home. And as the smoke cleared,' said West, with a sideways glance at Jack, 'there was the Admiral. "God damn you all," he cries, hitting Mr Hale – he thought Hale had fired the shot – with the flat of his sword. "God damn you all," fetching me a swipe on the top of my head. Then the ship, hauling her wind, showed her French colours, and Cochet, to save the Admiral's face, said "She is painted just like the *Invincible*" but . . .'

For some time now, as the veracity left West's account, the

ship had been heeling more and more: to counteract the lean those to windward, those on Pullings' right, braced their feet against the stretcher; but Reade's legs were too short to reach it and he slid quietly under the table, his eyes shut, his face pale. Stephen glanced at Padeen, who lifted the boy out and carried him away as easily as he might have carried off the folded cloth when it was drawn. There was no fuss, no comment; and West did not pause in his narrative.

Jack listened with half an ear, grateful for the sound but wishing that it might be replaced with something of greater interest. He was not a censorious man; he did not mind West's fiction, which he recognized as being composed for Mrs Oakes' benefit, any more than he minded Reade's collapse; but West was ordinarily the soul of truth, and his fiction was poor, embarrassingly poor, as well as far, far too long. It was with some relief therefore that he saw the long-expected messenger from the quarterdeck appear in the doorway. The gunner's mate looked into the gunroom and its formal array, hesitated for a moment, and then strode aft as if he were going into action. 'Gunner's duty, sir,' he said, very loud, bending over Jack, 'and the breeze is freshening. May he reduce sail?'

'Certainly, Melon. Tell him I am very glad to hear it and that I desire he will use his own judgment.'

'Aye aye, sir. Is very glad to hear it, and desires he . . .'

'Will use his own judgment.'

'Will use his own judgment it is, sir.'

'I am very glad to hear it,' said Jack to the table at large. 'We have been creeping over a mill-pond far too long, and the hands have been idle all this time.' A childhood memory to do with Satan and idle hands floated there, but he could not quite fix it and ended with the unuttered words 'Not only the hands, neither, God damn the wicked dogs.'

It was some time since he had dined with the gunroom. The last occasion had been rather a dull afternoon – Davidge and West were always indifferent company, their conversation either shop or twice-told tales, and Martin was always constrained when he was there – but a perfectly acceptable, traditional afternoon in a well-run ship.

Now the difference was very great. He could only guess at the causes: the effects, to a man who had spent most of his life at sea, were perfectly evident – the gunroom, as a civilized community, was almost at an end. But much more than their social comfort was at stake. Without good feeling between the officers, effective, willing co-operation was impossible, and without co-operation a ship could not be run efficiently: ill-blood in wardroom or gunroom was always perceived on the forecastle and it always upset the hands – apart from anything else each set of men had their own particular loyalty. And this ill-blood seemed to run in many directions: there was not only the obvious dislike between West and Davidge, but a series of other currents that seemed to affect Pullings as well and even Martin.

At present however there was this fine new flow of talk, initiated, he recalled, by Mrs Oakes – 'I shall always honour her for saving the feast from sinking with all hands' – and even the sullen Davidge had grown quite voluble.

Jack had missed the beginning while he reflected upon the situation, upon its possible causes and remedies, upon the ship's inner voice, now increasingly urgent in spite of sails having been taken in, and upon his own duties as a guest, and when he heard Stephen say ' "O Spartan dog, More fell than anguish, hunger, or the sea," ' he called down the table 'What was that, Doctor? Are you talking about the income-tax?'

'Not at all, at all. We were discussing duels and when they were, by general consent, permissible, when they were universally condemned, and when they were absolutely required. Mrs Oakes asked whether the military code did not oblige the officer who was beaten by Earl Howe to ask for satisfaction, a blow being an intolerable affront, and we all said no, because he was a very old gentleman and therefore allowed to be a little testy, because his immense deserts excused him almost anything, and because he could be said to have asked pardon by patting the lieutenant on the shoulder and saying "Well, so she ain't *Invincible* after all." '

'I am so ashamed,' said Clarissa. 'I lived very much out of the world when I was young, and that was one of my two pieces of fashionable wisdom. The other was that if you paid for anything in a shop with a bank-note you must always clearly state its value, so that there may be no argument about the change.'

'How I wish I had been taught that when I was a boy,' said Jack. 'Bank-notes did not often come my way, but the first decent prize-money I ever saw had one in it, a ten-pounder on Child's, no less; and the damned – I beg pardon, ma'am – the *shabby* fellow at the Keppel's Knob gave me change for five, swearing there was not a tenner in the house – I might look in the till if I wished, and if I found a tenner there I might have it all. But Doctor, how did the Spartan dog come in?'

'It seemed to me to express the state of mind of a deeply injured furious duellist when he plunges his sword into the opponent's bowels.'

'May I cut you a trifle of pudding, ma'am?' asked Pullings, moved by the association of ideas.

Clarissa might decline, but Captain Aubrey, feeling that he must do honour to the gunroom's feast, already tolerably damped, held out his plate; and now for the first time he realized with a pang that a third slice was going to be more of a labour than a delight: *non sum qualis eram* drifted up from those remote years when he was flogged into at least a remote, nodding acquaintance with Latin; the rest he could not recall. It might have had nothing to do with pudding at all, but the effect was the same.

'Mr Martin,' he asked, 'what is the Latin for pudding, for a pudding of this kind?'

'Heavens, sir, I cannot tell,' said Martin. 'What do you say, Doctor?'

'*Sebi confectio discolor*,' said Stephen. 'Will I pour you a glass of wine, colleague?'

'I beg your pardon, sir,' said Davidge, standing between Jack and Pullings, 'but it will be eight bells in two minutes and Oakes and I must relieve the gunner.'

'Lord,' cried Pullings, 'so you must. How time flies! But you must drink to the bride and bridegroom first. Come, gentlemen, bumpers if you please, and no heel-taps. Here's to the bride' – bowing to Clarissa – 'and here's to the happy man,' bowing to Oakes.

They all rose, and swaying on the roll they cried *Huzzay, huzzay, huzzay*, stretched out their glasses to Clarissa, crying *Huzzay, huzzay, huzzay* again, and then to Oakes, with a final cheer in which all the seamen servants joined, a fine deep roar.

When the party had broken up, Stephen took Padeen forward and they emptied Reade with a powerful emetic, undressed him, cleaned him, and put him back into his hammock, still three parts drunk and very unhappy. Stephen sat with him for a while after Padeen had carried off the basin, dirty clothes and dressings: Reade had the whole starboard midshipmen's berth to himself, immediately opposite the Oakeses, and very spacious it looked under the swinging lantern. The *Surprise* had from early times been a law unto herself as far as berthing was concerned, and now that she carried no Marines and a smaller body of seamen, the carpenter, bosun and gunner had taken advantage of the elbow-room to move themselves into cabins right forward, private triangular snugs, so that now the two midshipmen's berths were comparatively isolated, with the gunroom bulkhead and the ladder to the upper deck aft, the great screened-off space where the crew slept forward, and nothing in the broad passage between them but the captain's pantry, a stout erection the height of the 'tween decks, seven feet across and five fore and aft.

At one time Reade had spoken in a confused, incoherent way about Mrs Oakes; he *had* loved her so: he was sure his heart must break. But now he was asleep: even pulse, regular breath. Stephen dowsed his light and walked quietly out into the gloom of the lower deck. A movement on the far side, the larboard side, of the captain's pantry caught his eye, a dark coat that at once slipped out of sight: it was perhaps a little surprising that the dark coat did not call out to him, did not ask after Reade, but he thought nothing of it until he was climbing the ladder by the gunroom door, when he glanced to the left and realized that the man must now be standing against the forward side of the pantry, the only side hidden from the ladder. 'It would have been much wiser to hurry on through the screen,' he reflected. 'So much less furtive, so much more easily explained in the extremely improbable event of any explanation being called for.'

He climbed on, grasping the rail with both hands, the ring of his lantern between his teeth, for the *Surprise* was now capering like a wanton, the movement growing stronger as he rose.

It had early been laid down that there would be no beating to quarters today, and he found Jack Aubrey gazing out of the windward scuttle with his hands behind his back and a sombre look on his face. He turned, brightening, and said 'Why, there you are, Stephen. A pot of coffee will be up in a moment, if that wicked fellow has not upset his kettle again – she is grown a little skittish. You have been looking at Reade, I dare say? How does he do, poor little chap?'

'He will survive, with the blessing.'

'I suppose when you lose an arm there is less of you to take up your wine. I know Nelson was very abstemious and – Hold up,' he cried, 'Clap on to the locker.' He eased Stephen into a chair, saying, 'God's my life, Stephen, you absolutely turned a somersault. I hope nothing is broke?'

'Nothing, I thank you,' said Stephen, feeling his head. 'But had I not been wearing a wig, Martin would have had a depressed fracture of the skull to deal with. Surely, Jack, that was a very wild capricious bound?'

'She will do it sometimes, I am afraid, with a cross-sea and an increasing breeze that has not settled – that varies three or four points in as many minutes. There are all sorts of platitudes about ships being like women: unpredictable, if you know what I mean.'

'It was a shrewd blow,' said Stephen, rubbing the top of his head.

Killick came in with the coffee-pot slung in elegant gimbals and two thick, resistant, heavy-weather mugs that had seen service in many a furious sea. He instantly grasped the situation and told Stephen in a rather louder, more didactic voice than usual that he should always keep a weather-eye open, and have one hand for himself and another for the ship. 'Your best new-curled wig, too,' he said, taking it away. 'All crushed and filthy.'

'When we have had our cup, I shall take off my finery and go on deck,' said Jack. 'I believe the evening will be a little too lively for music, so what do you say to backgammon?'

'With all my heart,' said Stephen.

For many years they had played chess, with fairly even fortunes; but they played with such intensity, being extremely unwilling to lose, that in time it came to resemble hard labour rather than amusement; and they being unusually close friends remorse for beating the other sometimes outweighed the triumph of winning. They had also played countless games of piquet, but in this case luck ran so steadily in Stephen's direction, good cards and sequences flocked to him in such numbers, that it became dull; and they had fixed upon backgammon as a game in which the mere throw of the dice played so large a part that it was not shameful to lose, but in which there was still enough skill for pleasure in victory. As well as those of the usual kind, they had heavy-weather tables in which the men were provided with a peg, and Stephen had set them out long, long before Jack returned, wet, with his hair draggled down the side of his face. 'I believe you will have a quiet night of it,' he said. "The breeze has settled into the south-south-east, and steering east by north a half north we have it rather better than one point free: double-reefed topsails and courses.' He walked into the quarter-gallery, dried himself, and came out saying, 'And if the barometer don't lie, we shall have it for a good while yet – *long forecast, long last*, you know. A squall took my hat, a damned good Lock's hat, but a breeze like this is welcome to it – would be welcome to have a dozen more, and with gold lace on, too. I have rarely been so happy to see the glass sinking, with promise of more to come.'

'You conceal your joy with wonderful skill, brother.'

'Nay, but I *am* happy, uncommon happy. Perhaps I may look a little hipped, and feel it too, having over-eaten at your splendid feast, but at the same time I promise you I am extremely pleased with this blow. It may carry us as far as the Friendly Islands: in any event I mean to drive the ship and keep all hands busy night and day, very busy indeed. No idle hands. No goddam mischief . . . It is your turn to begin, I believe.'

By now the solid crash of the seas on the frigate's starboard bow and her motion had both become more steady, and the sweep of white water along her upper-works came at regular intervals: to ears accustomed to all the sounds of a five-hundred-ton ship being urged through a rough sea at nine knots by the force of the wind, the rattle and roll of dice was now clear enough, together with the cries of 'Ace and trey,' 'Deuce and cinq,' 'Aces, by God!' But after a while Stephen said 'Brother, your mind is not on the game.'

'No,' said Jack. 'I beg pardon. I am stupider than usual tonight. I had thought it universally true that however much dinner you had eaten, there was always room for pudding. But now,' – looking down and shaking his head – 'I find it ain't the case. I took a third piece out of compliment to Tom Pullings, and it is with me still. Not that I mean the least fling against your glorious feast, of course – a noble spread upon my word. Poor dear Tom had an anxious time of it, however. He would have been lost without Mrs Oakes talking away in that good-natured fashion. How I blessed her! And it was she that set West in motion.'

'West: aye, West. Tell me, Jack, how much of his account was historically accurate?'

'All the first part, until they were bearing down in line abreast, though the sequence was a little muddled and though he did not say enough about the *Charlotte*'s breaking the French line on the twenty-eighth. But then – well, perhaps it was a little fanciful. One tells such things to ladies, you know, like the black fellow in the play, in *Venice Preserved*: he rattled away, too, about fields and floods.' He looked thoughtfully at Stephen, hesitated, and said no more.

Stephen said nothing either for a while, but then observed, 'Pudding. Sure, it starts with pudding or marchpane; then it is the toss of a coin which fails first, your hair or your teeth, your eyes or your ears; then comes impotence, for age gelds a man without hope or reprieve, saving him a mort of anguish.'

When Stephen had set off for his evening rounds Jack brought out his half-finished sheet and carried on with his letter to Sophie: 'The gunroom has at last been able to give its long-overdue feast for the Oakeses, thanks to a providential sword-fish. He was prime eating – have never tasted a better – and with him we drank a capital light dry sherry of Stephen's, as sound as a nut though it has crossed the Line and both tropics at least twice. Yet I am afraid the party was heavy going, and poor Tom Pullings had but a sad time of it. He is never very happy, as you know, when he is obliged to take the head of a table, having, as he says himself, no genteel conversation. It began badly, with at least three officers doing themselves no credit, though it is true that after a while West gave us a long account of the First of June. Martin, to be sure, was properly hospitable, so was Adams, and so of course was Stephen when he thought of it; but we should have been nowhere without Mrs Oakes, who talked away nobly, never letting that deadly silence descend; and it must have been uphill work with three dumb sullen unsmiling faces opposite her. I smirked and drank wine all round and topped it the agreeable as much as I could, but as you know very well, my dear, I am not much gifted that way, particularly as I began to be oppressed by a set of shockingly unpleasant ideas. I did my best to help things along by perpetually passing dishes, helping people to more, pouring wine, and eating and drinking until I could no more: but what with nausea and the growth of these notions I was a pretty dismal companion by the end of the meal. For they did grow, increasing from a faint half-serious suspicion to something not far short of certainty.

'It is the very Devil that I cannot speak to Stephen about his messmates. I was in great hopes just now when he asked me whether West's account of the battle was to be taken literally. I had hoped I might lead on from that to the present situation, but when I found that he only wanted to know whether it was sound history I did not dare. If I had asked him, in effect, to peach on his fellow-officers even ever so slightly, he would have brought me up with a round turn – such a round turn! He has a greater contempt for informers than anyone I have ever met. Not that I really want him to peach but rather to give me the benefit of his lights: he knows more about the gunroom and more about mankind in general than I do, being such a very deep old file: but how to separate peaching and the lights is more than I can tell.

'For some time now, being taken up with writing notes for Helmholtz fair, and some pieces of my own, and dealing with estate papers (by the way, Martin has accepted the two vacant livings and is to have Yarell when it falls in) – I have kept rather to myself, apart from music and backgammon with Stephen; yet from odd words and exchanges on the quarter-deck, or rather from their tone, I had gathered that there was a certain amount of ill-feeling in the gunroom. But I had no notion of how much or how quickly it had developed until this afternoon. Can you imagine three what are ordinarily called gentlemen sitting in a row at a full-dress dinner with guests and never opening their mouths but to eat? It is true that Oakes, though a young fellow of some family and a passable seaman, is completely devoid of the graces and that Davidge had fallen down the companion-ladder. But it was not enough to explain the situation. In any case the livid bruise on the side of his head was like none I have ever seen given by a fall of that kind: it was much more like a blow with a mallet or a man's fist. And gradually it came to seem more and more probable to me that either Oakes or West had in fact hit him – a very heavy blow indeed, almost a knock-out blow. *Why*, of course, I cannot be sure; but this appears to me to be the explanation: nobody would call Mrs Oakes very pretty, but she is certainly good company.

'As for her having been a convict, which once caused such interest, it is neither here nor there: aboard ship, and I believe it is the same in prison – it certainly was in the Marshalsea, as you know very well, my dear – once you have been shut up together for some time, original differences scarcely matter. In the *Surprise* it is less obvious, because we are nearly all more or less white, but in the *Diane* there were black, brown and yellow men, Christians, Jews, Mahometans, heathens. We had barely doubled the Cape (though far to the south) before one took no notice – they were all blue with cold anyhow, and they were all Dianes. In the same way Mrs Oakes is now a Surprise, or close on; and as I say kind, good-natured, conversible, and a good listener, interested in their stories of the sea; and it so happens that they are all, except for Davidge, tolerably hideous. Most women would recoil from them, but she in her good nature does not. Cousin Diana told me long ago that there was a coxcomb to be found in almost every man, even the most unlikely; and these fellows I believe have misinterpreted her kindness as liking of quite another kind and have grown absurdly jealous of one another. It is not only absurd but where West and Davidge are concerned it is also extraordinarily unwise. They both long to be reinstated in the Service – it is their dearest wish – and having done well hitherto in the *Surprise* they are in a fair road to it: but they have to have my good word, their captain's good word, and my parliamentary influence behind them. What captain is going to speak well of officers who cannot command their passions better than this, let alone use his interest with the Ministry for them? During dinner they were talking about duels – Mrs Oakes had started that hare with the best of intentions, I am sure – and Davidge, coming out of his heavy stupidity, spoke very eagerly about the impossibility of putting up with an affront.

'I take what comfort I can from the fact that for a great while the ship has either been sitting still, slowly turning in the placid ocean, or swimming very gently along in light variable airs with the people fishing over the side; the weather has been hot and damp, and nobody has had enough to do. Even at quarters it is mostly dumb-show, since with the likelihood of trouble at Moahu I have to husband our powder. But now, thank God, we have a fair breeze, and I shall keep them busy, oh so busy, driving the ship as hard as I dare so far from stores. I believe it will grow to be a long-lasting close-reefed-topsail gale, and by the time it has blown itself out they may have come to their senses. If not I shall have to take very strong measures.

'I hear Stephen in the coach, trying to climb into his cot: he has already kicked the chair over twice. He dislikes being helped, however. He is in – I hear the steady creak. In this damp weather he has taken to wheezing and grumbling like an old dog: and this evening, when the ship pecked on a double crest, he took a most surprising toss, turning completely over on top of his head like a tumbler, quite unhurt; but how he has survived so long at sea I cannot tell.'

Jack laid this sheet aside to dry – the wet ink glistened in the lamplight – and took up yet another file of estate papers. Presently he found he was reading the same line twice, so he shut everything into his writing-desk and went to bed.

Lying there with the fine steady heave of the sea rocking him with a diagonal motion he mused for a while. Sleep did not come. Far from it. 'It is true that Clarissa Oakes is not really pretty,' he said, 'but how I wish she were lying here beside me.' A moment later he slipped out of his cot, put on shirt and trousers and went on deck. A dark, dark night, with warm rain sweeping across from forward: four hands at the wheel, West leaning on the barricade amidships, most of the watch under the break of the forecastle. He walked aft and stood there looking at the glow of the binnacle and the white water racing by under the frigate's lee; and in time the strong wind and rain blowing his long hair out behind like seaweed and soaking him from head to foot, calmed his spirit.

Chapter Five

The glass fell, the wind rose, and although Jack Aubrey could not drive his ship as hard as he would have done with a well-equipped dockyard under his lee, he took her to the uttermost limit of what he, with his intimate knowledge of her power, thought reasonable.

The wind was uncommonly welcome, to be sure, but there was too much east in it and too much rain for anything resembling comfort: day after day the *Surprise* sailed on a taut bowline, tack upon tack under a low racing sky across a sea as grey and white-capped as the Channel, though as warm as milk and phosphorescent by night. She ran fast, generally under double-reefed topsails and the array of staysails that Jack had found best to her liking: yet with both wind and sea inconstant this called for very close attention and her captain was on deck most of the time, as wet as a man could well be.

Next to the actual pursuit of an enemy, this was the kind of sailing he liked best, and if it had not been for his anxiety about the gunroom he would have been perfectly happy. He shook out a reef whenever he could, and often, as the ship responded with even greater life, leaning over and throwing her bow-wave broader still, the white water tearing aft and Reade's strangled voice calling 'Ten knots one fathom, sir, if you please' he felt a surge of wholehearted joy. He worked his officers and men very hard indeed, but they were used to it: the *Surprise* had sailed as a privateer and most of her people were privateersmen, who sailed more for the profit than the glory; and when Jack started beating to windward with such zeal they smiled at one another and nodded. In the ordinary course of events, when Captain Aubrey was sailing his ship from one place to another without a leading wind he rarely tacked but rather wore her. That is to say he did not bring her up to the wind as close as ever she could be, clap his helm a-lee, swing her head right up into the wind's eye and beyond, so that she filled on the other tack, but on the contrary he let her fall right off, present her stern to the breeze and so come round the other way. Wearing was slower, since the ship had to turn through twenty points of the compass rather than twelve; it looked somewhat old-womanish; and it lost a certain amount of windward distance; but it was much safer and it called for fewer hands, and less violent exertion, whereas tacking, above all in a strong wind and a heavy sea, put spars and sails in danger, as well as requiring the presence of both watches. They smiled even more when he spread so much canvas that even Pullings looked anxiously at him before relaying the order. They were very well acquainted with their skipper, an extraordinarily successful prize-taker who dropped on his prey apparently by intuition, and they were convinced that somehow he had got wind of a merchantman somewhere to the east: a seaman like Captain Aubrey would never gain a little windward distance by tacking in such a sea unless his chase had a beast in view, and they answered the frequent pipe of *All hands about ship* and the subsequent hard labour with perfect good will. 'Helm's a-lee,' they heard that huge familiar voice roar from the quarterdeck, and instantly, in darkness or fine weather, they let go the fore-sheet, fore-topmast staysails and jib sheets and waited for 'Off tacks and sheets', upon which those at their due stations let go the main tack and sheet and all the staysail tacks and sheets abaft the foremast, passing the sheets over the stays. Then came 'Main-sail haul,' and once she was round, with the main tack down and the breast backstays set up, 'Let go and haul.' Furious activity as the fore-tack and head bowlines were raised, the yards braced about just so, the bowlines hauled with the cry of 'One, two, *three*. One, two, *three*. Belay oh!' Some wet officer would hail the quarterdeck 'Bowlines hauled, sir,' the order to coil all gear would come back in reply and the watch below would pad off to drip through their hammocks in the steaming Turkish bath atmosphere of the lower deck.

His officers were of the same opinion: they too had served under him in the same privateering line; and since the ship, as a letter-of-marque, had carried no midshipmen they were perfectly accustomed to going aloft as reefers; in recent months, however, they had grown soft and now Jack rode them hard. 'Mr West, there: should you like your hammock sent up?' 'Mr Davidge, pray jump into the foretop again: the aftermost starboard deadeye is far from what it ought to be.' His voice became terrible to them.

The heavy weather brought its crop of injuries and the sick-berth had a number of sprains, cracked ribs, broken bones and a hernia, which together with the usual burns caused by lurching against the galley stove on those days when it could be lit, kept Stephen, Martin and Padeen busy and allowed some interesting developments of the Basra treatment.

Stephen's little girls, Sarah and Emily, were extraordinarily useful at a time like this. They were not in the least offended or surprised by the more squalid aspects of a sick-berth; they had been brought up to dissecting and to keeping Jemmy Ducks' quarters clean; and neither in their remote Melanesian island nor aboard the *Surprise* had they had a pampered nursery life. Now they carried, fetched, kept the sick men company, comforted, and gave them more informed news of the outside world than could be drawn from the medicoes. To the foremast jacks they talked forecastle English, seaman's English, with a broad West Country burr – 'Skipper auled down the main topmast staysail at one bell. "But," says e, "we'm going to ave another atful of wind more easterly soon; so do ee stow it in the fore catharpings, and pass a gurt old gasket round"' – and quarterdeck English to Stephen and Martin. 'Sir, Jemmy Ducks says he is going to ask Old Chucks –' 'Now, Sarey, where's your manners?' asked William Lamb, quarter-gunner, in an aside. 'Beg pardon,' said Sarah. '. . . is going to ask Mr Bulkeley the bosun to suggest to the Captain that hatches might be battened down: we are all aswim forward, and he is afraid for the sitting hen.'

'*Battened down*,' said Martin. 'There is a term I have heard again and again, like *bitter end* and *laid by the lee*, without

121

ever really understanding it. Perhaps, sir, you would explain them?'

'Certainly,' said Stephen. The seamen uttered no word; their vacant expressions betrayed nothing; only two exchanged covert glances. 'Certainly. But in these cases one drawing is worth a thousand words, so let us walk upstairs and find paper and ink.'

Hardly were they at the door, attended by Padeen, than there were cries on the ladderway and Reade was passed down, pouring with blood. A falling block had struck him so that he fell on to the marline-spike poised in his hand. It was awkwardly wedged between his ribs and he was half fainting with the pain.

'Hold him just so and sit on the step,' said Stephen to Bonden, who was carrying the boy. 'Padeen, two chests into his cabin and the great lantern this living minute.'

The two chests were lashed together, forming a table; Reade lay on his back on a spare studdingsail with his mouth tight shut, his breath coming fast and shallow; the surgeon looked down in the strong light, swabbing away the blood, gently feeling the spike and the wound and the crepitation of bone.

'This is going to be extremely painful,' said Stephen in Latin. 'I shall fetch the poppy.' Hurrying below he unlocked the hidden laudanum, poured a strong dose into a phial, caught up some instruments and ran back. Once there he cried 'Padeen, now, fetch me the long ivory probe and two pairs of retractors,' and as soon as Padeen was gone he raised the boy's head and poured the dose into his mouth. For all Reade's fortitude, tears were running fast.

Jack Aubrey was at the door. 'Come back in half an hour,' said Stephen. Half an hour, and the waves of pain rose and fell, reaching a shocking height before Stephen withdrew the splinter pressing on a thoracic nerve. Reade lay there, inert now, pale, running with sweat. 'There now, my dear, the worst is over,' said Stephen in his ear. 'I have not seen a braver patient.' And to Jack at the door, 'With the blessing he will do.'

'I am heartily glad of it,' said Jack. 'I shall look in again at eight bells.'

By eight bells Reade had drifted off and Stephen stepped to the door when he heard Jack's step. After a few low words Jack said 'Mrs Oakes asks whether you would like her to sit up with him tonight.'

'Will I first see how he comes along?'

'Aye: do,' said Jack.

'And may he have a cot rather than his hammock, and two strong men to lift him in?'

'At once.'

The cot was slung; Bonden and Davies, bracing themselves with infinite care against the heave of the sea, raised the boy on his taut sailcloth, lowered him so gently that he never stirred, and walked silently out.

Stephen returned to his seat, musing on a variety of things – the presence of a highly-developed olfactory system in albatrosses, its paradoxical absence in vultures – the easier motion of the ship, her less urgent voice – the situation in the gunroom – and at two bells Reade said, in a sleepwalker's voice, 'I doubt we are making more than eight knots now.'

'Listen, my dear,' said Stephen, 'should you like Mrs Oakes to sit by you a while? Mrs Oakes?'

'Oh, her,' said Reade. After a long pause he went on '. . . they go in and out of that door, like a bawdy-house. I see them from here,' turned his head away and drifted off again.

When Jack returned Stephen told him that a medical hand was still required – that the patient should be moved down-stairs tomorrow, if possible, for constant attention – and that Martin would relieve him in less than an hour.

'Surely the tempest has disarmed,' he said, walking into the lamplit cabin. 'The noise up here is less by half, and I climbed the stairs with barely a stagger.'

'The breeze has been dropping steadily,' said Jack, 'and after the last downpour – Lord, how it did pelt! Splashing from the deck up to your waist and gushing from the lee-scuppers like a fire-engine: if we had not battened down quite early you would have had a sopping bed – after the last downpour, the sky cleared . . . but tell me, how is the boy?'

'He is fast asleep and snoring. The wound itself was not very grave – pleura untouched – and extracting the marline-spike was no great matter, but it had driven a splinter of rib hard against a nerve, and withdrawing that was a delicate business. Now that it is out, however, he ought to be comfortable enough; and unless there should be infection, which is happily rare at sea, we may see him walking about quite soon. The young are wonderfully resilient.'

'I am delighted to hear it. And I dare say you will be delighted to hear that we know where we are. Tom and I had two beautiful lunars, the one on Mars, the other on Fomalhaut. If the wind had not hauled round a little north of east we might have made the Friendly Isles tomorrow.'

'You will never tell me, for all love, that you have been careering over this stormy ocean like a mad bull day and night without knowing where you were? And if you had run violently upon an island, Friendly or not, where would you have been then, your soul to the Devil?'

'There is dead reckoning, you know,' said Jack mildly. 'Shall we have something to eat?'

'How happy that would make me,' cried Stephen, suddenly conscious that he was clemmed, pinched and wasted with hunger.

'Which there is the best part of the hen that died,' said Killick, in one of those inferior pantomime appearances they knew so well. 'And since the galley stove is still hot, you might fancy a little broth to wet your biscuit first.'

'Broth and chicken, what joy,' said Stephen, and when Killick had left he went on, 'Tell me, Jack, just how would you explain the term *battened down*?'

A piercing look showed Jack that although this was almost past believing he was not in fact being made game of, and he replied 'First I should say that we talk very loosely about hatches, often meaning hatchways and even ladderways – "he came up the fore hatch" – which of course ain't hatches at all.

The real hatches are the things that cover the hatchways: gratings and close-hatches. Now as you know very well, when a great deal of water comes aboard either from the sea or the sky or both, we cover those real hatches with tarpaulins.'

'I believe I have seen it done,' said Stephen.

'Not above five thousand times,' said Jack inwardly, and aloud 'And if it also comes on to blow and rain uncommon hard, we take battens, stout laths of wood, that fit against the coaming, the raised rim of the hatchway, and so pin the tarpaulin down drum-tight. Some people do it by nailing the batten to the deck, but it is a sad, sloppy, unseamanlike way of carrying on, and we have cleats. I will show them to you first thing in the morning.'

For seamen first thing in the morning meant that dismal hour at the fag-end of an old and weary night when elm-tree pumps and head-pumps flood the already sodden forecastle, upper deck and quarterdeck with water, and the still sleep-sodden hands move aft in gangs, sanding, holystoning, sweeping and flogging more or less dry: for some seamen it also meant the time when Reade, still bleary with opium, was carried down to a sheltered extension of the sick-berth, there to be watched by Padeen.

For Stephen however it meant first thing in the Christian day, and it was in this sense that Oakes came below with the Captain's compliments and would the Doctor like to see the cleats they had spoken of? He was a pale, silent, dangerous-looking young man now, no longer an oafish overgrown youth; but he managed a smile for Stephen and added 'You might see something else too.'

The something else was a mildly ruffled sea, unvarying Prussian blue almost to the horizon under a pure pale sky: the sun just clear of the eastern ocean, the moon sinking into it on the other hand: and on the starboard bow a low domed island of some size, far off but already as green as a good emerald in that slanting light. The breeze, blowing directly from this island, was so faint that it scarcely whispered in the rigging, nor filled the towering array of sails with any firm conviction; yet it seemed to Stephen that the air brought the scent of land.

'Where is the Captain, Barber?' he asked a seaman on the gangway.

'He is at the masthead, sir.'

So, it appeared, was everyone else who could command an eminence and a telescope. Hammocks had not yet been piped up, but the watch below had come on deck of their own accord, and there they were, gazing at the distant island with great satisfaction, saying very little. Six bells, and John Brampton's spell at the wheel was done: he was a young smuggler and privateersman from Shelmerston, one of the Sethian persuasion, but less rigid than his fellows, and in his cheerful way he called out 'Good morning, sir,' as he went forward.

'Good morning, John,' Stephen replied, and pausing, Brampton asked him whether he did not admire the Captain. 'Never out. We knew he was not cracking on for sport; and there she lies!'

'Where? Where?'

'Right in with the island. Uncle Slade with his spyglass in the fore jack-crosstrees made her out directly, when the sun lit up her sails. You can't deceive the Captain, ha, ha, ha!' He was still laughing when he seized the foremast shroud and ran up to join his uncle.

'Good morning, Doctor,' said Jack, reaching the deck by way of a back-stay, his boyish agility making an odd contrast with his worn face. 'What news of Reade?'

'He is doing well so far,' said Stephen. 'No fever: some discomfort, but no very grievous pain – he can lie easy. Mr Martin is with him now, in the sick-berth.'

'I am so glad,' said Jack. 'And I beg pardon for being aloft when I sent word: a sail had been sighted. But, however, you are come to see these cleats. Shall we step down to the upper deck?'

'Would you first tell me about this island, and your sail?'

'Why, it is Captain Cook's Annamooka, exactly where he set it down.'

'One of the Friendly Isles?'

'Just so. Did I not mention it last night?'

'You did not. But I rejoice to hear it. And what of your sail?'

'It is right in with the shore. From the masthead you can still see it tolerably well with a glass: a European vessel, almost certainly a whaler – I saw a school of about twenty blowing at first light.'

'How I hope you will sail straight in, take your prize and turn us ashore for a thorough examination of the island's flora, fauna and . . .'

'Coffee's up, sir,' said Killick.

'Shall we go down?' asked Jack; and on the upper deck he showed Stephen the after-hatchway, its coaming and its cleats. 'A pin passed through this hole across the cleat, do you see, and grips the batten tight. It was not my invention but my predecessor's. You remember Edward Hamilton?'

'I believe not.'

'Oh come, Stephen. Sir Edward Hamilton, who commanded the *Surprise* when she cut out the *Hermione*. The man who was dismissed the service for seizing his gunner up in the rigging.'

'Must you not seize a gunner up in the rigging?'

'Oh dear me, no. He is protected by his warrant, just as you are. Anyone else you may seize up, and flog too; but all you can do to an officer that holds a warrant or a commission is to confine him to his cabin until he is brought to a court-martial. Hamilton was well with the Prince of Wales, however, and he was reinstated quite soon . . . It is whimsical enough to think that two captains of the *Surprise* should have been struck off and then brought back.'

Jack had invited Pullings and Oakes to breakfast, and since service matters were allowed to be discussed at this meal, the westward currents, the tide, the adverse breeze, the probable nature and nationality of the distant sail, the frigate's urgent need of water, livestock, vegetables and coconuts were canvassed, together with the desirability of intensive work on all the rigging, running and standing; but Jack did talk about other things, and he did ask after Mrs Oakes. 'She is very well, sir, I thank you,' said Oakes flushing, 'but she stumbled against a locker in the heavy weather, and she means to keep to her cabin for some time.'

Stephen excused himself quite early: apart from anything else this was as dull a breakfast as Jack had ever given, the host himself in poor spirits despite his landfall, guests obscurely oppressed, somehow shifty. Martin, relieved by Padeen and the little girls at eight bells, was already at the rail. 'I give you joy of the Friendly Isles,' he said, 'and of the prospect of a noble prize. All the hands who have made the journey to the main jack-crosstrees assure me that she is an American whaler, very deep-laden with spermaceti and no doubt great quantities of ambergris. Do you suppose the Captain means to go straight for her in the Nelson fashion, take her, and give us a run on the island? How I hope so!'

'So indeed do I. What mind is indifferent to a prize? And in addition to this splendid prize, a week of walking about on Annamooka – that indeed would be bliss. I believe it has a very curious chestnut-coloured cuckoo, and some rails, while the people are as amiable as can be, apart from a certain thievishness.'

'I have heard that there is an owl in the Friendly Isles,' said Martin.

'There she blows!' cried Stephen, together with a score of his shipmates: the familiar forward-pointing single jet, a hundred yards to windward, was followed by a black surging as the whale turned and dived, an ancient solitary bull with a lacerated tail. 'An owl, Nathaniel Martin? An owl in Polynesia? You amaze me.'

'I heard it on good authority. But here is the bosun, who has been to Tongataboo, no great way off. Mr Bulkeley,' calling down into the waist, 'did you see any owls in Tongataboo?'

'Owls? God bless you, sir,' replied the bosun in his carrying voice, 'there was one tree near the watering-place so thick with owls you could hardly tell which was tree and which was owls. Purple owls.'

'Did they have ears, Mr Bulkeley?' asked Martin, as one who doubts the value of his question.

'That I cannot take my oath on, sir; and I should hazard a lie if I said yea or nay.'

'Ears or no ears,' said Stephen after a while, 'I fear it will be long before ever we see either prize or fowl. Quite early Captain Aubrey used that ominous, ill-sounding word *still* – the ship could *still* be seen from a certain lofty point. And at breakfast he explained to me that not only was this wind, this breeze, this poxed half-hearted zephyr, breathing directly from the island to us, but that in addition to an adverse but presumably temporary tide there was also a permanent current bearing us to the west. He said it was by no means impossible that we should beat to and fro, perpetually receding in spite of all our efforts – see how the men brace the yard a little sharper, and haul on the bowline. Such zeal! They dearly love a prize.'

'So do I,' said Martin. 'I do not believe I could be called a worshipper of Mammon, but prize-money is different, and I am now like the tiger that has once tasted human blood. Yet I hope the Captain was making game of you, as the bosun was almost certainly making game of me just now.'

'It may well be; but I remember how we have lain to or sailed up and down trying to get into a port before this, or even out of one, for weeks on end, hungry, thirsty, and discontented. Let us not be dismal, however: let us suppose that we sail in tomorrow, butcher the whalers to a man, take their goods from them, and carry our butterfly-nets and collecting-cases into those verdant groves.'

The *Surprise* sailed gently on, slanting in towards Annamooka; and as they leant there on the rail, gazing out over a sea that had now turned a royal blue with lighter paths wandering over its smooth surface, and talking of their earlier expeditions and their hopes of those so soon to come, it seemed to Stephen that he had the old Martin at his side, open, ingenuous, amiable. How the change had come about Stephen could not tell with any precision: perhaps it was connected with prosperity and family cares, with jealousy, with causes as yet unperceived; but in any event their former close bonds of friendship had certainly grown looser. This morning however they talked away without the least reserve. They saw an unknown tern, and speculated upon its affinities with terns they knew; they saw what might possibly have been a Latham's albatross in the extreme distance; the sun shone down upon them with increasing force.

Once a boat was lowered down to tow the ship's head round when she had not quite enough way on her to go about; once they were desired to move further aft so that the awning might be spread. 'This would be a perfect day for Mrs Oakes to take the air,' observed Stephen. 'She has not been on deck since it began to blow: but unhappily it seemed that she hurt her head in the rough weather, and must stay below for a while. I asked Oakes whether he would like me to see her, but he says it was only a bruise and a shaking – a lee-lurch, no doubt.'

'The hound,' said Martin in a low, vehement voice, his face quite changed, 'the infernal young hound, he beats her.'

Captain Aubrey had not been making game of them. Day after day the *Surprise* tried to work to windward, and sometimes by favour of the tide or a stronger breeze she gained a little, so that the ship at Annamooka could be seen even from the deck, only to lose it in the flat calm of the night.

Although food was uncomfortably low, Jack did not like to bear away for Tongataboo while a possible prize lay in sight. A seaman and even more an officer of the Royal Navy was deeply attached to prizes, the only possible source of a fortune. But that love was not to be compared to the privateer's consuming passion, for his prize-taking was his whole way of life, his sole raison d'être. The Surprises therefore now sailed the ship with the closest possible attention to every shift in the breeze, anticipating orders and keeping her full, in spite of the fact that as the hours and days went by the likelihood of that distant whaler being fair prize grew steadily less. She showed a provoking stolidity, a disinclination to try to escape by night: morning after morning she was still there, her yards crossed, her sails bent. The mood in the *Surprise* changed from cheerfulness to something not far from restless discontent, with a tendency to be quarrelsome.

On the evening of Thursday, after quarters, Mrs Oakes came on deck again, sitting in her usual place by the taffrail. She had a black eye of some days age, now ringed with yellow and green, and as a partial shade she wore a piece of cloth over her head, as though a close-reef topsail breeze were blowing.

'I hope I see you well, ma'am,' said Stephen, bowing. 'Mr Oakes told us you had had a fall, and I should have called, had he not dissuaded me.'

'I wish you had, dear Doctor,' said Mrs Oakes. 'I have been sadly bored. It was nothing to make anyone keep her bed – only this squalid, ignoble black eye – but even if the dreadful weather had not kept me below, I felt I could not show myself looking like a female prize-fighter. I should not really appear now, if dark were not falling fast.'

Jack came aft, made civil enquiries and returned to his task of making a little windward progress in the most untoward circumstances. Pullings, Martin and West appeared and they talked with a fair amount of animation, but it appeared to Stephen that whereas their dislike of one another or at least the tension between them had increased, their attentiveness to Clarissa had declined in much the same proportion as her looks. She, for her part, was particularly agreeable to them all, particularly winning.

On later reflection it seemed to him that this was too simple. There was also another emotion abroad, perhaps best defined as a want of regard: just on whose part he could scarcely say. Nor could he recall any specific instance.

Yet the impression was there, and it was strengthened next day not only by the tone of the officers but by the attitude of some of the hands. Although many, indeed most, smiled upon her with the same genial warmth, there were some faces whose look was questioning, puzzled, even deliberately expressionless. The great matter of this next day however was the changing of the sails, each in turn for its lighter brother. Jack Aubrey, as sensitive as a cat to changes in the weather, had had the pricking of his thumbs confirmed by the barometer;

but so far he could not tell the direction of the coming breeze, and rather than disappoint all hands he had merely given the order. And since the *Surprise* owned a full wardrobe of well over thirty, a great deal of activity was called for; quite why, Stephen could not make out – the present suit of sails seemed perfectly adequate to him – but what he could make out, and make out quite clearly, was that when the Captain was not on deck there was much more damning of eyes and limbs than usual, and much more of the wrangling and contention and reluctant obedience not uncommon in a privateer but rare and very dangerous in the Royal Navy.

He also made out the fact that for one foremost jack who looked askance at Clarissa, there were half a dozen who cast a cold eye on Oakes. Yet it was not when Oakes was on duty that Jack, leaning over the side with Adams to measure the salinity, heard a voice float down from the fore crosstrees in answer to the cry 'Don't you know you must pass the selvagee first, damn your eyes?' a low voice but perfectly distinct: 'Who the Devil cares what you say?' Jack looked up, said 'Mr West, take that man's name,' and carried on with his task.

His breeze began to blow from the south, right on the frigate's beam, late in the forenoon watch. By the time the hands were piped to dinner the water was singing down her side, her deck had a slope of some ten or twelve degrees and the whole mood aboard had changed: laughter, merriment.

By the time the hands had eaten their dinner the island was so much nearer that it filled the eighth part of the horizon, and a fine great pahi, a double canoe with a deckhouse, could be seen putting off the shore, hoisting its immense peaked sail and coming out to meet them on the opposite tack.

'Killick,' said Jack, 'rouse out my box of red feathers, the chest of island presents, and whatever we have left in the way of sweetmeats.'

'Sir,' said Oakes, 'masthead says there is a white man aboard.'

'In a coat?'

'Yes, sir: and a hat.'

'Very good, Mr Oakes: thank you. Killick, the lightest coat

you can find, number three scraper and a clean pair of duck trousers. And pass the word for Captain Pullings. Tom, you know the South Sea islanders as well as I do. They are delightful creatures, but nobody is to be allowed below except those that I invite into the cabin, and anything movable on deck is to be screwed down, including the anchor. Doctor, of our people, who do you think speaks South Seas best, being at the same time intelligent, if possible?'

'There is the bosun; but he might prove a little over-facetious as an interpreter. I should suggest Owen or John Brampton or Craddock.'

Tom Pullings had barely time to make the ship presentable, and Captain Aubrey had spent no more than five minutes on the spotless deck in his spotless trousers before the swift-sailing pahi was within hail. The *Surprise* heaved to with her main topsail laid to the mast and the canoe, with naval politeness, ran under her stern and came close up along her leeward side.

Smiling brown faces gazed up, and an anxious white one; a young woman threw a sheaf of some strong-smelling green herb on deck; lines were passed and the white man came up the side, accompanied by an islander.

'Captain Aubrey, sir, I believe?' said the white man, advancing and taking off his hat. 'My name is Wainwright, master of the *Daisy* whaler, and this is Pakeea, the under-chief of Tiaro. He brings you a present of fish, fruit and vegetables.'

'How very kind of him,' said Jack, smiling at Pakeea, a tall stout beautifully tattooed young man shining with oil, who smiled back in the friendliest manner. 'Please thank him heartily for me. Nothing could have been more welcome.' And having named his officers and asked Pullings to have the presents brought aboard, Jack went on, 'Will you step into the cabin?'

In the cabin Killick handed some little round farinaceous objects fresh from the galley, spread with marmalade, and madeira; and after a few insignificant remarks Jack opened a drawer, showed Wainwright a bunch of red feathers, asking in an aside, 'Are they adequate?'

'Oh Lord yes,' said Wainwright.

'Oh Lord yes,' said Pakeea.

Jack handed them to him, together with a piece of scarlet cloth and a small magnifying glass. Pakeea raised the gifts to his head with a face full of pleasure, and made quite a long speech in Polynesian.

'I am afraid I do not understand you, sir,' said Jack, having listened attentively.

'Pakeea says he hopes you will come ashore. He does not speak English, but he can echo the last words he hears with wonderful accuracy.'

'Please tell him I should be very happy to come ashore, to water and trade for hogs, coconuts and yams, and to walk about this beautiful island.'

Wainwright translated this and some further civilities and then he said 'For my own part I am delighted that you will be coming. I have some very grave information for you; and aside from that my own ship is in a sad way for want of the carpenter and his mate and the cooper. As soon as I saw the *Surprise* heave up I said to Canning "My God, we are saved." '

'How did you know she was the *Surprise*?'

'Bless you, sir, there is no mistaking that towering mainmast, and in any case we have sailed in company many a time in the Channel and the West Indies. I often came aboard you in the Mediterranean with messages from the flag. I served my time as midshipman and master's mate and passed for lieutenant in ninety-eight; but they never would give me a commission, so in the end I bore up for the merchant service.'

'Like many another first-rate officer,' said Jack, shaking his hand.

'You are very good, sir,' said Wainwright. 'But since you are coming in, perhaps I may stay aboard, give you my important news and then show you the channel through the reef, while Pakeea takes his people back in the pahi. They are apt to be a nuisance on deck when it comes to the fine-work of threading the channel and dropping anchor.'

During this time the young chief, overcoming his natural gaiety, had sat with the gravity that became his rank, secretly counting his feathers and looking at them and the cloth through the magnifying glass, whose use he had grasped at once. On deck however there was no gravity at all, except on the part of Sarah and Emily. Once the fish, the yams, sugarcane, bananas and breadfruit had been brought aboard, most of the islanders followed them, leaving only a few to fend off. All the Surprises who had a word of Polynesian (and at least a score of them were moderately fluent) entered into conversation; and those who had not did the same, contenting themselves with incorrect English spoken loud: 'Me like um banana. Good. Good.' There were three young Friendly women, who had also had time to oil themselves afresh, which gave their bare torsos a charming gleam, and to ornament their persons with necklaces of flowers and shark's teeth; but the foremast jacks were shy of accosting them with the officers present, and in any case they seemed strongly aware of rank. One spoke only to Pullings, in his fine blue coat; one to Oakes and Clarissa; and one attached herself to Stephen, sitting by him on the carriage of a gun and entertaining him with a cheerful, very voluble account of some recent occurrence, often laughing as she did so and patting him on the knee. From the very frequent repetition of certain phrases Stephen was convinced that she was recounting a conversation – 'So I said to him . . . and he said to me . . . so then I replied . . . Oh, says he . . .' Her bubbling high spirits were agreeable for a while, but presently he led her, still talking, to the forecastle, where the little girls (and not so very little either, now that they had begun to shoot up) were watching the scene with displeasure. Jemmy Ducks had told them they were never to say 'black boogers' again, as it was not genteel; but these were the words they muttered from time to time. Stephen said they were to curtsy, and that if the young lady wished to touch noses they were to suffer it. This the young woman did as the most natural thing in the world, very gently, bending a little; and then she addressed them in Polynesian. Finding they did not understand she laughed heartily, gave Emily one of her necklaces and Sarah a mother-of-pearl pendant, and continued her flow of speech, pointing now at the island, now at the masthead, and laughing very often.

Presently Jack, Wainwright and Pakeea came on deck and the young chief called out with surprising authority. All the islanders began to leave the ship and Parsons, one of the South Seas speakers, said privately to Stephen, 'By your leave, sir: that young female prigged your wipe while you was a-looking at the mast. Shall I tell her to give it back?'

'Did she indeed, Parsons?' cried Stephen, clapping his hand to his pocket in a very simple way. 'Well, never mind. It was an old torn rag of a thing, and I do not grudge it to so pretty a creature.' 'But,' he added inwardly, 'she also took my little lancet, which I rather regret.'

The pahi shoved off, filled and ran smoothly for the shore at an extraordinary pace, making almost no wake and, because of its wide-spaced double hull, scarcely heeling at all. In addition to the modest voluntary presents, it carried five handkerchiefs, one pocket lancet, two glass bottles (one with a coloured stopper), and one tobacco-box, five iron and two wooden belaying-pins: yet what the islanders had brought so very far outweighed what they had taken that it was impossible for any except the man deprived of his tobacco to feel righteous or indignant.

'Now, sir,' said Wainwright, they having returned to the cabin, 'I must tell you that there is an English ship and several English seamen detained in the island of Moahu, which lies south of . . .'

'I know its position,' said Jack. 'But I have no accurate chart.'

'Perhaps I had better start by saying that my owners have six ships employed as whalers or as fur-traders to Nootka Sound and the northwards, and these ships often appoint to meet – and others do the same, it being so convenient – at Moahu to refresh and exchange news or owners' instructions before going on either to Canton for the Nootka ships or down into the Southern Ocean for the rest of their whaling cruise, right down, sometimes by way of Sydney Cove, to Van Diemen's Land or beyond. And if the fur-traders have not done well in their first season, they lie there and sail back early in the next, before the

Americans come round the Horn. Most of the year, when the north-east trades are blowing, we put into Eeahu; but the rest of the time we lie at Pabay, in the north.'

'Will you draw me a rough map?' asked Jack, passing pencil and paper.

'It is easy enough where Moahu is concerned,' said Wainwright, and he drew a large figure of eight with a broad waist. 'North to south is about twenty miles. The smaller lobe at the top, with the harbour of Pabay in the north-east, is Kalahua's territory. The division between the two rounds is very rough mountain country with forest going far down each side. The southern lobe belongs to Puolani. Rightly speaking she is queen of the whole island, but some generations ago the chiefs in the north rebelled, and now Kalahua, who has knocked all the other northern chiefs on the head, says he is the rightful king of all Moahu, Puolani having eaten pork, which is taboo to women. Everyone says that is nonsense. She certainly eats the usual pieces of enemy chiefs killed in battle, according to custom, but she is a very pious woman, and would never touch pork. So you see, sir, there is war between north and south. Our owners have told us to keep out of it, because we have to use the two harbours, Pabay in the north-east, a good harbour in a deep inlet with a stream at its head when the wet south winds are blowing, and Eeahu in the south, in Puolani's country, when the trades make it difficult to get out of Pabay. For my own part I should have backed Puolani, who has always been kind to us and true to her word, and who is after all only a poor weak woman, whereas Kalahua is an ugly scrub, not to be trusted. The forces used to be about equal, and both sides treated us civilly; but when I came into Pabay this last time, to join our ships *Truelove*, William Hardy, and *Heartsease*, John Trumper, I found everything was changed. Kalahua had a parcel of Europeans, some with muskets, and he had fallen out with our two skippers. He wanted to what he called borrow their guns, but he did not ask right out and make a point of it until Hardy was in a very awkward position, having heaved down his ship to come at a leak. They were still temporizing when I came in, but by then Kalahua had

137

seized a score of their men on one pretext or another – theft; fornication, by God; touching taboo fruits or trees – and when I went to see him he declared the ships should have no water, no supplies, and the men should not be released until his demands were satisfied. There was something odd and false and disagreeably confident about him, and he kept on putting off our meetings – he was gone up the country, he was sleeping, he was out of sorts.

'It was when he was really gone up into the mountains with his Europeans that a fourth ship of ours, the *Cowslip*, Michael McPhee, appeared in the offing. I signalled to her not to cross the bar, and sent off one of our Kanaka hands with a message, telling McPhee to water at Eeahu, Puolani's harbour, if necessary, and then to pelt down to Sydney Cove like smoke and oakum and tell them how we were being used.

'Before Kalahua returned a couple of big pahis came in, one of them belonging to an old friend of mine, a very good friend, an Oahu chief, last from Molokai in the Sandwich Islands, and I learnt why Kalahua was so confident. He was expecting the *Franklin*, a heavy privateer carrying twenty-two nine-pounders, sailing under the American flag but manned by Frenchmen from Canada and Louisiana: and to be sure, though Kalahua had kept his white men from us, I had seen something of them and they certainly spoke French among themselves or when they saw me a damned odd sort of English. And I heard that the French owner, who had been in Hawaii picking up hands, was a man who could not keep quiet, who had to be talking, and he had told a handsome Marquesas girl, half French herself, that he did not value Kalahua a pinch of snuff, an odious fellow, false through and through, and that as soon as the two sides, north and south, had weakened one another enough, Kalahua should be knocked on the head, Puolani's war-canoes (her chief strength) should be destroyed with a couple of broadsides and that Moahu, at the wish of its people and of those surviving chiefs who knew what was good for them, should be declared a French possession. The natives would be taught to cry *Vive l'Empereur*, which was fair enough, since it was the French government that had put up the money for the ship. But once the war was over there would be quite a different regime, with equality for everyone, all property held in common, justice, peace and plenty – everything settled by discussion.'

'That puts a different face on the matter,' said Jack, thinking of Stephen with great relief.

'Yes, sir. So I posted a sentinel to watch for the *Franklin*. There was nothing to be done about the *Truelove*. She was hove down right in the village and in any case the tide would not serve: but Trumper of the *Heartsease* and I prepared our ships as well as we could, though we only had what you expect in merchantmen. And that same evening the sentinel came hallooing down – there was a ship in with the land, making for the harbour under an easy sail. We had been delayed so long the trades were blowing again: the wind was north-easterly, but by the grace of God there was just enough north in it to let us scrape past the south headland close-hauled. *Heartease* went first, and she got off with no more than a hole or two in her topsails, but the *Franklin* cracked on to make all sneer again, throwing a bow-wave as wide as her fore-course and ranging up fast – the *Daisy* was never built for speed – and he gave us a broadside that killed our carpenter and his mate and shattered the boats on the boom. As cruel a broadside as ever I saw, and I thought if this goes on I shall have to strike. But it was only luck: his next went overhead and before he could fire again – damned slow, I may say, by your standards, sir – I had the satisfaction of seeing his fore topmast go by the board. I like to think it was the stern-chaser I had just fired that cut the backstay but it was more likely an absurd overpress of sail. Any gate, he came up into the wind, and he had not the command of his helm to follow me through the dog-leg passage in the reef.'

The way had been coming off the frigate for some time now, and Wainwright, glancing at the shore, said 'Speaking of channels, sir, perhaps I should show your helmsman just how this one lies: we are quite near, and it is no good following the pahi – they never can believe we draw so much water.'

On deck Jack found that they had indeed come very close to the reef. There were leadsmen in the chains on either side;

Davidge was on the fore topsail yard conning the ship; Pullings had hands at the braces and halliards, with the anchor dangling a-cockbill. 'Captain Wainwright will take her in,' said Jack to Pullings, and Wainwright, guiding himself by familiar landmarks, set about the awkward turns with such obvious competence that all hands relaxed.

All hands, that is to say, except the medical men and Clarissa Oakes: for her part she had never supposed that there was any danger, and her whole being was taken up with the shore, its brilliant coral strand, its coconut-palms leaning in every direction, their fronds streaming with infinite grace, the village of wide-spread little houses among irregular fields and gardens, a path leading into the green forest. Maturin's and Martin's eyes and telescopes, on the other hand, were fixed upon the whaler, lying close in-shore, leaning heavily; she had a stage over her side.

'I believe it is an ancient murrelet,' said Stephen. 'I saw it on the water.'

'How can you speak so, Maturin,' said Martin. 'An ancient murrelet in these latitudes?'

'It is certainly an auk,' said Stephen, following its rapid whirring flight. 'And I am persuaded it is an ancient murrelet.'

'See, see,' cried Martin. 'It circles the ship. It lands in the foretop!'

The frigate had passed through the channel and she was gliding gently towards the whaler. Wainwright brought her head to the wind, called 'Let go,' the anchor splashed into the sea – that welcome, welcome sound – and the *Surprise* drifted on with the making tide, paying out a good scope of cable, and bringing up in a comfortable five fathom water so close to the whaler that the bird could clearly be seen, watching them with every appearance of curiosity.

'If you will come across and dine with me, sir,' said Wainwright, 'I will finish my account. I am so sorry I cannot invite your officers, but the *Daisy*'s cabin is crammed with the more valuable bales from the *Truelove*, and there is barely room for even two to sit down.'

'I should be very happy,' said Jack, 'but first may I beg you to ask Pakeea to tell his people they must not come aboard until he gives the word? Mr Davidge, my gig. Captain Pullings, I am going aboard the whaler: there is to be no trading for curiosities until the ship has been victualled.'

While the boat was lowering down Stephen, from the gangway, said 'Captain Aubrey, sir, I appeal to you: is not that bird on the edge of the whaler's front platform – top – foretop – an ancient murrelet?'

'Why,' said Jack, considering it, 'I am no expert, as you are aware. But perhaps it does look a little elderly. Can it be ate?'

'Certainly it is an ancient murrelet, Doctor,' said Wainwright. 'It is our surgeon's ancient murrelet Agnes. He brought her up from the egg. If you would like to come across with us, I am sure he would be happy to show her to you.'

'I will not importune you at the moment, sir,' said Stephen, 'but I have a little small skiff of my own, and with your permission I shall wait upon the gentleman somewhat later in the day.'

'And so, sir – a trifle of crackling?'

'If you please,' said Jack, holding out his plate. 'How I love roast pork.'

'And so, sir, having left the *Franklin* astern, I ran as fast as I could to catch up with *Heartsease*: but that was not very fast, because the privateer's unlucky broadside had caught us on the heel, well below the waterline, and with the larboard tack aboard the water came spurting in like three conduits under anything more than close-reefed topsails. In any case, the weather turned thick and dirty that night. We never saw the *Heartsease* again though we kept pegging away with all the sails she could bear, pumping all day and most of the night. We managed to fother the worst of the leaks for a while and stuff some of the rest inboard, but heavy seas undid all our work after some ten days or so, and the hands were dropping with fatigue, so I was obliged to haul up for Annamooka. But how I hope the *Heartsease* reached Sydney Cove!'

'She did,' said Jack, 'and in consequence of her report I

have been sent to deal with the situation. I am now proceeding to Moahu with all possible dispatch.'

'Oh,' said Wainwright, laying down his knife and fork and gazing at Captain Aubrey. 'Are you, by God? I am prodigious glad of it for those poor men we had to leave behind, and for my owners too of course. The *Truelove* is a fine new vessel, Whitby-built, with a valuable cargo, apart from what we took out. May I come with you? The *Daisy* may not carry very heavy metal, but I know those waters, I know the people, I speak the language, and we have nineteen prime seamen as well as the officers.'

'That is a most obliging offer,' said Jack, 'but in this case speed is everything. A few degrees north we should find the trades blowing hard and steady, and the *Surprise* is happiest on a bowline. In those latitudes she has logged well over two hundred miles between noon and noon day after day, and I fear the *Daisy* could not keep up, even if she were in a fit state to sail.'

'She has made seven knots, with the wind on her quarter,' said Wainwright. 'But I must admit there is no comparison.'

'I hope to catch him at anchor,' said Jack. 'No great seaman, I believe you said?'

'That was my impression, sir. I am told he has not cruised before; and is a somewhat philosophical, theoretical gent.'

'Then the sooner his capers are cut short the better. Let us have no benevolent revolutions, no humanitarians, no God-damned systems, no panaceas. Look at that wicked fellow Cromwell, and those vile Whigs in poor King James's time, a fine seaman as he was, too. But tell me, what does your damage amount to?'

'Oh, sir,' replied Wainwright, brightening, 'I doubt there is much more than a day's work for a skilled carpenter and his crew, if we could but have the worst looked to, and just one boat patched so that it might swim.'

'Then if you will pass the word for my coxswain I will send him to bring Mr Bentley, a capital hand with a shot-plug or a fractured knee.'

*

142

In Dr Falconer, the *Daisy*'s surgeon, Stephen and Martin found a man after their own hearts. He had abandoned a lucrative practice in Oxford as soon as a modest competence was put by, and he took to the sea in his cousin's various ships for the sake of natural philosophy. Volcanoes and birds were his chief delight, but nothing came amiss and he had dissected the narwhal and the white bear of the north and the sea-elephant of the far south. Yet his interest in medicine, theoretical and practical, was undiminished; and as the two vessels were warping across the harbour to lie side by side for the benefit of the carpenters, they abandoned ornithology for the moment and turned to hydrophobia: hydrophobia philosophically considered, some of the cases they had known, and the variety of treatments.

'I remember a strong boy of fourteen who was admitted to the Infirmary having been bit that day month by a mad foxhound,' said Dr Falconer. 'There is a yellow-billed tropic-bird. The day after he was bit he went to the sea, where he was dipped with all the severity usually practised under so disagreeable an operation. A common adhesive plaster was applied to the part after the sea-bathing; and in the course of a month the wound was healed, except a small portion somewhat more than an inch in length, and in breadth about one tenth – it was in quite a cicatrizing state. Five days before he was admitted he began to complain of a tightness over his temples, and a pain in his head: in two days the hydrophobia began to appear. The disease was pretty strong when he came to the Infirmary. He was given a bolus of a scruple of musk with two grains of opium; then a composition of fifteen grains of musk, one of turpeth mineral, and five grains of opium, every third hour; an ounce of the stronger mercurial ointment was rubbed on the cervical vertebrae, and an embrocation of two ounces of laudanum and half an ounce of acetum saturninum was directed to be applied to the throat. But by this last he was thrown into convulsions; and the same effect followed though his eyes were covered with a napkin. The embrocation was therefore changed for a plaster of powdered camphor, half an ounce of opium, and six drachms of confectio Damocritis.'

'What was the outcome?' asked Stephen.

'The disease seemed somewhat suspended; but the symptoms returned with violence in the evening. His medicine was repeated at seven, and at eight five grains of opium were exhibited *without* musk or turpeth. At nine another ounce of mercurial ointment was rubbed upon the shoulders, and half an ounce of laudanum with six ounces of mutton broth was injected into the intestines, but to no purpose. A larger dose of opium was then given, but with as little effect as the former; and he died the same night.'

'My experience has been much the same, alas,' said Stephen, 'except in one case at Oughterard in Iarconnacht, where two bottles of whiskey, drunk at stated intervals during the course of one day, appeared to effect a radical cure.'

'I am not to speak of physic in the presence of two doctors of medicine,' said Martin, 'but I was once present when an embrocation of half an ounce of sal ammoniac, ten drachms of olive oil, six drachms of oil of amber and ten drachms of laudanum was applied.' The two ships came together with a gentle elastic thump. Martin raised his voice above the nautical cries and the laughter from the swarm of Friendly canoes, some paddled by children and very nearly crushed between the sides. 'Strong mercurial ointment on shoulder and back, as in Dr Falconer's case, and to induce ptyalism even more speedily, the patient received the smoke of cinnabar into the mouth . . .'

Above their heads Bulkeley started his call – the shrill urgent pipe of *all hands on deck* – followed by his hoarse roar of 'All hands on deck: all hands aft: look alive, look alive, you dormice.' Then Pullings' voice: 'Silence fore and aft,' and after a pause Captain Aubrey said, 'Shipmates, we must run north as soon as ever the ship can be watered and victualled. We shall start watering directly; then tonight half of each mess may have a run on shore. Tomorrow we shall complete our water and start trading, and tomorrow night the other half may have leave. The next day, after trading again in the morning, we must get under way at the beginning of ebb. There is not a moment to be lost.'

144

Chapter Six

It was a moonless, slightly covered night, and all along the shore the embers glowed a lovely red in the darkness, brightening at every breath of air from the sea, the deserted fires round which Surprises, Daisies and Friendly Islanders had danced and sung with such echoing zeal that at last both Jack and Stephen laid aside their bows and turned to the grinding and making of coffee over a spirit-stove (for Killick was one of the liberty-men and the galley fires were out in the sleeping ship) and then to backgammon.

When each had scored two hits they ate some of the piled tray of small, exquisitely scented bananas, and after a considering pause Jack said 'When we were off Norfolk Island I received orders by that cutter, as you know. I have not spoken about them until now because unlike most of my orders of anything but a purely naval kind they did not mention your name. They did not say "You will seek the advice of Dr Maturin". Then they not only told me that British ships and British seamen were being misused in Moahu, as you also know, but they went on to say there were two parties at war in the island, more or less evenly balanced, and that having dealt with the ships or rather that in addition to dealing with the ships I was to back whichever side was more likely to acknowledge King George. And since I know what you think of empires and colonies I did not like to make you a party to what you disapprove.'

He took yet another banana, deliberately peeling it, and ate it. Stephen was a perfect listener: he never interrupted, he did not fidget or look privately at the time. Yet although Jack was used to it, he found polite, neutral, attentive silence during so long and delicate a speech somewhat unnerving, and while he ate his banana and arranged his coming words some odd region of his mind said that this awkwardness was particularly unfair: he knew perfectly well that Stephen had received countless orders which he never disclosed or spoke about. 'Yet on the other hand,' he went on, 'it occurred to me then and it occurs to me now with far greater strength that the reason the orders did not mention your name was that the people in Sydney did not suppose you capable of giving advice about anything other than medicine. At present I am sure of it: furthermore Wainwright, who has just come from Moahu and who seems to be perfectly reliable, tells me that the two sides are no longer equally balanced. A French privateer-commander, sailing under the American flag but with a crew of Frenchmen, has joined the northern chief against the ruler of the south, a woman; and his intention, when both north and south have worn one another out, is to destroy the chief men of his allies and opponents and turn the place into a Paradise in which the survivors and the French colonists are to hold everything in common: no wealth, no poverty.' He reflected, paraphrased Wainwright's account more fully, more accurately, and said 'His name is Jean Dutourd.'

At this Stephen's face showed a sudden life, a glow of satisfaction. 'What joy,' he said. 'It could not be improved.'

'You know him?' cried Jack.

'I do too. He has written about equality, the perfectibility of human nature, and the essential goodness of mankind for many years – he judges others by himself, poor soul – and he has a considerable following. I was acquainted with him in Paris; and once to my surprise I saw him at Honfleur, sailing about in a very spirited way in a boat with two masts. In personal relations a kinder man never breathed, and in his system the whole purpose was for the good of others: he spent a fortune in trying to settle the Jews in Surinam and another – for he is very rich – in farms and manufactories for young criminals. But although I believe that the man who told Captain Wainwright of Dutourd's deliberate, Machiavellian desire of knocking his Polynesian associates on the head may have been a little excessive, I have no doubt that in defence of a

146

system Dutourd could be utterly ruthless – a very short way indeed with dissenters. And the result though perhaps not the sin might be much the same. One of his books on the Pacific paradise infected that American naval officer – Killick, what are you doing to that young woman?' he called through the open stern window.

'Nothing, sir,' said Killick instantly, and after a gasping pause, 'It is quite all right – perfectly natural. I was just saying good night. Which she pulled me across, the liberty-boat having gone too soon.'

'Killick, come aboard at once,' said Jack.

'Which the boarding-netting is rigged, sir. I thought to creep up by the quarter-gallery, but you ain't turned in yet,' said Killick in a tremulous voice; though he did extract some hint of grievance and hard usage from their sitting up so late.

'Come in by the sash-light,' said Jack.

The sash-light could be reached by a spring from the canoe: Killick, though totty from his swink, attempted it, fell back into the sea, sending up a phosphorescent splash like a moderately good firework, tried again and this time grasped the sill. But he hung there gasping, and it was not until the young woman, with a shriek of laughter, had shoved him from behind, that he came inboard, sodden, resentful, and sadly out of countenance, going straight through the door with a bowed head, a mumble and a gesture towards his forelock.

They sat back, each secretly pleased with having acquired a moral advantage over Killick at last; and Jack returned to the paragraph in his orders in which it was stated that in any event Moahu already belonged to the British crown, Cook having taken possession of the archipelago in 1778.

Stephen said, 'I believe the same applies to a very great many other places in the Pacific Ocean. I remember Sir Joseph telling me that Otaheite, or Tahiti as some people say, was called King George's Island when he was there observing the transit of Venus: though indeed it was Wallis rather than Cook who discovered and annexed it. He did not think the chiefs or their people took the matter at all seriously, and I do not

147

suppose the lady in question would do so either – a polite formality, no more.'

'Forgive me if I am stupider than usual, Stephen, but what lady is in question?'

'Why, Puolani, Wainwright's poor weak woman, the queen of the south. For I imagine it is she you mean to support, the privateer being allied to her enemy in the north, the doubly inimical privateer, both American and French?'

'Of course. I am sorry. She had slipped my mind.'

'Yet even if it were more than a political formality, being a subject of the very remote King George –'

'God bless him.'

'By all means, my dear – would seem a less dreadful fate than being under the immediate and present rule of France or America or the architect of a system that roots up every form of social existence known to man and that is very likely to hurry unbelievers or heretics to the stake.'

'So may I take it that you have no objections?' asked Jack, who was indeed very weary, sleepy and stupid by now.

'As you know very well,' said Stephen, 'I am in favour of leaving people alone, however imperfect their polity may seem. It appears to me that you must not tell other nations how to set their house in order; nor must you compel them to be happy. But I too am a naval officer, brother; long, long ago you taught me that anyone nourished on ship's biscuit must learn to choose the lesser of two weevils. On that basis alone I may be said to have no objection to Moahu's becoming a nominal British possession.'

It was far into the silent middle watch before they parted, and Stephen, having looked into the sleeping sick-berth, tiptoed along the gunroom with a dark-lantern to his lower cabin in the hope of escaping the infernal din of holystones and swabs, ritual cries, the wheeze of pumps and the clash of buckets that began before dawn: for he was a creature that needed sleep if his mind were to function at all, and he looked forward to his free day on Annamooka, a day of intense observation and discovery that would call for all his powers if it were to be carried out intelligently.

Jack Aubrey, on the other hand, possessed in an eminent degree that ability to plunge straight into a deep, restorative sleep without which sailors do not survive, and to wake bright, sometimes intolerably bright, and efficient after an hour or two, no more. He had bathed and he was cheerfully eating his first breakfast, served by a haggard, mournful, unnaturally submissive Killick, when word came below that a small canoe was putting off from the *Daisy*. It was Wainwright himself, and he brought the news that Tereo, the old chief, had arrived, had given orders that no market should be opened, no trading take place, before there had been an exchange of visits and presents. That was why the beach was empty; that was why there was no swarm of visiting canoes. 'He is a very authoritarian and formal old gentleman,' said Wainwright. 'He rebuked Pakeea for his free and easy ways and confiscated his red feathers. His presents should be coming off in about half an hour, and then you ought to make a return and visit him. I think it might be a mistake to start watering before you have asked his leave.'

'Is there likely to be any difficulty?'

'Not if you handle him right.'

'Captain Wainwright, I should be infinitely obliged if you would help me through the whole of this business. There must be no misunderstanding, no disagreement, no time lost.'

'Of course I will, sir. But it is I that am obliged: your Mr Bentley's mate is caulking our red whale-boat at this moment, and he himself is fashioning a new rider. Perhaps, sir, if you were to show me what you have in the way of trade-goods I could pick out a reasonable return for what you are about to be given. Pakeea told me to the last yard of tapa.'

They were turning over the adzes, axes, beads, glass balls, printed cotton, brass and pewter basins, when a pahi put off from the shore, paddled by girls and commanded by an immensely stout middle-aged woman. 'That is Tereo's sister,' said Wainwright. 'A jolly old soul. It might be as well to rig a bosun's chair.'

A jolly old soul she doubtless was, for the habitual expression of her face had lined it with smiling and laughter; but at present, as she was lowered gently to the deck, she behaved with a natural and impressive gravity. Three of her maidens ran nimbly up the side to join her; they too wore clothes from knee to shoulder, being, as Wainwright whispered in Jack's ear, women of high birth, related to the great families of Tongataboo. They were taller and a lighter brown than the cheerful bare-bosomed girls in the pahi, and they too were grave. They spread out the presents – bolts of tapa cloth, dark red, orange and its natural fawn, made from bark; young hogs confined in matting; baskets of live chickens and dead wildfowl, which included a purple coot and some rails that made Martin stiffen like a setter; billets of sandalwood; baked dogs; sugar-cane, fruit and berries; and two clubs made of a hard, dark wood with a sperm-whale's tooth set in each formidable head. The frigate's crew stood on the forecastle or along the gangways, some few leering at the paddlers or exchanging nods and becks with those they had met the night before, but most watching in silent admiration.

Jack said to Wainwright 'Please tell her that I am profoundly grateful for the chief's magnificent presents; that presently I shall do myself the honour of waiting on him with an offering of our own, necessarily less beautifully attended; that I shall ask his leave to water in his island and to trade with his people for victuals; and that at present I beg that she and these young ladies will walk into the cabin. Pray make it as elegant as you can.'

Wainwright certainly made it longer and probably more elegant, for the South-Seas speakers of the *Surprise* were seen to nod approvingly at several passages; and at the close the chief's sister turned a benevolent face on Jack. He escorted them to the cabin, where Wainwright seated them according to the Polynesian etiquette and Jack gave each a bunch of red feathers and some other little presents. The feathers in particular were very well received; the madeira that followed less so. Their looks of pleased anticipation changed to one of astonishment, in some cases alarm. But after a stunned moment the polite smiles returned and although they were a little artificial the meeting ended with expressions of kindness and esteem on either side.

Shortly after the pahi had left for the shore Jack followed it, his coxswain and bargemen in their best; and about an hour after his return, successful in all points, Stephen first appeared on deck. Admittedly he had slept late, and he had been long delayed in the sick-berth, yet even so he was astonished to see the sun so high and the day so bright, the ship such a hive of activity, the beach so thronged with people and dashed with colour: for in this brilliant light even a pyramid of coconuts on the white coral strand with aquamarine sea in front and the green of palms and gardens behind, was a fine living tawny brown: to say nothing of the heaps of bananas, yams, breadfruit, taro roots and leaves, the baskets of shining fish. He stared and stared again. A pahi came in, the men and women of its crew all singing; they turned their broad, elaborate, beautifully-built craft round the ship in the light breeze in the most seamanlike fashion, avoiding her cables (she was now moored fore and aft) and running up on the beach to unload yet more fish. A flight of medium-sized parrots he could not identify passed over the gardens beyond the strand: a green, fast flying pigeon. But the *Surprise* was a busy ship: the great water-casks were already coming aboard, rising up from the launch, swaying in over the deck with many a cry of *All together — way-oh — handsomely, there — God damn your eyes and limbs, Joe — half an inch, half an inch, half an inch forward, mate* and vanishing down the main hatchway to muffled but sometimes more passionate cries far below.

And water was not all by any means. It had been agreed between Jack and Tereo that all trading should take place on shore, in order to avoid the complexity of business with fifty canoes at once, and the market was spread out, wide, handsome and remarkably varied. The *Surprise*'s chief kinds of trade-goods, tools and everything metal; bottles and everything glass; cloth and the much valued hats; gauds, beads and trinkets, were in barrels with a seaman sitting on each; the bartering was carried out first by Wainwright, who set some kind of a standard, and then on that basis by the more knowing Surprises. Their purchases flowed aboard in a steady stream, to be received by Mr Adams, his steward, Jack-in-the-Dust, Jemmy Ducks where poultry was concerned, and Weightman, the ship's butcher, where it was a question of hogs.

These creatures had been arriving in ones and twos since well before Stephen was afoot, rather small, razor-backed, long-legged, dark and hairy swine, inexpressibly welcome to the little girls. They were the same as the hogs of their native Sweeting's Island in appearance, voice and above all smell: they brought back times past with such force that both girls wept, spoke to them in the Melanesian they had almost entirely forgotten, and comforted them in their distress – they were penned on the forecastle until there should be time to enlarge the quarters below where yesterday's hogs were kept, and the animals were both anxious and frightened. Yet those below were in a still more wretched state, and when they heard and smelt others of their kind overhead they set up a hideous din: this too was perfectly familiar to Emily and Sarah. They ran to Jemmy Ducks and told him the creatures were starved; they were calling out for food. For a great while Jemmy, who was much taken up with his chickens, put them off, saying that hogs was butcher's business; but at last they pestered him so that in a lull he went up to Weightman, one of the very few thoroughly disagreeable men aboard, and suggested that the hogs below sounded hungry. He received the abuse he expected – who did he think he was, telling the barky's butcher about hogs? Did Weightman tell Jemmy Ducks how to look after his fucking hens? Or turtles? Turtles, kiss my arse. In any case, the hogs below *had* been fed; had been offered every goddam thing the ship contained, from bread to tobacco, passing by a prime bucket of swill. And would they touch it? No, squire, they would not. And Weightman would be buggered if he offered them anything again: they should be salted and put up while there was still any flesh on their bones; and if Jemmy Ducks did not like it, why, he could do the other thing.

About this time repeated cries of 'By your leave, sir,' 'If you please, your honour' had driven Stephen off the gangway, then farther and farther aft along the quarterdeck to the taffrail itself, where, behind a great mound of netting full of yams, he found Mrs Oakes, gazing at the land, lost, enraptured; and her delight made her look more nearly beautiful than Stephen had ever seen her, and physically better in spite of the remainder of her black eye. 'Is not this capital, Doctor?' she cried. 'I always longed to travel and to make distant voyages, but I never did – except of course for . . .' She waved New South Wales aside and went on, 'And this is what I always hoped Abroad and the islands of the Great South Sea would be like. Dear me, such brilliance! How I wish I may always retain it in my mind's eye; and how passionately I yearn to go ashore! Do you think the Captain will give Oakes leave?'

'Forgive me, ma'am,' said Pullings. 'I am afraid we must clear the davits.'

Stephen and Clarissa were separated by a gang of seamen earnestly paying out an eight-inch hawser: she took refuge half-way down the companion-ladder, her head on a level with the deck, so that she might not miss anything that might be seen through the passing seamen's legs; and he was contemplating the ascent to the mizen-top when Padeen thrust his powerful form through the press. 'Gentleman dear,' he cried, his emotion drowning what little English he possessed, 'that black thief the butcher, Judas' own son, is tormenting the pigs, so he is, his soul to the Devil.'

'Pigs, is it?' said Stephen, but even before Padeen had finished speaking – it took him some time even in Irish, with his terrible stammer – pigs he knew it was. An eddy in the gentle breeze brought him a smell that he knew as well as even the little girls did or Padeen, and that was almost as much part of his childhood as it was of theirs, for he had been fostered with peasants in the ancient Irish way, and in their house particular swine walked in and out like Christians, as familiar as the dogs and upon the whole cleaner, more intelligent; while in one of his Catalan homes he and his godfather had reared up a wild boar from a striped, bounding piglet to a great dark beast of nineteen score with huge tusks that would come out of his beech-grove at a rocking-horse gallop to greet them, frightening all but the boldest of horses. For him too, although the pigs were eventually eaten and eaten with rejoicing, they had a particular sanctity, at least in part because they were individuals rather than members of a herd. He and Padeen walked forward along the waist, dodging between the baskets of turtles coming aboard on the one hand, the casks swinging in front from the other, and sacks of yams, sacks of yams. At the break of the forecastle Sarah, the braver and more vehement of the two girls, came running to meet them. 'Oh sir,' she cried to Stephen, 'listen to the hogs below. We keep asking Jemmy to tell the butcher they must be given taro, but he will not attend.'

Padeen began to speak, pointing down the fore hatchway: his stammer allowed him no more than 'Muc – muc – muc' but his pointing finger and the increasing noise from below were eloquent enough. Stephen climbed to the forecastle, where Martin was staring at the starboard pen. 'Good morning, sir,' he cried. 'Here's a pretty kettle of fish.'

'Good morning to you, colleague,' replied Stephen, 'and an elegant kettle it is.'

Over by the larboard pen, where he and some forecastle hands were reinforcing the barriers, Weightman was saying that he had fed the hell-damned swine – details of what they had been offered – swill that would have graced the cabin table – Lord Mayor's banquet – and they would not touch a morsel, drink a drop – and (lowering his voice) he would be buggered if he would try it again or listen to any prating poultryman – he was the barky's butcher, and he was not going to be taught his trade by any . . . His voice died away altogether.

'You don't want to starve pigs,' said Joe Plaice. 'They want feeding regular, or they go out of condition directly.'

'I call it a cruel shame,' observed Slade.

'Why don't you feed them poor unfortunate buggers below?' asked Davies.

Weightman answered these remarks and others, laying out his case with such increasing emphasis that his voice grew to resemble that of the swine at their shrillest and most passionate.

At this moment the frigate's executive officers were all either on shore or below. 'This is a matter for the Captain,' said Stephen privately. 'He has already put off.'

They walked back along the gangway, and sitting on the brace bitts, the most secluded place they could find, they watched the Captain's boat pull out through the many inshore canoes.

'Sarah and Emily tell me that just a little taro would do,' said Martin. 'They ran off, took a piece from that pile there, and the forecastle pigs flung themselves upon it. I pointed this out to Weightman, but he would have none of it. He is a disagreeable surly fellow at the best of times, and now he is beyond the reach of reason. Pig-headed, one might almost say.'

'Perhaps one might. How I long to be ashore.'

'Oh, so do I, Lord above! The moment we have finished our rounds, we may surely ask for leave with clear consciences. My nets, cases, paraphernalia, are all ready. What shall we find? The Polynesian owl, ha, ha, ha? But before I say anything else I must tell you two pieces of news that it was not fit to bring out on the forecastle. The one will rejoice your heart; the other I fear will sadden it. First, among the presents sent by the chief this morning were two rails of a kind unknown to the learned world, two *different* rails, and a great purple coot.'

'Never a gallinule, for all love?'

'No. Far larger and of a far richer purple. Without mentioning it to anyone, there being such abundance, I appropriated them, as objects more fit for philosophic examination than the gunroom table.'

'Very right and proper. What a treat in store! But you spoke of bad news.'

'Yes, alas. Last night I was turning over our collections, renewing the pepper and camphor, and on reaching the lories I went to bed, leaving the skins on the locker. This morning all the lories with red feathers had been plucked bald; and those of the cockatoos that had scarlet on their tails were mutilated.'

'The wicked false lecherous dogs know they can get anything on this island with red feathers: and there is only one thing they want. Pox and eternal damnation on the whole vile crew.'

Jack came aboard on the larboard side – this was no time for the slightest ceremony – and he was at once seized by Pullings and Adams with a host of questions: seeing that he could not be free for some time Stephen hurried below to see the rails and the coot. They were fascinating objects in their mere outward form, but they also promised osteological peculiarities and Stephen said 'It is our clear duty to skin them at once, and then Padeen will gently seethe the flesh from their bones in the sick-berth cauldron: the liquid will no doubt strengthen the invalids' soup and we shall have the skeletons entire. Carry them into your cabin – it would be more discreet – and I shall fetch the instruments.'

He was down in the dim sick-berth, rattling among saws, forceps and retractors, and he had just called 'Mr Reade there: I can hear you perfectly well from here, and if you persist in trying to get up I shall desire the Captain to have you whipped,' when Oakes appeared.

'There you are, Doctor,' he cried. 'They told me I might find you here. May I beg you to do me a kindness, sir?'

'Pray name it, Mr Oakes.'

'If you go ashore, please would you take my wife with you? She is wild to set foot on a South Sea island, and I cannot have leave with the ship to sail so soon and so much still to be done.'

'Very well, Mr Oakes,' said Stephen with a smile as cordial as he could make it. 'I should be happy to wait on Mrs Oakes in forty minutes time.'

'Oh thank you, sir. She will be so very grateful . . .'

Stephen followed him, but more slowly, up the ladders. 'Mr Martin,' he said, 'here are scalpels for two. If you will take the nearer rail, I will tackle the coot. I have just agreed that we shall take Mrs Oakes ashore. You have no objection?'

Martin's expression changed. 'I am so sorry,' he said after

156

a very slight pause, 'but I forgot to tell you I was engaged to Doctor – to the surgeon of the whaler.'

The Captain's gig ran hissing up the coral sand; bow-oar leaped out, placed the gangboard, and two seamen, one beaming, one severe, handed Mrs Oakes ashore; she thanked them prettily. Stephen followed: they passed him his fowling-piece, powder-flask, game-bag; Plaice, a very old friend, begged him to take care of the lions and tigers and them nasty old wipers, and the gig instantly put off again.

'Should you like to look at the market?' he asked.

'Oh, if you please,' cried Mrs Oakes. 'I am excessively fond of markets.'

They walked up and down in the sunshine, the object of lively but amiable curiosity, much less invasive than he had expected. Seeing that he was with a woman, even his talkative girl of yesterday said no more than 'Ho aia-owa,' with a discreet but knowing smile, and a wave of her hand; and importunate children were restrained.

Wainwright and the South-Seas speaking Surprises showed them the wonders Annamooka had to offer and even those who were not or who were no longer ardent supporters of Clarissa were pleased that she should behold their fluency and the extent of their knowledge.

Twice at least they made the tour, pausing sometimes to look at the exquisite workmanship of the canoes hauled up for caulking, of the nets, the matting of the sails, Clarissa as eager as a child to see and understand, delighted with everything. But while she was watching a man inlay mother-of-pearl eyes on the blade of his steering-paddle she caught Stephen's wistful eye following a pair of doves – ptilopus? – and after a decent pause she said 'But come, let us go a-botanizing. I am sure this island must have some wonderfully curious plants.'

'Should you not like to look at the newly-arrived fishes at the other end of the strand?' asked Stephen; yet although Clarissa could be imperceptive and even stupid on occasion there were times when no amount of civil disguise could hide a man's real desires from her; and in this case the disguise called for no great penetration. 'Let us take the broad path,' she said. 'It seems to lead to well you can hardly call it a village but to most of the houses, and I believe it wanders off into – could you call it a jungle?'

'I am afraid not. It is at the best but open brushwood until the distant reed-beds before the forest: but you are to observe that in true jungle, in the rainy season, there is no seeing a living creature at all. You may hear birds, you may see the tail-end of a serpent disappear, you may sense the vast looming form of the buffalo, but you may come home, if indeed you are not lost entirely, bleeding from the thorn of the creeping rattan, devoured by leeches, and empty-handed, with no acquisition of knowledge. This is much better.'

They walked along, following the stream and passing three or four wide-spaced houses – little more than palm-thatched roofs on poles, with a raised floor – all empty, their people being at the market: other houses could be seen no great way off, half hidden by palms or paper-mulberry-trees; but there was little sense of village. And since the breeze was blowing off the land they soon left the noise of the throng behind and walked in a silence barely altered by the rhythmic thunder of surf on the outer reef. When they had skirted three remarkably neat fields of taro and sugar-cane a little flock of birds flew up. Stephen's gun was at his shoulder in one smooth movement; he fixed on his bird and brought it down. 'A nondescript parrot,' he observed with satisfaction, putting it into his bag.

The shot brought out an elderly person from the last house in sight, quite close to the lane: she called in a hoarse old friendly voice and hobbled down to meet them, baring her withered bosom as she came. She invited them in with eloquent gestures and they walked across a smooth, bright green lawn to the grateful shade of the house, whose level floor was covered with thick layers of matting, and this, in places, with strips of tapa. On these they all sat down, uttering amiable, mutually incomprehensible words, and the old lady gave them each a small dried fish with a most significant look, emphatically naming it Pootoo-pootoo. Clarissa offered her a blue glass-headed pin, with which she seemed enchanted, and so they took their leave, turning to wave from time to time until the house was out of sight.

Now the rising path, such as it was, still following the quite copious stream, led through young plantations of mulberries and plantain, and the sun, nearing the zenith, beat down with increasing strength. 'Do not you find the solid earth wonderfully hard and unyielding after shipboard?' asked Clarissa, after a silence, the first since they had left the ship.

'It is always the same,' said Stephen. 'Dublin's streets might be made of plate-armour, every time I walk about them after having been afloat for a while. Furthermore, in a great city I feel obliged to wear leather shoes or even God help me boots; and with their unaccustomed weight after the packthread slippers I ordinarily wear aboard and the unforgiving nature of the pavement I am quite knocked up by noon; I grow fractious and . . .' At some ten yards distance on the top of an infant sandalwood-tree he saw a beetle, a large beetle, one of the lucani, begin the process of opening its wing-covers and unfolding its wings. In a moment it would be in the air. Stephen was not very deeply moved by beetles, least of all by the lucani, but his friend Sir Joseph Blaine was devoted to them – he was prouder of being president of the Entomological Society than of being the head of naval intelligence – and Stephen was much attached to him. He put down his fowling-piece and ran with twinkling feet for the sandalwood-tree. He was almost within reach when the animal took off in its stately flight, its long body almost vertical. But the breeze was blowing down the slope from the forest to the sea: the beetle could not gain height. It sailed on, making for the trees, at between six and eight feet from the ground, and by running with all his might Stephen could just keep up; but he could not have run another fifty yards when the inexpert creature blundered into an outstretched branch and fell to the ground.

Returning with his capture, Stephen found Clarissa in the shade of a breadfruit tree, bathing her feet in the stream. 'I have found something even better,' she called, pointing up; and there indeed, where the tree forked into four main branches, there was an improbable cascade of orchids, three different kinds of orchids, orange-tawny, white with golden throats, flamingo-red. 'That is what I mean by foreign travel,' she said with great complacency. 'They may keep their lions and tigers.' Having gazed about her for some time she said 'How happy I am.' Then, 'Can the breadfruit be eaten?'

'I believe it has to be dressed,' said Stephen. 'But when properly cooked, I am told, it will serve either as a vegetable or as a pudding. Do you think we might imitate the foremast hands and dine at noon?'

'That would make me even happier. There has been a wolf devouring my vitals this last half hour. Besides, I always dine at noon. Oakes is only a midshipman, you know.'

'So much the better. It is noon now: the sun is directly overhead and even this spreading umbrella of a tree, God bless it, only just affords us shade. Let us see what Killick has allowed us.' He opened the other side of the game-bag, took out a bottle of wine and two silver tumblers, roast pork sandwiches wrapped in napkins, two pieces of cold plum-duff, and fruit. In spite of the heat they were both sharp-set; they ate fast and drank their sherry mingled with the brook. There was little conversation until the fruit, but that little was most companionable. With the last banana-skin floating down the stream, the last of the wine poured and drunk, Clarissa mastered a yawn and said 'With the pleasure and excitement I am quite absurdly sleepy. Will you forgive me if I lie in the even deeper shade?'

'Do, by all means, my dear,' said Stephen. 'I shall go botanizing along the stream as far as the reed-beds, just before those tall trees begin. Here is my fowling-piece: do you understand how to use it?'

She stared at him as though he were making a joke that should be very strongly resented – Medea came to his mind again – then looking down she said 'Oh, yes.'

'The right barrel is charged with powder but no shot: the left has both. If you feel the least uneasiness fire with the foremost trigger and I shall come directly. But it is always possible that any approaching footsteps may be those of Mr

Martin and the surgeon of the whaling ship. They may join us.'

'I doubt it,' said Mrs Oakes.

Stephen Maturin lay along the branch of a tree that gave him a view over the reeds and into the little series of mud-fringed pools beyond. 'There is such a thing as being fool-large,' he said as a procession of coots, purple and violet, of stilts belonging to an unknown species with brown gorgets, and of other singular waders passed by within fifteen yards, going from the left to the right and then back again, the larger birds walking stately, the little things like ringed plovers darting among their legs, 'and there is also such a thing as being too complaisant by half. That woman did not even thank me for the gun.' He knew that in the last moments of their conversation the current had changed: he had no doubt said something tactless. He could not tell what it was, just as she, being no natural philosopher, could not tell what he was giving up – hours, irreplaceable hours of running about virgin country, never to be seen again, filled with unknown forms of life. Not that the analogy was sound, he reflected, climbing down.

He did not find her mood much improved when he came back to the breadfruit tree, carrying a respectable collection of botanical specimens, but never a bird, of course, without a gun. Yes, she had slept very well, thank you, sir, quite undisturbed; and she hoped the Doctor had found all he had hoped for. He had no sense of hostility or offence on her side but rather the impression that before and even during their meal she had reached too high a pitch of spirits and that now she was suffering from the usual reaction, coupled with physical fatigue: he also perceived that one of her heels was sadly blistered. Clearly it would not be possible to drag her as far as the forest. By way of restoring something of the earlier tone he told her about the little girls' triumph: how Captain Aubrey had brought the butcher up with a round turn, had ordered him to mingle a little taro with the hogs' swill and to sprinkle some on to their grain, how they had hurled themselves upon both with cries of swinish joy, and how the category of the animals themselves had been changed: they were now to be considered lambs, and therefore under the rule of Jemmy Ducks.

'Sarah and Emily were delighted,' he said, 'yet discreet beyond their years, very careful not to exult over the butcher or to wound his feelings in any way.'

'Yes, they are dear little things,' said Clarissa, 'and I love them much, although they have taken against me to quite a wounding degree.' An incautious mixed band of parrots passed within shot: Stephen chose two, killed them cleanly and brought them back. When she had admired their plumage she went on 'I do so dislike being disliked. That reminds me of poor little Mr Reade. How does he do?'

'He is so well and active that I am afraid he will get up too soon. I have left orders with Padeen that he is to be lashed into his cot, if he grow unruly.'

'I am so glad. We were such good friends at one time. Can he have any career in the Navy? I do hope so – he thinks the world of the service.'

'Oh, I have little doubt of it. Honourable wound, excellent connexions, glowing report from his captain: if he is not killed first he will die an admiral.'

'What about the other officers?'

'Captain Pullings will almost certainly be made post when we get home.'

'Will West and Davidge be reinstated, do you suppose?'

'As for that, I am no judge; but I doubt it. The beach is littered with failed sea-officers; many of them, I am sure, courageous and capable seamen.'

'Captain Aubrey was reinstated.'

'Captain Aubrey, apart from his martial virtues, is a wealthy man, with high-placed friends and an unshakable seat in Parliament.'

Clarissa considered this for a while and then with quite another look and in quite another tone she said 'How pleasant it is to be sitting in the shade, just not too hot, with those glorious flowers overhead, next to a man who does not ply one with questions or with – or with assiduities. *You* will not think I am fishing when I ask does my eye still show much? I have no decent looking-glass aboard, so I cannot tell.'

'It can no longer be called a black eye,' said Stephen.

Clarissa felt the place gently and went on 'I do not give a straw for men qua men, but I still like to look agreeable or at least passable: as I said before I do loathe being disliked, and ugliness and dislike seem to go together . . . Someone once gave me a confused account of the little girls' origin – they are not Aborigines, I collect?'

'Not at all, at all. They are Melanesians from Sweeting's Island, a great way off, the last survivors of a community destroyed by the smallpox. We brought them away because it seemed improbable they should live on by themselves.'

'What is to happen to them?'

'I cannot tell. An orphanage in Sydney could not be borne, and my present plan is to carry them to London, where my friend Mrs Broad keeps a warm comfortable tavern in the Liberties of the Savoy. I have a room there all the year round. She is a kindly woman; she has agreeable young nieces and cousins about the house, and I mean Sarah and Emily to live with her until I can pitch upon some better solution.'

Clarissa hesitated and made two false starts before she said 'I wish your Mrs Broad may keep them safe at least until they know what they are about – may keep them from being misused. Indeed I wish they may not have been misused already, plain little creatures though they are.'

'They are very young, you know.'

'I was younger still.' A fruit-pigeon landed on the other bank of the stream and drank a long draught. 'As a medical man you must have come across incestuous families?'

'Often and often.'

'Though perhaps incest is too strong a word as far as I am concerned: my guardian was only some remote connexion. I went to him when I was about the size of Emily. He lived in quite a large house with a park and a lake, very secluded: pleasant enough. I believe there had been deer in the park in his father's time, but he lived almost entirely indoors, in his library most of the time, and he took no notice of poachers: he had no notion of sporting. He was a shy, kind, nervous man, tall and thin; I used to think him very old, but he cannot have been, since his niece Frances, his older sister's daughter, was only a little older than I was myself. The servants really were old, however: they had been there in his parents' days. He was a learned man, and kind, and a very good and patient teacher; I was really fond of him, in spite of . . . I did not much care for Frances, though since we had no other companions we played together and ran about in the garden and the park. We were jealous of one another, jealous for his regard, and that did wonders for our lessons: my guardian – I called him Cousin Edward – for Latin and English reading and writing and a string of unfortunate French governesses for the rest. They never stayed, saying the place was too remote; and it is true that the lanes were so narrow and deep that there was no getting the carriage as far as the church in winter except when there was a strong frost. Yet we were not so very isolated after all. The tradesmen came, which was always an event; and people used to call on Aunt Cheyney, the old lady who lived upstairs, but never left her room for fear of taking cold. Mrs Bellingham drove over from Bishop's Thornton almost every week in summer, and when the roads were too dirty she would ride across, taking the high country. She and Aunt Cheyney taught us how to come into a room properly and go out closing the door behind us, and to sit up and be quiet and make our curtsy. There were some others, too, though my guardian disliked visits extremely. I said *in spite of* just now and I wonder how I can explain it without being gross. We had various games: Cousin Edward played chess and backgammon with us, and battledore and shuttlecock in the big hall; and then there was what we called the games in the dark, with lights put out, curtains drawn, a kind of hide and seek; and sometimes he would catch the one, sometimes the other, and pretend to eat us while we screamed. Yet after a while it took a different turn. He was always very gentle; he hardly ever hurt me; and he seemed to think that though our game was private it was of no great importance.

Frances and I never spoke about it to one another. But when we went to school in Winchester – do you know Winchester?' The question made the strangest contrast with her toneless monologue.

'Only by repute. I know little of England.'

'It was a convent of French Dominicans, and many of the girls were émigrés' daughters. But when we were there and we heard the whispering and giggling and wild suppositions about marriage, childbirth, and what went before it, we looked at one another with perfect understanding though we neither of us ever mentioned it in words. It was there that I began to have some notion of what had happened. Though I still could not make out why there was so much fuss. The first part of *foeda est in coitu et brevis voluptas* I could understand perfectly well, but not the second. I could not associate it with the least degree of pleasure, however short: and so a great deal that I read and heard – romantic attachments, swimming the Hellespont and so on – remained incomprehensible, in so far as they were for that end, the right true end. So we concealed our knowledge of these matters; and we soon learned to control our learning too. We knew far more Latin than the other girls. That was one of the reasons for our unpopularity: my violence was another.

'When we came back from school, for eventually the nuns would not keep me any longer and I cannot blame them, we found everything changed. Aunt Cheyney had died; many of the servants had been turned away; nobody called any more. Only the library and the lessons were the same; and the game in the dark. But then after a while Mr Southam joined in: he was the last remaining visitor, an officer in the army, a big, coarse, arrogant man with some very nasty ways. Cousin Edward said we were to be particularly kind to him. We hid as hard as ever we could when he was there: but that was mostly because of his smell and general unpleasantness – the thing itself was of no consequence.

'And so life went on, very slowly, and it seemed to be winter and chilblains most of the time: only the library was heated. Everything grew poorer and poorer. The silver disappeared. Gypsies camped in the park on the far side of the lake, where the wall had fallen down; and the garden was head-high with weeds. All the servants left except for two very old women who could get no other work and who preferred staying to the poorhouse. The tradesmen stopped calling. The coach had been laid up long since, and a little while before Frances was sent away into Yorkshire we dwindled from a gig to an ass-cart; and in this, when the roads were passable, Cousin Edward went to Alton with a basket. In winter, although he hated riding, he took the pony. I never saw Frances again, by the way, nor heard what became of her. Looking back now, I suppose they got her in child, and either bearing or getting rid of it killed her.' An orchid flower fell in her lap: she looked at it, turning it this way and that, and presently she carried on with her oddly jerking narrative, not unlike inward speech with its own references and allusions. 'It was the pony indeed that was the death of him. Some farm labourers found him thrown down on the road and brought him back on a hurdle. Mrs Bellingham of Bishop's Thornton saw him properly buried; there was a fair congregation and they said my friends would no doubt come for me. The only people who came were Mr Southam and some lawyer's men who went all over the house writing everything down. He told me I was penniless; no provision had been made for me, but he would find me work in St James's. Do you know St James's?' Once again her voice changed entirely to a waking tone.

'Certainly I know it,' said Stephen. 'Do I not stay at Black's every time I am in London?'

'So you are a member of Black's?'

Stephen bowed.

'I used to work on the other side of the road, or rather beyond the other side of the road, behind Button's. Yes, at Mother Abbott's. But I always had a kindness for Black's because it was a member that begged me off when I was to be hanged. Did you ever go to Mother Abbott's?'

'I have sometimes walked across and drunk tea with herself while my friends went upstairs.'

'Then you know the parlour on the right. That was where I worked, keeping the accounts: one of the few things the nuns taught me, apart from French, was keeping accounts neatly and accurately: there or in one of the little rooms beyond, keeping men company while they waited for their girl. Or sometimes they came in just to talk, being lonely. Mother Abbott was very kind to me. She taught me how to dress and undress and she let me have clothes on credit; but she never made me do anything I did not choose to do, and it was not until much later that I *obliged* as they say, when we were short-handed and the girls were very busy.'

'Forgive me,' said Stephen, leaning forward, seizing a small orthopterous insect and putting it into a collecting-box.

'It is an odd thing, living in a brothel,' said Clarissa, 'and it has a certain likeness to being at sea: you live a particular life, with your own community, but it is not the life of the world in general and you tend to lose touch with the world in general's ideas and language – all sorts of things like that, so that when you go out you are as much a stranger as a sailor is on shore. Not that I had much notion of the world in general anyhow, the ordinary normal adult world, never having really seen it. I tried to make it out by novels and plays, but that was not much use: they all went on to such an extent about physical love, as though everything revolved about it, whereas for me it was not much more important than blowing my nose – chastity or unchastity neither here nor there – absurd to make fidelity a matter of private parts: grotesque. I took no pleasure in it, except in giving a little when I happened to like the man – I had some agreeable clients – or felt sorry for him. It was sometimes from them that I tried to find out what the world in general really thought. Obviously on the face of it Mother Abbott's customers belonged to the less rigid side, but they reflected the rest and I did learn a certain amount from them. There was one lonely man who used to come and sit with me for hours and tell me about his greyhounds: he was part of a ménage à trois; his wife and mistress were great friends; he had children by both; and the mistress, who was a widow, had children of her own. And they all lived together in one house, a vast great house in Piccadilly. Yet he and they and everyone about him were received everywhere, prodigiously respected. So where is the truth of all this outcry against adultery? Is it all hypocritical? I am still puzzled. It is true that he was very grand when he had his clothes on: the blue ribbon is the Garter, is it not? So perhaps . . .'

They both raised their heads at the sound of a shot. 'That will be Martin and Dr Falconer,' said Stephen.

'Oh dear,' said Clarissa. 'I hope they do not come this way. I have so loved talking to you that it would be a pity to spoil it with how-d'ye-do's. But Lord how I have burdened you with my confidences! I have nearly talked the sun down. Perhaps we should be going back to the ship.'

'If you will give me your shoes, I will put them into my bag. You cannot wear them with that blister.'

As they walked down towards the sea, talking in a desultory way of the brothel's inhabitants, of their customs and the customers' sometimes very curious, occasionally touching ways, he said, after a while, 'Did you ever come across two men who were often there together, the one called Ledward, and the other Wray?'

'Oh yes: I had their names in my books many a time. But that was more on the boys' side: the girls were only called in when there was something quite special – chains and leather, you know. Surely, surely they were not friends of yours?'

'No, ma'am.'

'Yet surprisingly enough they did know some quite agreeable people. I remember one very grand person who used to join in their more curious parties. He had the blue ribbon too. But he never acknowledged them in public. Twice I saw them pass one another in St James's Street and twice at Ranelagh with not so much as a nod on his part, and they never even moved their hats, although he was a duke.'

'Did he have a limp, at all?'

'A slight one. He wore a boot to disguise it. Dear me, how hoarse I am – I have absolutely talked myself hoarse. I have not talked like this to anyone, ever. I wish I may not have been indiscreet as well as intolerably boring. You are such a dear to have listened to me; but I am afraid I have ruined your day.'

Chapter Seven

For many years Stephen Maturin, as an intelligence agent chiefly concerned with naval affairs, had been harassed, worried and deeply distressed by the activities of highly-placed, well-informed men, admirers of Napoleon, who from inside the English administration sent information to France. Their messages usually had to do with the movement of ships, and they had caused the loss of several men-of-war, the failure of attacks whose success depended on surprise, the interception of convoys with the capture of sometimes half the merchantmen, and (which wounded Stephen and his chief Sir Joseph Blaine even more intimately) the taking of British agents in all the unfortunate countries forming part of Buonaparte's shoddy empire.

With the help of a man belonging to one of the French intelligence-services, sick of his trade and fearing betrayal, Stephen and Sir Joseph had discovered the identity of two of these traitors: Andrew Wray, the acting Second Secretary of the Admiralty, and his friend Ledward, an important Treasury official; but the arrest was bungled; the pursuit lacked zeal; and they both escaped to France. Clearly they were protected by someone more highly placed by far, someone of their own way of thinking. Stephen had dealt with Ledward and Wray when the creatures went to Pulo Prabang, part of a mission designed to bring about the alliance between the Sultan and France, whilst Stephen was the political adviser to a mission with the contrary intent. He had indeed dissected them. Yet their protector, or possibly protectors, had still not been found, and after a discreet pause the flow of information had begun again, less ample, less purely naval, equally dangerous.

He squared to his writing-desk in the great cabin, the only

place where he could conveniently spread out his copy, his code-books and his dispatches. 'My dear Joseph,' he wrote in their first, private code, the code each knew by heart, 'how I wish, O how I wish, that this, the first of writing, may reach you by the whaler *Daisy* bound for Sydney, and then by the most expeditious means (India and then overland?) the Governor has at his disposal. I believe the million-to-one chance has served us. Pray think of a duke, well at Court, with the Garter though lame of a leg and with curious ways . . . Come in.'

'Which it's all hands, sir, if you please,' said Killick.

'Compliments to the Captain and beg to be excused,' said Stephen, darting a reptilian look at him.

All hands. Of course, that was the pipe he had heard some minutes before. '. . . with curious ways. Before he was a duke, before he had become attached to the ministry, before he was a Privy Councillor and before he had the Garter, I saw him in Holland . . . Come in.'

It was the little girls, smiling and bobbing, dressed in new frocks with blue bows on their sleeves. 'You said you would like to see us when we were ready,' said Sarah.

'And very fine you are too,' said Stephen. 'Turn round, will you?' They slowly revolved, holding their arms well away from their stiff skirts. 'The elegant frocks of the world, so they are. But Emily, my dear, what is that in your cheek?'

'Nothing,' said Emily, beginning to grizzle.

'Put it out, put it out: would you shame us all by chewing tobacco before the King of the Friendly Islands himself?' He held out a waste-paper basket and slowly, unwillingly, Emily let drop her quid. 'There, there,' he said, kissing them, 'blow your nose and run along. You must not keep Mr Martin waiting: there is not a moment to be lost.'

'You will come along, sir, won't – will not – you, if ever you can?' asked Sarah.

'. . . I saw him in Holland House,' wrote Stephen; and leaning back for a fresh vision of the scene he heard Jack, in another world, address the crowded deck; to starboard the liberty men, who had somehow, after a day of strenuous toil, found time and energy to put on their shore-going clothes of brass-buttoned light-blue jackets, white duck trousers, embroidered shirts, broad-brimmed ribboned hats, neat little shoes with bows; to larboard those now jaded souls who had had their fun the night before and a cruel hard day on top of it. Those who were to go ashore – and already the fires were burning for the feast – could hardly wait for their Captain to be done: they jigged up and down as they stood, as they jigged so the stolen nails, bolts, pieces of old iron for trading, jangled in their places of concealment. 'I repeat, shipmates,' he said loud and clear, 'we weigh with the first of the ebb. All hands are to repair to the boats the moment the second rocket goes up; they will have five minutes from the first in which to take their leave. And there are to be no women aboard the ship. No women at all, d'ye hear me there?'

'What about Mrs Oakes?' called a half-drunk voice from the sullen larboard.

'Take that man's name, Mr West,' said Jack, and those who had been close to the butcher moved away from him with expressionless faces, leaving him isolated. 'Gig's crew away,' called Jack: a few moments later he went down the side in some state and Stephen returned to his letter.

'I saw him in Holland House during the peace, when he had just come back from the Paris embassy. As the door opened Lady Holland was saying in that loud metallic voice of hers "How I worship that Napoleon". Some people looked embarrassed but for a moment he stood there in the shadow of the doorway with his hands clasped and his face shining as though he had been granted the beatific vision; then he composed himself and walked in with the ordinary commonplace remarks. Lady Holland ran to meet him: "What news from Paris? Tell us all about your dinner with the divine First Consul."

'Now this man shared in Ledward's and Wray's dirtiest parties, but although he had been to school with Ledward he never acknowledged him in public; nor of course Wray. But the point that carried total conviction with me was that their code for him was Pillywinks, and the name we found so often but could not interpret in Wray's criminally negligent papers.

'To carry the same conviction to your mind, let me tell you about my source: she is the lady who blew Mr Caley's head off with a double-barrelled gun some years ago; and as you will recall (which I did not at the time) our fellow-member Harry Essex had her sentence commuted to transportation. It was therefore in New South Wales that she joined our company.'

There followed a succinct account of their voyage, its interruption and its present aims: a more detailed account of his walk with Clarissa in which he could not refrain from the briefest notice of Sir Joseph's beetles; and then as detailed an account as he could remember of their conversation about Ledward, Wray and the lame man, both at the first mention of their names and during the walk down to the strand, a long walk, and made longer by the blister. The exact sequence was not always easy, and to fix it he sometimes gazed out of the window. The frigate lay stern-on to the shore, a shore lined with fires and as brilliant as could be: no moon to interfere: leaping flames above an incandescent heart, white sand, dark green looming behind, a blue-black sky; the whaler clearly lit upon his right; and all along the line straight young brown bodies dancing to the sound of rhythmic song and drums. But dancing in a series of exact, perfect evolutions that would have put the Brigade of Guards to shame. Advance, retreat and twirl; twirl, retreat, advance; a half turn and so back again, the close ranks and files interchanging, all with a perfect simultaneity of pace and waving arms. In the middle, beyond the fire, a temporary roof of palm fronds had been set up, and here by the chiefs' side sat Jack: then other notables: to their right Clarissa and her husband, then Wainwright and Dr Falconer, Reade, Martin and the little girls, now hung with wreaths of flowers, staring with amazement and delight. They were all slowly, absently sipping kava in coconut cups from the ancestral bowl in front of the chief.

Back to his coding, the fires dazzling in his eyes, and he struck out several lines in which the sequence was mistaken. To convey the perfectly convincing, ingenuous, nature of her words was, he feared, beyond his powers; but certainly their exact, inconsequential train might do something towards it.

When next he looked up he realized that for some time he had been hearing neither song nor drums but a confused din not unlike the roar of a bull-fight: it was in fact a boxing-match. He had heard of the sport for ever, but curiously enough he had never seen a formal contest – nothing more than scuffles among the boys in earlier commissions or dockside brawls. Yet this appeared to be a singular battle. He took up his small spyglass, never far from hand, and his first astonished impression was confirmed. There were two fine upstanding young women setting about one another with bare fists. Violent, wholehearted blows, and judging from the cries of the onlookers, well given and well received. Clarissa was laughing; the little girls hardly knew how they liked it; some of the seamen and all of the islanders backed one girl or the other with the greatest zeal. Yet at the very climax, and for no reason that Stephen could see, when neither was giving an inch, the old chief beat the kava-bowl, an attendant blew on a conch, the chief's sister intervened, the two young women fell back and walked off, one rubbing her cheek, the other her bosom: there was a cry of disappointment from the seamen who had enjoyed it, but almost immediately afterwards, from one end of the line to the other, came baked hogs, baked dogs, fishes and fowls wrapped in leaves, yams, plantains, breadfruit.

Stephen's watch uttered its tiny silver chime, and looking at the pile of sheets he had so inconsiderately filled he said 'Holy Mary, Mother of God, I shall never get all this recoded in time: and already my poor boiled eyes are dropping out of my head.' He put on his green shade, wiped away his tears, changed his spectacles and opened the new code-book.

He did not look up again until a great howl plucked him from his task, his mechanical work. There was Awkward Davies flat on his face with a burly islander sitting on him, pinning him down with an arm-breaking hold. Davies presumably gave some sign, uttered some word, for the islander got off, helped him up, and led him back to his friends in the kindest way.

Again Stephen's watch struck and while it was still striking the first rocket soared up. 'Oooh,' cried all the people, and 'Aah!' followed by cheers as it burst.

The second rocket, not a quarter of a page later, was followed by nautical cries and then by the arrival of the boats. Some few hands had contrived to get drunk on the chief's kava, but most came aboard very quietly, welcomed in a low voice by the harbour-watch.

When his sheep had been counted Jack looked into the cabin. 'Am I interrupting you?' he asked from the doorway.

'Never in life, my dear. I am only copying: let me finish my group and I am with you.' Many years before this Jack, no fool at sea, had perceived that Stephen was more than a ship's surgeon, more even than a man whose political advice would be sought by a captain where relations with foreigners were concerned; and gradually his close connexion with intelligence had become so evident that there was nothing strange about his coding messages, sometimes of surprising length.

The group finished, Stephen put a small lead weight upon the place and said 'I trust you had an agreeable evening.'

'Very agreeable indeed, thank you. The chief did the thing handsomely, uncommon handsomely: and then nobody ran, there were no harsh words, the only fighting was in play, and we ate like aldermen – such turtle, Stephen! But I am afraid Bonden and Davies will need your attention in the morning; and Emily was sick.'

'What happened to them?'

'Bonden boxed with an islander, and his nose is knocked sideways: Davies was cruelly wrenched and twisted in wrestling; and somebody told Emily how the kava she had drunk was made.'

'Then she is now wiser than I am.'

'Why, they sit round an enormous pot, chewing kava-root, and when it is chewed enough they spit it in, going on until there are gallons of it; and then they let it ferment. The notion made her vomit; though it is true she had already eaten an extraordinary amount of sugar-cane, and was already looking green about the gills.'

'She may survive.'

'I am just going to write Sophie something of a letter before turning in. Have you any message?'

'Love, of course. I had hoped to write to Diana, but I doubt I shall have time for anything more than the briefest note.'

'Then I shall not keep you a moment longer,' said Jack, moving over to a table at the far end of the broad cabin. Their pens scratched away bell after muffled bell: at one point Stephen heard Jack tiptoe off to his sleeping cabin; and slowly the first code turned into the perhaps impenetrable second.

At last, when his eyes could not bear the darting from one page to another any more, he took off his spectacles, covered his eyes with his hands and pressed hard for several minutes. While he was in this state of coruscating darkness he heard the bosun's pipe and his fine determined voice 'All hands unmoor ship. All hands, there. Tumble up, tumble up, you dormice,' and when he took his hands away he saw the first hint of coming day on the shore.

With a fresh urgency he recoded the words. 'How it can be accomplished I do not know, but I shall try to get her back to England with another copy of this: may I rely upon you to protect her? Little do I know of the law, but although she is now married to a naval officer I fear she may be molested as having returned before her time. She has already given us this piece of information, one of the most valuable that has ever come into our hands; she is potentially a valuable source of more, if handled with extreme discretion; and in any event I have a great kindness for her. Immunity would be politically sound; privately obliging. Lastly, my dear J, may I beg you to send the enclosed scribble down to my wife?'

All this last hour there had been confused roaring and bawling, beyond the reach of his concentrated attention. Now as he ranged his papers the cry of 'Heave and awash' came from forward: the cabin was already full of light. Mr Adams knocked at the door: 'Captain's compliments, sir, and if you have anything for Sydney, we should wrap it now. I have his own dispatch still open, and as soon as Mr Wainwright has seen us through the channel he will take it back to the *Daisy*.'

'Will you clap on to that God-damn cat-fall, there? Are you

asleep?' asked Captain Aubrey, very strong and clear, very far from pleased.

Dr Maturin and Mr Adams looked at one another, startled: they had both of them heard many more orders than were usual in unmooring ship, more, louder and angrier, but none so severe as this; and in a low tone Stephen, waving his last sheet, said 'Let us allow the ink to dry, and I am with you.'

They wrapped, sealed, taped, tied and sealed again: Oakes came below to ask if they were ready. 'In four minutes,' they said; and when they came on deck they found Captain Aubrey looking at his watch, Mr Wainwright poised by the gangway and his boat's crew looking anxiously up. Hurried farewells and the whaleboat shoved off: the *Surprise* filled her fore-topsail, and holding her breath she weathered the outermost spur of the reef.

Stephen stood right aft, watching Annamooka diminish astern, and then, quite small now, swing steadily round until it was abreast as the *Surprise* crossed that clearly-marked line in the sea, that sudden change from aquamarine to royal blue, which marked the limit of the local tides and breezes on the one hand and the steady wind from the east-south-east on the other; the long even turn, in which the ship was accompanied by three moulting man-of-war birds, brought the wind upon the beam, and Captain Aubrey, having increased sail steadily until she was under topgallants, gave the course north-north-east a half east and went below, leaving a nervous silence behind him.

His breakfast was ready, but although two places were laid his usual companion was not there. 'Which he is still in the sick-berth,' said Killick, 'setting Davies and Bonden to rights. I could fetch him in a moment.' Jack shook his head and poured himself a cup of coffee. 'Infernal lubbers,' he muttered to himself.

In point of fact Stephen was rolling pills in the dispensary and listening with half an ear to Martin's reasons for having deserted him in favour of Falconer. They were untrue; and Martin, feeling that they did not persuade, plunged deep into circumstantial detail, which diminished him in Stephen's opinion. He was not much opposed to falsehood in itself nor offended by its skilful use; but one of Martin's most amiable characteristics had been an ingenuous candour.

In the sick-berth itself, where Bonden and Davies were lying in as much comfort as could be expected, medical art having done what little it could, visitors had come below to tell them how lucky they were to have escaped the wrath on deck. 'I never seen him so wexed since he came back to the barky off the Dry Tortugas and found Mr Babbington had let her get a foul hawse,' said Plaice.

'A round turn and an elbow it was,' said Bonden in the voice of one with a very heavy cold or a nose newly broken, 'an horrible sight. He choked poor Mr Babbington off till he nearly cried, quite pitiful to see.'

'But that was nothing to this,' said Archer. 'That was ignorance and folly, the fruit of youth as the Bible says. This was ill-will between the oakapples and the rest, and it very nearly made us miss our tide. I shouldn't wonder if he flogged the whole ship's company, come Monday, with bosun touching up his mate.'

'My conscience is quite clear, any gate,' said Williams.

'That will be a great comfort to you when you get a bloody shirt on Monday, mate.'

'He had the smiting-line set up seven times before he was satisfied: swore something cruel.'

'Smiting-line, ha, ha. You'll grow acquainted with a smiting-line come Monday,' said Awkward Davies with his rare grating laugh.

Martin, abandoning justification as unprofitable and feeling shy of telling Maturin about his expedition with Dr Falconer, turned to the frightful din of the early morning, oaths such as he had never heard, objurgations. 'You were no doubt asleep with balls of wax in your ears,' he said, 'otherwise you could not have failed to hear the thunder of the captains and the shouting. It appears that the manoeuvres were so ill-executed that Captain Aubrey became uneasy for his tide – that in another five minutes the land-breeze would have headed us. I wonder that an officer of his experience . . .'

'Be so good as to pass me the quicksilver. We shall be needing it soon, no doubt. You know as well as I do that it is the one true specific for the pox.'

Martin reached the bottle across, and looking anxiously at Stephen he said 'I hope I have not offended you?'

'As far as I am concerned Captain Aubrey is wholly infallible in the conduct of a ship. Pray tell me about your walk with Dr Falconer.'

'It was not nearly so successful as I had hoped. While we were taking a short cut over a tumble of black rocks, Dr Falconer fell, twisted his ankle and broke his spy-glass. We could not go on, neither could we go back until the extreme pain had diminished, so we sat there on the rocks in the sun, talking about volcanoes; for this formation, it seems, was of recent igneous origin. Presently we decided to eat and above all to drink; but it was found that although we had collecting-bags, nets and specimen-cases in plenty, the knapsack and the bottles had been left behind. He desired me to go to some palms right down by the shore and bring back some coconuts; and when at last I came back empty-handed in spite of my most earnest endeavours to climb even the most oblique of the little grove, he was surprisingly impatient.

'Yet in time he recovered his equanimity and told me at length about the frequent volcanic activity in these regions. He believes there is an intimate connexion between eruptions, particularly submarine eruptions, and those great waves that devastate so many shores, wrecking ships and drowning thousands; and he was exceedingly put out by having to leave Moahu before he had climbed the volcano there, since he had hoped to establish a relation between its intermittent rumbling and the level of the sea. He had made his way up a far more important, far more active volcano in the Sandwich Islands, one of many; and I heard a great deal about scoriae, ashes, incandescent dust, the various forms of lava, lapilli and vitreous pumice. You will remember that Dr Falconer has an unusually loud voice: it seemed louder still under that torrid sun, and perhaps there was an effect of echo. We saw no birds, apart from two very distant boobies and a common sooty tern. Yet on our slow and halting return, which took us through gentler, more shaded country, I found him more interesting: he spoke of the importance of volcanoes to the Polynesians. Apart from anything else they are visible gods, and sacrifices are often made to them in the hope of evading the usual fate of the poor and lowly-born, whose souls are slowly eaten by the evil spirits who dwell inside the craters.'

'Why, Stephen, there you are!' cried Jack, his grim face breaking into a smile. 'I have kept half a pot of coffee for you, but I am sure you could do with another, having watched so late. Your eyes are as red as a ferret's. Killick! Killick, there. Another pot for the Doctor.'

'We are bounding along at a fine pace, are we not? At a rate of knots, I make no doubt. See how the table leans.'

'Pretty well. We have spread everything she can carry, perhaps even a little more than is quite wise; but I felt so hell-fire hipped and mumpish in the channel with that parcel of God-damned lubbers, nearly missing my tide, that I longed for a breath of fresh air. Try one of these toasted slices of bread-fruit: they eat well with coffee. The chief's sister sent me a net-full, dried.' He slowly ate a piece of crisp breadfruit, drank out his cup, and said, 'Yet, you know, it has not made quite the difference I had reckoned on. Perhaps it will be better presently, when we bring the breeze abaft the beam.'

The breeze, as he had foreseen, came abaft the beam late in the forenoon watch; the *Surprise* spread her weather stud-dingsails, and by the time the hands were piped to dinner she was running at eight knots three fathoms: fresh air in plenty, brilliant sun, and the taste of salt from the fine spindrift.

The officers on the quarterdeck watched their captain pace fore and aft as he had paced fore and aft uncounted times, but they remained silent, over there to leeward, and the men at the wheel and the quartermaster beside them stood unnatu-rally stiff as he passed by.

'Captain Pullings, if you please,' he said, after he had walked his measured mile. 'A word with you.'

In the cabin Pullings said 'I am glad you told me to come, sir. I was going to ask you to do the gunroom the honour of dining with us tomorrow, it being Sunday.'

'That is very kind in you, Tom,' he said, looking him right in the eye, 'but I must decline invitations to the gunroom at present. This is not a fling at you, however.'

'I am afraid the last time was not all we could have wished,' said Pullings, shaking his head.

'No, Tom,' said Jack after a considerable pause. 'The ship is falling to pieces. Where there is ill-will, really strong ill-will, in the gunroom a ship falls to pieces, even when she has a company like this. I have known it again and again. So have you.'

'Yes, by God,' said Tom.

'I had thought of remedying it, at least to some extent, by making Oakes acting-lieutenant.'

'Oh no, sir!' cried Pullings: he flushed, and his dreadful scar showed livid across his face.

'It would add to the number at your table and make rudeness, gross incivility, less easy; it would put him on an even footing, which would prevent any officer from riding him and so angering the hands in Oakes's division; he would stand his own watch, which would make him independent. He is quite seaman enough, for blue-water sailing.'

'Yes, sir,' said Pullings; and then barely audible in his embarrassment and protesting that he did not mean to carry tales or inform on anyone, he said 'But that would mean Mrs Oakes messing with us.'

'Of course. That is a part of my argument.'

'Well sir . . . some of the officers are sweet on Mrs Oakes.'

'I dare say they are – a very amiable young woman.'

'No, sir. I mean serious – bloody serious – cut-your-throat serious – fucking serious . . .'

'Oh.' Jack Aubrey was taken aback entirely. 'But you surely do not mean that last word literally?'

'No, sir. It is just my coarse way of speaking: I beg pardon.

But so serious that if she were there at the table day after day . . .'

After a silence Jack said 'The husband is always the last to know, they say. I am talking of myself, as being married to the barky, you understand. The sods. But I am sure she never gave them any encouragement. Well, Tom, thank you for letting me know: I see things in a new light now. Yes, indeed. Now passing on to the shameful bungling this morning, I shall speak to the officers concerned but there were also some hands who behaved ill: sullen and unwilling: neglect of duty. You must prepare a list and I must deal with them; a damned unpleasant business.' He walked over to his chart-table and measured off the distance yet to run to Moahu. 'We must pull them together before there is any question of action,' he said. 'Tom, will you dine with me and the Doctor tomorrow? And perhaps I might ask Martin and the Oakeses.'

'Thank you, sir. I should be very happy.'

'I shall look forward to it, too. And Tom, pray tell West and Davidge that I wish to see them.'

They were both expecting the summons. Jack had left the unmooring to them while he and Pullings finished their business with Wainwright below, and he had come on deck to find an everyday manoeuvre being shockingly bungled. But they had not expected this degree of cold fury nor the far-reaching nature of his observations. 'I am speaking to you about your public life,' he said. 'You know perfectly well that public ill-will stirs up division and brings discredit on a ship: you also know that officers' disagreements in wardroom or gunroom are public, since the mess servants tell their mates directly, so that they affect the whole ship's company even if they are kept under hatches, since any officer with a division has a following among the hands in his charge. But you have not even attempted to keep things under hatches. You are openly, blatantly, rude to one another, and you ride Oakes in a way that causes great resentment among his men, whom he looks after very well. Obviously, since your messmates are not tale-bearers, I have had no idea of your conduct in the gunroom; but you cannot deny that I have given you many a hint, aye and many an open check these last weeks about your rudeness and incivility on deck. One result of all this ill-feeling, division and contention was today's disgraceful exhibition when I came on deck and found you wrangling like a couple of fish-fags and the ship looking like Bartholomew fair: and all this in the presence of the *Daisy*'s master and her people. I can only thank God there was no King's ship by. Imagine such a state of affairs in action! Another result was that you disgraced the ship in your entertainment to Mrs Oakes and her husband: you, both of you, West and Davidge, made your dislike of one another staringly obvious. You showed no respect for your guests in what was essentially a public function. For my own part I have just declined Captain Pullings' invitation for tomorrow.'

'I was half stunned at the time, sir,' said Davidge.

'No doubt you presented your excuses to Oakes the next morning?' said Jack. Davidge reddened, but made no reply. 'As for your personal, private disagreements I have nothing to say. But I do absolutely insist upon your keeping up public appearances, officerlike outward appearances: in the gunroom when any hands are present, on deck at all times. I say nothing about my report to the Admiralty, but I do promise you this: unless I find you have taken great notice of my words by the time we have dealt with Moahu, by God you shall sow what you have reaped, and I shall supersede you by two of the master-mariners from before the mast. We have at least a score. That will do.'

'Dearest Sophie,' he wrote, 'A captain worth his name knows a great deal about his ship, her capabilities, her stores, her weaknesses and so on; and common daily observation shows him his people's seamanship and fighting qualities: but he lives so far from his officers and men that unless he listens to tale-bearers there is a great deal he does not know. These last weeks I have been worried by the obvious ill-will in the gunroom and its bad effects on discipline; I had both directly and indirectly told them to be more civil, but only this morning did Tom, horribly confused at informing on his messmates, tell me the reason for this ill-will. I had thought it the usual weariness of a long commission with the same faces, the same jokes, perhaps sharpened by some foolish raillery carried too far, losses at cards, chess, arguments – but all this carried much farther than I should ever have let it go. I am much to blame. Yet this morning, just before I called them in to reprove them for the horrible mess they had made of unmooring the ship, Tom let me know that they hated one another because of Mrs Oakes; and that it would not do to give Oakes an order as acting-lieutenant, because with her at the table their rivalry might well break bounds.

'It is a shame that such a modest, well-conducted woman should be so persecuted, and kept to the dismal solitary messing of the midshipmen's berth; I am sure she has given no encouragement, even in the most harmless usual shipboard way, has never said "Pray do up this button for me; my fingers are all thumbs," or "I hope you do not think my tucker too low." No. And at a most discreditable dinner the gunroom gave for her, with half her hosts as mute as fishes, she kept things going most courageously. I do like courage in a woman. By the way, I was quite mistaken about Stephen, when I feared he might be too fond: they went for a walk in the country yesterday and came back so pleased and affectionate together, carrying some extraordinary flowers and a bag of Stephen's birds and beetles. I have a mind to ask her and her husband to dine tomorrow, to mark the point; but I am not sure. I was so angered by seeing the ship exposed and mishandled this morning that I have little heart for entertaining; and Oakes himself, though a tolerable seaman, is a shocking drag. I shall ask Stephen: he is examining her in his cabin at this minute.'

Although Jack and Stephen had played some deeply satisfying music that evening, Stephen sitting with his feet braced against the heel of the ship on a batten shipped for the purpose and Jack standing to play his fiddle, the Captain woke early in the morning watch on Sunday with the humiliation of his ship's disgrace still strong in his mind, and a clear recollection of Wainwright's silent astonishment and tactfully averted eyes when they came on deck. The wind had begun dropping through the middle watch, as some inner recorder told him, and he was not at all surprised to find the ship ghosting along under limp, dew-soaked sails over a grey sea with barely a ripple on the heavy swell from the south.

'Good morning, Mr Davidge,' he said, taking the log-board from its place. 'Good morning, Mr Oakes.'

'Good morning, sir,' said Davidge. 'Good morning, sir,' said Oakes.

Although there were stars and even their reflexions in the west, the eastern sky was light enough for him to read the board: and from what the sky to starboard told he saw the calm would not last.

'Have any sharks been seen?' he asked.

Davidge hailed the lookout: no sharks, no sharks at all, sir.

'I will just peep under the counter, sir,' said Oakes. 'Sometimes we have a messmate there.' A moment later he called 'All clear, sir.'

'Thankee, Mr Oakes,' said Jack. He walked to the gangway stanchions, hung his shirt and trousers over the ridge-rope, breathed deep and dived deeper. The bubbles hissed past him, his whole weight changed; and the water was cool enough to be wonderfully refreshing. He swam powerfully for half a mile, and turning he contemplated the ship, her trim, her perfect lines, as she rose and fell, sometimes disappearing altogether in the trough of the swell. The sun had now turned the whole sky blue, light blue, and he could feel its warmth on the back of his neck. Yet even so some blackness remained; he did not rejoice with the whole of his being. The abiding fury was wholly dissipated however when within twenty yards of the frigate he caught sight of Mrs Oakes leaning over the quarterdeck rail, far aft.

'Heavens,' he cried inwardly. 'I may be seen naked,' and he

instantly dived, swimming as fast and far as he could on one breath.

He need not have feared nor held his breath to so near bursting-point: already Oakes was running in one direction to shield her eyes and Killick, with a towel, in the other, to shield his person.

Killick, seeing his captain's approach from afar, had also timed his first breakfast with particular care, rather as a keeper obliged to live in the same cage with a testy omnipotent lion might time his gobbets of horseflesh to the very first stroke of the zoological bell.

For once Stephen shared this first breakfast. He had been so much taken up with encoding that he had not looked at a tenth part of his botany specimens nor even at all his birds and their parasites with anything like really close attention, and the thought of them brought him out of his cot at first light with that almost trembling or rather bubbling excitement he had known from very early days – his first sight of St Dabeoc's heath when he was seven, of a dell filled with Gold of Pleasure the next year, and of the Pyrenean desman (that rare ill-natured cousin to the shrew) only a few weeks after that!

'I was very near offering Mrs Oakes a dreadful spectacle just now,' said Jack after a pause in which they each drank two cups of coffee. 'I was swimming back – was within pistol-shot – when I noticed her there at the rail. Had she looked my way she must have beheld a naked man.'

'That would have been very shocking, indeed,' said Stephen. 'Pray pass the breadfruit toast.' He remembered an earlier occasion on which Mrs Oakes had in fact beheld a naked man, through the scuttle of the cabin in which she had been examined, perfectly unmoved. Jack was standing in a boat, giving directions about the recovery of a hawser cut by the sharp coral rock and on the point of diving himself; and she contemplated him with a detached interest: 'Captain Aubrey would be considered a fine figure of a man even in Ireland, would he not?' she asked. 'But surely he has been most dreadfully cut about?'

'I should scarcely like to number the wounds I have sewn up and dressed, or the musket and pistol balls I have extracted,' said Stephen. 'You are to observe, ma'am, that they are all honourably in front; except for those that are behind.'

That was long before their walk in Annamooka: indeed it was the first time he had distinctly seen anything unusual in her attitude towards men, an almost clinical attitude that disconcerted him to some degree, since neither her face nor her everyday behaviour was marked by any irregularity of life. He was still thinking of her when Jack said 'Speaking of Mrs Oakes, it is long since I heard her howling on Martin's viola: or Martin himself, for that matter.'

'I believe I understood him to say that the neck was out of order: or possibly the head. How does it come about, do you suppose, that so few people play it? For a score that make their attempts upon a fiddle not more than one, nay less, tries the viola. Yet it has or can have the sweetest voice.'

'I cannot tell, I am sure. Perhaps they are less easy to come by. Perhaps they are even more difficult to master: think how rare it is to find a player of the very first rate, fit to answer a violin like Cramer or Kreutzer in say Mozart's . . . Come in. Come in and sit down, Tom,' he called, pouring him a cup of coffee.

'Thank you, sir. It was only that I forgot to ask whether you meant to rig church today.'

'Yes,' said Jack, his face clouding again. 'Yes, certainly: there is nothing like church for bringing a sense of order into things. But only the penitential psalms and the Articles.'

Church by all means, with awnings over the quarterdeck; yet before church came the ceremony of divisions, the formal inspection of all hands lined up under their divisional officers, and of their quarters. It was, as Jack had observed, one of a commander's best opportunities for taking the ship's company's pulse. As he passed along the ranks he looked eye-to-eye at every seaman, petty officer and warrant officer aboard; and he would be a dull fellow if the expression or lack of expression on these scores of well-washed, new-shaven faces did not give him some notion of the ship's general temper.

This worked both ways: the Surprises also gauged the state of their captain's mind; and his progress, accompanied by Pullings and by each divisional officer in turn, left gloom and dismay behind. In spite of his bathe, in spite of his breakfast and in spite of the fine steady breeze there was still a great deal of anger and resentment in his heart. The ship had been mishandled, made to look ridiculous – all that unofficer-like, unseamanlike swearing and shouting and noise in the course of an everyday manoeuvre that the old *Surprise* would have carried through without the slightest fuss and with little more than the single order 'Unmoor ship' – would have carried it through like a man-of-war rather than a slapdash privateer. It was a desecration; and very strong displeasure emanated from him as he walked along. He smiled only once, and that was when he came to the gunner's division, where Mr Smith was attended by Reade, making his first official appearance since his accident. 'I am happy to see you again, Mr Reade,' he said. 'You have the Doctor's leave I am sure?'

'Oh yes, sir: he declared I was quite fit for –' began Reade: but here his voice, which had just started to break, soared out of control before he brought out 'light duties' in a deep croak.

'Very good. But even so you must take care. We do not have so very many seamen aboard.'

On to Oakes and the foretopmen, a division that had always been the most cheerful in the ship and that was now the most disturbed. Guilt accounted for some part of their trouble as it did for their more than usually high perfection of cleanliness and Sunday dress – gestures towards averting wrath – but there was also something more that he could not define. He walked along past them with a grave face and none of the small remarks that so often attended divisions. On to the forecastle-men and so to Jemmy Ducks and his charges. 'How they shoot up,' he reflected. 'Perhaps Fanny and Charlotte will be as long in the leg by now.' Although he looked at them kindly and asked them how they did, they gazed up with even more anxiety than usual. In their very remote Melanesian small-childhood formal gatherings had sometimes ended in human sacrifice – a reasonable foundation for uneasiness – but in addition to this they were more exactly in tune with the people's mood than their captain; and so, raising upon the foundation to an uncommon height, they quavered as they replied.

In the empty sick-berth Stephen and Martin sat carefully in their good clothes, listening to the sound of Padeen putting the last touches of polish and exact order to the surgical instruments. Breaking the silence Martin said in a low tone, 'I owe you a fuller explanation for my conduct yesterday. I did not go with you and Mrs Oakes because for some time now I have felt – how shall I put it? – an inclination, a growing inclination for her that it would be criminal to indulge. I felt I must avoid her company even at the cost of a falseness and incivility that I do assure you, Maturin, I very much regret.'

'Never in life, my dear Martin,' said Stephen, shaking him by the hand. 'Sure, it is better to flee than to burn; and from the mere philosophical, as opposed to the moral, point of view, we covered rather more ground.'

'For the same reason I broke my viola,' said Martin, still with his first idea: then, the second having pierced through, he clapped his hand to his pocket and cried, 'Very true. And at one point in our return, when Dr Falconer and I were sitting among old and rotting tree-trunks, felled by some long-past hurricane – a kind of locality you did not encounter, I collect – I found a large variety of beetles. Here,' – producing a flat box from his pocket – 'is a selection I beg you will accept.'

Stephen opened the box and tilted it to the filtered light. 'Here's glory for you!' he cried. 'Longicorns to a man: no, these must belong to the Cleridae – such colours! How they will make Sir Joseph stare: and how grateful I am. They are all dead, I find.'

'Yes. I cannot bear that perpetual hopeless striving to escape, the scrabbling noise. So I pass them through spirits of wine.'

'Gentleman, dear, himself is upon us,' said Padeen in a nervous whisper and of course in Irish, thrusting his head through the hatch like a rabbit and withdrawing it at once.

'Perhaps I should tell you that Captain Aubrey means to invite you to dine with Pullings, the Oakeses and myself,' said Stephen.

'Oh, thank you,' said Martin with a harassed smile. 'Now that I am forewarned I believe I can keep my countenance for the space of a dinner.'

Yet when Jack, having gone through the motions of inspecting the sick-berth, said 'Mr Martin, may we hope for the pleasure of your company at dinner today?' Martin replied 'Alas, sir, I must beg to be excused. I am very far from well, and shall absent myself even from church: but allow me to say how very sensible I am of your goodness. Far from well – indeed, a man must be uncommonly disordered to decline an invitation from both his patron and his commanding officer.'

The refusal of a captain's invitation to dinner was extremely unusual in the service – an act assumed to be a declaration of hostility, very near neighbour to mutiny if not to high treason – but Jack, who could not look upon either Martin or Stephen as a truly maritime animal, took it quite calmly, suggested that perhaps he had ate something in Annamooka, recommended lying down – 'A man's pillow is his best medicine: though I should not say so in the present company' – asked his advice on the more lowering psalms, and carried on with his inspection.

As he and Pullings walked forward along the cable-tier a rat crossed their path and Jack cried 'Bless me! It was here that we found Mrs Oakes, looking like a boy. That was in fact no great while ago in time or course made good, if you consider; yet now she seems as much part of the ship as the figurehead.' Pullings, who worshipped and detested the figurehead equally and in torment, uttered a murmur of assent, and after a while Jack went on 'Where did she get those trousers from, do you imagine? They were much too small for Oakes.'

'They belonged to poor Miller, sir,' said Pullings, speaking of a midshipman killed in Jack's most recent action, 'and when his things were sold at the mainmast Reade bought the uniform, hoping he would grow into them when we were in New South Wales. But, however, he did not; and I suppose he passed them on – I only speak at a venture, sir. I have no real knowledge,' he added, unwilling to have the air of an informer.

'It is very likely,' said Jack, calling young Miller to mind. 'They were much of a size.'

He said no more until they were in the light of day once more, a light so brilliant that it caused them to narrow their eyes, but that also made it clear to the ship's people that nothing had happened below to change their skipper's state of mind, and that they still had a right Tartar on their hands.

Jack Aubrey's large open florid blue-eyed face could not by any contortion be made to look shrewish or mean, but indignation for his ship and deep anger against the men who could have used her so gave it a leonine ferocity that had a wonderfully daunting effect. It did not change during divine service, an austere ritual unrelieved by the presence of the Reverend Nathaniel Martin, who though no hand at a sermon added a greater humanity than was present today: after the regulation prayers, read in a strong, unforgiving tone, and the sin-confessing psalm, the Surprises heard their captain raise his already powerful voice a pitch or two and run through the dreadful Articles of War in a tone less forgiving still. He dwelt with more than usual emphasis on the words '. . . if any officer, marine, soldier, or other person in the fleet, shall presume to quarrel with any of his superior officers, being in the execution of his office, or shall disobey any lawful command of any of his superior officers, every such person being convicted . . . shall suffer death.' And on 'If any person in the fleet shall quarrel or fight with any other person in the fleet, or use reproachful or provoking speeches or gestures, tending to make any quarrel or disturbance, he shall, upon being convicted thereon, suffer such punishments as the offence shall deserve . . .' And on 'No person in or belonging to the fleet shall . . . negligently perform the duty imposed upon him, or forsake his station, upon pain of death.'

Mrs Oakes and the little girls being present he skipped Article XXIX, which dealt with sodomy by hanging the sodomite, but he came out strong on XXXVI: 'All other crimes not capital . . . which are not mentioned in this act, or for which no punishment is hereby directed to be inflicted, shall be punished according to the laws and customs in such cases used at sea,' ending with a glare at the congregation that reminded them of the more brutal customs used at sea, such as keel-hauling, and that caused Emily, who was less stout than Sarah and who had seen Jemmy Ducks' change of countenance, to start grizzling again.

After this and the midday observation he dismissed them to eat their dinner with what appetite they could summon with the help of grog, and began the most recent in a long, long series of measured miles on the windward side of his quarterdeck.

Heart of Oak beat for the diminished gunroom dinner: Martin retired to his cabin with two concealed biscuits: the Captain paced on and on in his elegant white waistcoat, as grave as a hanging judge. It did not foretell a particularly cheerful dinner-party.

Yet Jack had a high notion of hospitality: apart from anything else, on his first introduction to the Navy he had served under a nephew of the amiable Admiral Boscawen, a commander who carried on his uncle's tradition, famous throughout the service – a tradition that suited the natural bent of Captain Aubrey's genius, so that when Killick came to tell him that the Doctor was square-rigged and powdered, that his Honour's coat was hanging on the back of his chair, and that his guests were at single anchor, he brightened at once, hurried down the companion-ladder and into what was officially his sleeping-place, now for so small a party turned into his dining-cabin, with its usual blaze of silver (Killick's joy) among the orchids and his own coat hunched at the head of the table. He put it on, splendid with gold lace and epaulettes, gave the table and the great cabin a quick glance and walked into the coach, where his meagre store of gin, bitters and madeira stood ready to receive his guests.

They arrived in a body, and a little civil war of declining precedence could be heard on the half-deck: the war was lost before it began, however, and they walked in according to established order. Mrs Oakes, the Scarlet Woman, as the

Sethians and some others called her, came first, in a modified version of her wedding-dress; she dropped Aubrey the prettiest straight-backed curtsy, exactly timed to the frigate's roll, and made room for Tom Pullings, almost as glorious as a post-captain; then came Stephen, who as a mere surgeon, a warrant-officer, had no lace at all on his plain blue coat, though he was allowed an embroidered button-hole to his collar; and last of all Oakes, who had no precedence of any kind and whose only ornament was the extreme brilliance of his polished buttons.

He was nevertheless the most cheerful of the band, smiling and chuckling to himself; he had obviously fortified himself for the encounter with grog, and when Jack asked Clarissa what he might bring her she said she would be happiest if she might be allowed to share her husband's madeira in so wifely a manner that the married men, even Killick and his mate, smiled inwardly. But when on the stroke of the bell they moved into the dining-cabin Clarissa was seated on Jack's right, with Pullings opposite her and Stephen at her side; Oakes was on Pullings' left, removed from her by a broad expanse of tablecloth. It is true that he often looked at her with a doglike devotion, and her glance sometimes made him call 'Belay' when Killick had not even half filled his glass.

Yet neither being stinted of his wine nor the foreboding atmosphere in the ship affected his spirits and it appeared to Stephen, his vis-à-vis, that something must very recently have passed between him and Clarissa: a new understanding, per- haps physically ratified.

'Doctor,' he said, leaning over the table with a smile. 'You are a very learned cove; but do you know what it is, that the more you cut of it, grows still the longer?'

Stephen considered, with his head on one side, took a sip of wine, and in the expectant silence he asked 'Would it be celery, at all?'

'No, sir. Not celery,' said Oakes, with great satisfaction.

Others suggested hay, a beard, nails; and Killick whispered in Stephen's ear 'Try horseradish, sir.' But none would do and in the end, as soup was clearing away, Oakes had to tell them that the more you cut of a *ditch* the *longer* the ditch grew. They confessed it; even Pullings, rising from his state of guilt at the frigate's present condition, said it was very clever – one of the cleverest things he had heard; and Jack looked at Oakes with a new esteem. On the half-deck, as the fish was coming aft, Killick could be heard explaining the apparent paradox to his mate and Jack Nastyface.

Oakes wore his triumph modestly throughout the fish, a noble creature like a bonito but with crimson spots; and during this time Jack explained the theory of trade winds to Clarissa, while Pullings listened with a fixed look of polite attention and Stephen attended to the fish's anatomy. 'Doctor,' said Oakes, having wiped his plate, 'do you remember the Bathurst tavern in Sydney? Well, there was a soldier that used to come down with a couple of friends and we played halfpenny whist; and after every two or three rubbers he would call for a pipe of tobacco. Then one day, no pipe. "Ain't you going to smoke?" we asked him. "No," says he. "I lit my pipe last night with a broadsheet ballad folded lengthways, and there has been a singing in my head ever since. I am sure it is the ballad still."'

Stephen noticed an anxious expression on Clarissa's face, but her husband, enchanted by the reception of his piece, missed her look and plunged on into an account of a man who wore his hair over his shoulders and who, on being asked by a bald companion why he let it grow so long, answered, it was to see if his hair would run to seed, that he might sow it on bald pates.

'Very good, very good, Mr Oakes,' cried Jack, beating his hand on the table. 'A glass of wine with you, sir.'

During the roast pork he drank to each of his guests, particularly to Clarissa, whose looks he thought much improved from their exposure to the sun and the breeze. 'So returning to my trade winds, ma'am,' he went on, 'presently I hope we shall meet those blowing from the north-east; and then you will see what the ship can do, for we shall have to beat to windward, tack upon tack, and she is a good plyer – there is nothing she loves better than sailing close-hauled into a fine steady gale.'

'Oh I should love that,' said Clarissa. 'There is nothing so – so exalting as clinging on with both hands when the ship leans right over and the spray comes dashing back right along the side.' She spoke with unfeigned enthusiasm and he gave her an approving look – more than approving, indeed, and he quickly dropped his eyes in case his admiration should be seen. 'Doctor,' he called down the table, 'the bottle stands by you.'

Oakes had been silent for some time. He was silent while the plum-duff was passing round; he was silent while it was being eaten; but on swallowing his last spoonful he raised his glass and smiling happily round at the company he said

'So long as we may, let us enjoy this breath
For naught doth kill a man so soon as death.'

On the other hand there was little merriment on the forecastle in the last dog-watch though the evening was calm, beautiful and in every way fit for the dancing so usual at this time of day on a Sunday: only the little girls played the northern version of hopscotch they had learned from the Orkneymen – played it quietly, watched by the seamen with barely a comment.

There was if anything less on the quarterdeck, and when Stephen came up a little before sunset he found Davidge, the officer of the watch, standing by the barricade, looking haggard, middle-aged, wretched, and Clarissa sitting in her usual place by the taffrail, quite alone.

'I am so glad you have appeared,' she said. 'I was growing as melancholy as a gib cat, which is ungrateful after such a splendid dinner; and very strange too, because I never minded being by myself when I was a girl and I longed for nothing so much as solitude in New South Wales. Perhaps I feel it here because I do so dislike being disliked . . . Reade and Sarah and Emily – we were such friends, and I cannot think how I have offended them.'

'The young are notoriously fickle.'

'Yes. I suppose so. But it is disappointing. Look, the sun is about to touch the sea.' When the last orange rim had gone

194

and the rays alone were shooting up into the lemon-coloured haze, she said 'I suppose a sea-captain's life must be a very lonely one. Of course it is different for Captain Aubrey with you aboard, but for most of them, cooped up with nobody to talk to . . . Do many take their wives or mistresses to sea?'

'Wives are uncommon – almost unheard-of on long voyages, I believe. And mistresses are in general disapproved of by everyone, from the Lords of the Admiralty to the ordinary seamen. They take away from an officer's character and his authority.'

'Do they really? Yet neither seamen nor naval officers are famous for chastity.'

'Not by land. Yet at sea a different set of rules comes into play. They are neither particularly logical nor consistent, but they are widely understood and observed.'

'Really? Really?' she asked leaning forward with intense interest: then she sighed and shook her head, saying 'But then, as you are aware, I know so little about men – men in the ordinary sense, in ordinary everyday life: men by day rather than by night.'

Chapter Eight

Monday dawned pure and fair, lighting the starboard watch as they worked aft, cleaning the deck with wetted sand, then with holystones, and then with swabs. The sun heaved up as they neared the capstan, on which West was sitting, his trousers rolled up to keep them from the flowing tide: sunrise was usually the moment for a certain amount of discreet cheerfulness and ancient witticisms such as 'Here we are again, shipmates!' and 'Are you happy in your work?' But nothing was to be heard today apart from the conscientious grating of the stones, the clash of buckets, and a few low warnings: 'Watch out for sweepings under that old grating, Joe.' And this in spite of the brilliance of the day, the ship's fine long easy pace, slanting across the swell with a lively rise, and of the favourable easterly breeze that ruffled the sea, bringing an exquisite freshness with it.

At seven bells hammocks were piped up and the larboard watch came running on deck in the most exemplary manner, each carrying his tight, exactly-lashed cylinder, which the quartermaster stowed in the nettings, numbers uppermost, with the meticulous regularity usual before an admiral's inspection. There was no merriment among the larbowlines either: none at their first appearance in the sunlight, none half an hour later, when all hands were piped to breakfast.

The old Surprises, that is to say those who had sailed with Captain Aubrey in earlier commissions, naturally messed together, even though this entailed the often disagreeable and sometimes dangerous company of Awkward Davies; and they listened in silence to his description of the skipper's coming on deck at first light, his good morning to Mr West, cold enough to freeze his balls off – 'Just as well too,' said Wilson

– his gazing sternly to windward, and his pacing fore and aft in his nightshirt, like a lion seeking whom he might devour.

'They can do nothing to me,' said Plaice. 'I only done what my officer told me to do. "Belay there, Plaice, God damn your eyes" says he. So I belayed, though I knew it would bring us by the lee. Then "Let go, let go, forward there. Let go, Plaice, God damn your limbs," calls t'other, so I let go. It would have been mutiny else. I am as innocent as a drove of lambs.'

With some difficulty Padeen said that God had never created a more beautiful morning nor a more propitious wind: it would soften the heart of Hector or Pontius Pilate himself.

Padeen was esteemed for his kindness in the sick-berth and for his cruel hard times in Botany Bay; he was also thought to have absorbed wisdom from the Doctor, and some people took comfort from his words.

It was a flimsy sort of comfort, however, and it quite disappeared a little before six bells in the forenoon watch, when the officers and midshipmen appeared on the quarterdeck in their uniforms and cocked hats, wearing swords or dirks. Pullings gave orders to rig the grating, and Mr Adams came hurrying up the companion-ladder with the Articles of War. As soon as the sixth bell had struck, the bosun's mates piped *All hands to witness punishment* and the frigate's people flocked aft in a confused body, from which there arose a sense of collective guilt.

'All women below,' called Captain Aubrey. Sarah and Emily disappeared, and Pullings, at his side, said 'Mrs Oakes is already with the Doctor, sir.'

'Very well. Carry on, Captain Pullings.'

In her present state the *Surprise* carried no master-at-arms and Pullings himself called the wrongdoers from the throng, stating the crime of each to the Captain as he advanced. The first was Weightman. 'Insolence and inattention to duty, sir, if you please.'

'Have you anything to say for yourself?' asked Jack.

'Not guilty, your honour, upon my sacred oath,' said the butcher.

'Have any of his officers anything to say for him?' He waited

197

for a moment: the breeze sang through the rigging: the officers looked into vacancy. 'Strip,' said Jack, and Weightman slowly took off his shirt. 'Seize him up.' The quartermasters tied Weightman's wrists to the grating rather above shoulder-height and cried 'Seized up, sir.'

Adams passed the Articles. Jack, followed by the officers and midshipmen, took off his hat; he then read ' "No person in or belonging to the fleet shall sleep upon his watch, *or negligently perform the duty imposed on him*, or forsake his station, upon pain of death or such other punishment as the circumstances of his case shall require." Twelve strokes.' And to the senior bosun's mate, 'Vowles, do your duty.'

Vowles drew the cat from its red baize bag, phlegmatically took up his stance, and as the ship reached the height of her roll he laid on the first stroke. 'Oh my God,' cried Weightman, enormously loud.

Mrs Oakes and Stephen looked up. 'There is punishment carrying out forward,' he said. 'Some of the people behaved amiss in pulling up the anchor.'

'So Oakes told me,' she replied, listening to the successive shrieks with no apparent emotion. 'How many does the Captain usually give?'

'I have never known him give more than a dozen, and rarely so many. Flogging is uncommon in ships under his command.'

'A dozen? Lord, that would make them stare in New South Wales. There was a horrible parson, a magistrate, who only dealt in hundreds. Dr Redfern hated him.'

'I know it, my dear. So did I. Breathe deep, will you now, and hold it. Very well. That will do,' he said at last. 'You may put your clothes on again.'

'You say that in just the same tone as dear Dr Redfern,' said Clarissa from under the folds of her blue cotton dress: and emerging, 'How I adored that man when he told me that I was neither pregnant nor . . . nor diseased. I might well have been both. I had been raped often enough.'

'I am so sorry; so very sorry,' said Stephen.

'For some girls it would have been dreadful: it meant little to me, so long as there were no consequences.'

Flogging was indeed rare in Jack Aubrey's commands, but this time the ship had been outraged and humiliated and he punished severely, flogging seven and stopping grog right and left. Of those who were seized up, none called out except for Weightman; but none came away unmarked. As each was cast loose, Padeen stepped forward, tears streaming down his face, and sponged his shipmate's back with vinegar, while Martin swabbed the wheals with lint and passed the man's shirt, a gesture much appreciated. All this was done with the customary man-of-war formality – charge, response, evidence of character, attenuating circumstances, Captain's decision, relevant Article, sentence, punishment – and although the later sentences never exceeded six strokes, the whole took up a great deal of time which Stephen and Clarissa, for their part, spent in talking quite placidly about men in general, everyday men in their ordinary life.

The last of those to be beaten presented an unusual case. He was James Mason, a bosun's mate; he was a good seaman, and the officer spoke in his favour. But his offence had been very gross – direct disobedience – and Jack had him brought to the grating. 'In view of what your officers say, it will only be half a dozen,' he said. 'Mr Bulkeley, do your duty.' It was of course the bosun's duty to flog his mates, but the occasion very rarely arose: Bulkeley had not been called upon to officiate for years; he had lost the habit; and taking the cat from Vowles he stood there for a moment, combing its bloody tails through his fingers in a sad state of indecision. He was fond of young James, they got along well together; but the ship's company was watching most attentively and he must not be seen to favour his mate. No, indeed: and his first blow jerked a great gasp out of Mason, rock of fortitude though he was. When he was cast loose he staggered for a moment, wiped his face, and cast a reproachful look at the bosun, the embarrassed, confused and uneasy bosun.

In Stephen's cabin the conversation had moved on by way of a discussion of pain to the extraordinary difficulty of defining emotions or assigning to them any quantity quality volume or force. 'Harking back to pain,' said Stephen, 'I recall that when

Captain Cook was here he used to flog the islanders for stealing: it was no use, said he: one might just as well have flogged the mainmast. And I saw Aborigines in New South Wales who utterly disregarded burns, blows and cruel thorns that I could never have borne; while in the Navy a seaman will generally take his dozen without a murmur. Yet even when all things are considered, youthful resilience, fortitude, pride, habituation and so on, I wonder that your experience did not beat the softer, kinder emotions out of you entirely, leaving you sullen, morose and withdrawn.'

'Why, as for the softer emotions, perhaps I never was very well endowed; I disliked most cats, dogs and babies; I never cared for dolls or pet rabbits and sometimes I violently resented being crossed; but I never was sullen then and I am not sullen now. Nor am I morose and withdrawn: I think I am fairly kind, or mean to be fairly kind, to people who are kind to me or those who need kindness; and I know I like being liked – I love good company and cheerfulness.

Sic erimus cuncti postquam nos auferet Orcus
ergo vivamus dum licet esse, bene.

And I also know I am not a monster incapable of affection,' she said, laying a hand on Stephen's knee and flushing a little under her tan. 'Only I cannot connect it with that toying, striving, gasping – what can I call it without being gross? – with anything of a carnal nature. They seem to me poles apart.'

'I am sure they do. Sic erimus cuncti . . . so that was where Mr Oakes had his couplet yesterday? I wondered.'

'Yes. It was a doggerel version I made when I was putting on my gown. But I was astonished he should remember it.'

Stephen's only patients that afternoon were the butcher and the bosun's mate, both of whom, but particularly Mason, needed dressing. Martin had applied the ordinary pads, but he had had little experience with this kind of wound, the *Surprise*'s temper being ordinarily so mild, and a more practised hand was required to wind the cingulum that would enable them to move with something approaching ease.

Yet it was clear to the practised hand that he might have a well-populated berth quite soon. Not only was Jack tautening the ship in all points, but on excusing himself for missing dinner – 'he would take an extra bite this evening, and with the wind going down like this they might very well have some fresh fish with their music' – he had also thrown out a remark about a flying column. Quite what he meant by that Stephen had not gathered; but basing himself upon the axiom that what goes up must necessarily come down, he anticipated a fine crop of broken limbs, ribs, even skulls.

He reflected upon this as he dined in the gunroom, a rather silent gunroom, but one in which the malignance had been largely replaced by anxiety and even by a certain fellow-feeling. Martin ate wolfishly, twice desiring Pullings 'to cut him just a little more of this excellent roast pork', but when at last his empty plate was taken from him before pudding he told Stephen that he had seen a remarkable number of boobies towards the northern horizon, and that old Macaulay, who knows these seas, had confirmed him in his notion that this meant great shoals of fish. They might go a-fishing if the evening fell calm.

'You medicoes may go a-fishing,' said Pullings. 'But I very much doubt whether we do anything but exercise until next Christmas.'

Truer words he never spoke. The *Surprise* had by no means passed through the variables, and in the afternoon watch the breeze, which had been boxing the compass for some time, died away almost entirely; yet it did not do so until it had brought the ship within a mile or so of the zone where the boobies were fishing, and Stephen's skiff had long since been lowered down.

They rowed laboriously out, with rods, hand-nets, sieves for animalculae, pots and jars, baskets, all of which got in the way, impeding their artless progress and making them even slower, even hotter in the damp, unmoving air. Stephen, who had little sense of shame where nakedness was concerned and who had so often exposed his entire person that he feared no sunburn, took off his clothes; Martin, more shamefast by far, only unbuttoned his shirt, rolled up his trousers, and suffered.

But it was worth their toil. The fishing-ground was sharply defined, and as soon as they were over its border and among the boobies they found that it possessed at least two levels, a turmoil of squids pursuing pelagic crabs and the free-swimming larvae of various forms of marine life that neither could identify, though they were fairly confident of the pearl oyster, and two or three fathoms below these, clearly to be seen, particularly under the shade of the boat, swam schools of fishes, crossing and recrossing, all of the same mackerel-shaped kind, all flashing as they turned, and all feeding upon a host of fry so numerous that they made a globular haze in the clear green water. The boobies preyed on both, either making a slight skimming dive to snatch up a squid just under the surface, or plunging from a height like so many mortar-bombs to reach the depth where the fishes cruised. They took no notice whatsoever of the men, sometimes diving so close to the boat that they splashed water into it; and after some time the men, having classified the birds (two species, neither particularly rare), took no notice of the boobies. They scooped up the squids with their hand-nets and found that they belonged to at least eleven different kinds, two of which they could not name; they sieved great quantities of the squids' food, which they put into well-closed pots; and they caught the fishes – handsome fellows, weighing a couple of pounds – baiting their hooks with pork rind cut in the shape of a minnow.

'Paradise must have been very like this,' observed Martin, putting another into their basket: and then 'How happy they will be when we bring back our catch. There is nothing like fresh –' Here he looked towards the ship and his face changed entirely. 'Oh,' cried he, 'she has lost a mast!'

Certainly she looked horribly lopsided, or rather deformed; but Stephen replied 'Not at all, at all.' He reached among his clothes for a little pocket spy-glass, pointed, focussed, and continued 'Never in life, my dear sir: they are only shifting topmasts.'

He saw from the great activity in the maintop, where top-mast shrouds were being set up afresh, that they had begun aft and were working forward in one of the most strenuous exercises known to man.

Pullings and Oakes were on the forecastle; Davidge was in the foretop; West was perched in the maintopmast crosstrees; they and all the hands under their command were all in a state of extreme activity; and Jack Aubrey, with Reade on one hand and Adams on the other, was timing them with his open watch.

'I believe you have not seen it done before,' said Stephen, passing the glass. 'Will I tell you what they are at?'

'If you would be so good.'

'First they unbend the topgallantsails and send them down and the yard after them; then they strike the topgallant mast, a manoeuvre we are all familiar with – a matter of minutes for skilful mariners, attentive to their duty. But then they do the same to the great topsail, its mighty yard and then the very mast itself, a heavy task indeed. This they have evidently done to the mizenmast and the main; now they are operating on the foremast, and I perceive from the forms creeping along the bowsprit that they contemplate shifting the jibboom too, the creatures.'

'Do they look for flaws and change the defective pieces?'

'I suppose they do. But I believe the real aim is to make them brisker, to confirm them in their seamanlike activity, and perhaps to strengthen their sense of combined, exactly synchronous effort. Sometimes it is done, not from any desire to enforce discipline and instant compliance with orders but out of a spirit of competition if not indeed of vainglory and showing away. The old *Surprise*, with a crew that had been together a great while, all men-of-war's men, was extraordinarily good at it; and I remember that once, in the West Indies, shifting topmasts at the same moment as the *Hussar*, considered a crack ship, she did so in one hour and twenty-three minutes, the hands dancing hornpipes on the forecastle before the wretched Hussars had even crossed their main topgallant yards. See, the topmast is swaying up – it rises, rises, the capstan turns – higher, higher, secured by a complex system of ropes – high enough – Tom cries "Launch ho!" – it is fidded and safe – they fling themselves upon the shrouds and cast off this and that – the brave topgallant-mast follows . . .'

So it did; and once the frigate looked like a Christian ship again – for the shifting of the jibboom was neither here nor there to the medicoes – they returned to their squids, more active now than ever. 'I am almost certain that over there we have a species quite unknown,' said Martin. He leaned out with his long-handled net, but before he had even dipped it he started back. 'Oh,' he said in a shocked voice. 'Do not move. Do not hang your arm over the side. My image of Paradise was only too exact. The Evil One is with us too.'

They peered cautiously over the gunwale, and there under the frail skiff they saw the familiar form of a shark: one of the many kinds of Carcharias no doubt, though to tell just which they would have to look at its teeth; yet it seemed larger than most: far larger.

'Do you suppose it is likely to bump the boat?' asked Martin in a low voice.

'Sure he may well do so, by rising suddenly; or sometimes they are known to take a run and launch themselves bodily into the middle, or athwartships as we say, snapping right and left.'

'I wonder you can speak with such levity,' said Martin. 'And you too a married man.'

A silence fell, broken from time to time by the splash of a deep-diving booby and the remote shrilling of bosun's calls. A bird dived close at hand, down and down: the shark moved smoothly from under the boat: its bulk covered the diving form and carried on into the depths, growing steadily dimmer though still huge when it vanished. Three or four feathers floated up. 'Will he come back, do you imagine?' asked Martin, still gazing down with shaded eyes.

'I do not,' said Stephen. 'The flesh of the booby is acrid and rank, and I have no doubt he thinks we belong to the same genus at least.'

From over the sea came an urgent piping and Captain Aubrey's powerful voice urging haste. In rapid succession all the frigate's boats were lowered down; their crews leapt into them with the breakneck speed they would have shown if a valuable prize had just heaved up; and lines having been passed they began towing the ship in the direction of the boobies.

By the time the *Surprise* reached them the sun was already far down the sky. The fish had stopped biting; the squids and their prey had sunk out of sight; and as soon as the boats were hoisted in the hands were piped to a belated supper, with precious little rum served out.

'What a comfort it is to have solid heart of oak beneath one's feet,' said Martin as they took their pots fishes rods buckets and specimens out of the skiff. 'I had never felt the dreadful fragility of this boat – planking not half an inch thick – so much as when I saw that horrible creature almost touching it. I have never felt more uneasy in my life. As I peered down it rolled a little and gave me a cold look that I shall not soon forget.'

Supper was hardly swallowed before the drum beat for quarters. The cabins vanished in the usual clean sweep fore and aft; Stephen hid his specimens together with a large number of squids in the quarter-gallery and hurried to the sick-berth, his action-station; the great guns were cast loose, and the drooping officers reported 'All present and sober, if you please.'

They were soberer still by the time they had performed the great-gun exercise – running in the cannon (five hundred-weight to a man) – running the massive object out again as far as possible, laying the tackle-falls in neat fakes – pointing the guns in a given direction – going through the motions of firing – running in, going through the motions of worming, sponging and reloading – replacing the tompion – housing and making all fast – a dozen turns apiece, each separately timed by their inflexible Captain, and then a full broadside together: all this in dumb show. They were not indulged in a single round of live ammunition, for although the magazines were tolerably full (powder being one of the few things that New South Wales could supply) Jack Aubrey had no intention whatsoever of giving them pleasure: he was profoundly displeased with his officers and men, and with himself for not having detected this spirit of faction earlier. He was in no mood for indulgence of any kind, and the hands knew it.

There was no singing or dancing on the forecastle during what little remained of the sweetest evening. The hands sat about, dog-tired, until the setting of the watch. They did not resent the skipper's anger: they knew it was justified: they hoped it would not last.

A vain hope. All through the variables they were kept on the run, manning and arming boats, lowering them down and hoisting them in until they achieved twenty-five minutes twenty seconds for the one and nineteen minutes fifty seconds for the other: they could also send up lower yards and topmasts and cross topgallant yards in four minutes four seconds; and apart from shifting topmasts every now and then there was always the bending of new sails, painting ship and a remarkable amount of small-arms and cutlass exercise.

Throughout this time Jack kept his severity for the quarterdeck: once in the cabin he was as amiable as ever. He played his violin to Stephen's 'cello with his usual wholehearted enjoyment, and apart from the deep lines in his weatherbeaten face there was little to show the strain he was under.

'Lord, Stephen,' said he, after a day of particularly wearing exercise, 'I cannot tell you what a refuge this cabin is, and what a happiness it is for me to have you to talk to and play music with. Most captains have trouble with their ship's people from time to time – on occasion it is a continual sullen covert war – and unless they make cronies of their first lieutenants, as some do, they have to chew over it alone. I do not wonder that so many of them grow strange or bloody-minded; or run melancholy mad, for that matter.'

Even when they did reach the full north-east trades there was no relaxation of his manner on deck: he was fairly cordial to Pullings, Oakes and Reade, always civil to Martin and markedly polite to Clarissa when he saw her; but he remained stern, impersonal, remote and exigent with the other officers and the foremast jacks. Nor was there much relaxation in their daily and nightly toil, for the trade-wind proved more northerly and considerably less steady than he could have wished, and this called for the nicest management of the helm, a continual attention to brace and bowline and a frequent change of jibs and staysails if the *Surprise* were both to keep her course and run off her two hundred sea-miles between one noon observation and the next. He spent most of his waking hours on deck with Pullings, and he liked West, Davidge and Oakes to spend much of theirs aloft, supervising the exact carrying-out of his orders or even anticipating them. They grew worn and lean; they were haunted by the dread of being found asleep on their watch; and the gunroom dinners were silent less from animosity than extreme fatigue. None of them had ever known a ship driven so hard so long.

'My dear' wrote Stephen.

'We are now in the realm of the trade wind and we fly along at an exhilarating pace; but sailing against the wind (or as nearly against it as lies within the abilities of a square-rigged ship) is very unlike sailing before it, very unlike those luxurious days of rolling down to St Helena when one sits under an awning admiring the sea or reading one's book and when the mariners are not required to touch the flowing sheet. Now we lean over to a dangerous degree, and the spray or even solid water comes sweeping back with uncommon vehemence. Jack comes down soaked: not that he comes down often, because sailing of this kind requires his presence on deck. It would be much, much easier for all concerned if he would spread fewer sails and keep the wind one point free; yet he means not only to reach Moahu as soon as ever he can but he also, and above all, wishes to deal with the present situation by recalling all hands to their duty; and he is doing so with a greater authority than I knew he possessed.

'Whether he will succeed in his purpose I do not know. He sees the trouble as being caused by the enmity between the officers who are attracted to Mrs Oakes, and these officers being supported by their own men, so that there are rival clans in the ship. But there are complexities that escape him, and

207

now that I have time and to spare and the cabin to myself I shall endeavour to set them out as well as I can. The divisions, if I may so call them, amount to at least half a dozen: there are those (the majority) who condemn Clarissa for lying with any member of the quarterdeck at all apart from her husband; those who condemn her for lying with any officer but their own; those who support Oakes without reserve (they belong for the most part to his division and they are known as the Oak-Apples); those who condemn him for having beaten his wife; those who support their divisional officer whatever his situation with regard to her; and those who still look upon Clarissa with affectionate esteem – the sailmaker, for example, has recently made her a tarpaulin cloak, in which she now sits by the taffrail.

'Even if it were right for me to open my mind to Jack, I doubt it would be useful: I do not think I could ever make him understand that for her the sexual act is trivial, of no consequence. Our ordinary salute, the kiss, is held infamous among the Japanese if bestowed in public: with them, says Pinto, it is as much a deed of darkness or at least of total privacy as physical love-making is with us. For her, because of the particularity of her bringing-up, kiss and coition are much the same in insignificance; furthermore, she takes not the slightest pleasure in either. If therefore, through a variety of motives in which good nature and even compassion certainly have a part as well as a general desire to be liked, she has admitted some men to her bed, she has done so very innocently: "If an ill-looking pitiful fellow with say a thorn in his foot begged you to take it out, sure you would consent, even if doing so were rather unpleasant than otherwise." To her astonishment she had found herself loved and hated in various degrees, rather than merely liked, by those she obliged; and condemned by many who were in no way concerned.

'At different times I had tried to explain the violent male desire for exclusive possession – the standard by which a wide variety of partners if not promiscuity is laudable in oneself, vile in women – the want of sequence or even common honesty of mind coupled with unshakable conviction – the unreasonable yet very strong and very painful emotions that arise from jealousy (a feeling to which she is almost entirely a stranger) – and the very great force of rivalry. I also told her, with authority, that nothing can be done aboard ship without its being known. I spoke each time at some length, with real concern for her; she listened attentively and I think she believed me. In any event she is determined to renounce fornication: though how she will fare I know not. She has lit a fire that will not easily be put out; and although for the moment Jack keeps all hands in such a state of perpetual activity that the members of the gunroom mess can hardly put one foot in front of the other when they come below, these passions, confined as they are in space, may burst out later with a shocking force.'

He sat there, lost in his reflections, until Killick came in and said, as he had so often said before, 'Why, sir, you are sitting in the dark.' He brought a light, a lantern that swung in gimbals, and Stephen returned to his contemplation, holding his pen in the air.

'Scribble, scribble, scribble, Dr Maturin,' said Jack.

'You are not wet at all, I find,' said Stephen.

'No,' said Jack. 'Not to put too fine a point on it, I am quite dry; and was you to put your nose above the coaming and look at the dog-vane, you would see why. The wind has veered a whole point, and the spray goes well away to leeward. In any case the sea has gone down. Could you do with a cup of coffee and a breadfruit biscuit?'

'I could, too.'

'Killick! Killick, there.'

'Sir?' said Killick, still unnaturally meek, though a shade of the familiar shrewishness could now be detected. Indeed, he had recovered enough assurance to bring them only a meagre plate of the dried breadfruit slices, he being devoted to them himself.

The coffee came; and when half had been drunk Jack said 'Do you remember that I spoke to you about a flying column?'

'I remember it well; and I wondered at the time how and where it was to fly.'

Jack took a sheet from his desk and said 'This is Wainwright's chart of Moahu, and I am particularly grateful to him for the soundings of the reef off Pabay here in the north, and the channel into the harbour: the same for Eeahu down in the south. This hatching across the neck of the hourglass – a damned wide neck for an hourglass, I may say – represents the mountains that separate the two lobes, Kalahua's country in the top half, Queen Puolani's in the bottom. Now my plan is to sail straight into Pabay, preferably in the evening, but that depends on tide and weather, to sail in looking as like a whaler as possible, and to lay the *Franklin* aboard directly, dealing with her out of hand as we did the *Diane* at St Martin's. But time and tide may not serve, and she may have thrown up batteries on either side of the narrows, using the *Truelove*'s guns. I may have to lie off and deal with them first. So it seems to me that if things do not go as smooth as they did at St Martin's, we should land a body of men here' – pointing to a bay half a mile south of the harbour – 'to make a diversion – to take them from behind while we are battering them from in front. That is my flying column; and what I should like you to do as a medical man is to help me choose the most active, intelligent and of course healthy of the twenty or thirty men we can afford. I do not want any poxed hands – and I know you have the usual crop after Annamooka – or bursten bellies, however brave they may be, nor any ancients, above thirty-five. They must be extremely nimble. So please look at the list Tom and I have drawn up and tell me if there is an objection to any of the names from a medical point of view.'

'Very well,' said Stephen: and having run his eyes down the list he went on 'Tell me, are we far from Moahu?'

'About four days sail. I mean to ease off tomorrow, and give them a quiet Sunday: then target-practice on Monday, to air their intellects; and in the evening I may tell them what is afoot.'

'I see. Now as to your list, I have made a mark against the least medically sound: it is not necessarily discreditable at all.'

'Many thanks. Then of course there is the command; but I hesitate to question you about your messmates . . .'

Stephen's face closed: he said, 'Purely as the ship's surgeon, I should make no exception to any of them.'

'I am happy to hear it.'

There was a somewhat embarrassed silence, and to break it Stephen said 'Had we but world enough and time you could choose your band in the Irish manner. Did I ever tell you of Finn Mac Cool?'

'The gentleman that was so fond of salmon?'

'Himself. Now he commanded the forces of the nation, the Fianna Eirion, and none was accepted into any of the seven cohorts – I quote from a fallible memory, Jack, but at least I am sure of my figures – until he had learned the twelve Irish books of poetry and could say them without book: if the party to be accepted would defend himself with his target and sword from nine throws of the javelin from nine of the company that would stand but nine ridges from him at distance, and either cut the javelin with his sword or receive them all on his target without bleeding on him, he would be accepted; otherwise not. If the party running through the thickest wood of Ireland were overtaken by any of the seven cohorts and they pursuing him with all their might and main he would not be taken of them in their company. But if he had outrun them all without loss of any hair of his head, without breaking any old stick under his feet and he leaping over any tree that he should meet as high as the top of his head without impediment, and stooping under a tree as low as his knee and taking a thorn out of his foot (if it should chance to be in it) with his nail without impediment of his running, all which if he had done, he would be accepted as one of the company: otherwise not.'

'Twelve books, did you say?'

'Twelve, upon my soul.'

'And all by heart? Alas, with a Sunday coming between, I doubt it can be accomplished.

The Sunday in question was emphatically a day of rest, of as much rest as was feasible in a ship at sea. It is true that hammocks were piped up half an hour earlier than usual and that breakfast was swallowed fast so that the deck could be brought to a high state of perfection, with what little brass the frigate possessed blazing in the sun and all the ship's pigtails (the *Surprise*, rather old-fashioned in some respects, still had well over fifty, some of a most impressive length) untwined, often washed and always plaited afresh by the seaman's tie-mate, while all hands put on the clean clothes washed on Thursday and made themselves fine for divisions.

Divisions passed off perfectly well: the wind, though less powerful than it had been for some days, was steady and dead true to its quarter, with never a gust or a flurry; and the Captain, though scarcely jovial, could be said to have lost his wickedness; while when church was rigged it was observed that he had abandoned the Articles, leaving the sermon to Mr Martin.

Martin had no gift for preaching; he did not feel himself qualified to instruct others in moral, still less in spiritual, matters, and his few sermons in the *Surprise*, delivered long ago when he sailed as a chaplain rather than as surgeon's assistant, had been ill-received. He now therefore confined himself to reading the works of more able or at least more confident men; and as Stephen reached the half-deck on his way to the cabin from the sick-berth, where he had said a rosary with Padeen and some other Papists, he heard Martin's voice: 'Let no man say, I could not miss a fortune, for I have studied all my youth. How many men have studied more nights than he hath done hours, and studied themselves blind and mad in the mathematics, and yet wither in beggary in a corner? Let him never add, But I studied in a useful and gainful profession. How many have done so too, and yet never compassed the favour of a judge? And how many that have had all that, have struck upon a rock, even at full sea, and perished there?' And then some time later: 'What a dim vespers of a glorious festival, what a poor half-holiday, is Methusalem's nine hundred years to eternity! What a poor account hath that man that says, This land hath been in my name, and in my ancestors' from the conquest! What a yesterday is that? Not six hundred years. If I could believe the transmigration of souls and think that my soul had been successively in some creature or other since the Creation, what a yesterday is that? Not six thousand years. What a yesterday for the past, what a tomorrow for the future is any term that can be comprehended in cipher or counters?'

Jack dined that day, and dined well, off Stephen's fish, last year's lamb, and a thumping great spotted dog, his guests being Stephen himself of course, Pullings, Martin and Reade. With the ship running fast and easy, the water racing down her side in a speaking stream, they could not but be happy – a subdued happiness however in Pullings and Reade, still oppressed by the shameful exhibition at Annamooka – and after dinner they moved up to the quarterdeck for their coffee.

Mrs Oakes, who dined a little after twelve, had already been there for some time, her chair installed at the leeward end of the taffrail and her feet resting on a cheese of wads placed there by William Honey, an admirer still, like the rest of his mess. She was alone, her husband, West and even Adams being fast asleep, as indeed were almost all hands who were not actually on duty – the main and fore tops were filled with seamen asprawl on the folded studdingsails, their mouths open and their eyes shut, like Dutch boors in a harvest-field; and Davidge, the officer of the watch, had taken up his usual position by the weather hances. Jack led his troop aft and asked her how she did. 'Very well indeed, sir, I thank you,' she said. 'It would be an ungrateful woman that did not feel amazingly well, being carried over the sea in this splendid fashion. Driving fast on a turnpike in a well-hung carriage is charming, but it is nothing in comparison of this.'

Jack poured her coffee and they talked about the disadvantages of travel by land – coaches overturning, horses running away, horses refusing to run at all, crowded inns. That is to say Jack, Clarissa and Stephen talked. The others stood holding their little delicate cups, looking as easy as they could and simpering from time to time, until at last Martin contributed an account of a very wretched journey across Dartmoor in a gig whose wheels came off as night was falling, a rainstorm beating in from the west, the linch-pin lost in a bottomless mire and the horses audibly weeping. Martin was not one of those few men who can speak naturally when they are in a false position, and Stephen observed that Clarissa was secretly amused: yet she helped him along with polite attention and timely cries of 'Heavens!' 'Dear me' and 'How very horrid it must have been.'

From this, perhaps as an illustration of the greater ease of travel by sea, the conversation passed on to her foot-rest. 'Why is it called a wad of cheese?' she asked.

'A cheese of wads, I believe, ma'am,' said Jack. 'Cheese because it is a cylinder like a tall thin Stilton, and wads because that is what the cloth is filled with. I dare say you have seen a man load his fowling-piece?' Clarissa bowed. 'First he puts in his powder, then his shot, and then with his ramrod he thrusts down a wad to hold everything in place until he wishes to fire. That is just what we do with the great guns; only of course the wads are much bigger.'

Again Clarissa bent her head by way of agreement, and Stephen had the impression or rather the certainty that if she had spoken her voice would have been as unnatural as Martin's.

'Now that I come to think of it,' said Jack, gazing amiably at the eastern horizon, upon which Christmas Island should soon appear if his two chronometers, his last lunars and his noonday observation were correct. 'Now that I reflect, I do not believe you have ever seen the operation: you have always been below. We mean to have target-practice tomorrow, and if it would amuse you to watch, pray come on deck. You could see everything quite well, was you to stand amidships, by the barricade. Though perhaps you may not like the explosions. I know that elegant females' – smiling – 'do not always like it when one fires even a fowling-piece at anything like close quarters.'

'Oh, sir,' said Clarissa, 'I am not so elegant a female as to mind the report of a gun: and I should very much like to see your target-practice tomorrow. But now I think I must go and rouse my husband; he particularly desired me to wake him well before his watch.'

She rose; they bowed; and as she went down the companion-ladder the lookout at the masthead cried 'Land ho! On deck, there, land on the starboard bow. A low sort of long island,' he added in a subdued voice for the benefit of his friends in the maintops, 'with more of them fucking palm-trees.'

Early on Monday morning, with the sun slanting low across the long even swell so that its rounded summits, a furlong apart, were visible, though very soon they would be quite lost in the little fret of superficial waves, Captain Aubrey spread top-gallantsails, and the hands racing aloft very nearly crushed Stephen and Martin as they crouched in the mizen-top, train-ing the glass aft over the rail, gazing back at the land and the cloud of birds over it.

'I am persuaded that it is a vast atoll,' said Stephen. 'Vast; prodigiously extensive. Were we to climb higher still we might perhaps see across it, or at least make out a segment of the great circle.'

'I should be sorry to disturb the men at their work,' said Martin.

Stephen looked up as the hands came fleeting down, the outer men leaping in from the yardarm like so many gibbons, and did not press the point. He said 'We have been sailing past it almost all night: and though the rim of the lagoon may be no more than a musket-shot across at any given point, that still amounts to an enormous surface with no doubt a comparably enormous quantity of animals and vegetable life – the palms and the birds we have seen from afar, and some low bushes; but who knows what interesting predators, what wholly unexpected parasites they may have, to say nothing of undescribed forms of mollusc, insect, arachnid . . . there may even be some antediluvian mammals – a peculiar bat – that would confer immortality upon us. But shall we ever see it? No, sir. We shall not. Presently this ship will haul off, heave her wind, and spend hours, *hours* I say, bombarding the empty sea on the pretext of airing the mariners' intellects and in fact doing nothing but frighten the birds: yet she would never consider stopping for five minutes to let us pick up so much as an annelid.'

Stephen knew that he had said all this before, off the many, many islands and remote uninhabited shores they had passed, irretrievably passed; he knew that he might be being a bore; yet the tolerant smile on Martin's face, though very slight indeed, vexed him extremely.

After dinner – they had eaten alone – he said to Jack, 'At breakfast yesterday, when you were telling me about your first days at sea, I quoted Hobbes.'

'The learned cove that spoke of midshipmen as being nasty, brutish and short?'

'Well, in fact he was speaking of man's life, unimproved man's life: it was I that borrowed his words and applied them to the young gentlemen.'

'Very well applied too.'

'Certainly. Yet later conscience told me that my words were not only improper but also inaccurate. I looked out the passage this morning, and of course my conscience was right – is it ever wrong? – and I had omitted the words *solitary* and *poor*. "Solitary, poor, nasty, brutish and short" was what he said. And though *poor* may have been appropriate . . .'

'Appropriatissimo,' said Jack.

'The *solitude* had nothing to do with the overcrowded berth of your childhood. The false quotation was therefore one of those flashy worthless attempts at wit that I so much reprehend in others. Yet the point of all this is not to beat my breast crying mea culpa, mea maxima culpa, but rather to tell you that on the very same page I found that Hobbes, a learned cove, as you so rightly say, considered glory, after competition and diffidence, mankind's third principal cause of quarrel, so that trifles, as a word, a smile, a different opinion or any other sign of undervalue, were enough to bring violence about. Nay, destruction. I had read this passage before of course – it was on the same page, as I said – but its full force had escaped me until today, when just such a trifle . . .'

'Come in,' called Jack.

'Captain Pullings' compliments and duty, sir,' said Reade, 'and he believed you wished to know the moment the targets were ready.'

The targets were ready, rafts made of empty beef-casks and what odd pieces of plank and rail the carpenter could bring himself to part with, each with a square of bunting flying aloft. The gun-crews were ready too, and had been ever since the Captain's words to Clarissa were reported to the forecastle and confirmed by messages sent to the carpenter and the disappearance of the gunner and his mates into the forward magazine, where with infinite precautions they lit the lantern in the light-room and sat next door filling cartridges, stiff flannel bags made to take the due charge of powder, by the light that came through the double glass windows.

Each gun-crew naturally wished to wipe the eye of its neighbours, indeed of all other gun-crews aboard; but they were all eager to mollify their skipper, partly because it was more agreeable to sail under a captain that did not flog you and stop your grog, but even more because many were deeply attached to him and were eager to regain his esteem, while all hands freely acknowledged his seamanship and fighting qualities. Throughout the last dogwatch of Sunday, therefore, and in what few moments of leisure the forenoon and afternoon watches of Monday allowed, the captains of the guns and their crews titivated their piece, making sure that all blocks ran free, that all crows, worms, sponges, handspikes and other instruments that ought to be there were there in fact, smoothing their already well-smoothed roundshot, gently swabbing the name painted over the gun-port: *Towser, Nancy Dawson, Spitfire, Revenge*. This checking and re-checking was carried out by each member of the crew, by the midshipman in charge of a division of guns, by the officers, and of course by Mr Smith the gunner himself – everything was passed in review, from the upper-deck twelve-pounders and the long nines in the forecastle chase-ports to the twenty-four-pounder carronades on the quarterdeck.

No one therefore was either astonished or caught unprepared when, the drum having beaten to quarters and Mrs Oakes having appeared at the barricade, Captain Aubrey called 'Silence' in the midst of the expectant hush: a purely formal word, followed by 'Cast loose your guns,' and 'Mr Bulkeley, carry on.'

After this no more orders were called for. The bosun and his mates eased the first target over the headrail, paused until it was rather better than a quarter of a mile aft and to leeward, then launched another, and so until there was a string of five going away to the south-west. The *Surprise* had been sailing close-hauled under topsails and topgallants during this; and after a considering pause Jack bore up and brought the wind on her larboard quarter: the sail-trimmers, aware of his motions, left their guns without a word, clapping on to brace and sheet until she was steady on her new course, when they belayed and returned to the stations like automata, no words having passed.

With the wind so far abaft the beam there was much less noise in the rigging, less from the bow-wave and little indeed from the following sea. The men had mostly stripped to the waist; those with pigtails had clubbed them; many had tied black or red handkerchiefs round their heads. They stood or knelt in their set positions – the powder-man with his cartridge-box directly behind his gun far to larboard; the gun-heavers right against the ship's side with handspike or crowbar away from it; the boarders with their cutlasses and pistols, the fireman with his bucket, standing like statues; the match-holder kneeling clear of the murderous recoil; the captain glaring along the barrel; and as the target came in sight, fine on the starboard bow, a quarter of a mile away, murmuring words to his crew for pointing and elevation. And all this time the smell of slow-match in the tubs drifted along the deck.

'From forward aft,' called Jack as the first target came within range. 'D'ye hear me, there: from forward aft.'

The match-holders reached behind them, seized the match and knelt by the captain again, blowing the ashes off its glow.

'Starboard a point,' said Jack to the helmsman, and then much louder 'From forward aft: fire.'

The extreme tension broke as the bow-gun's captain

whipped the proffered match across to the touch-hole and the gun went off with a deafening crash, leaping bodily from the deck and instantly racing back between its minders with frightful speed. But even before it was brought up by the breeching, the scream of its trucks and the great twang of the rope was drowned by the crash of its neighbour and so down the line in a prodigious thunder-clap that went on and on, the jets of smoke stabbed through and through with orange flame, a roar that was taken up in a different voice by the quarterdeck carronades. The wind drove the smoke away to leeward and the later shot could be seen raising white fountains in the general boil where the raft had been or skipping with immense bounds over the sea towards or even beyond it.

Already the foremost guns, held in on the recoil, were being wormed, sponged and reloaded; but before they were run out again one after another with the usual rumbling crash, Jack heard a clapping, thin and remote to his somewhat deafened ears, and turning he saw Mrs Oakes' delighted face. Her eyes were dark with emotion and she cried 'Oh how splendid! Oh what glory!'

Jack said 'It was just a rippling broadside, not to strain her timbers. They will start again directly.'

'How I wish Dr Maturin were here. Such prodigious . . .' She could not find the word.

'Directly' in this case meant two full minutes after the first discharge, a leisurely performance compared with the *Surprise*'s three accurate broadsides in three minutes eight seconds which she had achieved in the days when she was manned entirely by highly-trained men-of-war's men; but now many of her people were privateers who had always shipped by the lay, having no wages but sharing in the proceeds of the voyage less the expenses. They therefore had a deeply-engrained hatred of waste and they could not be brought to add to the expenses by blazing away with powder at eighteen pence a pound, as though it were free – paid for by the King. In most cases Jack had mixed the gun-crews, to avoid jealousies; but *Sudden Death* for example was manned entirely by the frigate's Sethians, privateers and members of a religious body in Shelmerston, excellent seamen, sober and reliable, but even more unwilling than most to waste a shot, and very deliberate in their aim. Still, by training their guns as far aft as they possibly could they did manage to send most of their shots close to the remains of the target.

'That was rather a ragged ripple, I am afraid,' said Jack to Mrs Oakes. 'I trust we shall do better next time.'

They did better, much better: one minute forty seconds between broadsides, the first raising the target high on a turmoil of white water, the second scattering it all abroad. 'Make fast your guns,' cried Jack over the cheering – Clarissa's pipe could be heard as shrill as Reade's – and he took the ship across the line of targets to engage the next two with the larboard guns, already cast loose by the second captains.

Firing from to-leeward meant that the flight and pitch of the shot could be followed more exactly, and when Jack, having given the order 'House your guns' turned to Clarissa, not without pride, and asked her how she had liked it, she cried 'Oh sir, I am quite hoarse with hallooing and amazed with the sound and the glory. Dear me, I had no notion . . . What a terrible, splendid thing a battle must be: like the Day of Judgment.' And after a pause, 'Pray what do you mean to do with the fifth?'

'That, ma'am, is for the bow-chasers.' He looked affectionately at her face, glowing with candid excitement and enthusiasm – she had never looked so animated nor half so handsome – and for a moment he was inclined to invite her to come forward and see the fine-work of firing a gun. But he hesitated, put the notion aside as out of place and walked along the gangway over the happy, sweating gun-crew in the waist as they were securing their guns, bowsing all lashings taut and talking in the loud, after-broadside voice about their wonderful accuracy and speed. 'Though mark you,' said the captain of *Spitfire*, 'we should have been even quicker, if *some people* had been more *sudden* than *dead*.' His neighbour, the bearded Sethian Slade, captain of the gun called *Sudden Death*, instantly replied 'And we should have been even more accurate, if some other people had been more *deadly* than *sudden*.'

Respect for their Captain, immediately overhead, restrained the Sethians' joy, but they beat Slade on the back and shook both his hands, while even the *Spitfire* crew laughed and said 'That got you in the balls, Ned.'

The bow-chasers on the forecastle were what the Navy called brass long nine-pounders. They were in fact made of bronze rather than brass, but the force of the word was such that the hands polished them assiduously, producing all the shine that bronze was capable of: on the other hand they were long and they did take nine-pound balls; they were also as accurate as smooth-bore cannon could well be. They both belonged to Jack: one he had bought in Sydney; the other he had had time out of mind and he knew its temper, its kick, its tendency to shoot better from the third ball to the twelfth, when it called for a rest to cool – if this were denied, it was apt to leap and break its breeching.

Both Jack and Tom Pullings loved to fire a great gun. Each had his own picked crew and each pointed his own chaser: each now fired three rounds; and as Jack himself had taught Pullings, then a long-legged midshipman in his first command, how to point a gun, their style was very much the same. One shot, though true for line, a little long; the next a trifle short; while Jack's third scattered the barrels and Pullings' leapt skipping through the wreckage. With the ship taking the swell abeam, the roll scarcely affected guns firing ahead, and she hardly pitched at all; so with a range of five hundred yards, rapidly narrowing, this was no outstanding feat of gunnery; but it thoroughly pleased the gunners and delighted the hands. Mrs Oakes' congratulations could not have been kinder, and in the excitement both West and Davidge ventured 'Give you joy of your shooting, sir.'

All this had taken a remarkably short time measured by clock rather than by activity and emotion, and a little before sunset all hands were summoned aft. When they were assembled in their usual unseemly heap their Captain surveyed them with a benevolence they had not seen this many a weary day and night and in his strong voice he said 'Shipmates, we have warmed our guns and new-charged them: no fear of damp powder or charges that have to be drawn. And that is just as well, because we may have to use them in a couple of days or so. I will tell you the position. There is a British ship and her crew captured in Moahu, the island we are heading for, by the natives and their friend an American privateer, the *Franklin*, ship-rigged, twenty-two nine-pounders, French crew. The island is used by some English fur-traders on the Nootka—Canton run, and by certain South Sea whalers; and she may try to snap some more of them up. She nearly had the *Daisy*, as you heard in Annamooka. So we must put a stop to her capers. When we cut the *Diane* out of St Martin's I was able to tell you just how she lay. This time I cannot do so, although the master of the *Daisy* gave me a chart of the harbour and the approaches; but I do not think we shall go very far wrong by laying her alongside and boarding in the smoke.'

The Surprises, who had been listening with the utmost intensity, nodded their heads and uttered an affirmative growl, interspersed with 'that's right, mate' and 'board her in the smoke, ha, ha.'

'But we want no trouble,' said Jack. 'We do not want any of our people to be knocked on the head, if we can avoid it. So since she will be pleased at the sight of a whaler, English or American, our best plan is to sail in looking as much like one as ever we can. Of course there may be no sailing in: she may have thrown up batteries each side of the narrows and she may smoke what we are at: and we may have to deal with the situation some other way. But in any case the first thing to do is to make the ship into a whaler: we turned her into a blue Spanish barque once, as I dare say you remember; and that answered quite well.' General laughter, and a cry of 'God love us, how we sweated!' 'Now I know at least a score of you have been in the Greenland or South Seas fishery at one time or another, and I want those hands to choose the three longest-headed, most experienced men among them to help us change the barky into a whaler, a tired, shabby, down-at-heel, three-years-at-sea old whaler, short-handed and peaceful.'

Chapter Nine

An old tired shabby whaler, with a crow's nest aloft, trying-out gear and general filth on deck and deeply squalid sides stood into Pabay, the north-eastern port of Moahu, in Kalahua's territory, just making headway against the ebb under a single blue-patched foretopsail.

In her crow's nest stood her even shabbier master in a black-guardly round hat, crammed up against his unshaven mate, both of them gauging the wind and the distance between the two headlands on either side of the entrance. 'We should get out in two tacks at slack water or on the ebb,' said Jack, and they returned to their examination of the far end, where the wide, sheltered bay drew in before broadening into the harbour itself.

'We shall open the narrows any minute now, sir,' said Pullings.

Jack nodded. 'I do not see a hint of a battery on either side,' he said: and then as the narrows opened he called down 'Mr West, come up the sheet and drop the kedge.'

'Nor no privateer neither,' said Pullings. 'The fat round tub of a ship right down against the shore where the stream comes in is a Nootka fur-trader, if ever there was one.'

Jack nodded again: he had had her in his glass for some time and after a silence he said 'She must be the *Truelove*. She was hove down just there when Wainwright left her. They have come at the leak. She has crossed her yards and bent her sails, and she is riding low: stores and water aboard for sure.'

'Nothing could be a better example of Dr Falconer's general position,' said Stephen, standing with Martin in the mizentop. 'The whole is volcanic, with coral superimposed here and there and lying around the edge in reefs. That mountain, that truncated cone rising behind the jagged hills, certainly has a crater at the top. It is no doubt the volcano he wished to explore. Indeed, there is a little cloud of what may well be smoke just over it.'

'Certainly. Furthermore, the extreme luxuriance of the vegetation surely implies a volcanic soil: do but consider that impenetrable forest – I say impenetrable, but now I see a road along the stream.'

'Then again these strands, now coral, now lava-black, argue repeated eruptions.'

'We hear of submarine outbursts of extraordinary violence.'

'Iceland, says Sir Joseph Banks, is blessed not only with birds so remarkable as the gerfalcon, the harlequin duck and both phalaropes, but also with sensible volcanic phenomena at virtually all seasons.'

'There is something I do not like about that village,' said Jack. 'Wainwright spoke of it as full of people – crowded – and now there are very few walking about. And they are only women and children with here and there an old man; the canoes are all drawn up, most of them high up.'

Pullings was digesting this, and the absence of nets spread out to dry, when two girls, helped by a band of children, slid a small two-hulled canoe down the sand and put off, the girls managing the immense sail with no apparent difficulty, steering very close to the wind and travelling with extraordinary speed.

Jack heaved himself out of the deep crow's nest: the topgallantmasts gave a warning creak. 'Take care, sir,' cried Pullings: Jack frowned, let himself gently down to the cross-trees, reaching out for a standing backstay and shot down to the quarterdeck like a well-controlled meteor, landing with a thump and hands just this side the scorching-point. 'Pass the word for Owen,' he said; and to Owen, 'Hail the canoe in South Seas as it approaches the narrows: hail it very civil.'

'Very civil it is, sir,' said Owen. Yet he had no time to make his compliment, for in their friendly Polynesian way the girls hailed them first, smiling up and waving a free hand.

'Ask them to come aboard,' said Jack. 'Mention feathers, coloured handkerchiefs.'

Words passed, but the girls, though amused and half-tempted by feathers and coloured handkerchiefs, did not choose to come up the side; and to be sure, the few visible Surprises looked deeply unappetizing. Nevertheless they stayed long enough to make three rings about the ship, handling their craft with a skill that was a joy to behold, and to answer the question 'Where is the *Franklin*?' 'Gone to chase a ship.' 'Where are all the men?' 'Gone to war. Kalahua is going to eat Queen Puolani: he has taken the gun.'

Their third remark, though shrill and high, was uttered by both at once and much of what might have been comprehensible was lost in the wind as they sped off; but it seemed to tell the Surprises, who at this point were sailing under American colours, that they would find their friend in Eeahu when the *Franklin* had caught her ship.

'The *Truelove* is lowering down a boat, sir,' said Pullings.

An eight-oared cutter: and although some of those that lowered it were sailors, those that came down into the stern-sheets were obviously landsmen. Jack considered them and their ship, their thinly-manned ship, for some time as the cutter made its way from the shore. 'Mr West,' he said, 'let all boats be ready at a moment's notice. Mr Davidge,' – calling down the hatch – 'stand by.' Davidge was in command of the flying column, armed and prepared for any emergency that might arise and kept below decks, where they fairly stifled.

He then recovered the kedge, hauled the sheet aft and stood on through the narrows, looking very attentively at the country between the village and the mountains, where the stream came towards the harbour.

When the cutter was within hail a man stood up, fell down, stood up again holding the coxswain's shoulder and called 'What ship is that?' in an approximately American voice, drawing his face in a sideways contortion to do so.

'The *Titus Oates*. Where is Mr Dutourd?'

'Gone a-chasing. He will join us in Eeahu in three–four days. Do you have any tobacco? Any wine?'

'Sure. Come aboard.' With the wheel in his own hands Jack stood on past the cutter and turned so that the *Surprise* lay between the boat and the shore; speaking to the quartermaster, one of the few hands on deck, he said quietly 'When they hook on, hoist our own colours.' It was a sophistry: the colours, streaming directly towards the shore, would be seen neither by the *Truelove* nor by a boat attached to the *Surprise*'s windward mainchains. But certain forms had to be observed.

The man who hailed and three others from the stern-sheets came awkwardly up. They had pistols in their belts; so had the man they left behind. They were not seamen; the canvas strips that concealed most of the ship's guns did not surprise them, nor did her whaling gear, improbable when seen close at hand.

'The Liberator said we should soon have wine and tobacco,' said the leader, smiling as pleasantly as he could.

'Mr West,' said Jack, 'pray tell Mr Davidge that these gentlemen are to be properly served. Bilboes in the forehold might be most suitable. Go with him, Bonden,' he added, feeling that perhaps West might not quite have grasped the point of the last murmured words.

In point of fact everybody aboard, apart from these wretched white or whitish mercenaries, was aware of Captain Aubrey's motions, even Stephen and Martin, newly arrived from the mizentop; and when Jack, seeing Bonden return with a satisfied smile, said in an undertone, 'Doctor, pray get that ugly fellow in the sternsheets to come aboard,' he needed no explanation but called out in French, asking for news of Monsieur Dutourd's health and suggesting that the man should climb carefully up the side with a mariner or two capable of carrying heavy weights. One of the mariners he pointed to, stroke oar, had been gazing up for some time very earnestly, making discreet nods and becks, and Stephen was almost sure he was one of a thousand former patients.

The mercenary came up with no further persuasion and stroke oar after him. The seaman having saluted the quarterdeck instantly gave the mercenary a truly frightful kick that hurled him with stunning force against the capstan. Bonden took his pistol away as though they had practised the act for weeks; and the seaman, turning to Jack, pulled off his hat and said 'William Hoskins, sir, armourer's mate in *Polychrest*, now belonging to the *Truelove*.'

'I am heartily glad to see you again, Hoskins,' said Jack, shaking his hand. 'Tell me, are there many other Frenchmen in the *Truelove*?'

'About a score, sir. They was left behind to keep us at work and to stop the natives from stealing when the others went off to war with Kalahua. They cut capers over us something cruel, and spoke sarcastic, those that could speak any English.'

'Are the rest of the boat's crew Trueloves?'

'All but the coxswain, sir; and I dare say they have scragged him by now. A right bastard: he killed our skipper.'

Jack glanced over the side, and there indeed were the Trueloves busily, silently, drowning the coxswain. From a sense of duty Jack called out 'Belay, there,' and they belayed, coming aboard as nimbly as cats for a glass of grog, served out on the half-deck. 'We smoked you was no right whaler from the shore,' said one of them to Killick. 'But did we tell them infernal buggers? No, mate, we did not.'

During this time the *Surprise* had let fall her topsail and she was making for an anchorage close inshore on the south side of the harbour. The cutter was towing alongside and her own boats were in a high state of readiness for lowering down. 'Mr Davidge,' said Jack, 'it is of the first importance that you and your men should be on that road into the mountains, that road by the stream, before any of the Frenchmen from the *Truelove*. They are almost certain to run once we show them our guns, and if they get to Kalahua we are dished. He and his men are only a day's march away – perhaps not so much seeing they are trying to drag a gun.'

Even in a frigate as well worked-up as the *Surprise* the order 'man and arm boats' was rarely carried out in under twenty-five minutes, the system of tackles to the fore and main yardarms being so cumbrous; and the launch was scarcely in the water before the Frenchmen in the *Truelove* had grown suspicious. They were gathering on the shore and moving through the village southwards along the stream, carrying bundles.

The launch and blue cutter were already full of men, however, and Jack called 'Go ahead with what you have, Mr Davidge, and do your best to hold them until the rest come up.'

'I shall do my very best, sir,' said Davidge, looking up and smiling. 'Shove off. Give way.'

The boats raced for the shore and ran far up the sand; the men bundled out, holding their muskets high, and almost at once they disappeared into the tree-ferns.

When the other cutter and the gig were on their way Jack hurried up into the foretop. The deep belt of tree-ferns thinned out to a country of tall grass scattered with bushes and small but very thick patches of wood, full of lianas. The column could be seen here and there, still in reasonable formation, but much drawn-out, the leading men doing their best to keep up with the extraordinarily agile Davidge. Their muskets gleamed in the sun, and their cutlasses as they slashed at the lianas and the undergrowth.

The Frenchmen had now started running too, throwing down their bundles but not their arms. They, like Davidge, were clearly aiming for the point where the stream broke out of the mountains in a narrow gorge; and although the distance from the column's landing-place to the gorge was much the same as that from the village, the Frenchmen had the advantage of the road cut for the gun.

'Even so,' said Jack, clasping his hands with great force, 'we had half an hour's start.' The line was becoming still more drawn-out, Davidge going like a thoroughbred: he was running not indeed for his life but rather for his living, for all that made life worth while. The other boats had now landed their men, and they were tearing along the track already made – the tree-ferns could be seen waving as they passed. 'Oh no, oh no!' he cried as a body of Surprises, outstripped, tried to catch up by forcing their way straight through a brake criss-crossed with thorny creepers. 'Would God I had gone with them,' he said; and he was about to lean over and call 'Tom, try a long shot at the Frenchmen on the road,' when he realized that the sound of the gun would act as a spur, doing certain harm for almost no likelihood of good.

The Surprises had now come to fairly clear country and the two lines were converging fast. Davidge had reached the stream: he was across it: he climbed the far bank and stood in the gorge, facing the three leading French, his sword in his hand. He ran the first through the body, pistolled the second, and the third brought him down with a clubbed musket. From that moment on it was impossible to make out particular actions: more Surprises hurled themselves across the stream, more Frenchmen came up the road as fast as they could run. Dust rose over the close fighting, the hand-to-hand battle in the gorge; there was a steady crackle of musket-fire as the reinforcements came up taking the Frenchmen from behind and picking off those who were not yet engaged or those few who tried to run back.

The shouting died; the dust settled. It was clear that Davidge's men had won. Jack took the ship across to lie alongside the *Truelove*, landed in the jollyboat with Stephen, Martin and Owen to interpret, and walked fast along the road towards the gorge. He was silent, more exhausted than if he had taken part.

It was a small group they met, men of Davidge's division, carrying his body.

'Was anyone else killed?' asked Jack.

'Harry Weaver copped it, sir,' said Paget, captain of the foretop, 'and William Brymer, George Young and Bob Stewart were so badly hurt we dursn't move them. And there are some more their mates are helping down to the boats.'

'Did any French survivors get away?'

'There weren't no survivors, sir.'

By the height of flood everything was laid along: the wounded had been brought down, the Trueloves who had taken refuge in a puuhonua, a sanctuary so profoundly taboo that even

229

Kalahua would not allow the French to violate it, had been recovered, and the *Surprise*, followed by the *Truelove*, had warped across the harbour to the northern side of the narrows, waiting for the first of ebb to waft them through.

As Stephen came into the cabin Jack looked up and said 'How are your patients coming along?'

'Tolerably well, I thank you. At one time I was doubtful about Stewart's leg – I even reached for the saw – but now I believe that with the blessing we may save it. The rest of our people are mostly straightforward cut or stab wounds, though some poor fellows from the *Truelove* are in a sad way. Is there any coffee in that pot?'

'I believe so. I had not the heart to finish it; I am afraid it may be cold.' Stephen poured his cup in silence. He knew how Jack hated watching a battle rather than take part in it, and how he would brood over orders he might have given – ideal orders that would have meant victory at no cost to his own people. 'But at least I can give you some good news,' Jack went on. 'One of the Trueloves from the taboo place was born in the Sandwich Islands – Tapia is his name, a chief's son, intelligent, speaks uncommon good English and he knows these parts very well. He it was that told the others about the puuhonua when they had to cut and run after their captain and his mate were killed. And he says he is confident that once we get out, if we get out, he can pilot us through the reefs. I am amazingly glad of it, because although Wainwright's chart is a good one, picking up his bearings on a moonless night would be a damned anxious business.'

'Sir,' said Killick, coming in with a tray, 'which I brought you a pot and a decanter.'

'God shield you from death, Preserved Killick,' said Stephen. 'I could do with both. Faith, so I could.'

'And would your honour like some hot water?'

'Perhaps I should,' said Stephen, looking at his hands, which were gloved over with brown dried blood. 'It is a curious thing, but though I nearly always clean my instruments I sometimes forget my person.' Washed and drinking coffee and brandy in alternate sips, he said 'But tell me, brother, why should you wish to grope through the darkness? The sun always rises.'

'There is not a moment to be lost. Kalahua means to attack on Friday in the morning, whether he can get his gun there in time or not: his god says he cannot fail.'

'How do you know?'

'Tapia told me: he had it from his sweetheart, who brought him food in the puuhonua, and all the news. If we do not get out on this ebb and with this moderate backing wind we may lose essential days – we may even have to wait for the change of the moon. What I hope, what I very much hope to do is to run down to Eeahu by Wednesday, tell Puolani that she is about to be attacked and that we shall defend her against Kalahua and the *Franklin* if she will promise to love King George, and so make our arrangements to deal with either or both with at least a day in hand.'

'Very good.' Stephen considered for a while and then asked 'What have you learnt of the *Franklin?*'

'It appears that although Dutourd is no great seaman he now has a Yankee sailing-master, as they say in America, who is: the ship is a flyer, and he drives his people very hard. Of course, with only twenty-two nine-pounders, a broadside of ninety-nine pounds, she is scarcely a match for us, with a hundred and sixty-eight, not counting carronades; but a fight at sea can turn on one lucky shot, as you know very well, and I had much rather not have to cope with her and perhaps her prize at the same time as Kalahua. I ought to have said, by the way, that Dutourd took all his seamen out of the *Truelove* to run after this chase, so he would have plenty of hands to serve his guns. Come in.'

'If you please, sir,' said Reade, 'Mr West says the tide is on the turn.'

They waited until the gentle current had grown to a stream that gurgled round their stern and tightened the hawsers from ship to shore so that they rose above the surface, almost straight, in a low dripping curve, and the palm-trees, which acted as bollards, leant still more. 'Let go,' called Jack, and the two ships moved smoothly out through the narrows.

The wealth of precautions – tow-line to the launch anchored out in the bay to heave her head to windward if she sagged, hands poised to fend her off the rock, a complication of lines to the *Truelove* – proved unnecessary: they both passed through with ten yards to spare and instantly flashed out topsails to gather way enough to go about on their first leg. The *Surprise* had a remarkably clean bottom, even now, and she had always been brisk in stays; she came round easily. But Jack, watching the deep-laden bluff-bowed *Truelove*, had a horrible feeling that she was not going to manage it; and that since there was no room to box off, still less to wear, Tom Pullings would have to club-haul her: a perilous manoeuvre with an unknown crew. The critical moment passed, and with it his extreme anxiety: she filled on the starboard tack – she was round, and the Surprises would have joined the Trueloves' cheer – she was an uncommonly valuable prize – if Davidge's body had not been lying there, sewn up in a hammock with four cannon-balls at his feet and an ensign over him.

The next tack took them clear of the harbour, though the *Truelove* was within biscuit-toss of the headland. Tapia's sweetheart, who had kept pace in her canoe, said goodbye and he took the ship along the landward side of the reef and so through the dog-leg passage, the *Truelove* following. Here in the fading light they both heaved to the kind and steady wind. Aboard the *Surprise* the ship's bell tolled; Martin said the proper, deeply moving words; men from Davidge's division fired three volleys; and his body slid over the side.

They filled again, passed two small islands with their attendant reefs – Tapia pointed out their bearings against the dark peaks of Moahu – and then they were in the open sea.

Oakes took the first watch, and while he was on duty Stephen came on deck to breathe: the air of the sick-berth, in spite of the wind-sails, was uncommonly fetid. Apart from the heat and the numbers, two of the rescued Trueloves had shockingly neglected and mortifying wounds. Clarissa was sitting there in the light of the stern lantern and for a while they talked about the extraordinary phosphorescence of the sea – the wake stretched away in pale fire until it joined the *True-*

love's bow-wave – and the brilliance of the stars in the black black sky. Then she said 'Oakes was very deeply grieved not to be one of the landing-party; and I am afraid Captain Aubrey was sadly upset by – by the casualties.'

'He was indeed; yet you are to observe that if fighting-men, accustomed to battle from their youth, were to mourn for their companions as long as they might in civil life, they would run melancholy mad.'

Oakes came aft: he said 'Give you joy of our prize, Doctor. I have scarcely seen you since we took her. It is true that the *Truelove*'s guns were all spiked?'

'So I understand: all but one. Tapia told me that Captain Hardy and his mates were spiking the last when the Frenchmen killed them.'

'How do you spike a gun?' asked Clarissa.

'You drive a nail or something of that kind down the touch-hole, so that the flash of the priming don't reach the charge. You can't fire the gun till you get the spike out,' said Oakes.

'It appears that they used steel spikes, which the *Franklin*'s gunner could not deal with. He was going to try drilling new touch-holes when they went off in chase of the ship they are still pursuing,' said Stephen.

Two bells. 'All's well' called the lookouts round the ship, and Oakes went forward to receive the quartermaster's report of 'Six knots, sir, if you please' and to chalk it on the log-board. Coming back, he said 'I know it ain't genteel to talk about money, sir, but I must say the prize could not have come at a better moment for Clarissa and me.' He spoke with a touching earnestness, and by the light of the stern-lantern Stephen caught a look of tolerant affection on her face. 'All the hands are busy reckoning their shares. The *Truelove*'s merchant's clerk told them the worth of the cargo to the last penny, and Jemmy Ducks says the little girls may get close on nine pounds apiece – they walk about scarcely touching the deck, and thinking of presents. You, sir, are to have a blue coat lined with white, whatever it may cost.'

'Bless them,' said Stephen. 'But I did not know they formed part of the ship's company.'

'Oh yes, sir. The Captain rated them boys, third class, long ago, so that Jemmy might have their allowance, to ease his spirits.'

'Oh!' cried Clarissa. 'What, what is this?' She held up a writhing viscous object.

'A flying squid,' said Stephen. 'If you count, you will find he has ten legs.'

'Even if he had fifty, he would have no business spoiling the front of my dress,' she said quite mildly. 'Fly off, sir' – tossing it over the rail.

With the breeze steady on their larboard quarter they went easily along under single-reefed topsails, sitting in their island of lantern-light surrounded by darkness, and talking in a desultory, amiable fashion bell after bell, while the wind sang in the rigging, the blocks creaked rhythmically and the ritual cries were repeated at their due intervals.

Half-way through the watch Oakes left them. 'I am happy to have this chance of speaking to you,' said Stephen, 'because I should like to ask you whether you would welcome the opportunity of going home – of returning to England.'

'I have hardly thought about it,' said Clarissa. 'My only wish was to get away from New South Wales, *away* rather than *to* anywhere. I have not really thought at all. The present, with all its inconveniences, seemed to me the natural present; and if I had not with great perseverance contrived to make myself so generally disliked I could think of nothing better than sailing on and on and on.'

'Dear Clarissa, collect yourself. I must be back in the sick-berth very soon. Suppose Captain Aubrey were to send this prize away under the command of Mr Oakes, would you rejoice at the thought of seeing England again?'

'Dear Doctor, pray consider: of course I should like to be in England again, but I was transported, and if I were to return before my time I might be taken up and sent back again, which I could not bear.'

'Not, I believe, as a married woman; and if you were to keep away from St James's Street, the likelihood of your being recognized is less than that of your being struck by a thunderbolt. And even in that case I have connexions who are as it were lightning-conductors. I am speaking to you in this fashion, Clarissa, because I believe that you are a discreet and honourable woman, one who has a friendship for me as I have a friendship for her, one who understands the value of silence. If you return, I will give you a letter to a friend of mine who lives in Shepherd Market, a good, decent man who would like to hear all that you told me and more and who would certainly protect you in the extraordinarily unlikely event of your being taken up.'

After a long silence Clarissa said 'To be sure, I had rather be in England than anywhere else. But what could I do there? As you know, a midshipman has no half-pay; and I could not go back to Mother Abbott's: not now.'

'No, no, never in life. There is not the least question of that, at all. Captain Aubrey has considerable influence with the Admiralty; my friend more still; and if between them they did not get Oakes a ship at once, he having passed for lieutenant, you would set up house with him for a while. If they succeed, why sure, you might feel lonely, as perhaps my wife does when I am at sea, and you might stay with her. She has a vast great house in the county – whatever county it is behind Portsmouth. Far too big for a woman and she alone apart from our little Brigid and a few servants and the horses. She breeds Arabians.' He spoke a little at random; Clarissa was clearly troubled, and she probably did not attend.

'Yes,' she said, 'but suppose I had done something wrong in Botany Bay – suppose I had committed a capital crime like . . . like throwing a baby down a well, for example, and suppose that finding me gone they had sent word to England, might I not be sent back for trial?'

'Listen, my dear, with ifs you can put all Paris into a bottle. The protection I offer you will, with reasonable discretion on your part, cover you from a multitude of sins, many or even most of them capital. Here is Padeen, his soul to the Devil, and I must go. Think of what I have said, now: speak to no one – the whole thing is a mere hypothesis, since I may not persuade the Captain – tell no one at all what I have said, and let me know yea or nay with a look in the morning. Come and be examined if ever there is time. I am away. God bless, now.'

It was morning before he reached the quarterdeck again, a brilliant morning with the sun well up and green land, ending in Eeahu Point, all along the starboard beam. Tapia was at the foremasthead, guiding the ship through the passage in the south-eastern reef. 'All clear now, sir,' he hailed. 'Nine fathom water all the way till you open the bay.' He came down and continued his conversation with the two canoes that had been alongside for some time, and Jack noticed the jollyboat shove off from the *Truelove*'s side, with his armourer in it. 'Come up the sheet a trifle,' he said, to check the frigate's way: vain words – attentive hands had already done it.

'Which the coffee is getting cold,' said Killick. 'And the squids won't be worth eating.'

'Mr Smith wishes to tell you that the armourer has unspiked all the *Truelove*'s guns,' said Pullings, coming across the deck and taking off his hat.

The information came down the chain of command to the armourer, who stepped forward, wheezing and chuckling, gave Jack a handkerchief full of spikes, all with an internal screw-thread tapped into the thick end and all glistening with sweet oil. 'I learnt that ploy in the old *Illustrious*,' he said, chuckling still.

'And it was an *illustrious* deed, too,' said Jack. 'Well done, Rogers, upon my word. Good morning, Doctor. You could not have timed your arrival better: we have fried squids for breakfast.'

The squids dispatched, the proper enquiries after the sick-berth made, and a fresh pot of coffee begun, Jack said quietly, 'It may seem flying in the face of Providence to talk about what to do after a battle before you have fought it; but some things, like preventer-stays, have to be laid on before-hand, although in the event they may not prove useful. So I will say this: the gunroom's problems would be best resolved if I were to send Oakes in with the prize. But what would his wife think

of it? I do not want to order that good modest young woman
back if she don't choose to go. What do you think? You know
her so much better than I do.'

'I cannot tell. But I shall be seeing her later in the morning
and I will endeavour to find out. When do you propose to
land?'

'Not until after dinner. I am letting the canoes come alongside and gossip, so that Queen Puolani will know everything
about us and what is afoot. She will not be caught unprepared
– it is a dreadful thing to have a whole carriageful of people
draw up at your door and leap out grinning, the house all
ahoo, carpets taken up, a great washing going on, the children
bawling, yourself confined to the head, having taken physic,
and your wife gone to Pompey in hopes of a new cook.'

The Queen was not to be caught unprepared; nor was the
Surprise or her people. The quarterdeck carronades, so much
lighter than long guns, and at short range so much more
deadly, were made ready for carrying ashore, together with
powder and shot, mostly case-shot, in canisters of twenty-four
pounds apiece. The ship's blackened sea-service muskets were
blackened again, the seaman's natural propensity to polish
having made them shine more than they should, as Jack had
noticed at Pabay; and now, considering the country before
him and all that Tapia had to say about it, he had fair expec-
tations of laying an ambush. Pikes, bayonets, boarding-axes,
cutlasses, pistols and murdering-pieces were all laid neatly out
on the one hand, only waiting the order to go ashore; and on
the other bandages, splints, surgical needles and waxed
thread, silk or hemp. The civil side was naturally of great
importance too: presents – a large looking-glass, feathers, pat-
terned cloth, cut-glass decanters – had been laid in a sandalwood chest, while a crown piece, with King George's head,
ringed and hung from a sky-blue ribbon, lay in Jack's pocket
– and the officers, knowing the Polynesians' great regard for
rank, set out silver-buckled shoes, white silk stockings,
breeches, fine coats and cocked hats, and the Captain's barge-

men put by their uniform dress of white trousers, light blue brass-buttoned jackets and neat little pumps with bows, agony to wear on feet long flattened by bare contact with the deck. Because of the heat, and for fear of dirtying them, however, none of these things were put on until the *Surprise*, followed by the *Truelove* and accompanied by many canoes, rounded-to opposite Eeahu, brought up in five fathom water, and flashed out a fine display of bunting.

During this long interval Clarissa came to see Stephen and for a while they talked of her health, each feeling shy of approaching yesterday's conversation. He said 'I am better pleased with you today than ever I have been before. I shall leave off the mercury, which will do away with the slight salivation you mention. It is, as you know, a specific for the malady you dreaded, but Dr Redfern was quite right in his diagnosis and I exhibited it only to clear up the trouble for which you first consulted me. It has done its work; but I think we must continue the steel and bark for a little while, to consolidate the general improvement.'

'I thank you, dear Doctor, for your very great care of me,' she said, and sat with folded hands for a while before going on, 'I have thought about returning to England, as you desired me to do; and if the possibility were to arise I should very much like to go back.'

'My dear, I am heartily glad to hear you say so. The possibility *has* arisen. At breakfast this morning Captain Aubrey said that he had it in mind to give your husband the *Truelove* to take in, but he hesitated on your account, being unsure how you would like it. He asked me to sound you. I was so nearly certain that you would say yes that I have already prepared a letter for my friend: his name is Blaine, Sir Joseph Blaine, and he has a place under government. I must apologize for its being sealed, a necessary proof of its authenticity. In it I have told him nothing of your childhood and youth, only that you were employed to keep the accounts at Mother Abbott's – he is as well acquainted with the place as I – and that you knew a great deal about what went on in the house.'

'Did you tell him how I came to be sent to Botany Bay?'

'I said that a member of Black's – Sir Joseph too is a member – begged you off, and that is enough for him. He is discretion itself, the very heart of discretion, and you need fear no impertinent questions from him, no personal questions at all. If you will tell him all that you told me about Wray and Ledward and their friends he will be satisfied. And here' – holding up a small parcel – 'is a small parcel of beetles for him; he is passionately devoted to beetles, and nothing could be better to guarantee your good faith. You do not mind beetles, my dear.'

'I do not mind them at all. Indeed, I have sometimes tried to help them climb a stone, but always in vain,' said Clarissa.

'Very good. I do hate women that cry out "Oh beetles! Oh serpents! Oh mice or centipedes!" and long to knock their silly affected heads together. But now, my dear, things are likely to move very fast and we may neither of us have time to talk at our leisure. So let me tell you one or two things of importance: you will certainly go by way of Batavia, where the prize will be condemned and sold, and you will both travel to England in an Indiaman from Canton. Here is a letter to my banker in Batavia, who will provide you with funds to travel in something resembling comfort. And since East Indiamen usually put their passengers down in or near the Thames, here is a draught on my infamous London bankers that will tide you over until Mr Oakes can come at his pay and prize-money.'

'How very, very . . .'

'A small loan between friends is no great thing, my dear. And here is a note for Mrs Broad, who keeps a comfortable inn in the Liberties of the Savoy: I have mentioned her before. You would do well to stay there and send a note by ticket-porter to Sir Joseph Blaine, asking for an appointment in the evening and going there by hackney-coach. You need not be afraid of him: he is appreciative of tender young charms, but he is no satyr. You will not forget the beetles, Clarissa. And lastly here is a letter for my wife. If Mr Oakes passes for lieutenant and is appointed to a ship, which I think will be the case, I believe she will ask you to stay with her until we return from the seas . . . I hesitate to say anything about Mr Oakes's discretion.'

'You may rely upon it,' said Clarissa, with a curious smile, 'partly because he knows, really *knows*, nothing, and partly because –'

The rest of her words were drowned in a violent roaring above their heads, a piping and the rush of feet. 'Jesus, Mary and Joseph,' cried Stephen. He whipped off his canvas shoes and trousers, drew on the fine breeches laid out; she tucked his shirt in behind and fastened the strap, folding and pinning his neckcloth, put his swordbelt over his shoulders, held out his best though still sadly shabby coat, straightened his wig and passed his hat. 'God bless you, my dear,' he said and ran on deck, where a great voice was calling 'Hell and death, where is the Doctor? Will no one rouse me out that Doctor?'

They pulled ashore through the rows of Puolani's great double-hulled war-canoes, Jack and Pullings in a blaze of gold lace and epaulettes, the others in their respective degrees of glory, and they were received with a stately formal welcome; for although the *Truelove* was an old friend, nothing like the *Surprise* had been seen in these waters, with a crow's nest like a whaler but with no whale-boat at all and far, far too many guns.

Jack and Pullings, with Stephen and Martin, Oakes and Adams, with Bonden carrying the sandalwood chest and Tapia to interpret, paced up in twos from the sea, through ranks of elderly grave-faced men holding fern-palm fronds, towards a wide, open-walled building where a woman was sitting on a broad bench that ran the whole width of the house with several islanders on either side of her: Jack noticed that whereas she was wearing a splendid feather cloak all the others, old men, young men, women and girls, were bare to the waist.

When they were within ten yards of her, an ancient man, remarkably tattooed and with a white bone through the septum of his nose, gave Jack the leafy branch of a breadfruit-tree. The last men of the line threw down their fronds and Tapia said 'That is a sign they mean peace. If you put yours on top, that shows you mean peace too.'

Jack laid the branch solemnly over the fronds: the woman stood up, as tall as Jack and broad-shouldered, but not nearly so heavy. 'This is Queen Puolani,' said Tapia, taking off his shirt. Jack made his bow, his hat tucked under his left arm, an elegant leg stretched out; she stepped forward, shook his hand in the European manner – a firm, dry clasp – and led him in, seating him next to herself. He named the others by order of rank and she inclined her head to each, a welcoming, friendly smile on her handsome face, no darker than an Italian's and scarcely tattooed at all. Perhaps thirty or thirty-five. There were some forty people, men and women, sitting in this pleasant airy place, and when all the newcomers were settled there followed an exchange of compliments. A meal was proposed; Jack excused himself – they had just eaten – but happily accepted the suggestion of kava, and while it was handing round he called for the presents. They were well received, particularly the smaller bunches of feathers that, on Tapia's whispered advice, he offered to the aunts and cousins of Puolani's house. She herself, and her councillors, were clearly too anxious to pay very much attention to beads or even looking-glasses: it was also obvious, from the general course of the conversation, that many of her enquiries were a matter of form. From what her people had learnt from their friends in the *Truelove* and from other sources she knew most of what had happened, and asked only out of politeness.

Presently she sent most of the people away, accompanying some various distances across the square before the house, others to the threshold, while others were dismissed with a smile; and the assembly was reduced to Puolani and two councillors, Jack, Stephen and Tapia.

When Jack said 'Kalahua is about to attack you, with the help of the Americans,' she replied, 'We know. He has reached the Oratonga spring, the river that flows into our bay, with thirty-seven white men: they have muskets and a gun – a gun. They may be here early the day after tomorrow.'

'So I have heard,' said Jack. 'As for the gun, he may have dragged it up, but without a road he may never be able to drag it down – nothing so cumbrous as a gun. Yet even if he should, it is no great matter: we have many more guns, bigger and better; many, many more muskets. I must tell you, ma'am – put that as civil as ever you can, Tapia, d'ye hear me – I must tell you that the Americans are my King's enemies: the two states are at war and that we shall guard you from them and from Kalahua, who has misused our countrymen, if you will accept King George's protection – is that how I should put it, Stephen? – and promise to be a faithful, loving ally.'

The Polynesians brightened amazingly. After a few words with the old chiefs Puolani turned to Jack with sparkling eyes and a glowing face – the flush was clearly perceptible – and said 'I welcome King George's protection; and I shall be a faithful loving ally; as faithful and loving as I was to my own husband.'

Tapia translated the last words, added perhaps as an afterthought, with a particular flatness; and the councillors looked down. 'What a handsome creature she is,' thought Jack, and he said 'Very well: that is settled. Allow me to give you your protector's likeness.' He brought the shining crown from his pocket, and after a pause for the translation, hung it round her acquiescent neck. 'Now, ma'am,' he said, rising and looking at her with respectful admiration, 'if I may speak to your war-chiefs, we may start getting some of our guns ashore and making our preparations. There is not a moment to be lost.'

Not a moment was lost. By sunset both ships were moored outside the bay, under the lee of its southern headland, in good holding ground and completely invisible from the hills over which Kalahua must come; and although the emplacements had been chosen, even the carronades were not to be landed until dusk, in case some advanced party should see them being rolled up the open strand before reaching the impenetrable green. And by sunset Jack had explored the traditional battlefields, three places along the only route across the mountains for a considerable body of men, above all for men pulling a gun.

'I am so sorry you had to stay with your patients,' he said, taking his ease at last in the great cabin with a bowl of fruit to quench his thirst. 'You would have rejoiced in the birds. There was one with a beak.'

'That alone would have been worth the voyage.'

'A yellow bird, with a heavy great beak shaped like a sickle: and many others. You would have been delighted. However, you shall see them later. Well, now, there were three main battlefields by land. The first is a grassy plain between the sudden precipitous hills and the cultivated ground: there the southern people wait for the northerners, and they draw up in lines, throw spears and slingstones and then go for one another with clubs and the like in the old-fashioned way; but there is the disadvantage of three taboo groves, and if anyone passes within hand's reach, either pursuing or being pursued, he brings defeat on his side; and his soul, together with the souls of all those related to him, spend eternity in that volcano up there.'

'Is it active?'

'Pretty active, I believe. Then the next place is quite high up, a natural cleft of rather better than a cable's length, with remarkably steep sides. When our friends here learn that the northerners are coming they usually send a squadron of war-canoes up to Pabay – they are better at sea than on land – while another body hurries to this cleft and throws up a dry-stone wall: they are amazingly quick and skilful and they have the stone at hand. Sometimes they hold it, being picked men: sometimes they are overwhelmed, the attackers having the advantage of the slope. But even if that does happen, the southerners rarely suffer much, since the men from Pabay have to hurry back because of the war-canoes. The third place is where the really decisive battles have been fought. It is higher still, on a desolate lava plain flanked with cliffs; it has a damned unpleasant sulphurous smell, and it is still littered with whitened bones. I absolutely saw hundreds of skulls: perhaps thousands.'

'May I ask what you mean to do?'

'Oh, it is the cleft, every time. Kalahua knows that Puolani cannot send her war-canoes to Pabay with the *Franklin* likely to appear at any moment: he can use his whole force, demolish the wall at once if he has brought his gun so far, and in any case push on without fear. I will draw you the cleft. There: about two hundred yards long and twenty wide: room for Kalahua and all his men. My idea — I must repeat that they are astonishing hands at dry-stone building — is to post two carronades here at the north entrance, hidden by walls. Four more at the southern end, spaced out thus and similarly hid, two firing straight down and two, like those at the far end, firing diagonally: quite a slight angle, but enough to sweep the whole ground. I post a few of Puolani's people just beyond the cleft. When Kalahua comes up they skirmish a little to concentrate his men and then run hell-fire quick back towards us, drawing the northerners into the cleft. When they are in, the guns at the far end open fire. The northern rear presses hard up against its own van, and the guns at the southern end open up.'

'Have the northerners no retreat?'

'None.'

'I had imagined it was a military maxim that the enemy should always be left a line of retreat.'

'Perhaps that is so in the army; but the Navy is required to take, sink, burn or destroy. Pray don't look so low, Stephen. After all, the man who starts a war only gets what he asked for, you know, if he is destroyed. And he can always call for quarter.'

When Stephen had returned to the sick-berth, Jack sent for Oakes and said 'Sit down, Mr Oakes. As you know, tomorrow we shall be preparing to support Queen Puolani against the people from Pabay and the Americans. Captain Pullings and I and Mr West and most of the warrant officers will be on shore, and we shall probably sleep there, some way up the country. You will remain on board in command of the ship and Mr Reade of the prize. If during my absence the American privateer *Franklin* should make as if to enter the bay you are both to hoist our colours and engage her, but at no greater distance than a quarter of a mile. I shall leave you enough men to fight one side, with the gunner's mate to assist you. If you are obliged to slip rather than weigh your anchors, which is probable should the American appear, you are to buoy them with the utmost care. Should the *Franklin* withdraw, she is not to be pursued beyond a line joining the two headlands. I cannot emphasize that point too strongly, Mr Oakes. Have you any questions?'

'No, sir. But may I say, sir, may I say with all respect, that I never had a go at Pabay. I never had a go at what you might call – I never had a go at regaining your esteem.'

'No. It is true I was angry with you for bringing Mrs Oakes aboard, but since then you have behaved in a seamanlike, officerlike fashion and I think highly enough of your qualities to make you prizemaster of the *Truelove* with orders to take her to Batavia to be condemned, if the encounter goes as we wish and if you feel competent to command her.'

'Oh sir,' cried Oakes, 'I don't know how to thank you – I shall tell Clarissa – that is to say, oh yes, if you please. I am reasonable good at navigation, and I believe I know how to handle a ship – not like you, sir, of course, but tolerably well.'

'It should not be too difficult. She is well-found and you will have the monsoon with you. I shall, if all goes well, give you an acting order as lieutenant; and although she will still be a little short-handed, I shall let you have a couple of our master-mariners, Slade and Gorges for example, who can stand a watch and keep their own reckoning: the three French prisoners too – they can at least haul on a rope. And I shall make an advance on your pay and prize-money to bear your charge from Batavia home. Now, although the whole matter depends on our success the day after tomorrow, you had better go across and become acquainted with the *Truelove* and her people.'

'May I tell my wife first?' asked Oakes, almost laughing with pleasure.

'By all means – my best compliments wait on Mrs Oakes – and let Mr Reade know I should like to see him.'

*

245

The ship's boats were coming back in the darkness, having landed the very heavy material; they were hoisted in, and when the jollyboat was safely stowed inside the launch – for the small-arms men and the gun-crews were to be taken off at dawn by Puolani's canoes, by way of precaution – West reported to Pullings, who relayed the news to Jack that all hands except two of the most notorious lechers were aboard.

'Very well,' said Jack, and he went below, sharp-set.

At supper he interrupted his steady attack upon the sea-pie to say 'I was never so much surprised in my life. Just now I told Oakes I should give him an acting order as lieutenant to take the *Truelove* in, if all went well on Friday. He was amazed. Delighted and amazed. His wife had not given him the slightest hint. Yet she must have known it hours before, from your questions.'

'She is a jewel of a woman,' said Stephen. 'How I value her.'

Jack shook his head and returned to the sea-pie. Eventually, leaning back, he said, 'I never asked you what you thought of Puolani.'

'I thought her a magnificent queenly woman. Juno, with the same large expressive eyes, and I hope without her faults of temper.'

'She is certainly very kind. She set her people to work making a house for me to sleep in, but I told her that tomorrow night I must be right up by the guns.' A silence for pudding, and he went on, 'I do not think I told you how pleased I was with the war-chiefs and their men – thoroughly professional and well-disciplined – not the least jealousy of the Navy, as you so often find at home. They were perfectly ready to take any suggestions I made, and I had hardly mentioned a dressing-station for you on a convenient shaded little plateau half an hour short of the cleft before they started setting it up.'

'Half an hour short of the cleft?'

'Yes. It is not the custom here to take prisoners, and I can do nothing about it. I expect something of a slaughter-house; and I cannot have a battle of this kind interrupted for a moment on humane grounds.'

'Have you ever known me interfere in any battle?'

'No. But I strongly suspect you of a tender heart, and in such a case I think you would be far better in your proper place, which is a dressing-station well to the rear, corresponding to the cockpit in a ship of the line.'

It was in this dressing-station that Jack, Stephen, Pullings, West and Adams slept on Thursday night, having walked up the broad well-beaten track, smelling of crushed green, that the carronades had taken before them, stubby short-range guns that could be manhandled for this distance and on this slope with relative ease, they weighing no more than half a ton, three times less than Kalahua's piece.

And it was here, clearly, that Stephen woke at the first hint of light. His companions had already left, moving with that silence usual among naval men in the night watches; so had most of the warriors, but as he stood in the doorway, with birds singing and calling in the trees all round and below him, more tribesmen came hurrying up the path, big brown cheerful men, some wearing matting armour, all armed with spears, clubs and sometimes dreadful hardwood swords, their edges studded with shark's teeth. They called out as they passed, smiling and waving.

When the last had gone up, running not to miss the fight, Stephen sat outside the doorway in the rising sun. Presently the birdsong diminished to a few screeches here and there (they were not a melodious choir, upon the whole), and presently Padeen succeeded in striking a light, coaxing a fire into being, and warming the coffee.

A number of birds passed close at hand, some of them probably honeysuckers; but still he waited, listening rather than seeing. Kalahua's camp fires had showed clear last night only an hour's march beyond the cleft, and even with the gun the northern men and their white mercenaries should reach it before the sun had risen another hand's breadth.

At intervals he looked at it over the immense stretch of sea ending in a taut horizon. Immobile of course. He tried thinking of that glorious Queen Puolani: it was said that her late husband, her consort, proved a man of inferior parts and that she had him set in the forefront of just such a battle in the cleft. He tried repeating verses; but those which he knew well, which came easily, did not overlay his vision of the sheer-sided defile two hundred yards by twenty, filled with men and they being fired upon from back and front and diagonally. The twenty-four pounder carronades would be using canister, about two hundred iron balls at each discharge; and they would be served by expert crews, capable of firing, reloading, aiming and firing again in less than a minute. In five minutes six carronades would discharge at least six thousand lethal shots into those trapped bodies. In his harsh unmusical voice he chanted plainsong, which had a better covering effect: he had reached a Benedictus in the Dorian mode and he was straining for a high *qui venit* when the clear sharp voice of gunfire – carronade-fire – cut him short. Four almost at once, it seemed to him, and then two; but the echoes confused everything. Then four quick hammer-strokes again. Then silence.

Padeen and he stood staring up the mountain. They could make out a vague roaring, but nothing more; and the birds that had started from the trees below all settled again. Perhaps battle had been joined: perhaps the carronades had been overrun.

Time passed, though less slowly now, and presently steps could be heard on the path. A young long-legged man raced down past them, a messenger of good news, his whole face alive with joy. He shouted something as he passed: victory, no doubt at all.

After him, several minutes after him, came two more, each carrying a human head by the hair, Polynesian the first, European the second. Both heads had their eyes open, indignant in the one case, perfectly blank in the other.

Then loud and clear, helped by some eddy in the wind, came the cry 'one, two, three, belay-oh!' and it was plain that a carronade was coming down the path. Long before it reached them a group of small-arms men could be heard laughing and talking, and as soon as they came in sight Stephen called 'Wilton, are many of our people hurt?'

'None that I know on, sir. Ain't that right, Bob?'

'Right as dried peas, mate. And none of the Queen's men that I see, neither.'

'But them poor unfortunate buggers in the gulley,' said the captain of the hold, an old shipmate of Stephen's and entitled to speak freely, 'God love us, sir, it was bloody murder.'

By this time the mountainside was alive with men, islanders who knew scores of paths the guns could never have taken, most of them carrying their spoils: weapons, matting, ornaments, ears.

Presently Jack appeared at the turning, with Bonden a little way behind him, looking somewhat anxious. Stephen walked up the track and as they met he said 'May I give you joy of your victory?'

'Thank you, Stephen,' said Jack, with a sort of smile.

'Are there any wounded I can look after?'

'All that did not run away are dead by now, brother. Shall we take a side path? It will get us down so long as we follow the slope and hit the Eeahu river. Tom is seeing to the carronades. Bonden, give Padeen a hand with the medical stores, will you?'

They struck off to the left, a track that led steeply down through ferns to a little purling stream; the path was too narrow and abrupt for any conversation until the place where the stream ran across, making a pool under a spreading tree. Jack knelt down, washed his face and hands and drank deep. 'Lord, that is better,' he said, sitting back on a mossy root. 'Should you like to know how things went?'

'I am afraid it distresses you to speak of it at present.'

'Yes, it does. But these things soon pass, you know. Well, the scheme worked perfectly, like a drill-book. They were rather tired, having come uphill nearly all the way, dragging their gun and precious short of food; and our young men, posted at the far end to provoke them and bring them on into the cleft, had plenty of time to run back behind the guns and leave the field clear. I should never have believed case-shot could do so much damage. I must say the French came on very well, leaping and scrambling over the bodies: two rounds dealt with them. But even then Kalahua's people rallied and charged with a shout, some of them almost reaching the guns before the last broadside. We stopped firing then, and those that could run ran, pursued by some of Puolani's men – not many, and they will not go far, the war-chiefs tell me, because of the broken country. We took their gun, of course, and I dare say Puolani will get it down in time.' After a pause he said 'We only fired ten rounds, Stephen, but there was a butcher's bill like a fleet action. And though the hands were pleased, of course, scarcely anyone raised a cheer; and it was not taken up.'

'You did not follow your plan of closing the other end, I collect, since some were able to run away?'

'My plan? Oh no: that did not make very good sense. I was really trying to make your flesh creep, as you do mine with your surgical horrors. It is my belief, Stephen, that you do not always know when I am being droll.'

This was the first sign of a lifting, at least a superficial lifting of his depression, and by the time they had made their slow and often mistaken way down to Puolani's village he was perfectly capable of responding to their extraordinarily happy and triumphant welcome. He had been expected by the main path through the sugar-canes, where arches of greenery with two carronades under each had been set up: the Queen led him back by a side way to the first and then through the middle of all three to an immense sound of cheering and the thunder of wooden drums. Then he was taken from one group to another – Tapia, recovered from the throng, explained that these were the various branches of the tribe – and each group in turn fell flat, though not quite so flat as to hide their delighted smiles.

The tribe had a great many branches, but the repeated cere-monies, the incessant beating of drums and blowing of conches, the feeling of great friendliness and affection as Puolani led him about and the great beauty of the day – a brilliant sky and white clouds sailing evenly from the north-east and the heat of the sun tempered by a charming scented breeze – set a barrier between now and the slaughter of the morning, and he walked into the Queen's house perfectly ready to be pleased with his entertainment. Here the whole company, all robed, stood up as he came in; and to his astonishment he saw Stephen, Pullings, West and Adams among them, wearing splendid feather cloaks, and as he stood there Puolani placed one on his shoulders, crimson from top to bottom. She smoothed it with great satisfaction and made a confidential remark. 'She says it belonged to one of her uncles, now a god,' said Tapia.

'Any god would be flattered by such a cloak,' said Jack, 'much less an humble mortal.'

'It is a present,' whispered Tapia.

Jack turned and bowed, returning his best thanks: Puolani looked modestly down, an unusual attitude for her, and motioned him to a seat beside her on the bench, or perhaps firmly padded sofa would be the better description. A yellow-feathered Pullings was on her other side; Stephen, in blue-black, on Jack's left, and to him he said in an undertone 'Are you hungry? I have never so famished in all my life. It came over me suddenly.' Then, seeing Tapia whispering to an immensely tattooed chief beyond him he said 'Tapia, pray ask the chief if Bonden can be sent back to the ship in a canoe to tell Mr Oakes that all is well and that the boats are to come round tomorrow morning. I shall sleep ashore.'

Puolani's grandfather had acquired three ship's coppers. These vessels rarely appeared, since almost all Polynesian cooking was carried out with hot stones in an underground oven, the dish being wrapped in leaves, but now, gleaming like red gold, they were brought out by strong men and set on hearths in front of the house. An extraordinarily savoury smell wafted in and Jack swallowed painfully; to distract his mind he desired Tapia to tell the Queen how much he admired the orderliness of the gathering – to the right hand, outside the house, sat the starboard watch in due order of precedence, on the left, the larboard, all hands wearing garlands of flowers, while beyond them, closing the square, were the densely-packed islanders; and on every hand attendants were preparing food.

As well as the coppers seven china bowls had reached Moahu, and these were placed on little cushions before the Queen, Jack, Stephen and Pullings, West, Adams, and an ancient chief, together with spoons and wooden platters of mashed taro. A chorus of conches blew three great blasts. Servants stood by the coppers, looking expectantly at the Queen. 'Turtle on the left, fish in the middle, meat on the right,' whispered Tapia. The Queen looked at Jack with a smile and he, returning the smile, said 'Oh meat, ma'am, if you please.'

The bowls were filled all down the line: the Queen had chosen to begin with fish, nearly all the *Surprise*'s officers with meat. But it was exceedingly hot, and while they toyed with their taro, slavering as they did so, Stephen noticed the unmistakable helix of a human ear in his bowl and said to Tapia 'Please tell the Queen that man's flesh is taboo to us.'

'But it is Kalahua and the French chief,' said Tapia.

'Even so,' said Stephen, and leaning to speak behind Puolani's back he said rather louder 'Captain Pullings, Mr West: this is forbidden meat.'

When the news reached Puolani she laughed cheerfully, changed bowls with Jack, and assured them that his hands were in no danger: they were being fed on pork, which happened to be taboo to her – so many taboos, she said, smiling still.

And indeed there were so many taboos, personal, tribal, national, woven into the texture of the island's life that this little gaffe passed almost unnoticed, certainly without any embarrassment on the part of Puolani, and the feast went on and on, most of the sailors soon recovering their appetite. After the fish and turtle – the best turtle in the South Seas – came fowls, cooked in the Polynesian manner, dogs, eggs and young fat pigs; all this with great quantities of chief's kava, a more heady brew than usual.

The feast, and there was a great deal of it, eaten over a very long time, was accompanied by singing, the music of flutes, drums of various pitch, and something between a harp and a lyre: and when even fruit would scarcely go down, the dancing began.

There were some of the exactly-timed evolutions and manoeuvres they had seen far to the south, in Annamooka, and they were received with applause; but not with nearly such hearty applause as the much freer hula, danced with great skill, grace and enthusiasm by a number of young women.

'I am glad Martin is not here,' said Stephen in Jack's ear. 'He could never have approved these licentious postures and wanton looks.'

'Perhaps not,' said Jack. 'For my own part I do not find them objectionable, however.'

Nor did West. His appetite had been more severely checked than most by the sight of the Frenchman's ring-finger in his bowl, but now he had recovered entirely and he was leaning forward, gazing with passionate intensity at the second girl from the left.

Jack did not object: not at all; but sleep was rising up with such force that for some time now he had not dared shut his eyes for fear of dropping off and more than off – deep, deep down. He stifled a yawn and looked wistfully at the stimulating kava bowl – the cup-bearer too was engrossed by the motions of the second girl on the left. Puolani caught his glance, reached out and filled him a bumper with kind, comforting, apologetic words.

More conches, a great howl of conches. The girls withdrew to a thunder of applause, with whistles and cheers from the frigate's crew, and to his surprise Jack saw that the sun was already dipping. Silence returned at last; and a figure eight feet tall, a man entirely covered with basket-work, came into the square before the Queen. He had two drummers with him, one deep, one shrill, and when they had beaten three measures he broke out in a high falsetto of surprising volume, rising and falling to a rhythm that certainly existed for many of his hearers, since they bowed and nodded, but that neither Jack nor Stephen could make out. Tapia whispered 'He is telling the Queen's family right back and back.' Again and again Jack tried to seize the pattern but always at some crucial point his attention wandered and all was to begin again: he closed his eyes to concentrate on the chant alone, and this was fatal.

To his extreme confusion he woke to find the whole table smiling at him. The wickerwork figure was gone, and already the fires showed red in the more than twilight.

Two powerful men heaved him gently to his feet and led him away. On the threshold he turned, as in a dream, and made his bow. Puolani, with the kindest look, returned it: then there was a warm darkness and these sure hands; they took his feather cloak, he slipped off his clothes and they lowered him on to the wonderful ease of the long, flat, soft couch in the house that had been built for him.

He had rarely been so tired, had rarely gone so very far down; yet he rose up clear and fresh, no muddiness, no staring about; he knew, as a sailor knows, that it was near the end of the middle watch, and the tide was on the turn; he knew that there was someone in the room, and as he sat up a strong arm pressed him back, a warm, scented arm. He was not altogether surprised – perhaps his half-waking mind had caught the scent – nor at all displeased: his heart began to beat violently, and he made room.

First light was coming through the door when he heard Tom Pullings' agitated whisper, 'Sir, sir, excuse me, sir. The *Franklin* is in the offing. Sir, sir . . .'

'Pipe down, Tom,' he murmured, pulling on his clothes. She was still asleep, flat, her head back, her mouth open, looking perfectly beautiful. He slid round the opening and they hurried down. The village was still asleep, apart from a few fishermen: Oakes had sent the boats in and already a second carronade was moving down over the rollers.

'Mr Oakes's duty, sir,' said Bonden, 'and *Franklin* was seen in the west as soon as it was day: she stood in, doubted all was right, let fall her courses and steered south-west. She will show round the headland any minute now, sir. And sir, he sent the drum.'

'Very good, Bonden. Watkins, beat to arms. Doctor, Mr Adams, come along with me. Captain Pullings, carry on.'

As the jollyboat pulled out across the bay the *Franklin*

appeared: quite unmistakable. Long and low, a right privateer. She was suspicious, but not particularly alarmed – no
topgallants, and she had not even let the night-time reef out
of her topsails.

Jack felt extraordinarily well as he ran up the side. 'Good
morning, Mr Oakes,' he said, 'well done indeed.' To Killick's
mate (for Killick was still on shore), 'Breakfast in twenty
minutes,' and to Mr Adams, just arrived, 'Mr Adams, pray
write out Mr Oakes's acting order in due form, and the dispatches and letters we drafted.' He glanced at the shore,
where the laggard Surprises were now hurrying about like
purposeful bees, flung his shirt and trousers on to the capstan-
head, and dived deep into the clear green water.

Even after breakfast the *Franklin* was obviously in two
minds, for she threw out a signal intelligible no doubt to her
countrymen; a sign to which Jack, old in deception, replied
with a vague hoist that went up and down, the halliard constantly jammed, wasting irreplaceable minutes.

The carronades were coming home with incredible speed,
and their munitions: there was an appearance of hopeless
chaos, with people coming up the side from helping the *Truelove* to weigh, very heavy weights being lowered, boats swinging inboard; but soon after Pullings had said 'All hands have
reported, sir, and the bosun's chair is rigged,' Jack turned to
Oakes. 'Here is your acting order, Mr Oakes, and the large
wrapper holds all the other papers: so now, if Mrs Oakes is
ready, perhaps you should go aboard your command.'

Clarissa stepped from the rail and said in her high clear
voice 'Please let me thank you, sir, for your great goodness to
me; I shall always be extremely grateful.'

He said 'We have been very happy to have you with us. A
prosperous voyage to you both, and pray give my dear love to
England.'

She turned to Stephen, who kissed her on both cheeks, said
'God bless, my dear,' and handed her to the bosun's chair,
which lowered her into the *Truelove*'s boat. He watched them
go aboard and heard the shout 'Three cheers for the *Surprise*,'

followed by 'Huzzay, huzzay, huzzay!' with all the force and conviction that the rescued crew could give.

'Three cheers for *Truelove*,' cried Jack, and suspending their work the Surprises answered 'Huzzay, huzzay, huzzay!' with great good humour, for many of them were very fond of Oakes and all had the tenderest regard for their prize.

Now the *Truelove* was drawing away: Clarissa appeared at her taffrail, and she and Stephen waved.

'All hands unmoor ship,' called Jack, and to Pullings, in a conversational tone, 'We can demolish the crow's nest as we go.'

Stephen stood there while behind him the capstan turned and clicked to the usual cries; each anchor rose in turn to the invariable orders and responses; and all at once he realized that the frigate too was under way, rapidly making sail and moving faster and faster eastwards after her flying quarry, so that the distance between the ships was increasing with dreadful speed; before he was prepared for it the *Truelove* was no more than a remote ship upon the sea; and there was no longer any human contact at all.